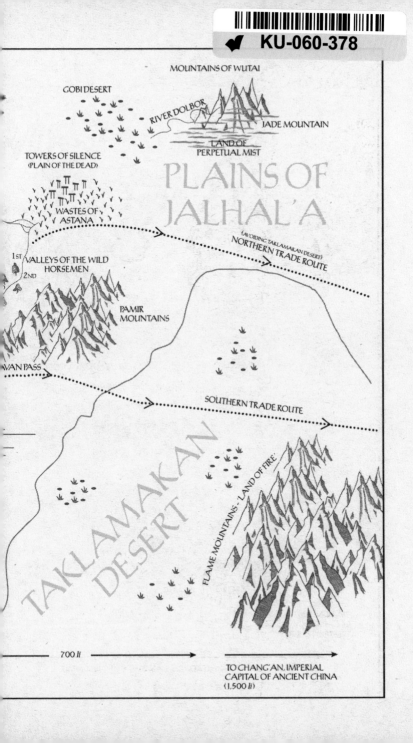

MOUNTAINS OF WUTAI

GOBI DESERT

RIVER DOLBOR

JADE MOUNTAIN

LAND OF
PERPETUAL MIST

TOWERS OF SILENCE
(PLAIN OF THE DEAD)

PLAINS OF
JALHAL'A

WASTES OF
ASTANA

(AVOIDING TAKLAMAKAN DESERT)
NORTHERN TRADE ROUTE

1ST
2ND

VALLEYS OF THE WILD
HORSEMEN

PAMIR
MOUNTAINS

...VAN PASS

SOUTHERN TRADE ROUTE

TAKLAMAKAN
DESERT

FLAME MOUNTAINS - 'LAND OF FIRE'

700 li

TO CHANG'AN, IMPERIAL
CAPITAL OF ANCIENT CHINA
(1,500 li)

CHARACTERS

Gods, Immortals and Guardian spirits

The Wise Lord, supreme deity, creator of Heaven and Earth
and all things in them

Chu Jung, Spirit of Fire and Heavenly Executioner
(first servant of the Wise Lord)

Corhanuk, higher guardian spirit and messenger to the Wise Lord

The Shadow-without-a-name, fallen higher guardian spirit
(formerly favourite of the Wise Lord)

The Crimson King, fallen higher guardian spirit, keeper of the
Gates of Hell

The Jade Spirit, fallen higher guardian spirit, keeper of the Wheel
of Rebirth

Beshbaliq, fallen lower guardian spirit, accomplice to the Shadow

Spirit of the Four Winds, spirit of nature

Kuan Yin, goddess of mercy and protector of travellers

Guan Di, god of merchants, scholars and warriors

Shou Lao, storyteller

Horses and Dragons

Stargazer, lord of the horses, grey stallion, servant to none

Breeze Whisperer, chestnut mare, Cetu's mount

Storm Gatherer, black stallion, brother to Breeze Whisperer
and Zerafshan's mount

Han Garid, lord of the thunder dragons

The Wild Horsemen

Cetu, Waymaster, mentor to Rokshan and unelected leader of the
Fifth Valley clan

Draxurion, clan leader of the Plains Horsemen

Gandhara, clan leader of the First Valley of the Horsemen

Akthal, clan leader of the Second Valley of the Horsemen

Mukhravee, clan leader of the Third Valley of the Horsemen

Sethrim, clan leader of the Fourth Valley of the Horsemen

Lerikos, brother to Gandhara, a scout

Kezenway, his son, a scout

Salamundi, a young warrior of the First Valley Horsemen

Sisters of the Serenadhi, horse-singers

Sumiyaa, lead horse-singer

Maracanda
Teeming capital of China's Western Empire

Naha, founder of the Vaishravana trading business

Zerafshan, his brother, formerly military attaché to the imperial
court and commander of the Imperial Cavalry Corps

An Lushan, Naha's elder son

Rokshan, Naha's younger son

Jiang Zemin, leader of the Council of Elders

Kanandak ('Kan'), an acrobat and Rokshan's best friend

Ah Lin, the family servant

Vagees Krishnan, the head clerk

Gupta, his son, head cameleer

Chen Ming, caravan master and friend of Naha

Qalim, caravan escort

Bhathra, caravan escort

People of the Darhad, wandering nomads of the north

Sarangerel, spellweaver and shamaness

Lianxang, her granddaughter, friend of Rokshan and An Lushan

Dalgimmaron, lawsmith

Zayach, tracker

Mergen, tracker

The citadel monastery at Labrang

The abbot, First of the Elect, governing body of the Fellowship
of the Three One-eared Hares

Sung Yuan, warrior monk

Elsewhere in the Empire

Emperor H'sien-tsung, despotic ruler of China and all Known Lands,
'Son of Heaven'

General Arkan Shakar, of the Imperial Light Cavalry Brigade

Vartkhis Boghos, rich Armenian merchant and bitter rival of Vaishravana's

Currency: *celehks* and *taals*

Measurements: li – the Chinese mile, approximately one third of a mile
yin – approximately one metre

1 candle ring = 1 hour

... In the beginning the Wise Lord was alone. Master of all creation. He longed to share the wonders of the world He had wrought, and He looked anew at the five precious elements from which He had shaped all things - water, earth, wood, fire and metal.

He breathed afresh on each of them, and conjured countless colours, shapes and feelings from the elements, and they danced a wild dance of life. But the Wise Lord grew tired of the dance, and made spirit creatures of them. He called them dragon spirits, because they burned so brightly with the fire of life.

He sent them to live in the world, where they became invisible spirits of the forests and mountains, rivers and streams, lakes and oceans, valleys and plains and deserts. The Wise Lord then created guardian spirits to serve Him, some of these guardian spirits He sent into the world, where they became men and women. But in time they forgot the dragon spirits with whom they had shared the world in the beginning. The dragon spirits became jealous, believing that mankind had turned the Wise Lord away from them, and in the madness of their envious rage, they turned into monsters.

The dragon spirits of fire were the fiercest and most powerful of all them. Shedding their invisibility, they assumed the most terrifying countenance and grew wings, commanding the skies and terrorizing the people as dragons ...

Source: unknown, but believed to be part of *The Book of Ahura Mazda, the Wise Lord*; partial scroll found in 807 AD by an imperial envoy en route to Maracanda.

PROLOGUE

Chu Jung, Spirit of Fire and Heavenly Executioner for the Wise Lord, stood like a colossus straddling the oceans and continents of the world as he confronted the last and mightiest of the rebel dragon spirits. Consumed with jealousy of mankind, Han Garid and his kind had become monsters, killing and devouring those who had once loved them as spirits of nature.

'Why have you risen against the Wise Lord?' Chu Jung thundered. He held his Talisman high as he moved his arm over the oceans, and the distant cries of a thousand demon gods erupted from the depths. At Chu Jung's command, they drew the water of the oceans upwards, higher and higher into a shimmering, towering cascade that reached the sky. The world turned dark as the sun was blotted out, but Han Garid roared his defiance.

'I am Han Garid, lord of the thunder dragons! Not even the waters of all the oceans of the world shall ever quench my fire. Join us, Chu Jung, and together we will rule the Earth and hold sway over the Heavens!'

Han Garid loosed a fearsome bolt of fire that roared and crackled around them, but Chu Jung's own mantle of fire protected him, and in the jagged half-light he looked upon the monster that Han Garid had become.

The lord of the thunder dragons was huge – at least nine horses' lengths long – and his wingspan must have been five across. There were bony ridges across his face, and his long reptilian head had a single horn the length of a man's outstretched arm, which swept back and curved into a peak. His piercing red eyes shone with a cruel intelligence, and the brilliant coloration of his skin – a shimmering gold and green, shot through with the palest blue – was the only reminder of the beautiful spirit creature he had once been.

'You joined forces with the rebellious guardian spirit who was once the favourite of the Wise Lord. He and his two fellow spirits sought to bring evil into the world and banish good for ever, but he has been vanquished,' Chu Jung told Han Garid. 'Even now he awaits his punishment. You must also come before the Wise Lord to learn of your fate and to witness his.'

Han Garid snorted a derisive bolt of fire as he spread his wings, but Chu Jung brought the cascading towers of water crashing down on him, swirling them around like an enormous net. Han Garid struggled in vain as the waters of all the oceans of the world extinguished his fire for ever.

Chu Jung then gathered the fiery dragon up and took him before the Wise Lord, who waited for them, unseen, at the edge of the universe.

There He who had created the Heavens and Earth, and everything in them, first pronounced His terrible verdict on his favourite among the guardian spirits who had dared to rebel against Him:

'From henceforth you shall be known as "the Nameless One", and you will be no more than a shadow, a sigh of the wind in the dark. I expunge all memory of you from every mortal creature. My messenger, Corhanuk, will bear witness and tell your fellow guardian spirits what has become of you.'

Then the Wise Lord spoke the sacred words and created an Arch of Darkness between the fallen guardian spirit and the living world, sealed with the recitation of his name, which would never again be spoken. And the fallen guardian spirit, thenceforth known only as the Shadow, was banished for ever.

The Wise Lord then turned to Han Garid, sorrow in His

eyes as He looked upon what the foremost of his glorious creation had become. But the Wise Lord could not bring Himself to destroy him and His first-born creatures.

'Take Han Garid to the Pool of Life, to be with the dragon spirits of air and water and all his kind,' the Wise Lord commanded Chu Jung. 'There you will raise them up, to be born again.'

Chu Jung did his bidding, and his master in His wisdom wrought the essence of the dragon spirits of fire such that they would never die, placing the smallest spark of Han Garid's immortality deep in the souls of the gentlest and most beautiful of his creatures, which came to be called *dragon horses*.

Meanwhile Corhanuk hurried to witness the Wise Lord's punishment. But something had stirred in him as he witnessed the terrible fate of the Shadow – and a raw hunger for the power he had so nearly succeeded in wresting from the Wise Lord began to gnaw at him. A very different plan was forming in the scheming heart of the Wise Lord's messenger: a plan so ambitious he realized it might take many aeons to bring about. He knew he must be patient and cunning if he was to serve a different master – one who surely would reward him well if he, Corhanuk, succeeded in releasing him from his perpetual imprisonment.

From that moment on, above all things he bent his sole purpose to bringing the Shadow back from beyond the Arch of Darkness – to be free once more to stalk the Earth and rule the Heavens.

PART ONE

MARACANDA, 818 AD

Chapter 1

The Unexpected Return

Kan raced through the deserted, dusty streets of Maracanda as the first slanting rays of the sun cast long shadows over the capital city of the Western Empire. He leaped over the sleeping bodies of the street people in the Grand Bazaar, gulping in the cool air. In an hour or two the extreme heat of the last few weeks would be settling like a pall over the city.

It was high summer, and the maze of winding alleys that surrounded the Grand Bazaar were overflowing with un-collected piles of waste. There had been no wind on the plains for many weeks now, so that the summer grass, usually so lush and green, was turning a scorched brown colour. The cooling northerly winds had not come, and Maracanda baked in the heat – the people muttered that it was a bad omen, another troubled sign of the times.

Kan was an acrobat. He was only thirteen but had travelled with his circus people up and down the trade roads that criss-crossed the Empire longer than any of his friends. His best friend, Rokshan, was the younger son of one of the city's richest merchants, a powerful trading family headed by the formidable Naha Vaishravana. Kan couldn't wait to tell him that their favourite storyteller, Shou Lao, known to everyone as the Old Man of the Markets, had travelled back with the circus people from their last show.

Shou Lao had not been in Maracanda for many years – and now he was back, right here, and Kan was prepared to bet ten silver *taals* that he had plenty of wonderful new stories to tell.

Kan rapped on the heavy double-fronted doors of Rokshan's house. The house servant, Ah Lin, heaved one of the doors open a crack to see who it was at such an ungodly hour; her wrinkled old face creased into a delighted smile of welcome when she saw who it was.

'Kanandak, master acrobat, is returned at last to the Western Empire's City of Dreams,' Kan sang out in his best ringmaster's voice, bowing low and beaming at her after executing a perfect circle of cartwheels.

'Come in, come in, before you wake the whole household – *master acrobat* indeed,' Ah Lin chuckled.

'No, I can't stop. Is Roksy up? He must come straight away to see somebody he hasn't set eyes on for years and years! Tell him Shou Lao, the old storyteller, is here. I'll meet him outside the school in two candle-rings.'

And he was gone, disappearing down the street in a whirling flurry of forward flips and cartwheels.

Ah Lin remembered the last time the old storyteller had been in Maracanda. Not long after he had moved on, the young mistress of the house, adored mother of Rokshan, had caught a mysterious fever and died. Ah Lin had always thought it was a strange coincidence, and maybe that's all it was, but she hadn't been able to get it out of her mind then – and now it all came flooding back.

As she watched Kan go with a worried smile on her face, she absently made the sign of the dragon – an s-shape representing the coils of the mythical creature, drawn with the nail of her thumb on her forehead, mouth and breast to ward off evil spirits. Then she shut the door as quietly as she could and disappeared inside.

The Maracanda School for Special Envoys attracted scholars – girls and boys from all over the Empire – to train as envoys for top diplomatic posts throughout all Known Lands. At fourteen,

Rokshan had another two years of study ahead of him.

The school was not far from the Grand Bazaar in the city centre. The buzz and hubbub from the great market provided a constant background hum that Rokshan found strangely comforting. To wake himself up, he shook his head and ran his hands through his thick brown hair, which he grew long to cover up a deformity from birth which had left him with only one ear. It didn't bother him – he could hear perfectly well through his good ear – but all the same he liked to cover the little stub of cartilage that marked where his other ear should have been. Right now he wished he could shave his head – it would have been a lot cooler in the heat, which even at this early hour was already uncomfortable; his linen tunic was damp with sweat and his feet were slipping and sliding in his light leather sandals. Where *was* Kan? Typical of him to leave an excited message and then not turn up.

He watched the steady stream of people making their way to the Grand Bazaar – absolutely everything from all over the Empire was bought, bartered, sold and exchanged here: a family of cotton traders went by, staggering under the swaying rolls strapped to their backs.

Trading, buying and selling was the city of Maracanda's lifeblood. It was Rokshan's family's business, and that of hundreds of others too. He helped out whenever he could get time off from studying, and loved to sniff out the bargains when the caravans came in from the east, or on their way to imperial capital.

Rokshan's family traded not only in cotton but also in damask and silk, spices, herbs and garden produce. They bought and sold everything for the home too: tables and chairs, cupboards, couches, altarpieces, earthenware pottery goods and the finest porcelain tableware for rich merchants' tables. They imported exquisitely carved ivory chess sets and chequers boards of hardest ebony, all the way from the jungle kingdoms of the Southern Empire, as well as intricately worked jade carvings of dragons of every shape and size, which guarded the entrances of all self-respecting households in Maracanda, bringing luck and good fortune. Dragon spirits were also considered harbingers of floods and rain, so there had been a brisk trade in the jade carvings.

'Roksy! Are you coming or are you going to stand there all day?' Kan had appeared from nowhere – an old trick of his – and was now standing on his head with his legs against the wall just a short way down the street.

'I'm coming!' Rokshan shouted, pushing his way through the throng of people. 'So what's this about Shou Lao?'

'It'll cost you two silver *taals*!' Kan replied, arching his back, leaping upright and running off as Rokshan shot out an arm to grab him. 'Follow me, Roksy – and keep up!' Kan laughed over his shoulder.

He ducked off the main street and sprinted through the maze of narrow winding lanes towards the East Gate of the city, which marked the beginning – or end – of the road to Chang'an, the imperial capital. With a shout of exasperation, Rokshan set off after him. They raced round the stalls and workshops that cluttered this part of the city, hurtling along as if their lives depended on it.

'Whoa, boys, whoa! Are you riding dragon horses?' a carpet-seller yelled at them as they slowed to take a corner. At that moment a bullock cart stacked high with tall wicker baskets came creaking around the same corner. Rokshan realized they had no chance of avoiding the placid beasts drawing the cart. *Kerrumph!* Kan gasped in pain, clutching his chest as he bounced off the great thick-boned skull of one of the beasts.

He landed in a crumpled heap – Rokshan couldn't avoid him as he came skidding round the corner and went head over heels. The bullock and its bemused partner stopped dead in their tracks for a split second before rearing back in shock and confusion.

'Whoa, whoa!' the basket-trader cried, desperately trying to control the animals. 'Idiots! Get away from them!' The two boys were trying to calm the frightened animals.

'Cursed spawn of dragon's breath!' the basket-trader swore as he cracked his whip at them. The bullocks' sudden movement had upset the load and launched a tumbling cascade of wicker.

The furious basket-trader leaped down, whip in hand, and gave chase – the two boys had wisely decided not to hang around and help clear up the chaos they'd caused.

'Clumsy oafs! By the fiery whiskers of Han Garid – get back here!' the basket-trader bellowed after them, but they had disappeared.

'Fools! I'll skin you alive if I ever catch you . . .' they heard faintly as they sped laughing on their way.

They were nearing the East Gate barbican now. Its double towers were twenty yin high, each flanking the enormous fortified gates that were tightly barred every night at dusk. As they approached, they could see guards with spears raised patrolling the walls. There were eight barbican gates to the city, all heavily guarded.

They jostled their way through a steady stream of people to the caravanserai – a maze of winding alleyways, teashops and guesthouses with open courtyards that lay just outside the city walls. It was home to a shifting population of hundreds of traders and travellers who passed through Maracanda every day – any storyteller worth his salt would find a ready audience here, and the boys knew that Shou Lao was one of the best.

They soon found where he was. A crowd had gathered in the large courtyard of one of the grander guesthouses. It was shady and cool, with a fountain splashing in the centre. Mothers and small children, boys and girls, old men and women, travellers and even some market traders taking a break – all waited patiently for the Old Man to appear. There was a hum of expectant chatter. The two boys settled down on the steps of the covered balustrade that enclosed the courtyard.

'Look – over there by the entrance.' Kan nudged Rokshan. 'Your brother – and Lianxang! I haven't seen her for a while.'

Rokshan followed his gaze and waved a hand in greeting, but they were deep in conversation and hadn't spotted them. An Lushan – everybody called him An'an apart from his father – was three years older than Rokshan and had just finished his last term at the School for Special Envoys. But he wasn't going on to the Han Lin Academy in Chang'an, to continue studying to be a diplomat; he lived for the family business. One day when they were both very young, he'd solemnly told his little brother that he was going to be even richer and more important than the great Vartkhis Boghos, a merchant famed throughout all the Known Lands, and so rich, it was whispered, he only had to breathe on something and it turned to gold. Rokshan was surprised to see An'an there – his brother always dismissed the old tales with a sneer; business and trade were what he lived for.

The friend he was with was a girl from the school called Lianxang. She was a year or so older than Rokshan, and was from the remote north of the Empire; she had only been at the school for a year but had impressed everybody with her quickness. Slight and light-footed, she wore her hair cropped short and carried a long stiletto dagger at her side. Rokshan had often asked her about her people, the mysterious Darhad, wandering nomads of the north, who had always kept themselves apart from the rest of the Empire, but she always gave an evasive answer, or laughed and gave a little shrug. But Rokshan knew that Lianxang – just like him – loved the old stories. He had often seen her in the library, immersed in the scrolls, and he suspected that the old myths and legends meant more to her than she would like to admit. Doubtless her being there explained why his brother was amongst the crowd.

A hush descended as a little boy in the front of the crowd pointed towards one of the arched entrances surrounding the courtyard. There was a shuffling of feet and clearing of throats as everyone wondered when the Old Man was going to appear. A minute or two passed before there was an intake of breath and the crowd strained to catch a glimpse of the renowned storyteller as a faint tap-tapping beyond the archway could be heard . . .

CHAPTER 2

THE STORYTELLER

All eyes were on the Old Man as he made his frail, shuffling progress along the covered walkway. He leaned heavily on a carved ivory staff, which struck the stone floor with every step. He would have barely reached the shoulders of even the younger boys in the crowd, so bent with age had he become. Rokshan was as amazed at his appearance now as he'd been at the age of eight or nine when he'd last seen the storyteller – he could have sprung out of any of the paintings on the scrolls in the city library that depicted the emperor's courtiers of long ago. He probably smelled of the library too, Rokshan thought: slightly musty.

His progress was slow, so everyone had a good stare. His wizened head was completely shaven apart from the long plaited ponytail, white with age now, that hung all the way down his back. His hooded eyes looked as if they were almost shut. His nose was large and fleshy and his long grey-white beard was oiled. He wore a belted wide-sleeved silk coat of faded crimson, long enough to cover his sandalled feet. A small perfume bottle hung from his belt on each hip.

At last, at the top of one of the sets of steps that led down to the fountain, the Old Man stopped and turned slightly.

'My greetings, people of Maracanda; may Kuan Yin, goddess of mercy and protector of travellers, always watch over you.'

Shou Lao spoke in a surprisingly clear voice, offering the traditional greeting of travellers on the ancient trading routes

14

before making his way down and eventually settling himself on the cool marble bench around the fountain.

In the midday heat, the hubbub from the caravanserai and the Grand Bazaar had quietened to a low murmur. The audience hardly dared breathe as they waited and wondered what the Old Man of the Markets was going to say. A mother hushed her young child, who had begun to cry. Kan started to say something but Rokshan jabbed him with his elbow to be quiet.

'People of Maracanda,' Shou Lao began, his voice echoing around the courtyard as he gestured towards the younger children at the front of the crowd. 'Girls and boys. Some of you have heard me tell of the old myths and legends, of when the Earth was young and all Known Lands and Unknown Lands were one. Remember them well, for one of them tells a tale which may be taken up by some of you here today.'

The old storyteller paused for breath, looking sternly at the smallest children who'd wriggled through the crowd and gathered at his knees, their faces alight with expectation as they fidgeted impatiently. Rokshan smiled as he recalled how excited he had always felt, waiting for the storyteller to begin one of his tales.

'But perhaps I should begin with the story of how the fallen guardian spirit who became the keeper of the gates of Hell got his name.'

Shou Lao's eyes twinkled as the children clapped and cheered in anticipation of one of their favourite tales. Rokshan remembered how frightened he had been when he'd heard it first: he couldn't have been more than four or five years old, but the story of the Crimson King – so-called because, chained close to the roaring fires of Hell, his skin was perpetually alight as he suffered his eternal punishment for rebelling against his divine master, the Wise Lord – had made a deep impression on him.

Shou Lao told the familiar tale; the older children – if An

Lushan was anything to go by – would now tease their younger siblings mercilessly with scary imitations of the fiery but fallen guardian spirit.

Now the old storyteller produced a battered-looking leather basket, which he passed into the crowd. The clink of coins being tossed into the basket was the only sound as the old man addressed them again.

'People of Maracanda – I said that one of the tales of long ago might one day be taken up by some of you here today. You may think this is just an old man's fancy – you will tell me that the history of our ancestors, which became legend and then passed into myth, has been forgotten, along with the prophecies, and are now lost for ever . . .' Here Shou Lao paused, wanting, it seemed, to fix everyone in the crowd with his hooded, beady stare. Rokshan looked away as his gaze fell upon him and lingered.

'. . . or so some of you may conclude from your studies here at the famous Maracanda School for Special Envoys!'

'He still remembers us – or you at least.' Kan looked in amazement at his friend. Rokshan jabbed him with his elbow again; he didn't want to miss a word of what the Old Man was saying.

'And that is what I am here to tell you about today, for there is much our ancestors knew that should not have been forgotten, but not all of it is lost. Listen now, for this, of all my stories, you should heed.

'You have all heard tell of the story of Chu Jung and his vanquishing of the ancient dragons . . .' At this the children again clapped and cheered, thinking they were going to hear another of their favourite stories. Nods and murmurs of agreement rippled across the rest of the crowd.

'Of how the evil of the ancient dragons was crushed; after mercifully being reborn in water, they once again became the spirits of nature with which you are familiar to this day. The legend recounts how some of the dragons were reborn as "heavenly horses" – or so the ancients called them – part horse, part dragon, able to fly; creatures which, so our emperors have always believed, would take them to Heaven when their span on Earth was done. The legend lives on in the dragon horses of the Kingdom of the Wild Horsemen. This much you all know.'

Shou Lao had his audience spellbound, even though he was only telling the very end of the story now.

'And you all know how Chu Jung kept apart the Talisman he used to capture the fiery breath of the dragons and the Staff he made from the Tree of Heaven as a gift for the Wise Lord, so that they would for ever afterwards be powerless, the one without the other, and so it is that they must never be united.' Shou Lao's voice rose a little as he proclaimed the ancient verse that Rokshan had heard so many times before.

> 'Whosoever through the ages wields the Staff
> Will be commanded by the evil one, grown bold –
> "Seek, seek the Talisman of old!"
> And he will be drawn, and lose his way.
> Yet he who serves the Wise Lord
> Treads the righteous path, and will never stray.'

He paused for breath, and again, it seemed to Rokshan, fixed him with his hooded stare, before giving a little shrug and leaning forward with both hands clasped at the end of his staff.

'So it is, and so it goes: a legend is just a legend. What does it tell us? The Wild Horsemen have their dragon horses, so called because they are venerated as the descendants of the heavenly horses, but ordinary horses they are, nonetheless.

'But if this is all you thought the legend tells us, you would be wrong,' Shou Lao said quietly. Now his eyes were blazing as he looked out fiercely over the crowd.

'People of Maracanda, your kingdom borders the valleys of the Horsemen, and I tell you a shadow grows here in the west which is spreading across all Known Lands, and creeps even towards the Lands of the Barbarians. It seeks the ancient powers given to Chu Jung so that it can command a magic so great that even the Wise Lord trembles at its destructive powers. The ancient scrolls foretold this, and I tell you even now, events unfold that bear witness to their truth.'

The old storyteller leaned heavily on his staff and hauled himself up, summoning all his energy so that his voice rang out. 'I speak of the end of empires, people of Maracanda! China and all Known Lands – even stretching beyond the Unknown Lands – all shall wither and die. The ancient power is stirring and shall be corrupted anew: the sleeping dragon awakes!'

'What sort of story is this, old man? Who awakes the sleeping dragon?'

Shou Lao glanced to where An Lushan stood with Lianxang at his side – it was as if the old storyteller knew immediately who had asked the question that was on everyone's lips. 'You would want to know, An'an?'

Rokshan wondered with a start how the Old Man knew his brother – he couldn't have seen him for nearly ten years, and then he would have been just another small, excited face in the crowd. His brother looked surprised too.

'The servant of the Nameless One is the one I speak of,' Shou Lao replied. 'He serves the Shadow-without-a-name, the Lord of Evil. He pores over the ancient lore and is plotting to use the power of the dragons of old for his own ends. He must be stopped, before it is too late. But there is one small hope – an ancient scroll unearthed in the Kingdom of the Wild Horsemen, which foretold this very moment: I speak of the riddle of the Staff – the Staff of the mighty Chu Jung himself, Spirit of Fire and Heavenly Executioner, first and most devoted servant of the Wise Lord.'

Exhausted, the Old Man slumped down on the bench and once more passed his leather basket into the crowd as everyone started to talk at once.

'I thought he was losing his touch there for a second,' a man behind Rokshan said; 'then as soon he talked about a riddle, I knew we were going to be all right. Well, you can't just end a story hanging in the air like that, can you? Wouldn't be a story then – I mean, with no ending – now would it?'

A young boy shyly handed the leather basket back to Shou Lao, who gave a small nod and rose to his feet again, a small scroll in his hands.

'People of Maracanda. Hear the riddle of the Staff:

> 'The horse of Heaven has come,
> Open the far gates.
> Raise up my body, o beloved,
> I go to the Mountain of K'unlun.
> The horse of Heaven has come,
> Mediator for the dragon.
> He travels to the Gate of Heaven
> And looks on the Terrace of Jade.

'People of Maracanda, you have heard the riddle – it must be solved . . . before it is too late . . .'

Shou Lao carefully rolled up the scroll and tucked it into his belt, saying nothing more. Excited murmuring hummed around the courtyard.

Rokshan didn't hear it – the noise of the crowd seemed far away as Shou Lao's words echoed round his head; for some reason they seemed especially important, as if the storyteller had been talking to him and him alone. Was everyone else thinking the same? he wondered, shaking his head and looking around. He saw An Lushan and Lianxang turning to go; but then his brother suddenly stopped and stared directly at him before being hurried along as the gathering broke up, the crowd's fleeting interest in the story waning, the riddle forgotten – and Shou Lao gone.

'Roksy! What is it? Come on . . . Roksy?' Kan was looking with concern at his friend, shaking him gently by the shoulder. 'What's the matter?'

But there was nothing Rokshan could say. He could only wonder at his reaction to Shou Lao's words – and whether he might seek out the Old Man again to ask him more.

They had the courtyard to themselves as the last few people wandered away. Rokshan scooped some water from the fountain, murmuring a prayer of thanks to the dragon spirit of the underground spring for the cool freshness of the water as he splashed it on his face.

'Feeling better?' Kan asked. Rokshan nodded.

'You still look as if you've seen a *kuei* – an evil spirit of the road!' his friend joked, trying to cheer him up. 'But what about that ending of the last story? This ancient scroll unearthed in the Kingdom of the Wild Horsemen . . . Of all the kingdoms in the Empire, it had to be the Wild Horsemen . . .' he went on excitedly.

'What do you mean?'

'I know from talking to people in all the places we visit when we're touring that there are some strange goings-on in the lands of the Wild Horsemen. Haven't the rumours reached Maracanda yet? I bet your father is interested in what's going on there – it's the Horsemen who control the Terek Dhavan Pass.'

'Yes, I know – it's the main northern route over the Pamir Mountains to the imperial capital. But why would I listen to rumours? Better to wait until we hear from my uncle, Zerafshan – I bet even now he's with the Horsemen, going about the emperor's business.'

'Are you *sure* you haven't heard anything from him? Or *about* him? All the rumours say the emperor's business is the last thing he's going about.' The look Kan gave his friend was a mixture of intense curiosity and exasperation. 'Tropical storms in the middle of winter when the temperatures at the height of the pass should be low enough to freeze the flesh off your bones? Animal shrieks echoing around the valleys up there that don't sound like anything anyone has ever heard? A new, self-appointed leader of the Horsemen inciting them to rebellion? Could that be your uncle? That's what some people are saying . . . You haven't heard *any* of this stuff?' Kan looked expectantly at him.

'Look,' Rokshan replied, trying not to sound irritated, 'my father told me that my uncle was sent on a special mission to soften up the Horsemen because the emperor wants more of their so-called dragon horses, but we don't know for sure what's happened to him, or what's going on in their valleys – and even if we did, it still might not help us understand what Shou Lao was talking about. I haven't seen my uncle for ages, almost five years! So how can I possibly know what's happening?'

'You really think the Old Man was serious – it wasn't just another one of his stories?'

'What – with all that stuff about ancient scrolls and riddles? And a warning to everybody as well! Of course he was serious! Except I don't think his warning was meant for everybody . . .' Rokshan trailed off, staring at the spot where Shou Lao had stood.

Kan followed his gaze as if he half expected the Old Man to suddenly appear again. 'What – you think it was meant just for you?' he asked, not sure if Rokshan was joking or not.

'Through my uncle, my family is involved with the Horsemen whether we like it or not. I'm sure that's not all he meant though,' Rokshan said, seeming to make up his mind. 'There's something else going on here . . . I can feel it, deep down. Kan, where did the Old Man go – did you see?'

'Shou Lao? I don't know – he always seems to disappear like that. I can ask around . . . He may be staying a few days.'

'Thanks, Kan. If you see him, tell him I'd . . . I'd like to speak with him,' Rokshan said hesitantly. 'For now, I think I'll go to the school library to see if I can find anything that might help explain the riddle – you never know . . .'

'You never know, but I think you'll be wasting your time. I've got to go. We've got a show on at Moon Lake this evening and it'll take the rest of the day to get there. Meet you tomorrow, same place?'

Kan cartwheeled off, whirling round just before he reached the guesthouse entrance. 'Roksy, nearly forgot! Your father's old friend, Chen Ming, the caravan master – bumped into him in the caravanserai when we'd just got back. He's ready to set off on his summer caravan to the imperial capital. He said he's staying at the Drawn Scimitar. Why don't you speak to him? He knows all the Old Man's stories.'

The familiar smell hit Rokshan as he entered the Empire's biggest and most famous library. He savoured the cool mustiness and felt himself unwinding after the strange events of the morning. But where to start unravelling the riddle?

He sat down and looked around; it was very near the end of term and there were only a handful of students scattered about. The racks of dusty scrolls and loosely bound manuscripts encircled the whole room and stretched up to the vaulted ceiling . . . His heart sank: it would take him the rest of the summer just to go through Legends & Mythology . . .

Feeling daunted by the task, he decided he would at least make a start. He pulled out a scroll at random, carefully unrolled it and was soon absorbed in the battles of good against evil in the ancient past, long before the history of the Empire had ever begun.

Time and time again, however, he found himself drawn back to the great myth the Old Man had referred to in his last story: Chu Jung and his taming of the dragon spirits. The very thought of the dragon horses that some of them had ultimately become – or so the legend told – thrilled him in a way he could not explain or understand.

He was having one last rummage around among the dustiest of the hundreds of volumes when he suddenly discovered an old scroll that had been tucked away behind the other books on a shelf. It was only a single page, but its subject – about an ancient secret society, the Fellowship of the One-eared Hares – drew his attention, as if he was somehow meant to see it.

The Fellowship of the Hares is a secret society dedicated to the worship of just one god, Ahura Mazda, the Wise Lord, creator of Heaven and Earth and of all things at the beginning of time.

The Wise Lord created Eight Immortals – guardian spirits who took human form – to act as his emissaries and maintain the balance of harmony and disharmony on Earth. The Fellowship of the Hares is made up of ordinary men and women who can be commanded by all or any one of the Immortals – who may adopt ordinary human appearance in whatever guise they choose – whenever they need to intervene directly in the affairs of men.

The Elect makes up the commanding body of the fellowship – twelve high-ranking priests. Each member is known by the number of his election – First, Second, Third of the Elect – but it is a non-hierarchical organization, except that the First Elect is acknowledged as the 'first among equals'. The priests have their own spirit-birds or animals, which they and no one else can communicate with in their minds.

The three hares of the fellowship represent Light, Life and Truth – the three intertwined faces of harmony.

The Fellowship of the Hares embraces the worship of all gods and spirits as either creations or manifestations of the Wise Lord, but does not under any circumstances extend this to worship of the emperor as the 'Son of Heaven'. For this reason, it was banned throughout the Empire and is now a secret organization.

Source: unknown.

CHAPTER 3

IMPERIAL MADNESS

By the time he got home later that day, Rokshan was tired and hungry and looking forward to the evening meal. His reading hadn't turned up anything that shed light on the Old Man's riddle. Feeling let down by his lack of success, and hoping that Chen Ming could at least point him in the right direction, he was even more disappointed when he called in at the Drawn Scimitar only to find that the caravan master wasn't there. All he could do was leave a message.

Arriving home, he'd hardly heaved the heavy front door shut, grateful to escape the sultry heat, before Ah Lin came bustling up.

'Out in this heat, Rokshan? Come, you must drink and then lie down before dinner.'

She clucked around him, as she always did. Following his mother's death some years back, Ah Lin had naturally filled her place. He hugged her affectionately, and having been reassured that, no, he hadn't got into any trouble, and no, he really wasn't so tired that he needed to have a little nap before dinner, she seemed satisfied and hurried off as Rokshan's father called out a greeting.

The rooms of Rokshan's home were uncluttered and elegant, with high ceilings and wide doorways. Brightly coloured friezes decorated the walls; rich silk carpets lay on the cool marble floors. The front entrance led straight into the large ceremonial hall with its carved wooden pillars and vaulted brick ceiling; strongboxes of dark hardwood lined the walls.

His father used this area for conducting his business and for occasional meetings of the city's richest and most powerful trading families; right now he was pacing up and down, obviously distracted. Rokshan recognized the warning signs straight away: the knotted brow, the exasperated sighs, the bunched fist smacking the scroll he was reading.

'What is it, Father?' Rokshan asked as his father waved his arm about in exasperation. 'Is it another report?'

'Yes, yes . . . another report . . . unbelievable . . . completely unfounded, I'm sure . . .' He trailed off, muttering and mumbling, and continued his pacing.

Rokshan's father, Naha Vaishravana, was a typical Sogdian – stocky and round-faced, with a thick, bristling black beard flecked with grey. He had a booming baritone laugh, and his brown eyes were surrounded by a crisscross of laughter lines. He had worked hard for his success, having built up his business from humble beginnings with a market stall to one of the biggest trading houses, well-known and respected in Maracanda.

Rokshan was concerned to see his father so agitated – he had been getting more of these reports in the last year than at any time he could remember. This one was probably from his chief spy in the court of the emperor. As one of the richer merchants in the kingdom, Naha had an unrivalled network of spies from Maracanda to Chang'an acting as his eyes and ears in every trading post, village, market town and military garrison along all the trading routes of the Empire. And he obviously did not like what he was reading. Perhaps his chief commercial rival and old enemy – the legendary foreign merchant, Vartkhis Boghos, of the neighbouring Kingdom of Armenia – had beaten his father to a trading contract he had specially wanted?

Rokshan often helped his father draw up the inventory of goods to be traded on the 3000 li journey to the imperial capital. It was one of the most arduous journeys you could ever undertake and it was possible to take over two years to travel just one way. At any one time the trading house of Vaishravana might have two or even three caravans of fifty or more camels crisscrossing back and forth along the trading routes.

Even though he was training to be a special envoy, Rokshan longed to go on his first caravan. As his father paced up and down, he started to drift off into a delicious daydream of soaring mountain passes and unending deserts. His father's explosion soon snapped him back to reality.

'*What!?* Has his imperial highness gone mad? He will ruin us. *Ruin us*, Rokshan. I cannot . . . He cannot . . . It's utterly preposterous!' In a shaking, foot-stamping fury, he flung the spy's report to the floor.

Rokshan quickly checked around the hall to make sure there weren't any prying servants; sometimes his father said things that shouldn't be heard by anyone but family. This looked like it was going to be one of those times.

'Calm yourself, Father,' he said, feeling anything but calm in the face of one of Naha's volcanic outbursts, 'and watch what you're saying; walls have ears, as you're always telling me.' He hurried to retrieve the scroll. 'Surely the news cannot be so bad,' he soothed, glancing quickly through the report.

His father had stomped off to the far corner of the hall and was now stomping back again, hands held to his temples. He shook his finger at his son. 'How can it get worse? Unless your uncle succeeds in securing *three hundred* of the Wild Horsemen's dragon horses, the emperor is threatening to close the Terek Dhavan Pass. He wants to add not just a *few more* mounts to the imperial stables by increasing the annual tribute, but an *entire regiment* to the imperial army – "An elite dragon-horse cavalry corps," it says here.' He snatched the report back. 'So *that's* why your uncle was sent on his so-called diplomatic mission to the

Kingdom of the Horsemen . . . Hah! He's obviously failed, so far . . .' Naha lapsed into a fuming silence.

'*Three hundred,*' Rokshan repeated, awestruck. 'The emperor really has gone mad! The Horsemen will never agree to such a number. Everyone knows they're reluctant enough to deliver the annual tribute of two horses a year, let alone supply enough for a cavalry corps – of dragon horses?'

'They have refused your uncle's entreaties, and the emperor will use that as an excuse to invade, destroying them completely and capturing all their precious mounts . . . Pah! He is mad – utterly mad!'

'*Father,*' Rokshan implored, his finger against his lips.

Naha glowered, and then seemed to make up his mind. 'Well, the emperor can keep his dragon horses. We are Sogdians, master traders. Our language is spoken by all along the trading routes, from the streets of Yarkand to the southern valleys of the Karakoram, and across the deserts in Kuche, Shorchuk and Gaochang – all the way to the imperial capital itself. The whims of our emperor, three thousand li away to the east, will not stop us.'

It was true: Rokshan's people, the Sogdians, were recognized throughout all Known Lands as merchants – traders, carpet-makers, glass-makers and woodcarvers. At the age of five, all boys in Maracanda and throughout the Kingdom of Sogdiana were taught to read and write as the essential basis for their future commercial skills.

'Father, listen. The Kingdom of the Wild Horsemen borders our own. The emperor will destroy the Wild Horsemen, so the report says, and take all their horses away from them. Maracanda's trade to the east will be threatened as a result, because no one will be able to cross the Terek Dhavan Pass, which is the only route across the mountains and is closely guarded by the Horsemen. The emperor will close it for however long it takes to crush the Horsemen.'

'We don't need a report from my spy at the imperial court to tell us that.' Naha was grim-faced.

'Yes, and we know the Horsemen guard it with their lives,' Rokshan added, 'and if you take the wrong path, you risk wandering into their sacred breeding grounds . . .' He left the rest unsaid.

The cruelty of the Wild Horsemen's Law of the Transgressor was legendary throughout the Empire, even though it had long been outlawed: none but the Horsemen's Waymasters – teachers of the Way of the Horse – or their mysterious horse-singers were permitted to know the exact location of the sacred breeding grounds. It was whispered that the Horsemen still secretly carried out their barbaric ancient punishment: any trespasser in their valleys was blinded so that he would never point the way to the sacred place, and his tongue was cut out so that he would never talk of it.

'The Horsemen will disappear into their secret valleys and hidden caves. The imperial troops do not know the land and they'll never find them. The Horsemen will pick them off, one by one. It could take years, but the Horsemen will hold out. They will never surrender.'

'You may be right, Rokshan. If you are, then we will simply take the longer southern route and avoid the pass altogether.'

'But the southern trading route can add six months to the journey to the imperial capital – and what about the warring states our caravans would have to pass through? There's no sign of peace there.'

'I know, I know,' Naha replied, sighing deeply. 'By the time we'd paid the warlords to pass through their territory, we wouldn't have any goods to trade in Chang'an.'

Rokshan noddded. Now seemed as good a time as any to bring up this morning's events.

'Father, you remember Shou Lao, the old storyteller?'

Naha nodded distractedly, only half listening. 'He's back in Maracanda,' Rokshan continued. 'Well, he was – he may have gone again already – but the last story he told this morning was . . . rather different from his other stories. In fact, it wasn't really a story at all – more like a riddle.'

'A riddle?' Naha said dismissively.

'Yes . . .' Rokshan said nervously; it did sound rather ridiculous now, but he pressed on anyway. 'He said we must solve it, before it's too late—'

'Too late for what? Why are you bothering me with these ramblings?' his father muttered impatiently.

'He didn't say where it had come from, Father, only that the riddle was unearthed in the Kingdom of the Horsemen. Kan says there are lots of rumours to do with the Horsemen too – you must have heard of them. One says—' Rokshan stopped as a thunderous scowl clouded his father's face.

'Rumours, my boy! Circus people live and breathe them! I don't rely on rumours to inform me about what I need to know – I make it my business to know everything that's going on. Your uncle, Zerafshan, is doing his best to win the Horsemen over – these matters take a great deal of time and diplomacy. Now, I know my brother and I have had our differences, but that is all in the past. Zerafshan didn't want to help me when our business was struggling and still in its infancy, and he went his own way – he always was . . . *headstrong*, shall we say. But he made up for it by doing us a lot of favours when he was at the imperial court. We should not forget that.'

Rokshan's memories of his uncle were hazy – he had not seen him for many years, not since he was eight or nine – he couldn't recall exactly. He had recollections of a swashbuckling adventurer who smelled of sweat and horse leather and never stayed for more than a few days at a time. His mother had always seemed to laugh a lot on his uncle's infrequent visits.

'But, Father—' Rokshan protested.

'That is all I have to say on the matter, Rokshan. The ramblings of an old storyteller do not concern me: the pass is not yet closed, and I have other plans, even if the emperor does carry out his threat.'

Rokshan knew his father better than to stretch his patience further, and quietly excused himself, saying he would see him at the evening meal. Naha disappeared into his study, slamming the door behind him.

Wondering what on earth those 'other plans' were, Rokshan went into the family room, where there were couches and low, finely lacquered tables for dining. The kitchen and family room adjoined the hall, with servants' quarters leading off from the kitchen and a large cellar that could only be accessed from that part of the house. His father's study was tucked away next to the family room. It was getting dark when Rokshan stepped onto the balcony that looked out over the city.

As his eyes grew accustomed to the gloom, he saw a small shuffling figure he thought he recognized making its way slowly towards the house.

'Shou Lao?' he called down incredulously. What on earth was the storyteller doing here? The shadowy figure gestured with his arm for him to come down. Rokshan signalled he would be there in a second, sneaked quietly past his father's study, padded through the ceremonial hall and slipped out through the heavy double doors.

The storyteller bowed creakily as Rokshan hurried up to him. 'May Kuan Yin, goddess of mercy and protector of travellers, always watch over you,' he said solemnly – the traditional greeting of travellers on the trade roads – holding up his hand as Rokshan started to say something. 'We must have some minutes alone,' he went on, 'by your house shrine – no one will overhear us there.'

'Y-yes, we can offer a prayer to the goddess,' Rokshan stammered; confused and a little alarmed at the Old Man's sudden appearance, without thinking he made the sign of the dragon. A lantern-seller, bent almost double under a clinking load of assorted brass lamps, looked at them hopefully for a sale as he went by, shouting out his wares.

'Oil for your lamps! Lamps for sale! Exchange new for old! Oil for your lamps . . . !'

'The gods will look favourably on your devotion. Come,' Shou Lao muttered as he hobbled over to the front door.

CHAPTER 4

THE FELLOWSHIP OF THE HARES

Rokshan swung the front doors shut and they made their way to the shrine at the end of the hall, which was dedicated to the patron goddess of the house, Kuan Yin. On the altar, delicately carved in green soapstone and adorned with silver earrings and gold amulets, stood a half life-size statue of the serenely smiling goddess. A finely sculpted crouching dragon in bronze, all rolling coils and glaring eyes, guarded the shrine.

Rokshan approached the altar, bowed and prayed to the dragon spirits to send cooling rains. Then he bowed to the statue of the goddess, his lips moving soundlessly in prayer, before turning to Shou Lao, who had remained a respectful few paces behind while the ritual of worship was observed.

Now the old storyteller shuffled forward. Rokshan caught his slightly musty odour before it mingled with the incense burning on the altar.

'My young friend, I can no longer keep your destiny from you; a destiny that will prevent you following the trading traditions of your people. You must go on a journey,' the Old Man explained, 'far to the east, across the Flame Mountains in the Land of Fire. There you will find the court of the Crimson King and the Guardian Monk – who you alone must help; all else will fail if you do not succeed in this.'

Rokshan did not like the sound of this at all. 'What destiny?' he burst out. 'The mountains you speak of are nearly one thousand li from here! And the Crimson King is just a myth; one of your stories. And who is this Guardian Monk?'

His mind was whirling. Shou Lao seemed to be saying that he had no choice but to do what he was telling him. Why? And when? Were the characters he'd heard and read about in stories actually living? Was it possible to meet a real guardian spirit? But the old storyteller only answered his questions with one of his own.

'Are you not training to be a special envoy at the school?' Shou Lao asked. 'So you would expect it to be a long and difficult journey. Death will be your constant companion. But always keep this in your heart, whatever may befall you: be true to yourself, and the answer you seek will find you. Remember this, and I will be with you on your journey.'

'I . . . I still don't understand,' Rokshan stammered.

'Your elder brother is going to take over the family business,' the Old Man replied patiently, 'but you . . .' He produced what looked like a copper coin or token. Without a word, he handed it to Rokshan. 'Look carefully. What do you see?'

Rokshan examined the token, turning it over and over in his fingers. 'It is too large for a coin and I . . . I cannot make out what the wording is around the edge, it is too worn. But the three hares − they must be hares, with such long ears − they each represent Ahura Mazda, the incarnation of Light, Life and Truth, in the old religion of long ago,' he said, handing it back. 'Strange, but I was only reading about the legend of the three hares this afternoon—'

'Keep it − it is a token of the ancient Ahura Mazda priesthood,' Shou Lao interrupted, 'formerly known as the Fellowship of the Three One-eared Hares . . .' He put his hand gently on Rokshan's arm, suddenly deadly serious. 'You must believe this, Rokshan . . . your scrolls and dusty documents in the library may deny it, but the fellowship and ancient priesthood are alive still. Men and women, from the imperial capital in the east to your own city here in Maracanda and throughout all Known Lands, even to Byzantium and yet further west, to the cold, grey Lands of Ice – all are united in one common purpose: to protect us from evil. It is a peaceful organization; the three hares, as you rightly say, represent the harmony of Light, Life and Truth. Each is inseparable, one from the other, in the dance of life. That is why they are always depicted, wherever you see their symbol, chasing each other. And they each share an ear, because to understand our own dance, we have to listen to our hearts as if they were one, shared by all men.'

'But . . . why do you want me to keep the token? Even when Ahura was worshipped far and wide, long ago, its priesthood was a secret one, and the scroll I read in the library said the same thing: that the Fellowship of the Hares was disbanded hundreds of years ago. It is forgotten now, just like Ahura – so who or what do they worship now?'

'Ahura is still worshipped; he just goes under many different names – Kuan Yin and all our gods, the Buddha too; Ganesh the elephant god and all the beneficent dragon spirits of the rivers and oceans, mountains and valleys: they are all one and the same, Rokshan,' Shou Lao explained. 'Ahura, the Wise Lord, sees all and hears all. It does not matter to him that men and women worship all forms of different gods, as long as—'

'As long as what, Storyteller?'

An Lushan stepped through from the adjoining family room. Rokshan realized with a start that his brother could not have come through the front entrance but must have entered the house through the servants' quarters.

'Why should we take all that old religious stuff seriously? Would you have us believe that the incarnation of darkness, death and evil is still the same? That he is known as the Shadow-without-a-name, according to your "ancient priesthood", as you call it?'

Shou Lao's beetling brows furrowed as he smiled thinly. 'Whether you believe it or not, An'an, the Shadow is ever intent on his purpose . . . which is why we should always be on our guard, mindful of his deceiving ways. Wouldn't you agree?'

'Perhaps so . . . but what is written in *The Book of Angra Mainyu* — or *Book of the Dead*, as it is more commonly known?' An Lushan asked, almost absently.

Rokshan looked at him, surprised.

'I'll tell you: "And in the ages to come, the Shadow-without-a-name will stir, waking as if from a sleep of the dead, intending still to break his eternal chains of space and time that bind him in the Arch of Darkness, once more to challenge his divine master, the Wise Lord." '

An Lushan stared coolly back at them as he proclaimed the old text. Shou Lao had himself only told the tale that morning, but An Lushan was quoting from the oldest written version of the story of the Wise Lord's punishment of the rebellious Shadow-without-a-name; how Corhanuk, messenger to the Wise Lord, had witnessed his eternal imprisonment but had hidden himself away from his divine master, choosing to serve the Shadow instead. An Lushan crossed the room and walked over to the altar.

'You are well-informed for one who does not believe in all that old religious stuff, as you put it,' Shou Lao said sternly, his hooded eyes flashing as he fixed An Lushan with a long, hard look. 'Perhaps you should read the ancient texts and prophecies again, my friend; they may tell you something important — about yourself and your place in the world.'

'I have learned from my father the importance of being well-informed, Storyteller,' An Lushan replied brusquely. 'It is a lesson we cannot learn well enough in the world today.'

He looked at the Old Man quizzically. 'Anyway, if your prophecy has truly come from this scroll unearthed in the Kingdom of the Wild Horsemen, why don't you tell us about their refusal to increase their tribute to the emperor? Even Rokshan could tell you that may lead to serious trading problems for our family,' he said with a malicious smile directed at his younger brother. 'And what of our uncle, Zerafshan, and his role in all this?' he went on, ignoring Rokshan's murmured protest. 'Have the Horsemen proclaimed him their new khagan? Could he be this mysterious leader that all the rumours tell of? My mother, if she was still alive, would have been greatly interested by anything you'd have to say about him,' he added sarcastically, almost as an after-thought.

'Peace, An Lushan. You must speak to your father of these matters,' Shou Lao said reprovingly. 'As you said, you learned from him the importance of being well-informed,' he added with just a hint of a smile. 'I will take my leave now.'

He took Rokshan's arm; Rokshan gave his brother a fierce look before walking the old storyteller to the door. Before he shuffled off into the night, Shou Lao paused, looking up at Rokshan.

'I will not see you again until many things have come to pass,' he said mysteriously. 'May Kuan Yin bless and protect you.'

Rokshan bowed respectfully, his mind churning. What could the old storyteller mean? But when he looked up, the Old Man had gone.

He went to rejoin his brother, who was standing on the balcony, looking out over the city.

'What's got into you, An'an – why were you so disrespectful to Shou Lao?' Rokshan asked indignantly.

An Lushan didn't reply and remained with his back to his brother. Rokshan was only a few paces from him when he noticed his brother was shaking slightly. Something made him stop still as An Lushan stretched out his arms as if trying to gather up the whole city. Suddenly a large crow swooped down from nowhere and cawed noisily.

'Where did that come from? Ugly thing – get away, go on, shoo!' An Lushan flapped his arms and the bird flew off.

'What were you doing just then?' Rokshan asked.

'Doing? I was just standing on the balcony, having a stretch. What an odd question, little brother.' An Lushan leaned against the thick-beamed timber and folded his arms, looking expectantly at his brother. 'You asked me a question, didn't you?'

'I asked you what you were thinking of, talking to Shou Lao like that?'

An Lushan shrugged. 'We need to know what's happening – it's a simple matter of economics: if the pass is closed, we will have to look elsewhere to make up the business we will lose as a result, and fast, before every other trading house does the same. If Shou Lao has the information to help us make that decision now, he should tell us. The timing is crucial, Rokshan, you must see that.'

'Of course I see that!' Rokshan retorted hotly. 'Father already has the information he needs to make that decision. He has already spoken to me of "other plans"—'

Just then they heard the study door slam and their father's brisk tread before he emerged through the ornate arched entrance of the family room.

'Boys!' he boomed delightedly. 'I thought I heard you at prayer downstairs, but here you are,' he said before stopping in mid-stride and spreading his arms questioningly. 'Why all the long faces? Too much prayer is just as bad as too little, I always say . . . Come, come, what troubles you?'

Rokshan looked at his father affectionately as Naha poured himself a goblet of wine and took an appreciative gulp.

'Well?' he growled, glaring at them both, but with an unmistakable twinkle in his eye.

An Lushan glowered at his brother. 'Tell Father everything the old storyteller was talking about,' he said softly, but with a slight edge to his voice.

'Storyteller? That old mischief-maker! I've already heard about his latest nonsense,' Naha exclaimed.

'No, Father, this is something else,' Rokshan jumped in quickly. 'He . . . he's just paid us a visit—'

'Here?' Naha sounded as surprised as Rokshan had been when he'd first seen the Old Man outside their house, and listened intently as his younger son told him everything the storyteller had said.

With a fixed expression on his face and clutching his wine, Naha heard him out and then strode over to the balcony to look out across the city he loved. The minutes passed slowly. Only the distant clatter of pans and sizzle of food being prepared for the evening meal disturbed what had become a thunderous silence. Rokshan looked anxiously at his older brother. None of them spoke.

'Very well . . .' Naha spoke at last as he turned to face them. 'It is time the truth was out – and the truth is sometimes hard to face. I of all people understand this,' he said reflectively, taking a large draught of wine before continuing. 'The simple truth is that the emperor wants to destroy the Wild Horsemen because of his obsession with what the Horsemen see as their sacred charges. But they are a proud, fierce people who will fight to the last man to save their dragon horses. And there are some who say we should help them – because of what the legends say the dragon horses were once, long ago—'

'May I speak, Father?' An Lushan interrupted.

'Go on, boy.'

'It is well-known that the Wild Horsemen have long been restless and resentful of the imperial yoke, refusing to increase their tribute payments to the emperor, as he wishes. But they have brought their own doom upon themselves through their leader's incitement to open rebellion – or so the rumours would have us believe. What then has all this got to do with us?'

'Everything – or nothing, depending on your point of view,' Naha replied grimly, putting his goblet down with a thud. Rokshan noticed his father's hands clasping and un-clasping as he paced about – a sure sign, he knew, that he was agitated.

'I can tell you, boys – and you know my sources are hardly ever mistaken – that the Wild Horsemen will give no more of their dragon horses until the emperor declares their independence. And, yes, it is true they have a leader who has united them and incites them to open rebellion. And I can tell you it is also true' – Naha lowered his voice just a fraction – 'that the Horsemen's leader, as I have long suspected but kept to myself, even in the face of all the rumours, is indeed my brother and your uncle – Zerafshan.'

Rokshan felt a wave of dismay break over him at the sight of his father's ashen face as he spoke; it seemed they must finally accept what had already begun to be whispered in the marketplace, the tea houses and the opium dens of Maracanda – that his uncle, Zerafshan, was a rebel and a traitor.

CHAPTER 5

SHOU LAO'S MESSAGE AND THE IMPERIAL MESSENGERS

Towards the eleventh candle-ring the following day, Rokshan wandered through the caravanserai just outside the East Gate. The winding alleys were already busy with small-time traders and merchants all shouting their wares, trades and services at the same time.

'Scrolls, paintings, booklets, prayer sheets and almanacs? Come and get them – all for sale here,' a wily-faced old stall-holder sang out. 'See what the future holds – it is all foretold in the stars. The year of the dragon, young master! Surely this'll be your lucky year . . . come . . .' The stallholder plucked at Rokshan's sleeve, unrolling with a flourish a star map full of complicated-looking astronomical charts and diagrams. 'Only one *taal*, young sir!'

'I already have all the almanacs I can study and they make my head spin!' Rokshan said with a laugh, shaking his arm free.

'Medical services for the young master?' another shouted, sensing a sale. 'Come, you look in need of my revitalizing medicaments . . . or something else perhaps? Please, this way.' The lanky herbalist in the long robes and conical hat of his trade indicated his dried flora and fauna neatly laid out on colourful cloths.

Next to him was a sharp-eyed acupuncturist with his gleaming rows of polished ivory needles: 'Dragon tattoos very cheap, if you have no ills. Bless the temple of your body, young master, with a fiery dragon spirit that will never fade. Please! This way!'

Palmists and pulse doctors, masseurs, and even 'demon doctors' specializing in exorcism – the caravanserai had them all.

The smell of incense and spices mixed with the different fruit and vegetables from all over the Empire hung in the air; food stalls with their charcoal stoves and braziers started to give off the most mouth-watering, delicious smells; suddenly Rokshan felt very hungry.

He pushed his way through the jostling crowd and grinned as he spotted the juiciest-looking apples just sitting on a stall, asking to be eaten. If Kan had been with him, it would have been a familiar routine for them: Kan would've gone in first – a whirl of cartwheels to distract the stallholder, who wouldn't notice a thing as Rokshan pocketed the prize . . . But then, to Rokshan's dismay, the sharp-eyed stallholder recognized him and, reaching underneath his gleaming display, threw a couple of rotten apples at him.

'Not from my stall, you won't – go on, hop it!' he shouted.

'Next time!' Rokshan shouted back as he ran off.

He ducked into a teashop; laughing and out of breath, he sprawled in a chair and was about to order a refreshing mint tea when suddenly a bulky figure loomed in the doorway. As Chen Ming stepped inside, he seemed to fill the whole of the little shop.

'So,' he chuckled, 'Rokshan, Special Envoy-to-be, I believe . . . I got your message.' He clapped an enormous hand on his shoulder.

'Blessings of the goddess,' Rokshan said, leaping up in surprise and bowing deferentially to the caravan master.

Chen Ming made an extravagant, sweeping bow in return. About the same age as Rokshan's father, he was a giant of a man with luxurious auburn hair which he wore in a mass of highly decorated braids. He had deep-set green eyes, rows of gold and silver earrings in both ears and a long drooping moustache after the fashion of his people, the Torgut Mongols of the Kingdom of Agni, neighbours to Rokshan's own land. The north-eastern boundaries of Agni bordered the Kingdom of the Wild Horsemen and the Torgut Mongols had long been their close allies.

Chen Ming sat down and waited to be served. The old woman who ran the shop brought his tea, her eyes lighting up as he offered her a handsome amount to close her doors for a while as they conducted their business. She murmured her assent and, shooing the handful of other customers out, disappeared to sit outside, shutting the rickety doors behind her.

Chen Ming toyed with the sprig of mint floating in his tea. 'Shou Lao has spoken to me,' he said at last. 'Rokshan, I do not know his ultimate purpose, but the Old Man has told me that I must help you. As a friend of your family for so many years, I am at your service.'

Rokshan nodded awkwardly. Chen Ming had been chief cameleer for his father for many years. He was an independent trader now, respected and sometimes feared, but known to any-one who had any sort of dealings in Maracanda and beyond.

'The Terek Dhavan Pass – the Summit of the Goddess – is the most direct and only northerly route over the Pamir Mountains, on the way east to the Flame Mountains,' the giant caravan master continued. 'Shou Lao has told me that you are to travel to these mountains and asked that I accompany you. You will reach the foothills of the pass with my late summer caravan to the capital. From the pass it will take as much as six full cycles of the moon to travel to the Flame Mountains – if you're following the northern caravan road. This is what Shou Lao told me to tell you, and to make clear that it is an arduous journey – no one would be mad enough to undertake it on their own, but it seems . . .'

Rokshan's head was throbbing so hard with the things that had happened over the last twenty-four candle-rings that he didn't hear the rest of what Chen Ming was saying. Shou Lao had only spoken to him of a journey – he hadn't said that he expected him to leave right now. Or had he? His mind was in a spin, trying to make sense of it all.

Chen Ming smiled, trying to reassure him. 'That is all the Old Man told me. He has gone, but he would not say where he was going, and I do not think he will return.'

In a daze, Rokshan felt Chen Ming's hand on his shoulder.

'Send word to me at the Drawn Scimitar. I will delay the departure of my caravan by two days, no more, to allow you sufficient time to make up your mind whether you will come with me or not.'

Just as Chen Ming pushed back his chair to go, Kan burst through the door.

'Come on, Roksy,' he cried breathlessly. 'We're going to miss the biggest show that's come to Maracanda since you and I were born – imperial dispatches being delivered to the city by the East Gate, with imperial messengers riding the emperor's dragon horses all the way from Chang'an! Luckily I know how to get the best ringside seats. Let's go! Sorry, Chen Ming . . .' He calmed down and bowed low under the towering scrutiny of the giant caravan master, who looked at him with an amused smile.

'Kanandak the acrobat, I believe,' he chuckled. 'May the blessings of the goddess be with you.'

'Will you come?' Rokshan asked Chen Ming.

The gold and silver rings in Chen Ming's ears jiggled as he shook his head. 'I will find out soon enough what their news is . . .' he said, stooping as he went out. The two boys bowed hastily to the broad expanse of his departing back.

'Not a moment to lose, Roksy! Stick with me!' Kan cried, diving out of the door.

They were immediately swirled along with the crowd, all heading in the same direction. Rokshan wondered how long it had taken the imperial messengers to bring the royal dispatches. They would be riding dragon horses from the emperor's own stables, and would have galloped in relay all the way across the Empire – 3000 li at least. Dragon horses! He had never seen one before.

'Come on, Roksy. Keep up!' Kan shouted over his shoulder, dodging and weaving in and out of the steady stream of people. 'Half the city's probably by the gate already.'

They were now nearing the East Gate barbican, where a thronging mass of people strained to get a glimpse of the imperial messengers.

At the foot of one of the towers there was a small door. A burly, heavily armed guard looked at them with a bored expression on his face as they approached.

'No, you can't go up on the battlements. If I've said it once I've said it a thousand times. N – O. No,' he said. He looked grim enough to mean it too, Rokshan thought.

'We have a pass, signed by your sergeant-at-arms,' Kan said confidently, producing a scrumpled piece of parchment with a flourish. 'Let us through. At once, please.'

The guard stared dubiously at the piece of parchment. 'What's it say? It's in some funny language. I can't let you through just because you produce some sort of pass thing. That's not the signature of my sergeant-at-arms either,' he said, jabbing at Kan's 'pass' with a grubby finger.

At this critical stage in the negotiations, three notes from the mournful-sounding horn blasted out across the ramparts. The crowd surged forward in anticipation.

'Look, the imperial messengers!' cried Kan excitedly, jumping up and down and pointing towards the gates. The guard turned his head, distracted by the commotion. In a flash, they had barged past him, hurled themselves through the doorway and leaped up the winding stone staircase that led to the top of the tower. They were astonished to discover that the entrance was open, and unguarded.

Kan peered around very cautiously. The nearest sentry stood some way along the battlements, but they could just see over the top from where they were.

Across the parched plains, through the shimmering heat haze, they could make out a thin column of dust. Three riders were approaching: the imperial messengers, one carrying the dispatches, one carrying the imperial standard and one escort – an expert archer with orders to shoot any who dared approach, and to ask questions later.

The riders were still a long way off, but the horses they rode were clearly no ordinary horses. These were dragon horses, taken in tribute-payment from the Wild Horsemen. Larger than ordinary horses, they were sixteen or even eighteen hands high. Deep-chested and with immensely powerful shoulders, they were grey or bay in colouring and their coats were sleek, their backs marked with three dark stripes; their long manes and tails streamed out like pennants. Their dark-green eyes, flecked with gold, smouldered with a fiery intelligence, and in the centre of their foreheads was emblazoned a writhing, brilliant-white winged snake – emblem of their ancient lineage and the fearsome beasts their ancestors had once been. Only the most courageous and intelligent riders could master them.

'Just think, Roksy, we're actually going to see an imperial dragon horse,' whispered Kan, his eyes straining to make them out in the hard glare of the afternoon sun.

The riders were fast approaching – they could now make out the leaping gold and green dragon of the imperial standard. They were riding abreast, three magnificent grey dragon horses, galloping so fast they seemed to float in a dusty blur. The riders wore short battle-robes of brilliant green with shoulder pads and protective leggings under short pleated skirts of sky-blue. All three wore russet-coloured caps and had long plaited hair.

Now, in a cloud of dust and thundering of hooves, they were nearly at the gates. Almost too late the messengers saw the mass of people awaiting them and had to rein in their mounts savagely. The horses whinnied in protest, steaming and frothing with quivering exhaustion. The urgent note of the escort's horn silenced the buzz of excited chatter. The imperial standard-bearer sat impassively.

The messenger acknowledged the elders of the city – Jiang Zemin, the thin, hatchet-faced leader of the Council of Elders, stepped forward to receive the dispatches. Before he handed them over, the messenger's voice rang out so that all could hear:

'Let the divine edicts of the celestial Jade emperor, Son of Heaven, ruler of the mighty Kingdom of China and all Known Lands, be known to his loyal subjects, the people of Maracanda.'

A dusty silence hung over the crowd as the messenger passed the dispatches to Jiang Zemin, who bowed deeply and then withdrew with the rest of the elders. The dispatches, and whatever divine edicts they contained, were soon forgotten as a low murmur of voices broke out in the crowd and a few brave souls ventured towards the dragon horses. As soon as they saw what was happening, Rokshan and Kan rushed down from their vantage point and pushed their way to the front.

The magnificent animals whinnied and blew noisily, as if they were greeting the Maracandians. Rokshan felt inexplicably drawn to one in particular, which pranced proudly, shaking its head and flicking its tail; he edged close enough to run his hand through the long silken mane. All Sogdians learned to ride at an early age, but the sturdy steppe ponies Rokshan was familiar with were different animals from the noble creature that stood in front of him, gazing at him gravely. The horse bowed its head as if in greeting, encouraging Rokshan to reach out; gently he traced the winged creature emblazoned on its forehead. The dragon horse whickered softly, as if trying to talk to him.

Rokshan bent closer and gazed into the dragon horse's eyes, and for a moment he felt as if he was drowning in the depths of green oceans. He grabbed instinctively for something to hold onto as he was swept into a whirlpool of colours that pummelled and tugged at him, pulling him this way and that. Strangely, he felt himself relaxing, and the more he let go, the more easily he seemed to float along with the pulsing colours that streamed about him . . . He felt himself laughing with joy at a sensation that was unlike anything he'd ever felt before—

'Stand aside, boy!'

Rokshan was jerked back to reality as the imperial messenger and his escorts prepared to leave. He stepped back in a daze, trying to make sense of what had just happened. As the messenger and his escorts wheeled round and trotted towards the gate, he felt a longing in his heart that he couldn't explain.

When Kan asked him whether he was feeling all right, he could only mumble a reply and had to turn away to hide the welling tears. He felt changed in some subtle, deep way, but wasn't sure how, or why . . . All he knew was that the heaviness of heart he felt was something to do with the dragon horses he had just seen for the first time in his life – and now they were gone.

CHAPTER 6

AN UNWELCOME VISIT

An Lushan, Rokshan and Lianxang were all gathered in the family room waiting for the master of the house. Naha had invited Lianxang to share their evening meal with them. Although she had visited their house many times since coming to Maracanda, she felt a little nervous. Rokshan was glad she was there − it would make it a far less gloomy affair than supper the day before.

'You've met Father before,' Rokshan tried to reassure her, 'he won't eat you, but to people who don't know him that well he can appear a bit overpowering.'

'I'll make sure he doesn't say anything embarrassing,' An Lushan laughed.

'Were you there when the imperial messengers came?' Rokshan asked, suddenly changing the subject − he'd hardly been able to get them out of his head. 'Half the city must have been there . . . And their horses − did you ever see such wonderful animals?'

'The famous *dragon horses* of the Wild Horsemen,' An Lushan said, sprawled on the cushions, eating nuts as fast as he could shell them. 'We only got a glimpse of them − we were right at the back of the crowd. You know, my mind's still on Shou Lao and his stories; have you found out anything about that riddle?'

Rokshan admitted he hadn't, deciding not to say anything about his meeting with Chen Ming. It was all still whirling in his head: a journey he was supposed to make, Shou Lao's riddle, the secret society of the Fellowship of the Hares that was still in existence not only in the Empire and all Known Lands but elsewhere in the world too . . . What was he supposed to do? He knew he had to decide fast – Chen Ming was waiting on his answer.

'Well, anyway, forget it for now. It won't be what Father wants to discuss tonight – I'm certain of that,' An Lushan said, glancing at Lianxang, who smiled nervously as they heard the slam of the front doors and the unmistakable heavy tread of their father's feet across the marbled floor. The two brothers looked at each other: they both knew what was coming next.

'Kuan Yin, sweet mother of mercy!' they heard Naha boom, but evidently he hadn't stopped at the house shrine, as his footsteps grew louder. 'Look kindly on your humble servant whose stomach rumbles and protests so groaningly that it must be fed at once . . . Ah Lin!' he bellowed as he bustled into the family room, shrugging off his jacket. 'Wine . . . before we all die of thirst!'

He clapped his hands in the unlikely event that Ah Lin hadn't heard him, and then stood in the middle of the room, a welcoming smile on his face.

'Lianxang, we are privileged indeed to be visited again by the sole representative in Maracanda of the people of the Darhad,' he said, bowing low but with no mockery in the courtesy.

'Thank you, Merchant Naha,' Lianxang replied, jumping up and bowing herself. 'An'an and Rokshan have always made me welcome in your house. They have been good friends to me ever since I arrived in Maracanda, as you know. I am very grateful to your family . . .'

'Of course, of course,' Naha said proudly, clapping both sons on the back before enfolding them in a crushing double hug, 'but there is no need for such formality, Lianxang – you are always welcome in our house . . . Ah Lin, at last!'

The house servant entered and set down a tray of wine

and house delicacies. Rokshan smiled his thanks at her.

'Come, let us drink,' Naha said. They all settled themselves on some cushions next to the low table and waited while Naha carefully poured the wine. He took a long draught and sighed appreciatively.

'Excellent!' he exclaimed. 'The finest sweet wine, made from the best mare's teat grapes in Kocho – a valued ally in these troubled times.'

Ah Lin brought some steaming bowls of lamb and rosemary soup with sweet bread, a Maracandian speciality, and soon the noise of satisfied slurping took over from the conversation. In between noisy gulps of soup, Naha asked Lianxang how her studies were going and what her plans were for the long summer break.

'My studies have gone better than I dared hope, Merchant Naha, but now I must return to my people . . .'

'Of course, they haven't seen you for nearly a year. You must be missing them,' Naha said sympathetically. 'But you will be back in the cooler months, ready for your final two years – I rely on you to keep an eye on my rascal of a younger son.' He beamed at Rokshan.

'I don't think Rokshan needs anyone's eye on him – certainly not mine! He is a natural scholar and will make a very special special envoy.' Lianxang smiled back, then suddenly looked very serious. 'But I have to tell you that I will not be coming back. My people allowed me only one year away from them . . . and . . . my . . . well . . . the fact of it is – my grandmother needs me.'

Silence fell around the dinner table as they looked at her in amazement – it had not occurred to them she would break off her studies.

'Your grandmother needs . . . ? But you are fifteen, nearly sixteen!' Naha exclaimed. 'In our country, plenty of girls of your age are already betrothed to be married and preparing to lead their own lives. Surely your people will allow you to finish your studies?' He seemed mystified.

'Merchant Naha, what I want more than anything else in the world is to become the Darhad's first special envoy,' Lianxang replied, looking around the table at the concerned, expectant faces of the family she had grown to love during her time in Maracanda. 'I want to represent my people so that at last we have a voice in the world. We have been silent nomads, stuck in the hinterland of the north for too long; it is time we played our part on the great stage of the Empire – and I want to be the first of the Darhad to lead our people onto that stage. If I was allowed to finish my studies here, I could go on to the Han Lin Academy in the imperial capital . . .'

'. . . and by the time you'd finished your studies there you'd be old enough for your people to take the dreams you have for them seriously – that sounds a very sensible plan, but do they want to be led, my girl?' Naha asked kindly. 'Aren't they happy in their old ways, keeping themselves to themselves, looking after their Dark Forests, as they've – *you've* always done?'

'Yes,' she replied, 'but that's the problem: we've always kept ourselves to ourselves and been shunned by the world *because* of our guardianship of the Dark Forests – which is why we cannot see that we live in poverty and ignorance!' Pushing her bowl away, she suddenly burst out, 'Before I came here, I had no idea . . . But when I saw your city for the first time, you cannot imagine how overwhelmed I was! I had never seen paved streets, or fountains, or brick houses so high that it seemed they almost reached the sky. And the riches of the markets – so much for sale! I wanted to sweep it all up into my arms and have it all to myself, for ever!' She stopped, embarrassed. 'But then I realized how selfish that was, and how much better it would be to be able to share' – she paused, and gestured with a wide sweep of her arm – 'all this . . . with my own people.'

'I remember when you first came to the school,' Rokshan said, trying to fill the awkward silence. 'You looked like you'd seen a ghost – but you soon settled in . . .'

'Of course you did, and now you have a second family, here with us,' Naha said, rubbing his beard vigorously – a sure sign, Rokshan knew, that he was thinking hard about what he was going to say next. 'If you want something badly enough, there is always a way to get it,' he reflected, staring towards the balcony. 'Your people have sent you out into the world, Lianxang. I imagine that is not a decision the elders of the Darhad took lightly: perhaps they can be persuaded more easily than you think of the need for change. You do not see it, but doesn't their decision already show a glimmer of acceptance that a people can improve their lot in life? That perhaps the old ways should be questioned? Look at us Sogdians! We have not been masters of the trade routes for ever – we were once nomads, like your people—'

'Many generations ago, Father,' An Lushan interrupted.

'Exactly so, my son – which only goes to prove my point! Now, Lianxang, what if you were to go back to your people with a proposition that would show them you were full of ideas and dreams for them; more than that, would prove to them that you had the ability to make your dreams for them come true? Isn't that something that would help them to agree to your continuing with your studies?'

Naha looked expectantly at Lianxang. Rokshan wondered what on earth it was his father had in mind.

Lianxang glanced at An Lushan, who smiled reassuringly at her. 'What were you thinking of, Merchant Naha?' she asked politely.

Just at this point, Ah Lin came hurrying back into the room carrying a tray laden with steaming, delicious smelling dishes.

'Excellent! Thank you, Ah Lin,' Naha said, eyeing the

dishes appreciatively, ladling his bowl full of rice and meat almost before they had been set down.

'My idea is this,' he continued between mouthfuls. 'Your Dark Forests . . . are absolutely vast . . . stretching from the near borders of the Land of the Darhad to – where?'

'The Dark Forests stretch from the most southerly borders of our land – not so very far from yours – to the edge of the Lands of Ice in the frozen north, where we have also wandered in the past. The swiftest of your dragon horses would gallop for seven days and as many nights and still not be halfway across them,' Lianxang concurred.

'Quite so, vast indeed, by all accounts.' Naha took a large draught of wine as he eased himself back against the cushions with a satisfied burp. 'So large that if – and I say if – your people were to harvest a small amount of the forests for trade as timber, it would hardly be missed; and of course those trees that are felled would be replenished in a carefully managed plan of renewal . . .'

Rokshan wondered about the knowing look his father gave An Lushan as he said this. Lianxang, however, flinched, and momentarily struggled to maintain her composure.

'It is an interesting idea, Merchant Naha,' she said politely but as if it was really of no interest to her, 'and now I understand why An'an has been so unusually interested in talking to me about my people and our way of life.' She flashed an angry look at him.

So that was why his brother had been spending so much time with her during the last few weeks – months even, Rokshan thought; this was at the heart of his father's 'other plans' if the pass to the east were to be closed. No wonder they had kept it a secret. But even so, he felt a stab of jealousy that his father had told only his brother about it, and not him.

'But consider this,' Lianxang was saying. 'Our Dark Forests

are sacred to us. It is an implicit trust that has been placed in us to safeguard them. What you're suggesting . . . to my people it would be unthinkable.'

'But possibly not to you?' Naha asked, either ignoring or quite blind to Lianxang's obvious sensitivity on the subject. 'I'm sure the Wild Horsemen thought it was quite as unthinkable when the emperor first imposed his tribute on them, and that was not so long ago.'

'Perhaps if your people had more time to reflect on it, Lianxang, having heard what we proposed first-hand . . . ?' An Lushan asked quietly, looking at his father.

'Sometimes we have to think the unthinkable if we want our dreams to come true, Lianxang,' Naha said. 'Unfortunately I think it may be too late for reflection . . .' He paused while Lianxang looked anxiously at him. 'Let me explain,' he went on quickly. 'If you, with our help, succeeded in opening up a new trade in exotic timber from the trees of the Dark Forests, it would break the monopoly the powerful merchants from the Southern Empire have with the timber from the jungles of the south-west. These presently supply all the needs of the Empire, and have guaranteed immense riches for the merchants of the south, who have grown fat and complacent.'

'Father . . . we know this from our studies,' Rokshan said hesitatingly.

'That may be so, Rokshan, but there is much more that your studies do not tell you – if you would permit me?' he said sternly but with a twinkle in his eye.

Rokshan squirmed uncomfortably and nodded humbly in apology.

'Good. Now consider: everyone knows that Maracanda's Council of Elders has long sought to break our southern rivals' stranglehold on the Empire's timber trade but has never found an alternative source of timber to rival that of the southern jungles . . . because the Dark Forests were always considered untouchable; until now.'

'Only if my people willingly consent,' Lianxang interrupted.

'Exactly so, my girl . . . except that someone else is already planning precisely what I have suggested. And his wealth and power is such that he will do it by force, if need be. He will trample all over your people, Lianxang, believe me – I know him of old – he stops at nothing to get his own way. He has the leader of the Maracanda Council of Elders, Jiang Zemin, in his pocket. And he is much closer to the Dark Forests than we are, here in Maracanda. He may already be approaching your sacred groves – from the west.'

'From the west! That can only mean Armenia . . . Not Vartkhis Boghos?' An Lushan asked in disbelief.

'Our old enemy,' Naha sighed.

'Who is this Boghos?' Lianxang whispered, looking dumbfounded at Naha's revelation.

'You may have heard us mention him before, in general talk of trade and commerce,' Naha said dismissively. 'He is from the Kingdom of Armenia. He is certainly the richest merchant of that country, and probably of Sogdiana too, if you include all the trading families he extorts money from . . .'

'Extortion? I . . . I . . . don't understand,' Lianxang stammered.

'Because he is so powerful, he has the monopoly on many different varieties of goods passing both east and west along the trade routes. So if other merchants want to trade in the same goods, he extracts a payment from them for the privilege,' An Lushan explained patiently.

'Do *you* have to make these . . . payments?' Lianxang asked naively.

'Certainly not!' Naha replied contemptuously. 'Boghos and I have an agreement: he stays out of my affairs, and I out of his.'

He pushed his bowl away and, heaving himself up, paced over to the balcony, gazing out over the city in his familiar stance, hands clasped firmly behind his back. Dusk had faded into starry darkness, the evening's muffled silence broken only by the cry of the lantern-seller as he began his night's work.

'So you see, Lianxang,' he said, turning towards them, 'with our involvement, your people, the Darhad, have a choice: come to an agreement with us, which will mean a controlled timber business of strictly limited felling and planned renewal. Or submit to Boghos and be forcibly removed from your land – and all you will be able to do is watch as he cuts a swathe through the Dark Forests from which they will never recover. I can get the documentation for such an agreement drafted very quickly – you will need to take it with you, for your people to consider. But time is of the essence – you should leave within the week. Even with your people at the most southerly part of their wanderings, camped at your winter settlement, the journey there and back will take at least two full cycles of the moon – and we must not allow Boghos to start his operations before we have put our case to the good people of the Darhad.'

He paused, then turned to leave the room. 'I must go now, but let me know when you have made up your mind. I will be in my study if you have anything you may want to ask me tonight.'

The two boys and Lianxang were so stunned by what they'd learned that none of them said a word. Just then, there was a loud, insistent knocking at the main entrance to the house.

'Are we expecting further guests?' Naha stopped in mid-stride and looked sharply at An Lushan, who shook his head.

'Rokshan . . .' His father jerked his head in the direction of the front entrance. Rokshan ran out of the room and through the ceremonial hall; Ah Lin was making her way across as quickly as she could to see who their unexpected visitor was.

'Who is it who calls unbidden at the house of Merchant Naha Vaishravana?' Ah Lin asked, politely but firmly.

'It is Jiang Zemin, leader of the Council of Elders,' came the muffled reply. 'I come unescorted, on private but urgent business with the Merchant Naha. Please announce me to your master.'

CHAPTER 7

THE ARREST

Rokshan's heart missed a beat – Jiang Zemin, at their house, unescorted? Such a thing was unheard of; it must be very, very serious. Frantically he indicated to Ah Lin to keep the council leader there for two minutes. Wide-eyed with alarm, she nodded her understanding.

'I will inform my master,' she managed to blurt out as calmly as she could while Rokshan rushed back to the family room.

'Jiang Zemin?' his father exclaimed. 'What can he want?' He hesitated for a second before taking control of the situation. 'Rokshan, escort him directly here. We must not keep the council leader waiting.'

Rokshan needed no second bidding, nodding to Ah Lin to let their visitor in. She swung the heavy front doors open, and Jiang Zemin swept in impatiently, his long robes rustling.

'Greetings, Rokshan,' he said in a low voice, as if he did not want to draw attention to himself. 'Your father is here, I trust? Please take me to him at once – I have little time.'

Naha was gazing out over the balcony and turned to face his visitor as they entered. 'Jiang Zemin, greetings,' he boomed, as if the leader of the Council of Elders' unannounced visit was perfectly normal. 'Rokshan, some wine for our honoured guest . . .'

'Merchant Naha, I have no time for pleasantries, but thank you,' Jiang Zemin replied brusquely, his eyes narrowing as they flicked around the room. He made the smallest of bows to

Lianxang, who was standing close to An Lushan; she took a moment to react before respectfully returning the formal politeness. 'I will stand,' Jiang Zemin said when Naha indicated a seat for him.

'The news must be of great importance for you to deliver it personally. We are honoured, Council Leader,' Naha said stiffly.

'Important? Indeed it is, Merchant Naha – and shocking. I shall come straight to the point. Amongst the dispatches that the imperial messengers delivered today was one that gave the Council of Elders grave concern.' Jiang Zemin's tongue flicked over his lips as he seemed to savour the moment.

'Yes?' Naha said with a hint of impatience in his voice. 'What is this *concern* you speak of, and how does it involve me and my family, Council Leader?'

'It is a warrant for your arrest, with immediate effect, Merchant Naha,' Jiang Zemin replied coolly.

Above his thick beard the blood drained from the merchant's face. Lianxang suppressed a little gasp of surprise and looked wildly at An Lushan, who had gone deathly pale but otherwise displayed no emotion. Rokshan sat as if in a trance, looking straight ahead. The seconds seemed to stretch into minutes.

Naha looked as if he'd been slapped hard across the face and blinked uncomprehendingly at Jiang Zemin. 'What is the charge, Council Leader?' he asked.

'Sedition and incitement to rebellion, through association with the rebel leader, Zerafshan Vaishravana, your brother, formerly military attaché to the imperial court.'

'What alleged association is that, exactly, Council Leader? Does the imperial warrant offer any details, any evidence?' Naha asked incredulously.

'None, other than you are close blood-kin, and . . .' A sly look stole over Jiang Zemin's face.

'*And . . . ?*' An Lushan asked pointedly.

Naha rebuked him for his rudeness and murmured an apology on behalf of his elder son.

Jiang Zemin smiled thinly in acceptance, then looked at Rokshan and An Lushan meaningfully and back again to Naha.

'As this concerns all my family, my sons should stay – our guest too: she has become one of our family even though she is not blood-kin,' Naha said firmly, ignoring the council leader's malicious look.

'As you wish,' Jiang Zemin replied. 'It is to do with the previous relationship of your wife, Larishka – may the gods watch over her spirit – to your brother, Zerafshan . . . previous, that is, to her marriage with you. The charge is that in the past you have knowingly harboured a rebel who now openly stirs rebellion against the emperor.'

'Who gave you that information?' Naha whispered.

'It is common knowledge that Zerafshan visited your house regularly in between diplomatic and military missions in the service of the imperial court,' Jiang Zemin replied smoothly. 'That is – before his current *assignment*,' he added meaningfully.

'Not *that* information, Council Leader,' Naha replied, icily calm now. 'I mean about my wife's previous relationship . . .'

Jiang Zemin's eyes flickered in alarm as Naha stepped menacingly towards him, seething with suppressed anger.

'I have my sources, Merchant Naha . . . After all, you and I have known each other since we were young, and full of youthful imprudence,' the council leader said with an edge of mockery in his voice – which he must have regretted when Naha lashed out at him with a cry of rage. He staggered back with the force of the blow, which caught him on the side of the head. 'You will regret that, Merchant Naha,' he spat out, scrabbling across the floor.

An Lushan sprang to restrain his father, who was bearing

down on Jiang Zemin to renew the assault. 'Father! It will make matters worse . . . calm yourself!' An Lushan cried, his face contorted with the effort of restraining his powerfully built father. But he was equal to the task, being as muscular and slightly taller. Naha struggled briefly but then slumped against An Lushan. His elder son steered him to sit beside Rokshan, who was still frozen rigid with shock and disbelief at what was happening. Lianxang crouched beside him, trying to offer what comfort she could – but his heart was thumping and there was a pounding in his head as the council leader's words echoed around it: *It is a warrant for your arrest . . . It is a warrant for your arrest . . .*

'I would remind you, Council Leader,' An Lushan said coldly, 'but you are probably well aware of it, that our uncle, Zerafshan, has not been here at our house for at least five years, long before the start of all these rumours of sedition and incitement to rebellion.'

'Nonetheless, the association remains,' Jiang Zemin replied. 'If the emperor considers that sufficient for your father's arrest, it is not for us to question his judgement – especially as the emperor is disposed to direct his anger against Maracanda, as well as against the actual person of your uncle . . . and your family.'

As he listened to Jiang Zemin's reply, their father's head drooped. The helpless look on his face changed to disbelief at the final confirmation that his own brother, through his treacherous disloyalty to the emperor, had swept away everything he believed in. Rokshan felt sick. All the fear he'd felt welling up in him evaporated as shame and pity and anger exploded in his heart. He turned to his father and hugged him, burying his head in his shoulder.

Jiang Zemin continued to speak directly to An Lushan. 'I regret that despite your father's longstanding service to Maracanda's business community and the high regard in which he is held, he is to be imprisoned in the citadel with immediate effect.'

At this, Naha let out a strangled cry. Jiang Zemin glanced at him before clearing his throat with a dry little cough. 'An armed guard is making its way to escort the prisoner as I speak,' he continued. 'In the circumstances, I felt it was the least I could do to give you warning.'

'I must protest, Council Leader. We demand a hearing in front of the full Council – and we will want to see the imperial warrant with our own eyes,' An Lushan said, with a slight tremble in his voice.

'I have made it plain,' Jiang Zemin snapped. 'Your father is to be imprisoned with immediate effect, to be detained at the emperor's pleasure, until the guilt or innocence of his brother, Zerafshan, can be established beyond any doubt.' He paused and smiled his thin-lipped smile. 'Either that, or your uncle delivers what the emperor has asked of him.'

'Which we all know is impossible,' An Lushan snapped back.

'Perhaps that is something your uncle should have considered before he accepted the emperor's mission,' Jiang Zemin smirked.

'You do not accept or decline an order from the emperor, Council Leader, as you are clearly demonstrating by what is happening here . . .'

'Then you will *accept*, An'an, that when your uncle is captured and executed as a traitor – as he most assuredly will be – all assets, goods and chattels of the Vaishravana trading business will be seized by the Council, including this house. Furthermore I could not guarantee that your lives would not also be forfeit,' Jiang Zemin concluded with deadly finality.

At this, Naha jerked forward, his eyes staring and his mouth working but unable to force out any words.

'You cannot threaten us like that, Council Leader!' An

Lushan started towards him, his fists clenching and unclenching.

Jiang Zemin gave a slight shrug of his shoulders; they all followed his glance towards the balcony as the rhythmic tramp of the armed escort could be heard making its way to their house. Rokshan put his arm round his father as he started to rock on his stool, in time to the guards' footsteps as they approached. Suddenly the sound of marching stopped, and there was silence for a few seconds, before a thunderous rapping at the door made them all jump.

'In the name of the Council of Elders of the city state of Maracanda, capital of the Western Empire, the first officer of the City Guard demands entrance with an imperial warrant for the arrest of Merchant Naha Vaishravana, resident at this address. Open up!'

Just then, Ah Lin appeared; she had been listening just out of sight since Jiang Zemin's arrival and had heard everything. She hovered apologetically at the entrance to the family room. 'I have packed a bag for the master,' she said, tears streaming down her face. 'Shall I open the door to the first officer?'

As if in response, the banging on the doors and the announcement were repeated. Nobody moved. It was as if they were all frozen in the nightmare of the moment.

Jiang Zemin broke the spell. 'Yes, thank you,' he said decisively. 'I shall come with you, as shall Merchant Naha. An'an, please assist your father.'

Gently An'an helped his father up. 'Come, Father, do not worry – I can take care of the business – I will instruct the chief clerk tomorrow.' But he wasn't sure if his father heard him – it was as if he wasn't there. Naha stared listlessly ahead, and shuffled off between Jiang Zemin and An Lushan while Ah Lin hurried ahead of them to open the doors to the first officer of the City Guard.

Just before they passed through the arched entrance of the

family room, Lianxang ran towards them. 'Wait! Merchant Naha – we will not fail you, I promise it.' She clung to his arm, and with a look full of compassion and resolve tried to reassure him.

Naha looked at her sadly, shaking his head. 'It is too late, Lianxang, too late . . .'

'No, Father, we can still—' An Lushan murmured but stopped abruptly as he saw Jiang Zemin looking intently at Lianxang.

'I know who you are, young woman,' he said, his voice quiet but full of menace, 'and you'd best keep yourself, and your people, well out of the affairs of this family – they are all tarred with the same traitor's brush.'

Lianxang gave him a defiant look, but said nothing. Jiang Zemin nodded towards the front entrance and they moved off.

Rokshan did not accompany them. His vision blurred with tears as he heard the tramp of the armed guard receding in the direction of the massive citadel where his father was to be imprisoned, at the indefinite pleasure of the emperor.

But for how long? If it wasn't going to be for ever, it would surely be for a very long time. The pain and fear and anger boiling within him finally erupted in a howl of anguish as he threw himself onto a pile of floor cushions, smashing his fist into them again and again.

CHAPTER 8

A FAMILY CRISIS

An Lushan strode back into the room, head down, deep in thought.

'It may be best if you don't stay here, Lianxang,' he said. 'I will demand a hearing. They cannot do this – I'll fight them all the way through the law courts . . . I'll . . .' An Lushan, his face grim and determined, lapsed into a fuming silence.

'You'll be wasting your time, An'an,' Lianxang said brusquely. 'Your father has been arrested by imperial warrant: no court of law in the land would dare rescind it, no matter what we may learn in the school about respect for the letter of the law. And it'll be just be a matter of time before the rest of what Jiang Zemin threatened comes about. Don't you understand? Your lives may be in danger!'

'He would not dare – that was an empty threat,' he muttered unconvincingly.

'What are we to do? Your poor father . . .' Ah Lin quavered, repeatedly making the sign of the dragon in her alarm and confusion.

Rokshan put a comforting arm around her, then turned back to his brother. 'I wouldn't be so sure,' he said. 'What would you suggest we do?'

Lianxang spoke and there was something in her tone of voice Rokshan hadn't heard before. She looked at him steadily, her deep hazel-brown eyes smouldering. 'We must ensure that your father is more useful to Jiang Zemin alive than dead. Greed will ensure that. We must return to my people and persuade them to accept your father's plans for trading timber—'

'But you heard what Father said: it is too late. Boghos will obtain all the necessary permissions from the Council,' An Lushan said dismissively.

'But he will never get my people's approval.'

'Doesn't make any difference. Boghos will just trample all over you – you know his reputation.'

'He will *not*. I can guarantee this—'

'How?'

'My grandmother is the spellweaver of the Darhad and one of its most respected elders – this I have told you before. What I have not told is that when she dies, I will take over her mantle. This is why I must return to my people, so she can pass on all the lore and traditions she has not taught me already. These are not *stories*, you know – they are the truth.'

They all looked at her in stunned amazement. Ah Lin nodded as if she had known this all along.

'You? But what can this . . . "spellweaver" do against Boghos and his hired mercenaries?' An Lushan asked.

'The spellweaver will speak to the spirits that guard the Dark Forests. They would not allow any trespass or violation. That is why the forests have remained untouched these past hundreds of years. The souls of our dead have fed the spirits there since the Darhad were first entrusted with their safe-keeping, one thousand generations ago.'

Ah Lin made a little whimpering noise at such sacrilegious talk and hurried off, muttering that they could find her at the house shrine, where she was going to say some prayers for them all.

'Well, whatever they are,' An Lushan said, tight-lipped as he watched her go, 'your spirits will have to work strong magic against the saws and axes of Boghos's men. The silver *taals* he will be paying them will work their own magic, you can count on it: do you think he will be bothered by your spirits of the forests? Of course he won't,' he added impatiently.

'You do not have to believe me; you will hear it from my grandmother, the spellweaver herself. And if you don't believe her, you will hear the same from all the tribal elders.'

'But who will look after the business if you go with her?' Rokshan asked his brother in a rising panic. 'We can't both go.'

'There won't *be* a business for you to look after unless we *do* something,' Lianxang said tightly.

'Wait a minute – what do you mean, "We can't both go"? Both of us *won't* be going.' An Lushan stared at his brother, waiting for a reply.

'From what Shou Lao has said to me, and now with Father's arrest, I don't think I have a choice—'

'What nonsense is this, Rokshan? What has that old man been telling you?' An Lushan demanded.

Rokshan told them of Shou Lao's message and his meeting with Chen Ming. 'I think Shou Lao is telling us that we – I – must find our uncle. If there's a chance it may help us straighten all this out and get Father out of jail, then maybe I don't have a choice. I have to tell Chen Ming by tomorrow night whether I am to go with him.'

There was silence in the room when he had finished speaking. The lonely cry of the lantern-seller echoed through the night, and far off the piercing screech of a hunting owl carried on the humid air.

'It is late,' An Lushan said at last, 'and we have much to think about. We shall decide in the morning what you should do, Rokshan. Lianxang, you must stay the night; Ah Lin will show you to your room. We should all try and rest now.'

CHAPTER 9

THE REVELATION OF CHEN MING

Rokshan woke and wondered in a sleepy fug if it had all been a bad dream, but he heard none of the familiar morning sounds: the muffled clatter and sizzle of his father's breakfast, which Ah Lin always cooked for him, his good-natured haranguing of traders and dealers who would already be clamouring to do business, bustling in little groups around the ceremonial hall.

He put his head under his pillow and screamed a silent scream, but already a little nugget of certainty was beginning to grow in his heart. He knew he had to do something to help his father. He scrambled out of bed and padded barefoot down to the house shrine. It was still early but the heat was already draping itself like a sodden blanket around his shoulders.

'Merciful spirits of water and bringers of rain,' he murmured, placing some incense in the bronze dragon's mouth, 'release Maracanda from the fiery grip of Chu Jung and grant us your cooling rains.' Then he turned to the serenely smiling statue of the goddess. 'Help me, mother of mercy. I must do whatever I can for my father . . . Help me do whatever that is.'

He finished his prayers and then went to the family room. An Lushan had just finished his breakfast and was glancing through a pile of papers and scrolls. He grunted a greeting as Rokshan took some fruit from the table and sat down.

'An'an . . . I . . . I've been thinking: maybe you shouldn't go,' Rokshan started hesitantly. 'Father would've wanted you to stay to look after the business – you know that.'

'But he also said that time was of the essence, and that's even more the case now he's in prison. Lianxang was right: we've got to appeal to Jiang Zemin's baser instincts to keep Father alive – and besides, if we succeed where Boghos fails, our trading house will become rich and powerful enough to crush him, and the council leader . . . and all his cronies – I will crush them all . . .'

An Lushan stared past his brother, a light burning in his eyes that Rokshan hadn't seen before. It made him feel so uncomfortable that he found himself turning round to see if his brother was actually looking at something.

'You, of course, will have to stay,' An Lushan said suddenly, snapping out of his reverie. 'Carry on with your studies and – main priority, Rokshan – keep on at the Council about visiting Father. If you pester them enough, they'll let you see him. As chief clerk of the family business, Vagees will be doing the same, but obviously that'll be about the business—'

There was a knock at the door.

'That'll be him.'

'Who?' Rokshan asked nervously, the noise bringing the nightmare of the previous evening flooding back.

'Vagees. I'll talk to him in the study.'

An Lushan went to let the chief clerk in. Rokshan listened to the brisk click-clack of his footsteps through the hall and the familiar clunk of the front doors. Inside he was seething at the presumption of his older brother, ordering him around like a little child. It chipped away at the little nugget of certainty he'd felt earlier.

With a sigh he got up and stepped out onto the balcony. He gazed across the city; this was where he had stood so often with his mother and father when he was younger. A flower-seller was pushing his cart, laden with produce, up the busy street, weaving his way through market traders, hawkers and peddlers on their way to the Grand Bazaar. Shouting, laughing children dodged in and out of them. The flower-seller passed directly beneath the balcony and the powerful scent of sweet basil and other fragrant herbs and flowers wafted up to Rokshan.

In an instant, he could see his mother standing beside him – it was the same smell as the crushed herbs and flowers she'd kept in a small, delicately embroidered silk-gauze bag that hung from her waist, filling each room with their heavy, sweet scent wherever she was – it was *her* smell. He saw her in his mind's eye, tall, with an imperious look, the loose-fitting vivid yellow dress of fine silk rustling about her feet when she walked.

Now he heard her voice, soft and persuasive, emphasizing the importance of his studies at the school, and how the family would benefit and prosper even more from the prestige of his appointment as one of the emperor's special envoys. It cut him up inside, and suddenly he was no longer sure he could go through with the task he had been set.

A sudden gust of wind blew a spiralling eddy of dusty grit up from the street; it whipped into his face, stinging his eyes. The flower-seller's cart creaked slowly by, and the moment was gone. He heard his brother talking to the chief clerk as he shepherded him into the study.

Rokshan wrestled with the unwelcome thought that his brother was probably right: he would have to stay – it'd kill his father if he found out that both his sons had left the city. His resolve evaporated the more he thought about it. Naha, abandoned and betrayed – surely that is how he would feel? No, he could never inflict that on him. He would have to go and talk to Chen Ming – he of all people would understand that with his father in jail and his brother leaving the city, he couldn't possibly go . . . Perhaps he could explain to Shou Lao for him?

He heard Lianxang stepping quietly into the room behind him. 'I will say farewell now,' she said. 'An'an is arranging two guards and a packhorse with Vagees – we leave at dawn tomorrow.'

'Already?' Rokshan asked. Suddenly things seemed to be moving very fast, and he didn't like the direction they were going in.

'Your father said we have no time to lose. I think he was right.' She gave Rokshan a hug. 'I hate goodbyes. We will send word – and don't worry: things will work out.'

She walked quickly away, without looking back.

Rokshan had sent word to Chen Ming as he'd said he would, and had just as quickly received a message back from the caravan master to meet him at the Drawn Scimitar. An Lushan had emerged briefly from the study, but was still deep in discussion with their father's clerk when Rokshan left the house.

In the heat of the mid-afternoon the streets were deserted: all the shops and stalls had closed and the street traders sought shade from the relentless, flaming furnace of the sun. The stench from the accumulating rubbish was overpowering, and Rokshan held a cloth drenched in rosewater to his mouth and nose. He noticed a beggar lying sprawled in the dirt by the side of the road.

'Water . . . please, water. I'm as parched as a dragon's gob . . . water . . . Please, young sir,' he croaked, holding out a claw-like hand. Rokshan flipped him a single *celehk*, but then stopped and, stooping down, gave the beggar some sips from his water pouch before continuing on to his appointment.

Chen Ming had ordered a fresh jug of water and limes. The two of them now sat, alone, in a shady corner of the courtyard of the Drawn Scimitar. They waited in silence as the innkeeper filled their glasses. Chen Ming nodded his thanks.

'I suppose it's all over the city already – about my father?' Rokshan asked glumly.

'I am sorry about your father, Rokshan, truly I am. He has

been good to me over the years,' Chen Ming said. 'But nothing will be achieved by your remaining in Maracanda now, apart from being a comfort to your father. Unfortunately being a comfort to him is not enough to disprove his guilt by association with your uncle, which is what the emperor seems to have accused him of. My concern now is Zerafshan: how to expose him and what he may be planning with the Horsemen, and how to contain him so that we avoid all-out war – and maybe worse . . . far worse . . .'

The caravan master stared out over the peaceful courtyard as if contemplating the awful consequences he hinted at, and then looked fiercely at Rokshan.

'This is a burden which Shou Lao has placed upon my shoulders and I cannot be certain that what he has asked of me is the right thing to do. But one thing I do know: Maracanda will be finished as the trading capital of the Western Empire if this business with the Horsemen isn't sorted out. If you can persuade Zerafshan to call off the rebellion – if that is what he plans – it would be better for all of us.'

'Chen Ming . . . I . . . My father would die of worry and a broken heart if he found out that both his sons were lost to him. I cannot go, for that reason alone,' Rokshan replied uncomfortably, squirming under his gaze.

'You are wrong, Rokshan. I have known your father since we were both about the age of your elder brother: he would not hesitate if he thought there was some chance of success, however small that chance may be. The stakes are too high, and I am not just talking about his freedom, important though that is.'

There was a long silence. Rokshan drained his glass. Chen Ming stroked his long moustaches and seemed to be contemplating something. Then he looked around, making sure nobody was about.

'Listen to me,' he said, leaning so close that Rokshan could smell the limewater on his breath. 'Shou Lao's riddle was a warning, I'm certain of it – a warning we must heed and act on before it is too late; this is why he has asked me to help you, and why you must accompany my caravan.'

Long moments passed as Rokshan tried to make sense of what was being asked of him, but in the end he knew it came down to one thing: he must do anything he could to help his father. Everything else, it seemed to him, was unimportant – rebellion, trade, Shou Lao's warning. Whatever he did, he couldn't just stay at home in the hope that things would some-how work out.

The caravan master's fierce gaze softened as he saw from the look on Rokshan's face that his mind was made up.

'We will face my uncle – and what he has become or is intending to do – together; and there's no one I'd rather have at my side, Chen Ming.' Rokshan's attempt at a confident smile looked more like a painful grimace.

'It is bravely spoken, my young friend,' Chen Ming said gravely, placing his enormous hand on the boy's.

Rokshan felt anything but brave. What would his brother say? Rokshan had always longed to go with his father's caravans on the long journey to the imperial capital, but not like this – sneaking away and with no real idea of what he would be facing. The enormity of the undertaking suddenly hit him, and his resolve faltered for a moment.

Chen Ming must have read his thoughts. 'Gupta, my chief cameleer, will keep you so busy you'll hardly have time to think, let alone doubt whether you have done the right thing,' he said with a wry smile. 'He will tell you what your duties are.' He stood up to go. 'We leave at dusk tomorrow – we can travel by night while we are within two or three days' ride of the city – it's much cooler. Meet us outside the East Gate. And don't forget – we travel light,' he said over his shoulder as he ducked out of the courtyard.

CHAPTER 10

FAREWELL TO MARACANDA

Wisps of pink cloud smudged the silver-pearl dawn sky the following morning. The great portcullis of the North Gate was raised for three horsemen and a single horsewoman, who galloped out onto the road, raising a hazy dust cloud in their wake: Lianxang and An Lushan and their two guides had started out on their long journey to the land of the Darhad.

For Rokshan, the rest of the day passed agonizingly slowly. He had packed and re-packed a small travelling bag with a blanket, a change of clothes, some dried fruit, a leather water pouch and a small medicine bag of herbs and charms. That was all. Anything else he would be able to pick up or trade on the journey.

As dusk began to fall, he waited nervously for Vagees to come to the house, when it would be time for him to go. Earlier that day, the chief clerk – now acting head of the Vaishravana trading house – had asked Ah Lin to visit his elderly sick father; she would not return until well after dark, when Vagees would break the news to her of Rokshan's departure.

Rokshan decided to have a last look around his home to fix it firmly in his mind's eye. The family's bedrooms opened onto a gallery with an open walkway. In the winter the walkway was completely shuttered and enclosed, with decorative screens made to fit the bedroom doors. For the last time he walked along the gallery, then down the stairs to the ceremonial hall and towards the opening behind the house shrine, which led directly to the kitchen and servants' quarters.

He stood in the small kitchen with its low cooking brazier and long table for chopping and preparing food; he'd spent countless happy hours here when he was small, helping Ah Lin prepare the family meals.

He walked down the passageway leading off from the kitchen. Passing Ah Lin's room, he noticed the rough mat she slept on. On the table beside it were a small oil lamp, her prayer beads and an amber comb that he remembered Mother giving her. He went through the warren of small storage rooms which he had raided in search of rare woods and spices to make incense sticks. Ah Lin had shown him how to grind aloes, sandalwood and camphor together, mixed with honey to make a dip for the sticks. Then they had made their own little altar to Kuan Yin in the cellar to burn home-made incense offerings.

These, and memories like them, came flooding back to him and he realized with a heavy heart how much he was going to miss his home. Just then he heard the front doors being opened, followed by footsteps in the hall – and Vagees Krishnan softly calling his name. Rokshan hurried back to meet him.

The chief clerk was a silver-haired Kashmiri in his middle years, a tall, imposing figure with a hawk-like face burned a deep copper-brown after many years of travelling all the different trade routes. His son Gupta, Chen Ming's cameleer, now trod the trade routes in his stead.

'Are you ready, Master Rokshan?' Vagees asked, bowing politely. 'It grows dark already and it would be unwise to keep the caravan master waiting.'

'I have no intention of doing that, Vagees. I am ready,' Rokshan said, taking a last look around the hall. 'Offer a prayer to the goddess for me, and please, look after Ah Lin. Can you tell her . . .' He wondered what he would have said if she'd been there. 'Tell her . . . that sometimes we have to do things that we're not really sure about . . . and . . . if we don't, we are letting down not just ourselves, but everybody we love. Will she understand that, Vagees?'

Vagees murmured that he'd make sure she did. Rokshan nodded gratefully, and without another word slipped out through the front doors.

Soon he was part of the milling mass of Chen Ming's caravan getting ready for departure just outside the East Gate.

The crack of the camel-drivers' whips mixed with the whinnies of the horses and the grunts of the buffaloes and yaks that would take them and their cargo on the first leg of the journey. The first of the mountain passes was the Summit of the Goddess, which they would be crossing after some ten to twelve weeks' hard travelling.

Up and down the caravan there was a deafening clamour of shouting, prodding, cajoling, yanking and pulling to make ready the beasts of burden. The flickering light from the oil brands cast strange, misshapen shadows, and the smell of tarry smoke mixed with animal and human sweat was overwhelming.

Rokshan hurried along the line to find Gupta, the chief cameleer. The tall figure was haranguing a group of heavily armed escorts clustered around three camels and a pair of buffaloes.

'You are to guard this cargo with your lives!' Gupta thundered at the escorts. 'Rotate your shifts when we are on the move, and especially when we're camped. Do you hear me?'

'What's so special about this lot?' Rokshan asked one of the escorts as he eyed the heavy iron-bound chests being loaded onto groaning buffaloes and camels.

'Can't you smell it?' he was told dismissively. 'In the long chests? That's hundreds of silver *taals* worth of sandalwood and camphor. The smaller chests are full of spices like cloves, cardamom, frankincense – and maybe even myrrh, the way Gupta's shouting his head off about it: the perfume of kings and emperors, they say. Now, hop it – we've work to do!'

The burly escort shouted a command and the buffaloes lurched forward. Rokshan leaped out of the way, nearly knocking Gupta off his feet.

The chief cameleer was unmistakably the son of Vagees Krishnan: he had his father's hawk-like features. He was only a few years older than Rokshan but, already an experienced traveller on the trade roads, had an unmistakable air of authority.

'Chen Ming asked me to look out for you,' Gupta shouted above the clamour, waving aside Rokshan's abject apologies. 'Make yourself useful now – any help you can give the camel-drivers readying the animals . . . But your main job – get yourself some sacks and collect all the dung from the animals: no dung, no fuel for our fires, nothing to cook with – most important job of the lot! Can I trust you with that?'

'Of course.' Rokshan responded with as much enthusiasm as he could manage.

'Well, get on with it then, there's plenty already to be picked up,' Gupta laughed, striding off.

'Dung collector!' Rokshan muttered to himself in astonishment as the first of the three blasts from the caravan master's horn signalled that the caravan should prepare to set off. It was a doleful sound, like a lament, as if to warn the travellers of the hardships and dangers to come on their journey to the imperial capital.

Rokshan tried to make himself useful to an old camel-driver as he made the final adjustments to his cargo, tightening the odd loosely tied rope, easing a chafing saddle strap, murmuring words of encouragement to the horses and emitting a series of the oddest-sounding clicks and clacks to the camels.

'Get out of the way, boy, and be about your business,' the old camel-driver said testily as he watched Rokshan's efforts.

Spitting disdainfully, he pointed to a steaming pile of fresh camel dung. 'Catch!' he shouted, tossing him a hessian sack.

Rokshan wrinkled his nose in disgust but dutifully set about his task. His mind wandered to what lay ahead of them: he knew enough about his family's business to realize that some of the most inhospitable territory on Earth awaited them. He recalled vividly his father's and Chen Ming's tales of their journeys – the searing heat of the desert day and the bitingly cold nights, the near impassable, snowbound mountain passes and suffocating sandstorms, and the altitude sickness and snow blindness that could afflict both man and beast along the precipitous, boulder-strewn tracks.

Then, to add to all the natural hardships and dangers, there were the marauding bandits. Renowned and feared for their barbaric cruelty, they were always on the lookout for smaller caravans that did not have the benefit of an armed guard. Evidence of their brutality littered the trading routes: crucifixion was the bandits' favoured form of execution; sometimes whole caravans were massacred in this way. Rokshan shuddered at the thought.

'What was crossing the Taklamakan Desert really like, Kan?' Rokshan had asked his friend the night before, trying to sound unconcerned about it. Kan had made the journey twice before with his parents – as travelling acrobats they had performed at every garrison, market town and oasis settlement the length of the trading routes. Compared to him, Kan was a seasoned traveller.

'Ah, Taklamakan,' Kan had said in a sinister whisper. 'Better believe everything you hear about the great Taklamakan Desert, Roksy: the spirits of the desert talk. By night they'll call your name, and you'll follow them off the path – and you'll never be able to find the caravan again. Then there are the demons of the Singing Sands that conjure up the tramp and hum of a thousand people away in the distance, and whole caravans will follow the noise and leave the road. Then, in the morning, they are lost, and there is no hope for them.'

Rokshan had paled.

'I have heard music being played,' Kan had gone on, enjoying making his friend even more nervous, 'and demon drums beating all night, until they drive you' – here he had paused dramatically – '*mad!*' he'd shouted, slapping his knees with his palms in imitation of the demon drums of the desert.

But Rokshan remembered one thing above all that Kan had said.

'I have seen men break. You try to block their screams out of your mind, but it's the poor horses that go mad with fear first . . .'

The mournful horn of the caravan master sounded again, snapping Rokshan out of his glassy-eyed contemplation of the rigours that lay ahead.

'I must be mad already, to be going in the first place,' he muttered to himself, wishing his friend was there with him. Kan had been desperate to accompany him, but had to go with his troupe on a tour of the Southern Empire, which meant he would be away all through the long winter months.

At the front of the column, Chen Ming stood high in his saddle on his magnificent grey mount, and gave the signal for his caravan of fifty beasts of burden, and perhaps as many as one hundred camel-drivers, guards and camp followers, to advance on the first stage of its long journey to the east. From the Summit of the Goddess the rest of the caravan would go on to Chang'an, the imperial capital – it was a journey that could take anything up to two years.

Rokshan looked for the last time at the East Gate, through which he'd passed so many times before on his wanderings in the caravanserai, and wondered if he would ever see his City of Dreams again.

PART TWO

AN LUSHAN AND THE DARHAD

Of Spellweavers and Dark Forests

The following is recorded in The Book of Ahura Mazda, the Wise Lord

The Darhad are wandering nomads of the north, a reclusive people who have always kept themselves apart from the rest of the Empire.

Of all the forest legends that run through history, the Darhad myth of the Tree of Heaven is surely one of the most fervently maintained. The Darhad cling to the old ways and believe that their spirits of the woods and earth make up the life-force of the Dark Forests, which is fed by the souls of their people when they die, the same life-force that also maintains the harmonious balance between good and evil.

The rebellion of the guardian spirits against the Wise Lord threatened to overturn this delicate balance when the most favoured of these spirits - known for ever afterwards as the Shadow-without-a-name - grew tired of his servitude and sought to overthrow the Wise Lord and rule the Heavens and Earth himself. The Shadow was joined by two other higher guardian spirits: the Crimson King and the Jade Spirit, a third, lower spirit, Beshbaliq, also fought with them. When the Wise Lord overcame them, He asked Lao Chun, sorcerer to the gods and one of the Immortals, to make his most devoted servant, Chu Jung, a Talisman of the dragon spirits to help him defeat them.

After Chu Jung had defeated the dragons, he was tempted to use his new-found power on the side of evil and wandered far and wide across the Earth, wrestling with his demons of temptation. Eventually he found himself in the Dark Forests. Here, driven half mad, he buried his Talisman as the Wise Lord had commanded so that it would never tempt him again.

As he buried it, the tears of relief and gratitude which fell on the earth caused a shoot to sprout up; this grew into a young sapling and finally turned into a tree, which Chu Jung called the Tree of Heaven, thinking that the Wise Lord himself had caused it to grow. From this same tree he fashioned the Staff as a gift for his master. To make sure his Talisman could never again be used, especially if it fell into the wrong hands, Chu Jung put a spell on it, making it powerless unless it was joined with his gift of the Staff – the gift which he thought would always be in the safe-keeping of the Wise Lord – the same gift that Corhanuk, the Wise Lord's messenger, stole.

The Darhad believe that Chu Jung passed on to them some of his special powers, including the ability to speak with certain birds – known to these people as spirit-birds. Their guardianship is entrusted in one person, known as the spellweaver of the Darhad, a shaman-like figure, always a woman, possessor of secret powers and a healer of mind and body. The spellweaver's mantle passes directly from one generation to another, in an unbroken line.

Source: the secret Fellowship of the Three One-eared Hares; origin: discovered in the ruins of the citadel monastery of Labrang, spiritual centre of the old Western Empire.

CHAPTER 11

JOURNEY TO THE DARHAD

An Lushan, Lianxang and their two escorts, Qalim and Bhathra – veterans of many journeys up and down the trade roads and trusted implicitly by Merchant Naha – had been travelling hard. They were almost at the first full cycle of the moon since they had set out, and even the sturdy little steppe pony they were using as a packhorse was tiring.

The rocky terrain of the high uplands they were crossing stretched like a rumpled quilt into the distance, broken only by the occasional straggling line of skeletal pines that followed the course of a long dried-up river bed. So far-off that they were only just visible, the snow-capped peaks of the Tianshan Mountains glittered in the bright sun.

'The Tianshan – it can't be far now!' An Lushan turned in his saddle and shouted to Lianxang, who was lagging behind, trying to encourage the little pony on the leading rein. She murmured some words of encouragement and spurred her horse on. Reluctantly the pony stepped up its pace behind her.

'A few more days – we do not go as far as the mountains.' Lianxang smiled, falling into step beside him.

'That would take us a round moon and then another full cycle after that – we would be as old as your grandmother by the time we reached your people,' An Lushan said, laughing.

'Then we would be old indeed,' Lianxang replied, 'and I would be the spellweaver, so then my people would have to listen to what I said, wouldn't they?'

'They will listen to you, but will they listen to the trader from Maracanda? I – we would've completely failed in what we set out to do if they don't.'

'They won't have a choice,' Lianxang said passionately, 'if Boghos has already started what your father said he was going to do.'

An Lushan looked at her sharply. 'Barely an hour goes by when I do not think of my father. He must be going slowly mad in prison – and there's not a thing he can do about it,' he added quietly.

'I'm . . . I'm sorry about your father, An'an, truly I am . . . but it's not your fault he was arrested, and doing what we're doing is the best way to get Jiang Zemin on our side, once he realizes he's not going to get what he wants from Boghos. My people will have a surprise waiting for Boghos and his men if they dare attempt anything in our Dark Forests without our permission. The dryads of the woods will see to that. Never in the history of our people has any harm come to the forests, such is the power of the trust placed in us – a trust we have cherished since it was first handed to us. And we have been well-rewarded for it.'

An Lushan wasn't listening to her: he was still battling against the guilt he felt at abandoning his father; it gnawed away at him, surfacing in uncontrollable flashes of anger that were becoming more frequent. 'There you go again, talking about your *dryads*, guardian spirits of the forests – whatever they are – the same spirits that will warn against *us*, not just Boghos!' he snapped.

'No they won't! Not once we have explained to my people that there will always be others like him, to feed the coffers of the emperor,' Lianxang shot back, stung by his angry rebuke. 'And the best way to curb men's greed for our forests is for *us* to control the supply of timber – An'an, you explained this many times before we left; now you must trust me.'

'I do, Lianxang, I'm sorry . . . I don't know what came

over me,' An Lushan said, rubbing his forehead anxiously. 'It's just . . . sometimes I feel the words bursting out of me and I can hear myself, but it's not what I want to say at all.'

'Don't worry, we're all tired – perhaps we've been pushing ourselves too hard; why don't we tell the guards we should slow d—?'

'No!' An Lushan shouted. 'I mean, no,' he apologized, looking sheepish, 'we must get there quickly. The longer we take, the longer Father has to stay locked up.'

'Of course . . . it was just a suggestion,' Lianxang replied, looking at him with friendly concern. Suddenly she jerked upright in her saddle, pointing excitedly at a tiny speck in the sky.

'What is it?' An Lushan asked curiously, straining his eyes in the direction she was looking.

'The royal eagle! I told you about her. She was born in the Five Holy Mountains, beyond the Tianshan, many hundreds of li from here. I have only ever seen her twice before. She knows, An'an! Sarangerel knows we are coming and is sending us a message!'

Her excitement was infectious, and he marvelled at how she recognized the bird from such a great distance. He shielded his eyes against the sun and at last spotted her: the great bird spiralled closer in huge arcs, effortlessly riding the air currents.

'So this is your grandmother's spirit-bird,' he said, gawping at its enormous wingspan, almost twice the length of a full-grown man. 'Only a spellweaver can summon her and become one with her spirit,' he murmured to himself. Was the magic Lianxang had told him about real? He'd never seen these magnificent birds, and had only ever heard about them in childhood stories. 'Will you speak to her?' he asked, unable to take his eyes off the eagle. The guards had also seen her now, and were pointing and shouting.

In answer, Lianxang let out a shrill cry, piercingly loud and long. The eagle seemed to answer her back with a screeching cry of her own before flying off, silhouetted against the clear blue of the sky.

'What did you say? Did she have a message for us?' An Lushan asked eagerly.

'She is Sarangerel's spirit-bird, but I can speak to her and understand the messages she carries,' Lianxang said, still gazing up at the sky. 'Sarangerel has seen us through the eagle eye, and will tell the tribe that we are coming. She says it will be a happy day when we arrive at the winter camp, An'an – and my people are honoured indeed that the eldest son of the most powerful trading family in Maracanda accompanies her beloved grand-daughter. Here, catch!' She laughed, throwing the packhorse's reins to him, and with a joyful shout spurred her horse on and cantered ahead of the guards. 'Race you!' she shouted over her shoulder, sitting high in the saddle.

'Wait!' he cried. 'Wait! I'll show you how Sogdians ride!'

But by the time he'd left the pony with the guards she was already some way off. He slowed his horse to a walk as a raucous and insistent cawing caught his attention. He looked up, squinting at the sun. It was a crow, directly overhead.

Again it called its ugly cry, and a sense of unease crept over him which he couldn't shrug off. His horse sensed it and whickered, tossing its head. He had to suppress an urge to follow the crow as it flew off; calming his horse with some soothing words, he caught up with Lianxang. She was still smiling at the appearance of her grandmother's spirit-bird, and he decided to keep his misgivings to himself.

They travelled in companionable silence for the rest of the day. At dusk they were sitting by the campfire preparing their evening meal when, without a word, An Lushan suddenly rose to his feet and left the others, not saying where he was going or why. Lianxang called out to him but got no response. Sensing that something was wrong, she followed him at a discreet distance, giving a little wave as the guards laughed and told her to be back soon if she wanted anything to eat.

That afternoon they had been following the course of a dried-up river flanked by sheer-sided cliffs of sandstone. Where the river had once been wide and free-flowing it was now dry shingle and gravel, home only to the hardiest wild flowers and weeds. An Lushan was half running along the river bed.

'An'an!'

Still some distance from him, for a second she thought it was a large animal of some kind, burrowing into the riverbank. But then, as she strained her eyes in the half-light, she saw An Lushan, on all fours, scraping and clawing at the dry earth, which he was repeatedly throwing over his head and body, then rubbing it in as if he was trying to wash himself.

'An'an!' she shouted again, running towards him and cursing as she tripped over in her hurry. She was about to call out to him again when she noticed a large crow hopping about on the bank in front of him. A crow! Lianxang stopped short, a chill stealing over her; she had noticed one a couple of times, cawing and wheeling high above them, usually at dusk. Could it possibly be the same bird?

As she got closer, she could hear An Lushan muttering to himself as he dug and tore at the earth. He was repeating the same phrase, over and over:

'And if I should fail, what then? What then, if I should fail? My father? My brother?' He stared at the crow, which cocked its head and then cawed as if responding to him. 'It cannot be . . . it cannot be . . . it must not be!' he shouted, scrambling up and lunging at the ungainly bird, which hopped away, just out of his reach.

Lianxang raced up, grabbing him by the shoulders. She gasped when she saw his mask-like face and empty, staring eyes, and slapped him. 'Stop it! Stop it! What are you doing?

What's the matter? An'an! It's me, Lianxang!' she shouted, and was about to slap him again, but as the crow flew off into the dusk, An Lushan wrenched himself away from her and stumbled after it, his arms hanging by his sides.

Frightened that he'd lost his mind, Lianxang hung back. Desperately she shouted for the guards, but they were well out of earshot. Hearing her cries, An Lushan suddenly stopped and turned slowly towards her.

'Why are you following me? And where is the camp? What are we doing here?' he asked in a puzzled voice, looking around. 'And what's all this?' he added, brushing the dirt off his clothes as he walked back up the river bed towards her.

'You don't remember?' Lianxang asked, as puzzled as him. 'You just got up and went off, without saying a word. I followed you, and . . . well, here we are.' She laughed, but it sounded strained and hollow. 'You were talking – you don't remember that either?'

'No. What was I saying?'

'Oh, nothing, sounded like nonsense – something about failing, and then you mentioned your father and brother, as if you were asking about them.'

'Asking who? About what?'

'An'an, I don't know! There was a crow hopping about . . . it was as if . . .' She fell silent.

'As if what?'

'As if you and the crow were talking to each other. I know it sounds stupid but . . . that's how it looked, anyway.'

'It looked like I was talking to a crow? But I thought it was just you and your grandmother who talked to birds,' he joked, putting his arm around her. 'Come on, don't look so worried. I feel fine now – apart from a raging hunger in my belly! Let's get back to the camp before those greedy guards hog all the food – if they haven't already, that is!'

She looked at him with concern shining in her eyes.

'Honestly, I'm all right,' he said quietly, smiling and squeezing her shoulder.

A little after the first round moon of their journey, just as Lianxang had said, the little group at last approached the most southerly part of the lands in which the nomadic Darhad wandered through the changing seasons. They had tracked west to the foothills of the Tianshan Mountains, and it was growing colder. Summer was already drawing to a close, and they were glad of their furs at night.

They drew close to Lake Baikal – a huge expanse of water which stretched from one end of the horizon to the other, marking a daunting natural boundary between the outside world and the Darhad. Beyond this they could just make out a dark smudge of featureless terrain.

'The Dark Forests, An'an! A few days' ride and we shall be there!' Lianxang shouted, with relief and joy in her voice, and even though the shoreline of the lake was still some distance away, she galloped towards the water. Her companions, weary and saddlesore, waved her on, content for her to go ahead.

'Lianxang! Wait!' An Lushan yelled, but he was far behind and could have saved his breath. Nothing could have stopped her – she had been too long in the land-locked Western Empire, and Lake Baikal was one of her people's most sacred sites.

As he set off after her at a brisk canter, it occurred to An Lushan that in only two to three days they would be entering the winter settlement of the Darhad. He couldn't help wondering what was in store for them there.

CHAPTER 12

ARRIVAL AND UNEXPECTED NEWS

'This is my home, An'an,' Lianxang said simply, pointing down into a valley ahead. They had been travelling for several days since leaving Lake Baikal, and this was their first sighting of her people. The valley was dotted with dozens of yurts – tents made of sturdy poles lashed together and covered with felt and animal skins. Thin plumes of smoke curled from the holes in the roofs.

The settlement lay perfectly secluded on the fringes of the Dark Forests, which stretched away to the north and east. They had just ridden across, and were now descending, a small range of lightly wooded hills.

Dusk was falling, and after travelling for a full cycle of the moon An Lushan felt only a deep weariness. Winter was threatening, and he longed for the heat of Maracanda. A freezing wind blustered and clawed its icy fingers through their thick furs so that even his bones felt numb with cold. He buried his face, now covered with a straggly beard, deeper into the animal skins around his shoulders.

'No one to welcome us?' he joked, but the wind whipped his words away.

As they picked their way carefully down the hillside, they were spotted by some children playing a game on horseback, who started pointing and shouting excitedly. Two of them, braver than the rest, spurred on their ponies and came trotting towards them.

'Who comes to speak with the people of the Darhad?'

piped one of them cheekily, halting his mount some way from them, although news of Lianxang's homecoming had spread through the settlement like wildfire a few days before.

She held up her hand in greeting. 'Tell the spellweaver her granddaughter is safely returned from the imperial city of Maracanda, accompanied by a friend and representative of one of its foremost trading houses – An Lushan of the Vaishravana family – and two escorts.'

The other boy approached, peering closely at her. His head was shaven under his crownless fur hat and he obviously didn't notice the cold – he wore only an armless tunic of animal skins similar to the one Lianxang wore under her furs.

'Lianxang, is it really you?'

'Yes, it is I; now go – be quick!'

The boy grinned in recognition. 'Lianxang – she has returned!' he shouted as he cantered away, his companion following. 'Lianxang! She is back . . . tell the spellweaver . . . Lianxang has returned . . .'

She turned and smiled at An Lushan. 'The news that we are here at last will soon be all round the camp.'

Their progress was slow as more and more members of the tribe poured out of their yurts and milled around them, shouting greetings to Lianxang and slapping her pony's haunches. An Lushan noticed some of the older ones touching her and then making a gesture to their foreheads.

'What are they doing?' he asked her over the din, astonished by the joyous reception she was getting from her people.

'For luck and good fortune, An'an – I am the spellweaver-to-be, and their future.' She looked at him with pride and happiness shining in her eyes, and he saw her as if for the first time, wondering what sort of woman her grandmother must be if this was the respect and warmth shown to her grand-daughter. The escorts soon gave up trying to clear a way for them and, after their initial alarm, dismounted and cheerfully put up with all the prodding and pulling directed at them with wide-eyed wonder.

They were being jostled towards a large building in the centre of the camp, which was different from the rest of the dwellings. This was the people's high yurt, where they gathered for feasts and storytelling and important announcements. It was an eight-sided construction made of logs, with a solid roof and a smoke-hole in the middle. A massive granite boulder marked the entrance; on its partly hollowed-out surface a fire blazed, and on either side stood a pole capped with a bear skull; the bear was revered as an ancestor and regarded by Lianxang's people as one of the highest-ranking of the animals.

As they approached, the people fell back and a hush descended. In the flickering twilight they saw a small hunched figure, leaning heavily for support on a child of ten or eleven years. Lianxang held up her hand and the little group came to a halt.

An Lushan noticed that whoever it was by the boulder was dressed in animal skins, with buckskin fringes hanging from the arms, and twists of cloth hanging in bunches from both shoulders, making her look almost bird-like. This effect was heightened by the feathered headdress, and the bird skull hanging from her neck was too big, he thought, to be anything other than that of a royal eagle like the one they had seen on their journey. He knew at once that this was Lianxang's grandmother, the revered spellweaver of the Darhad.

'Hail, Sarangerel, spellweaver and soothsayer! Your granddaughter has returned to the land of her people.' Lianxang's voice rang out.

The child whispered something to the old woman.

'Welcome, spellweaver's daughter. You have been too long away, and your people have missed you,' Sarangerel replied in a clear, lilting voice. 'You have brought strangers – ferangshan –

my young eyes tell me,' she added, stroking the head of the child, who stood impassively beside her. With a jolt, An Lushan realized she must be blind, and wondered why Lianxang hadn't told him.

'That is so, Grandmother, the same *ferangshan* I told your spirit-bird of when we were still some days away from our land.'

'They will be made welcome here. Come, let me touch you, so that I can be sure it is you,' she joked.

Without further bidding, Lianxang jumped down from her pony and ran into the outstretched arms of her grandmother. The tribespeople – who had been silent until then – clapped and cheered and then started to wander off, chatting and laughing. Some of the younger children came up to An Lushan, staring solemnly at him and his two companions until they were shooed away by their embarrassed parents. One family bowed elaborately and offered to share their yurt with Qalim and Bhathra, who gladly accepted their hospitality.

A little later An Lushan, Lianxang and her grandmother were sitting on roughly woven matting on the floor of the old spellweaver's yurt, their faces reflecting the red glow of the fire. Most of the smoke from the dried animal dung curled towards the circular opening at the top of the yurt, which could be closed with a small flap. The rest drifted in hazy layers, adding to the gloomy effect.

'Grandmother, we have so much to tell you . . .' Lianxang was saying excitedly. 'I'm going to start right at the beginning, when I first arrived in the city of Maracanda and spent days just wandering on my own gazing at the buildings and the markets and the *people*. Grandmother, you never saw so many people all in one place, and from so many different lands!'

Sarangerel sat contentedly, gently rocking back and forth, nodding and smiling, her eyes closed. An Lushan wondered if she was listening at all, and thought perhaps she was happy just to hear the sound of her granddaughter's voice. His eyelids grew heavier and heavier and he felt himself drifting away, jolting himself awake when he heard Lianxang mention Shou Lao and the storytelling.

'Has the spirit-bird told you more about the riddle, Grandmother?'

Sarangerel nodded but did not speak. At last she opened her sightless eyes and raised them towards the smoke-hole. 'My spirit-bird ranges far and wide across all the lands of the Empire, granddaughter, and those who can speak to it tell me of many things.'

'You mean, there are others who have this power?' An Lushan asked, politely but incredulously. The spellweaver nodded. Lianxang looked smugly at him – her grandmother had just confirmed what she'd told An Lushan more than once; in his heart he hadn't believed her. It struck him that he needed to learn more about these people.

'And did the old storytel— Did Shou Lao speak to your eagle? Is that how you know of his riddle?' he queried, his tone full of respect now.

Again Sarangerel nodded. 'Though I have pondered long on it, I cannot unravel its meaning – except that we must be on our guard, my children, and keep our forests safe from the prying eyes of the *ferangshan* . . . strangers, who do not believe in the ancient powers of the spirits of the woods and earth.'

'There are many who no longer believe, honoured Spellweaver,' An Lushan replied courteously. 'The Empire thrives today, and at its heart is trade. Unscrupulous traders who have no respect for the ancient powers you speak of will drive your people away from the forests you love – there are already too many "prying eyes" who covet the riches in timber. There is one in particular who will stop at nothing to extract those riches . . . he is known to my family—'

'And to us,' Sarangerel said.

'You know – about Vartkhis Boghos . . . and his plans?' An Lushan asked in amazement.

'I do not know who he is, but it is clear what he intends to do. Why else would such a gathering of men armed with saws and axes be assembled on the north-west borders of the forests?'

'North-west? Are you sure?' An Lushan asked urgently, glancing at Lianxang.

'My spirit-bird roams far and wide; he never lies,' Sarangerel replied quietly, gently rocking.

'Boghos! I knew it.' An Lushan whistled softly. 'He's moved incredibly fast – he must have known we were on our way here, Lianxang. The nearest entry point to the forests from his country would be from the north and to the west. He's started already!'

He shook his head, wondering why the spellweaver seemed so calm in the face of such looming disaster – a disaster for everything they had hoped for too, he thought bitterly. He gazed despairingly into the red embers, feeling exhausted and defeated, chiding himself for not foreseeing that their old enemy would move so quickly; hadn't his father said it could be too late already?

Questions raced through his mind: what did the Darhad intend to do about Boghos? Surely they weren't going to rely on their wood spirits to stop him? How could he get them to understand that, even if by some miracle they managed to stop Boghos, there would always be more like him? Had he trusted too much to Lianxang's enthusiasm to win her people over? He couldn't fathom the spellweaver at all.

'Once one man has done the unthinkable, there will always be others who follow him,' Sarangerel mused, as if she'd read his thoughts.

Lianxang looked puzzled at the startled look on his face. He started to say something but Sarangerel raised her bony hand and stopped him.

'You must both rest now, once you have eaten – all this talk has wearied me.' She pointed towards a far corner of the yurt. 'We have made ready a place for you to sleep.'

An Lushan murmured his thanks for their hospitality. After a simple meal of dried meat and oat cakes, they settled themselves snugly into the felt blankets and animal skins and fell into a deep sleep.

CHAPTER 13

OLD AND NEW WAYS

The bright morning light flooded into the spellweaver's yurt through the half-open entrance flap. The noises of the settlement drifted in: the bleating of goats mixed with the whinnying and blowing of horses and the shouts of the men and women going about their business. A group of giggling children played nearby, curious to catch a glimpse of the *ferangshan* from the capital city of the Western Empire where, they whispered excitedly amongst themselves, even the clothes were made of spun gold.

'Your grandmother seems very unconcerned by the news about Boghos,' An Lushan said to Lianxang. He still felt tired and scratchy even though he'd slept a long time, and the news about Boghos preyed on his mind.

'Our forests will be protected, as they always have been.' She smiled, tossing from one hand to another the butter and oatmeal cakes she was making. 'Here, try one,' she said, taking one off the fire. 'Don't turn your nose up at it! It's what we always have for breakfast.'

'I'd rather have melon and sweetmeats,' he said wistfully, his tummy rumbling at the memory of Ah Lin's cooking. 'I had bad dreams last night, Lianxang,' he added, munching anxiously on the oatcake.

'What sort of bad dreams?'

He could recall only dark, fleeting glimpses, but they had frightened him because the odd snatches he could remember were the same nightmares he'd had as a child.

'I was alone, in the Taklamakan Desert – not just *on my own* . . . it was as if I was the only human being left in the world. But there was somebody else talking to me. I called out to . . . whoever it was, but they wouldn't show themselves; they just kept saying I must go with them, but I didn't know where they wanted me to go. And it was so *cold*. Then I was falling, so far down I thought I'd never stop, and I ended up lying by the shore of a lake. The water was black as night and I could feel its chill. Then something else happened . . . but . . . I can't remember any more.' He shuddered at the memory of it.

'Well, it's already getting cold – and we did pass by Lake Baikal on our way here. It was just a dream, An'an.' Lianxang tried to reassure him. 'You're here now, with friends. Sarangerel understands dreams – perhaps she could unweave its meaning for you. We have herbs and roots, special fungi that grow only in our forests – she would make these into a potion for you to drink, then when you sleep it's like she's with you in your dreams, and when you wake, you understand them clearly.'

'What if I didn't dream the same dream though?' An'an replied, looking a little uncomfortable at the suggestion.

'You would,' Lianxang laughed. 'Here, have some more oatcake.'

He waved it away and looked around the yurt, watching the smoke from the fire curling in and out of the light. There was a pair of wooden bellows by the cooking stove; beside it lay neat stacks of brightly coloured earthenware jars, bowls and plates. Piled up in a heap on one side were felt rugs, quilts and furs. On the other side were sacks filled with what smelled like animal dung to feed the fire that was constantly kept burning. Beside the sacks was a mound of kindling and small branches.

Lianxang saw An Lushan looking at the wood. 'You see, we use what we need from the forests – not everything about it is sacred.' She smiled. 'Even though our husbandry is limited to tiny areas, it yields enough for our cooking and altar fires,' she went on. 'Long ago, there were altar fires with shrines tended by the priestesses of the spellweaver throughout the length and breadth of the forests, but there are too few of us now to tend them as we should. Huge areas are thick with brambles and ivy and dead wood – all choking the life out of them.'

'Which is where we come in,' An Lushan said, brightening at the prospect. 'Just a small amount of logging will supply us with our timber to trade and help make your forests healthier.' He looked at her intently. 'Lianxang, perhaps fate has played into our hands after all – I mean, with Boghos getting here before us.'

'How?' she asked doubtfully.

'Your people will see what Boghos is doing and understand how important it is for the Darhad to control the supply of timber themselves – with help from my family business, of course – and not be at the mercy of fraudulent, ruthless marauders who are unfit to call themselves merchants of the Empire.'

'And then?' Lianxang asked.

'And then?' An Lushan looked at her in surprise. '*And then* is the heart of it! A successful agreement between the Vaishravana trading house and the Darhad will expose Boghos for what he is – the most ruthless, corrupt merchant of them all. When we meet with the Council, Jiang Zemin will be forced to recognize the legality of the Vaishravana trading agreement; his greed will then ensure Father's survival, because Zemin will be slavering for a big slice of the profits . . .' He looked expectantly at her but got no reply.

'An'an, I have just come home after a long time away. I . . . I suppose I had forgotten, or pushed to one side with all the excitement of living and studying in Maracanda, just how deeply my people are attached to the old ways. Yes, you're right, if they saw what Boghos intends to do – or is already doing – it would help us persuade them to our way of thinking, but . . .' Lianxang paused, searching for the right words.

'But . . .?' he asked impatiently.

'But they will not see Boghos's destruction, because it won't happen,' Lianxang said quietly, in a way that told him she was utterly convinced of the truth of what she said. The look on his face told her he was still unsure. 'An'an, I have told you – our spirits of the forests are not warlike in the way you seem to imagine. They are like the dragon spirits of the air, and water, and earth – they are everywhere!' she said excitedly, taking his hand. 'I have been back for less than a day, but already I can feel their power. They are the life-force of the forests, An'an – a life-force that has been fed for many, many centuries by the souls of all our people. The same life-force that maintains the balance between good and evil in the world is concentrated here in our forests – it is at the heart of the sacred guardianship that we have been entrusted with, passed down from generation to generation—'

'Sacred guardianship! Of what? What is it that you guard against? How can I believe in something that you don't know about for sure; that is just based on some ancient legend.'

'An'an, calm yourself,' Lianxang said, troubled by the vehemence of his outburst. 'Our guardianship has never been so strongly challenged before,' she went on, suddenly very serious. 'My people's natural instinct will be to rely on the old ways – it will be up to us to persuade them that if we are to see off this challenge, and all the others that are sure to come after it, we can fight trade with trade. It will not be easy, but we must try.'

'Father was convinced there was no other way,' An Lushan said, relieved at her new resolve. 'Anyway, who will sign the agreement on behalf of your people – if they sign it? Would it be your grandmother?'

'Yes and no . . .' Lianxang replied uncertainly. 'As

spellweaver and chief elder of the Darhad, she will have to approve it, but it is our lawsmith who will actually sign it. His signature would be recognized in a court of law in Maracanda.'

'Ah . . . your lawsmith. Yes, I remember . . . When can we meet him?' An Lushan asked her, serious again. 'It must be soon. Every day we're away is another day in jail for Father.' He rummaged around in the big leather bag that had accompanied him all the way from Maracanda, producing a handful of scrolls that were all officially stamped and bound together with red silk. 'Here they are! This will impress your lawsmith – all the legal stuff Father's chief clerk drew up for me after his arrest. Can we leave your lawsmith with all the documents to have a look at while we have a little reconnaissance trip into the forests? Would he allow that?'

'Yes, I don't see why not. Come on, we'll see if we can speak to him now!'

They ducked out of the yurt. The children who had been playing close by stopped their game and regarded An Lushan in silence. Playfully he stuck his tongue out at them and they rushed off, laughing and chattering like a troop of monkeys.

CHAPTER 14

A MEETING IN THE HIGH YURT

They made their way across the camp, which was bustling with activity. More children had gathered as soon as they heard that the *ferangshan* had come out, and they whooped and danced around them. Lianxang clapped her hands to shoo them away as An Lushan good-naturedly pretended to lunge and grab at them.

Some older boys shepherded a herd of goats towards the scrubby pastures that edged the woods around the camp, before the trees thickened into the Dark Forests. The bells on the goats' collars tinkled, and the shepherds pretended to be busy with their charges while they sneaked looks at the stranger in their midst. Lianxang called out cheerfully to them, and An Lushan noticed that each one made the same gesture to his forehead he'd seen when they'd first arrived. A line of slow-moving oxen were being herded into a long, low-roofed building, and further off the clang and hammering of a smithy rang round the camp. He looked enquiringly at Lianxang.

'Tools, not weapons, An'an.' She smiled. 'Our winter crops of root vegetables need tending, as do our forests.'

'It is well-established, for a nomads' camp,' he said, taking in as much as he could as they made their way through the settlement. Dotted about the camp were simple shrines of piled-up stones with small fires burning in them – regularly tended by whoever was passing by.

'They are votive offerings to Chu Jung, Spirit of Fire,' Lianxang explained. 'As long as they never go out, our forests will be protected against the ravages of the dragon spirits of fire when they turned against mankind.'

'You are a superstitious people.'

'The old ways are not lost to us; not all of them at least,' she replied proudly.

A steady stream of people were coming in and out of the high yurt. They passed the great boulder that marked the entrance and entered the gloomy interior of the tribal meeting place.

Flickering torches of oiled hemp threw long shadows onto the wooden walls but it was difficult to make anything out clearly after coming in from the bright sunlight.

Lianxang took An Lushan's arm. 'Look' – she pointed to a raised dais with a long, low table – 'on the north side, the most important place in the high yurt: this is the *hoimor*, reserved for our sacred objects.' He struggled to see anything but could just make out a bear-skin draped over the table.

'The seating space next to the *hoimor*,' Lianxang went on, 'is the most honoured part of the building and is always reserved for the elders and respected guests at a gathering of the tribe.'

As his eyes grew accustomed to the light, An Lushan could see a small group of tribespeople gathered round a stooped figure who leaned heavily on a staff. He recognized the bird-like figure of Sarangerel sitting on some cushions and heaped-up furs. They were chattering away as if they were in his favourite teashop in Maracanda, An Lushan thought to himself.

The knot of people parted respectfully as they approached.

'Sarangerel, your granddaughter joins us,' an elderly, stooping man said joyfully, 'and our honoured guest. Welcome, An Lushan of the trading house of Vaishravana. I am Dalgimmaron, lawsmith of the Darhad. We have heard much about you.'

'As I have of you, sir,' An Lushan said, bowing deeply and murmuring an acknowledgement to Sarangerel. The lawsmith's face was square and heavily lined, with deep-set eyes.

'Lianxang, you are happily returned to your people – this is an auspicious day upon which the sun shines unusually brightly!' Dalgimmaron exclaimed rather ponderously.

She returned the greeting and, extricating herself from his fatherly hug, went to sit beside Sarangerel. There was an embarrassed silence; the little group of tribespeople tore their eyes away from An Lushan and shuffled their feet. He looked anxiously at Lianxang – perhaps he was expected to make some sort of speech? He was just about to open his mouth when Dalgimmaron stepped in.

'With your permission, Sarangerel, I would like to say just a few words,' the lawsmith said. He certainly sounded like a lawyer, An Lushan thought wryly, wondering just how long his 'few words' would go on for. He put on a friendly smile as the lawsmith looked at him.

'An Lushan of the trading house of Vaishravana, on behalf of our people, we thank you and your family for befriending Lianxang during her time at your city's famous school. Sarangerel has told me of your family's kindness, and how your father treated her as his own. Anyone who has shown themselves to be a friend of the Darhad in this way has earned our respect and gratitude.'

'Thank you for your kind words, sir,' An Lushan said respectfully, feeling the lawsmith would appreciate a formal reply, 'and for the hospitality you have shown me – and our escorts. The city of Maracanda will not take the gratitude and respect of the Darhad lightly, I assure you.' He ended with another smile and a bow.

Dalgimmaron looked very pleased but then glowered good-humouredly at the tribespeople, who were watching this exchange in silent, wide-eyed fascination.

'Do you not have work to attend to, children to look after? Go on – about your business! We will speak privately with our honoured guest.' Dalgimmaron waved his staff at them and they hastily dispersed, murmuring their respects.

'Thank you, Dalgimmaron,' Lianxang said. 'Grandmother, may I speak?'

'Of course, Granddaughter. We cannot hear too much of your voice, now that you are returned to us at last.'

As Lianxang started to tell the lawsmith about her time in Maracanda, An Lushan found his mind wandering. He looked around the high yurt and wondered about the Darhad's way of life. Now that he was here, among them, he began to understand why they had not changed these past hundreds of years: there was a simplicity of purpose about them that struck him, an outsider, as deeply ingrained. And then there was the implicit trust in the forests: they seemed certain that what Boghos was undoubtedly about to attempt – or was already attempting – posed no threat.

He could understand their reliance on the past – hadn't their guardianship always worked against intruders, as Lianxang had assured him it would prevail against his family's hated enemy? The forests had always been considered untouchable ... until now, and it was up to him, An Lushan, to convince the Darhad that his plan was both honourable and honest – it was the only way he could see of safeguarding his father's life.

'An'an?'

He glanced with a start towards Dalgimmaron, who was looking at him curiously.

'I ... I'm sorry, I am still a little tired from the journey,' he stuttered apologetically. 'You were saying?'

'I was asking if I might look at the documents Lianxang says your father's clerk has prepared – and I should say we are truly sorry to hear of your father's misfortune. Why they did not have a meeting of the people of your tribe to decide your father's fate is beyond me, but' – the old lawsmith shrugged his shoulders – 'the ways of the Empire are strange indeed.'

'They must seem that way,' An Lushan acknowledged politely, handing his bag of papers and documents over to Dalgimmaron.

'I will study these carefully,' the lawsmith said, looking at An Lushan keenly. 'Lianxang says that your city has many marvels: paved streets as wide as our high yurt; fountains that flow ceaselessly; and that your family's caravans trade their precious cargoes in all the different parts of the Empire, vast as it is.'

'All this and much more,' An Lushan said proudly.

'And we should be part of this . . . *hubbub*, she says, although that wasn't the word she used,' the lawsmith said, glancing warmly at Lianxang. 'It would seem that the capital of the Western Empire has bewitched her, would it not, Sarangerel? Not for nothing is it called the "City of Dreams".'

The spellweaver made a curious clacking noise from the back of her throat which An Lushan took to be amusement. Dalgimmaron received it as a sign of approval from her to carry on.

'As for our forests – they have seen off plunderers such as Boghos many times. Sarangerel's grandmother told of a whole army of barbarian invaders from the north who entered them and were never heard of again. We do not turn anyone away who wishes to tread their paths, for the dryads of the woods know their intentions before they have even set foot in them, and whoever betrays our trust suffers the fate they deserve. On that score, you have nothing to fear – a friend of the spellweaver's granddaughter is a friend of the Darhad, and of the forests. As for your startling plans – or what I understand of them . . .' He trailed off, turning to Sarangerel.

'There is no precedent, Spellweaver, in the history of our

people, for a merchant who has troubled to seek our permission to harvest a limited amount of timber. Perhaps in these times of change it would be prudent to consider what your granddaughter has told us – and her friend, from a powerful and influential trading family known throughout the Empire.' Dalgimmaron bowed in An Lushan's direction.

'My granddaughter is young, Lawsmith, and her head is full of ideas she has learned at that school of hers,' Sarangerel interrupted, gazing up at something only she could see, in her mind's eye. 'Perhaps when she is spellweaver, she may think differently, and change her mind. Until then, I say the old ways have served us well.'

'Grandmother!' Lianxang protested indignantly. 'I did not say the old ways haven't served us well, just that we need to consider other ways too . . .'

'I know this – and therefore they *shall* be considered, Granddaughter, but the lawsmith must first consider the documents that have been so carefully prepared, otherwise why would our honoured guest have troubled himself to bring them so far?'

'That is so, Sarangerel, just so,' Dalgimmaron clucked as he gathered up the various scrolls he had started to examine and put them back in the bag. 'I will scrutinize them most carefully.'

He gave An Lushan a quizzical look and a polite bow, and bustled off as fast as his old legs would carry him. An Lushan suppressed a smile as Lianxang caught his eye. Just then a young man and woman approached, carrying a small child. They looked troubled, and lingered hesitantly a few paces away.

'Come!' Lianxang called to them. 'Would you speak with the spellweaver?'

They nodded, and stepped forward shyly. An Lushan felt he was intruding on a private matter, and indicated to Lianxang that he would take his leave. He made his way to the entrance of the high yurt and, deep in thought, walked back through the settlement, oblivious to the curious stares and occasional muted acknowledgements of the tribespeople.

The sun shone from a cold, bright sky but he felt a long way from home and realized how much he missed the reassuring presence of his father. At the same time he was excited about seeing the Dark Forests for himself: not even his father, or for that matter the seasoned traveller Chen Ming, had ever ventured into them.

He pushed aside a sense of foreboding as a sudden glimmer of the bad dream he'd struggled to recall flashed through his mind, and decided to occupy himself by writing a report to his father. He knew that between them, Vagees and Rokshan would find a way to deliver it, even though it would be old news by the time Naha read it. Feeling a little calmer in himself, he settled down in the yurt, blew on the embers of the fire and, pulling out a scroll and pen and ink from his travel bag, began to write.

CHAPTER 15

THE DARK FORESTS

Sarangerel had insisted that two experienced trackers accompany them on An Lushan's reconnaissance expedition into the forests, despite Lianxang's protests that she was familiar enough with those parts: after all, they were within two or three days' march of the settlement.

'Winter approaches, Granddaughter, and you know that the fierce storms can overwhelm unwary travellers, forcing them to stumble from the path and lose their way; some never make it back again,' she had warned. The spellweaver had given Lianxang an eagle feather to invoke the protection of her spirit-bird: 'The eagle-eye will warn you of danger, my granddaughter,' she had said; Lianxang had taken it with great reverence, mindful of the guardianship being bestowed on her.

An Lushan had been secretly relieved at the spellweaver's precautions. Faint echoes of childhood stories and superstitions about the woods came drifting back to him. Above all others, man had always been wary of the Dark Forests; no one who was not of the Darhad, it was said, had ever crossed the length or breadth of them and lived; over the generations, the superstition and stories surrounding them multiplied, becoming in time part myth, part legend, part truth.

He looked around. Their guides, a grizzled tribesman of many years, Zayach, and a taciturn, much younger woman named Mergen, were ahead of them by some way.

'They say that the Dark Forests are enchanted,' he said hesitantly, 'and that the whispering you can hear near a certain tree is the death-song of all the people in the world who have ever taken their own lives . . .'

'. . . and what you hear are their sighs of pain and loss at being perpetually denied entry to the Wheel of Rebirth – I know; and a thousand other stories like them.' Lianxang smiled a little sadly. 'All are made up by ferangshan, An'an, who have always been jealous of us and our forests.'

'So, there isn't a tree of the guardian spirits?'

'Maybe there is. If there is, then of course we believe that it is our Dark Forests that are home to it – that is what we have always believed.' She paused as if waiting for him to say something. 'I'll ask the question for you,' she said affectionately: 'How do we know for sure?' She glanced up the trail to make sure Zayach and Mergen were out of earshot.

'Exactly!' An'an laughed. 'You must be a spellweaver's granddaughter, because you just read my mind! For all you know, the tree of the guardian spirits, your Tree of Heaven, could be somewhere else. Think of all the forests that must cover the Barbarian Lands – they have no cities or towns like the Empire.'

Lianxang was silent in the face of his scepticism.

'Even so,' he went on, craning his neck and looking around, 'could there really be bigger forests than these anywhere else in the world? And would they be as quiet as this? It's unnatural; it's so . . . still.'

A gentle soughing of the wind was all that could be heard, apart from the occasional rumble of thunder. No birds sang, no squirrels chattered. The Dark Forests breathed to their own rhythm, as they had done for millennia, long before man had intruded and made his noisy entrance into the world. The trees were packed close together and soared skywards, taller than any he had ever seen. Many had branches high up, with a cream-coloured silky-smooth bark; their canopies of lustrous yellow leaves were just beginning to drop as winter approached, making the path they followed shimmer in the half-light like a golden thread weaving its way into the distance.

An Lushan didn't tell Lianxang, but he found it forbidding and oppressive – in some areas, such was the denseness of the trees that only a little light found its way through the thick canopy. Despite this he noted with a practised trader's eye the quality of the timber, and thought it was little wonder that with the expansion of the Empire, attention had focused on the vast, potential riches of the Dark Forests. Surely it was just a question of time, he mused, before they were opened up and traders like him made their fortunes out of them?

His eyes narrowed at the prospect, and he looked guiltily at Lianxang. It was greed and duplicity that motivated the likes of Boghos, and he was here to show the Darhad that the trading house of Vaishravana was different. But whether he was successful or not in this endeavour, he had resolved to make the journey back to Maracanda before the bitter bite of winter in these regions made travel impossible: the family business and his father needed him, and he wondered too how his brother was coping. If he failed here, he would have to find another way to influence Jiang Zemin and ensure his father's safety.

For two days they had been following a route close to the western boundaries of the forests – An Lushan was eager to go as far north as they could to see for himself evidence of Boghos's presence, but Zayach had pointed out this would take them a full cycle of the moon, and Sarangerel had given them clear instructions to turn back after two to three days.

They changed direction on the third day, heading for the interior of the forest so that they could loop back towards the settlement rather than simply retracing their steps. An Lushan kept it to himself, but as they headed further into the woods, the dark oppressiveness he'd felt since they'd first set out became more intense, preying on his mind so that he hardly spoke. He became pale and withdrawn.

Lianxang noticed the change in him. 'An'an, you don't look well,' she said with concern after trying unsuccessfully to draw him into conversation. 'You've hardly said a word all day. What's the matter?'

But he just shook his head, muttering something about feeling the cold more than her and waving her on ahead.

Towards the late afternoon they were walking through a more lightly wooded part of the forest when Zayach came pounding back down the track, holding something up in his hand and shouting at the top of his voice. An Lushan caught Lianxang's anxious glance as he hurried to catch up with her. Zayach came rushing up, his chest heaving and sweat pouring from his face. Without a word, he handed Lianxang what looked like a piece of bark.

'What is it? What has happened? What is this?' Lianxang asked, twisting it round and round in her hands as if it could speak and tell her.

'It is from one of the trees up ahead!' Zayach managed to blurt out. 'It has become . . . blighted with some foul pestilence,' he cried despairingly.

'Blighted? By what? How can this be?' Lianxang whispered, turning it over and over before handing it to An Lushan. If it had once been a piece of the pale, almost trans-lucent bark from the trees that surrounded them, it would have been difficult to tell now. What he held was twisted and gnarled, covered in black, wart-like growths; what was strange were the glossy, almost glass-like patches in between the growths that were so polished they invited stroking.

As he brushed it lightly with his fingers, he thought he felt it pulse slightly . . . He stared at it in wonder, but then hurriedly handed it back to Lianxang as a wave of nausea swept over him. Stepping aside, he retched violently, slumping against a tree as dizziness and faintness overcame him.

Lianxang offered him some water, murmuring words of

sympathy. 'An'an, you're shivering,' she said, rubbing his shoulders. 'Here, take my cloak.' She draped it over his shoulders. 'We'll rest here a while. Mergen will have some herbs and roots we can make into a hot drink that will help bring out the fever.' She glanced towards Zayach. 'Where is Mergen?'

'She carried on deeper into the forest to see if any more trees were affected.'

'There are more?' she asked angrily, as if the blight was Zayach's fault. 'Take me to where you left her. Is it far?'

An Lushan looked at her in surprise – he had not heard her speak so imperiously to her people before. Zayach mumbled something apologetically and started to make his way back up the path.

'Stay here, An'an. You must rest. We won't be long,' Lianxang assured him, looking up at the sky, which was rapidly darkening with thunderclouds. 'We will need to find shelter soon. There's a storm coming.' And she hurried off after Zayach.

An Lushan raised his hand in acknowledgement and, shivering violently, pulled the cloaks closer around him. The strengthening wind moaned through the treetops and he grimaced to himself as he recalled the story of the lost spirits – *ferangshan* superstition, that was all, he reminded himself as a sudden gust ripped through the forest canopy and the storm that had been threatening suddenly broke.

Another thunderclap brought with it a downpour of torrential rain. He was sitting slightly off the track but not far enough to escape the worst of the storm. With a groan he heaved himself up and, his head spinning, made his way further into the forest, selecting a spot where he could still see the path. Waves of nausea overcame him again, and he leaned heavily against a tree, gulping in lungfuls of air to steady himself. He slid down the trunk and, covering himself up as best he could, closed his eyes . . .

He woke with a start. The rain had not eased. He glanced anxiously up and down the trail to see if his companions were making their way back. He had no idea how long he had slept, but he felt a little better. It was difficult to see clearly through the pelting grey gloom, and, peering absently into the dark interior of the forest, he was startled to see a distant shadowy shape slowly moving through the trees towards him.

'Strange . . .' he muttered, expecting the others to have returned the way they'd come. They probably hadn't realized he'd moved, he thought.

'Over here!' he shouted, scrambling up. 'Over here!' He waved his arms but got no wave of recognition back. It was difficult to make out exactly who it was; if it wasn't one of his companions, who could it be?

Whoever it was, he was bent almost double under an enormous load of twigs and branches strapped loosely together on his back; his arms were tucked behind him, supporting the load. His black tunic was ragged and the rain dripped off his stiff, wide-brimmed peasant's hat. He came to within hailing distance, and then stopped.

The stranger's head hung down, his hat completely obscuring his face. Slowly and deliberately, he eased the load off his back. Straightening up, he revealed himself to be surprisingly tall.

'A long way from home, to be gathering wood?' An Lushan asked warily as the stranger advanced slowly towards him. He now saw that the man was young, with golden hair that tumbled to his shoulders. His eyes were the deepest blue, glittering with an intensity that drew An Lushan into their depths.

'We are both a long way from home, are we not?' the stranger asked with a friendly smile.

'Are you?' An Lushan replied, surprised at the question and on his guard now. 'Where is "home"? Are you of the

Darhad people? We are three days' travel from their winter settlement, and I have not been there long enough to have seen you about the camp . . . we are returning there.'

'No, I am not with the Darhad,' the stranger said, not taking his eyes off An Lushan, 'but I know of them – who wouldn't, around these parts?'

An Lushan nodded, warier now that the stranger had avoided answering his question.

'It is unfortunate, what is happening to their sacred groves,' the man continued, looking around. As if in response, thunder rumbled threateningly overhead.

'You . . . you have seen other trees that have been affected?' An Lushan asked, concerned that the blight might be more widespread than they had feared.

'You have seen it too?' the stranger asked.

'Yes – did you see my companions? They were checking around the area where they'd come across the blight. Have you seen this happen before in the forests?'

'Questions, questions, my friend.' The stranger smiled. 'No, I did not see your companions. But my travels take me far and wide through the forests, and I can tell you the north-west is badly affected. The blight is spreading from there, it seems . . .' He trailed off, looking keenly at An Lushan.

'The north-west?' An Lushan looked stunned. If this stranger spoke the truth, he had saved him a long journey – he found it hard to believe, but had the spirits of the woods already moved against Boghos, as the Darhad had said they would?

'What is happening there? What did you see exactly? Were there people there . . . not of the Darhad?' An Lushan asked carefully, not wanting to give too much away – this peasant already seemed to know a lot, and there was something about him that made him feel uncomfortable.

'What more do you need to know? The forests are safe. The

greedy eyes of men will quickly lose interest in them – diseased timber will not add to the trading might of the Empire. In time the trees will recover, under the watchful eye of the Darhad.'

An Lushan recognized instantly the truth of what the stranger said: no one would want to buy diseased timber, not from him or Boghos or anyone else. Maybe the trees would recover, in time . . . but time was the one, precious thing he did not have.

'You look stricken, my friend,' the peasant said softly. 'Is this not what you wanted to hear? The dragon spirits of the earth, of water and fertility, are at their most potent here in the Dark Forests: they can destroy, and just as quickly they can recreate again the silent beauty of the sacred groves that you yourself witnessed when you entered them for the first time. You felt this – yet it troubled you.'

An Lushan stared at him. How did this . . . woodman, or whatever he was, know how he had felt two days ago? He tried to tear his gaze away, but the blue depths of the man's eyes would not let him go; it was strange, but he no longer felt so faint and sick.

'There may be another way, An Lushan.' The quiet tones washed over him, drowning out the roar of the wind and the steady downpour of rain.

'How do you know my—?' he heard himself ask.

'It is of no consequence,' the stranger interrupted, holding up his hand. 'I know about the Armenian, Boghos, too. You wanted to side yourself in alliance with him and carve up the forests between you. But this blight will destroy your plans to trade in the timber. Do not deny your scheming: it was only the barest glimmer of a thought in your mind, but you seized on it! You are no different from all the others of your kind.'

'No, it's not true, the Darhad – they trust me; I would do nothing without their permission . . . My father, he said it was the only way . . .'

The stranger stepped closer, holding him in his steady gaze. 'Then think on this, An Lushan: I can give you the power to release your father from his captivity and destroy Jiang Zemin – and destroy your enemy, Boghos, too. The way will be clear for you then to become the richest, most powerful merchant trader in the Empire and all Known Lands. Would this be your deepest desire?'

'To secure the release of my father is my dearest wish. I . . . I do not need the other things,' An Lushan replied hesitatingly. 'But how can you help me in this?'

'Walk with me a while and I will show you, but I must have your answer. I have a puzzle to solve, which I need your help with.'

'What is this *puzzle*?' An Lushan asked, playing for time. Who *was* this stranger, and could he really help him? Trying to calm his whirling thoughts, he found himself drifting deep into the forest at the stranger's side, allowing himself to be drawn ever further from the trails.

'Why, the one the old storyteller has already spoken to you about,' the stranger replied softly. 'It was a curious story, was it not, but nevertheless one that you should heed.'

'I don't really know what you're talk—'

'My master and I see and hear many things in the world of men,' the man cut him off. 'We think we have found the source of the ancient powers that is at the heart of the old storyteller's riddle. My master believes that what was *lost* should be returned, that is all . . . And then the puzzle is solved.'

'Do you mean the old storyteller's *riddle* is solved?' An Lushan said, astonished. 'But who is your master? And why is a riddle so important to you? It is all about ancient myths and legends – a "curious story", as you said, something to amuse children, that is all. I have more important things to deal with.'

'Your father's freedom, your trading agreement, the family business – you have much on your mind.' The stranger nodded sympathetically. 'But it is a small favour I ask, and if it will secure the release of your father—'

'How? How will it secure the release of my father?' An Lushan demanded. 'If I am to help you, how do I know that whatever it is you want me to do will help my father?'

'You will be a hero for solving the riddle and removing the threat that the old storyteller spoke of: "I speak of the end of empires, people of Maracanda! China and all Known Lands – even the Unknown Lands – all shall wither and die" – these were the words the storyteller used, were they not? Whatever you want shall be yours for the asking.'

'Yes, but the Council of . . . the leaders of my people – like myself – do not see an old storyteller's ramblings as a threat!' An Lushan replied with a dismissive laugh. 'We are all more concerned with the loss of trade that the closure of the pass through to the east will bring.'

'Yes, of course – the pass that goes through the Kingdom of the Wild Horsemen; and their rebel leader – your uncle, the source of all your family's woes.'

'You seem to know a lot about my family.' An Lushan glared at the young stranger.

'The leaders of your people will be much more . . . biddable when they witness the power of what will be revealed to you – if you help us,' the peasant replied persuasively.

'If you know what this source of the ancient powers is, and where it is, why don't you get it yourself? What is it to do with me? I must return to Maracanda, where my father is imprisoned,' An Lushan said carefully, weighing up the stranger's words and glancing around quickly as he realized with growing unease how far they had walked away from the trail.

'I . . . I cannot take it myself, small though it is for something of such power,' the man replied, sounding strangely hesitant. 'I must retrieve my wood – we have wandered far from the track.'

Was it his imagination, An Lushan wondered, or was the wood-gatherer's voice growing fainter?

'There is much your ancestors knew that should not have been forgotten, but not all of which is lost . . .' The man's voice *was* getting fainter. He turned to go. 'Stand back from the tree,' he said in a hoarse whisper. 'What I speak of will reveal itself to you—'

'Wait! Where are you going? Who are you? If I decide to help you, how shall I know where to go with . . . whatever it is?' An Lushan called after him. 'And what of my companions?'

'It is your decision, An Lushan: how will your father be freed if you return to Maracanda empty-handed? And if my master favours you, he may decide that what I speak of is yours to keep. Think on this: such power in the hands of one mort—man. You will know where to go – a crow will follow you and lead you when there is a need to. Return the way you came. No one must know what you have with you.'

Long after the stooped figure had melted into the rain, An Lushan stared after him, starting violently when a thunderclap detonated directly above. Almost too late, he remembered the warning he'd been given, and ran for his life.

Two lightning bolts, one directly after the other, crackled through the air and exploded into the tree he'd been leaning against only a moment before. It erupted in a blinding flash and he was flung to the ground, buffeted by the shock waves. When he looked up, where the tree had once been was now a smoking pit, about ten paces across. He picked himself up and crawled towards it.

Just as he peered cautiously over the edge, a deep rumble shook the ground. He gasped at the size of the rent in the Earth – it was more like a subterranean cavern – that the explosion had exposed. He couldn't even see the bottom of it at first, but then his eye was caught by what looked like a tiny spark glinting in the far-off depths. Was this – whatever it was – what the stranger had been talking about? He saw the sides of the pit were not too steep to prevent him climbing down, and there were roots and rough ledges he could hang onto.

Getting down might be possible, he calculated, though getting up again was a different matter altogether. Again the spark-like glint caught his eye.

He churned things over in his mind: his trading plans lay in ruins, so even if what the stranger promised turned out to be a worthless trinket, could he risk ignoring the opportunity if it really was what he'd said – a source of great power? And if he delayed? Lianxang and the others would find him, and the opportunity would be gone, or he would have to share anything he found.

After some agonizing moments of indecision, he realized there was only one way to find out; the stranger was right, he thought, with a little shrug: it was better than returning home empty-handed. Taking both cloaks from around his shoulders, he carefully rolled Lianxang's up as tightly as possible and tucked it into his belt, thinking it might come in useful to wrap up whatever it was down there.

He took a deep breath, and for the first time in many years, muttered a prayer to the dragon spirits of the earth; then he swung his legs over the edge and started to inch his way down.

CHAPTER 16

A PARTING OF THE WAYS

The light began to fade, but An Lushan's prayers that the storm would pass were answered. As he clambered slowly down, his legs ached and his hands were numb and sore from holding onto whatever his grasping outstretched fingers could find. The moon shone in a clear night sky, providing just enough light for him to see, and he calculated he could reach the bottom and make his way up again well before dawn.

The object gleamed dully in the moonlight as he inched his way towards it. It lay in a lattice of tangled roots and sharp, flinty stones, just below a natural ledge of compacted earth. Exhausted from the descent, An Lushan crawled onto the ledge and rolled gratefully onto his back. The muscles in his arms and legs were trembling from the arduous descent. Wearily, but with his heart thudding, he turned over onto his stomach and gazed at what he had risked his life to obtain. It was partially obscured by the roots, but he could see it was a figure of a rearing dragon, snarling and serpent-like. It was slightly longer than a man's outstretched hand, and beneath the dirt and grime of its long entombment, he imagined it would be exquisitely crafted in gold, bronze and silver, perhaps even studded with precious stones. He was too tired to wonder how it had glinted so brightly when he'd first seen it from the top of the pit. Swinging himself halfway off the ledge, he was just able to get his hand on it.

Gently he pulled it from its resting place and clambered back onto the ledge. Scraping away some of the dirt of centuries, he saw he'd guessed correctly: it was encrusted with rubies, sapphires and emeralds. Reverently he lifted it up, as if making an offering.

'So, I have you . . .' he whispered exultantly, turning it around in his hands. For a moment he thought he felt the faintest of pulse-like beats, and dropped it into his lap as if it was a branding iron. Nervously, he wrapped it in his cloak and wedged it securely in his belt.

His heart sank as he contemplated the ascent. The moon seemed many, many li away, a tiny saucer in the sky. With an exhausted sigh, he spat on his hands and began the long climb back up.

'An'an!' Lianxang shouted at the top of her voice, but her cry was whipped away by the howling wind.

'Perhaps he sought shelter off the trail,' Zayach shouted, looking all around. 'We have been gone longer than we thought.'

They had returned to where they thought they had left An Lushan, but there was no sign of him. When they had caught up with Mergen, they had been dismayed to find dozens of trees affected with the same blight, and had spent longer than they'd intended studying their condition. Lianxang kicked herself for being so unthinking, and wondered despairingly where An Lushan could have disappeared to.

A short way up the trail Mergen gave a shout, pointing excitedly into the forest. 'There! I think I saw him – difficult to tell which direction he's going . . . I think away from us!' she yelled, heading off at a run.

With a cry of relief, Lianxang followed Mergen in the direction she'd indicated. With a worried shake of his head, Zayach followed.

Some time later it was Zayach who called a halt. 'It cannot have been An'an that you saw, Mergen. He would have heard us and stopped.'

'If it wasn't him, who else could it have been?' the young tribeswoman replied sharply. 'Not one of our people, that's for sure. And how can you be so certain he'd have heard us? The storm was at its height – he could have been disorientated – and he is sick. Even if he heard us, perhaps he thought he was being pursued.'

'Zayach is right, Mergen,' Lianxang intervened. 'We just have your glimpse to go on. I saw somebody too, shortly after we left the trail, but then nothing. We must return to the settlement as quickly as we can and send our most skilled trackers out to find him. We can take a faster route through the forest itself, away from the trail, to save time.'

'As long as we don't get another storm like that one, it should be quicker,' Zayach agreed, rubbing his beard. 'If we head in a south-westerly direction, we should end up at the spot where we first entered the forest before tomorrow sundown – that's if we go at a steady pace through what's left of tonight and all tomorrow,' he said, glancing up at the night sky.

'Mergen and I can manage that,' Lianxang said. 'When we get nearer to the settlement, we'll go on ahead if you need to rest.'

'As you wish,' Zayach said with the barest of nods. 'Until then, I will lead the way.'

The weather held, and they arrived back at the settlement at the time Zayach had predicted. Despite being exhausted and cold, the three of them immediately conferred with Sarangerel and Dalgimmaron in the high yurt.

'This is most irregular,' Dalgimmaron fussed, as soon as he heard what had happened. 'Most irregular. I cannot recall anything like it in the annals of our history, Sarangerel: to have responsibility, *as hosts*, for the safety and wellbeing of an honoured guest – only to lose him! We can only pray the spirits of the woods will lead him back to us,' he added, looking disapprovingly at Lianxang.

'We must do more than that, Lawsmith,' Sarangerel said with just a hint of impatience. 'The dryads of the woods are bent on destroying the ambitions of the marauding merchant in the north-west, and have sent the blight we have learned of for just this purpose. We must summon more of our spirits to guide An Lushan back. Zayach, gather the most tireless drummers of the tribe. Mergen, assemble a dozen of the most experienced trackers. At first light you must lead them back into the forests. Go! Get what rest you can.'

At daybreak the following day An Lushan woke from a sleep of the dead. The day before, he had finally scrabbled his way to the top of the pit just as the dawn rays of the weak autumnal sun were slanting through the trees. He had stumbled back onto the trail and stuck to it, as the stranger had advised, and thought he recognized that part of the forest nearest to the settlement the closer he got.

He groaned and shook his head, which ached dully like a throbbing drumbeat. He was famished and shook the small leather bag he carried, emptying out a hunk of bread and some pieces of dried meat for his breakfast. There was a small spring nearby; he drank some of its icy water and then did his best to clean himself up, washing the worst of the muddy smears from his legs and arms.

He splashed water onto his face and felt his thickening beard. His head still throbbed, but he suddenly stood stock-still: it wasn't a throbbing in his head he could hear – it was definitely a rhythmic, pulsating drumbeat . . .

It could only be coming from the settlement, he guessed, realizing he must be closer than he thought. He patted the rolled-up cloak in which the statuette of the rearing dragon was hidden, and considered having another look at it – he liked the feel of it in his hands, and he wondered if he would be able to feel it pulse again, like a heartbeat, as if it was alive.

Furtively almost, he unwrapped it and held it reverently in both hands as he gazed at it. He realized he must be careful when he got back to the settlement. Somehow he would have to try and secrete it in his travelling bag as quickly and inconspicuously as possible. It occurred to him that a much better hiding place might be the bag of documents and legal papers that he had given Dalgimmaron to have a look through. Well, he wouldn't be needing those now, would he? A sneer flickered across his face.

'Bumbling old fool,' he muttered, shaking out Lianxang's cloak and wrapping the Talisman back up in it. He was suddenly seized by a feeling of such impatience to be away from these simple people, with their centuries-old traditions and ignorance of everything the Empire stood for. The sneer still lingered faintly as he strode off, following the sound of the drums.

An Lushan could almost feel the trees leaning and swaying as he followed the faint but unrelenting drumbeats, as if they were trying to steer him back to safety.

As the drumbeats grew louder, he stumbled onto the track they had followed when they had set out, and soon met some of the trackers, who welcomed him joyously, relieved to find their guest very tired and hungry, but alive and well.

As they walked back into the camp, An Lushan realized he did not have much time before the pit was discovered: some awkward questions might be asked of him. He resolved to leave as quickly as possible – they would surely understand that he had to get back to his family in Maracanda.

As they passed by the spellweaver's yurt, he quickly ducked in, taking the opportunity to hide the statuette under a heap of clothes at the bottom of his travel bag. He gathered up Lianxang's cloak to return to her.

On their way through the camp, some of the tribespeople came up to him with shy greetings of welcome and safe return which he politely acknowledged. Three young men were grouped around the huge boulder outside the high yurt, each beating out his own pulsating song on individual drums, which came together in one mesmerizing, hypnotic flow.

Lianxang stood at the entrance, a relieved smile lighting up her face. 'An'an, you're safe! Thank the spirits for your safe return! Are you feeling all right? You look better than when we left you.' She seemed slightly surprised as she brushed his cheek with her lips. 'What happened? Quickly, tell me,' she went on excitedly, taking him by the arm. 'You will have to recount to Sarangerel exactly what happened. Dalgimmaron will be so relieved to see you – we're all relieved, of course . . .'

'I don't really remember much at all,' he said as they walked down to the far end of the *hoimor*. 'I felt very feverish, and you seemed to be gone so long that I decided to go and find you. I . . . I must have got lost, but luckily wandered in the right direction, then I heard the drums – and it was strange, but I swear the trees seemed to know I was lost and tried to point me in the right direction – which is how I ended up on the track we were on when we first entered the forest.'

'But it wasn't very long before we returned to where we'd left you.' Lianxang shot him a questioning look but he didn't reply. 'Well, you decided to try and find us – it must've seemed the right decision at the time.' She smiled at him. 'We thought we glimpsed you going in the opposite direction, north. We shouted and shouted but couldn't attract your attention.'

'It couldn't have been me – I didn't hear anyone shouting for me,' he said uncomfortably, relieved to see Dalgimmaron bustling towards them.

'An'an! Welcome, the warmest welcome indeed, most honoured guest. Come, be seated – you must be exhausted after your ordeal . . . come . . .'

'He soon will be exhausted, Lawsmith, with all your

flapping and fussing like a mother hen,' Sarangerel remarked dryly. 'Welcome, An'an: the spirits have granted your safe return.'

She indicated for him to sit, and asked him to tell them everything that had happened. He recounted the same version of events he'd just given Lianxang. When he'd finished, he waited nervously for the spellweaver to say something. Sarangerel rocked back and forth, her eyes raised.

Finally she spoke. 'The forest is weeping; something long forgotten by men stirs. The spirits can feel its power – it is in the water, and in Mother Earth. Sometimes I can sense it: darting like a wraith in and out of the shadows of the night, it comes and goes . . . there! In my dreams I catch it, but it slips through my mind's fingers like an eel in the deeps of Lake Baikal, hiding, slippery and unseen – until it pounces on its unwary victim.'

She paused and bowed her head. An Lushan wished even more fervently to be away from the Darhad and, shivering, drew his cloak around him.

'An'an, you may still have a fever,' Lianxang said with concern. 'Grandmother, we must let him rest. He has been through an ordeal.'

He smiled at her, thinking if she only knew the truth of what she said.

'Quite so, Lianxang,' Dalgimmaron clucked. 'Sustenance and repose are what's called for. We can discuss the legal papers you kindly gave me to peruse, An'an, once you are fully recovered. I found them fascinating, quite fascinating – but I fear, with the forests blighted as they are . . .' He looked sympathetically at him, giving a little shrug of his shoulders.

'I understand, sir,' An Lushan replied, relieved at the change of subject. 'I understand fully. I trust you will understand, too, that my plans have now changed.' He addressed all three of them. 'My father and brother need me, and our trading business needs my attention. I must return to Maracanda without delay.'

'An'an, we haven't spoken of this.' Lianxang looked shocked. 'Must you go back straight away? Our woods – they will recover. And your plans . . . we can press ahead with them in time.'

'Time is what I do not have, Lianxang – you know that.' He smiled at her, but his voice was cold. 'Will the trees recover? I sincerely hope they do – and then we can talk again. Dalgimmaron has all the papers' – he gave a little bow towards the lawsmith – 'and once I am home, and have received word from you that the blight has gone, I will dispatch a full report detailing our proposals for his respectful attention. Until then, every day I am away is one more day's imprisonment for my father. I must return.'

Lianxang could only nod, but her eyes betrayed her confusion at the matter-of-fact way he was walking out of their lives.

'Of course . . . of course, our honoured guest must do as he sees fit, but we hope he will draw the attention of his tribe's elders to what has happened here – that our forests have suffered the unwelcome attention of the marauding merchant, as the spellweaver has said.'

An Lushan murmured he would indeed mention it to the Council of Elders and, hopeful that he could withdraw without further questioning, offered his thanks for the hospitality and warm welcome he had enjoyed.

'I will come with you to help you prepare for your departure,' Lianxang said. 'You must eat and rest before you leave at first light.'

'No!' he said brusquely, but recovered himself quickly. 'I mean, thank you, Lianxang, but I think I should leave immediately, while the weather holds, don't you think?'

She nodded and, jumping up, kissed her grandmother.

Dalgimmaron made one final, elaborate bow and wished him well.

'If you have no further need of my bag, sir – it is of no value but my father gave it to me as a token of his appreciation when I had successfully completed my first inventory for our annual summer caravan, a few seasons ago,' An Lushan lied, smiling warmly.

The lawsmith needed no further prompting and said he would go and fetch it straight away. An Lushan and Lianxang turned to go.

'I would know who the stranger was, in our forests,' Sarangerel said suddenly, gently rocking. An Lushan froze.

'Grandmother?' Lianxang asked, puzzled. 'I told you, Mergen and I only caught a glimpse of him, and he – or she – whoever it was was a long way off.'

'Did the stranger make himself known to you, An'an? You saw no one?' Sarangerel's questions hung in the air.

'I . . . I saw no one,' he replied quietly, with a tight smile at Lianxang. 'No one.'

A little later that day, An Lushan, Bhathra and Qalim were ready to depart.

'You will send me word as soon as there is improvement, or if it gets worse,' An Lushan said to Lianxang as he mounted up.

'Of course. And you will write to me – tell me how your father is, and Rokshan – and Ah Lin, of course, and Kan.' She held on tight to his horse's bridle. 'And you, let me know how you are, An'an . . . promise?'

'I promise.' He smiled. 'And you will let us know if you are to return to the school to finish your studies.'

'Yes,' she whispered, her eyes filling with tears, 'but you have seen how old my grandmother is: she may not let me go, especially now, with the forests . . .' She trailed off, smiled bravely, then slapped the horse's haunches hard. 'Go! May the dragon spirits of the wind speed you on your way!'

She gazed on long after they had disappeared over the hills they had crossed, weary but full of hope, only a few short days ago.

With a heavy heart, she walked back through the camp. The first squalls of a cold winter's wind buffeted her and she longed for spring to come, when – if her grandmother and people permitted it – she would be able to return to Maracanda.

PART THREE

INITIATION ON THE ROAD EAST

The Legend of the Sacred Scroll

The following is recorded in The Book of Ahura Mazda, the Wise Lord

The Sacred Scroll is the parchment on which the words of the Divine Commandment are said to be written.

It recounts, the legend tells, how the Wise Lord put in place the Arch of Darkness to keep the Shadow-without-a-name in perpetual imprisonment, outside the universe of all things and even time itself, following his rebellion and fall.

In ancient times when this took place, the Wise Lord did not intend it to be written down, but as he made his Divine Commandment, he was accompanied by his faithful messenger, Corhanuk. Corhanuk's role was to act as witness, on behalf of all his fellow guardian spirits, to the terrible punishment of the Shadow, formerly the best-loved and most favoured of all the Wise Lord's spirit-creatures, second only to Chu Jung.

But despite his imprisonment in the Arch of Darkness, the malevolence of the Shadow was still so strong that he could instill evil in the hearts of those who might serve him. And as Corhanuk witnessed the justice of the Wise Lord, he fell under the sway of the Shadow. He was persuaded by his new master to make cosmic mischief by recording the words of the Divine Commandment and 'losing' them in the world of men, so that if the Wise Lord found out, he would not be able to produce it even if he was commanded to. Thus what became known as the Sacred Scroll was created and came into being in the world of men.

And when Chu Jung - who was not mindful of the treachery of the Wise Lord's messenger - searched out Corhanuk and asked him to take his gift of the Staff to the Wise Lord, Corhanuk took the Staff for himself. The Wise Lord found out and sought vengeance for the theft of the gift, but Corhanuk hid himself and the Staff away from men and all living things.

Throughout the ages, Corhanuk now served a different master - the Shadow, who set his servant the task of finding the Talisman of Chu Jung, for without the Talisman, the Staff was incomplete and its power could not be realized ...

Historian's note: the legend of the Sacred Scroll has never been proved or disproved, as the parchment which the Divine Commandment was meant to have been written on has never been discovered. But the Fellowship of the Three One-eared Hares dedicated itself to ensuring that, should it ever be found, it would not fall into the wrong hands. Members of the secret organization swore on their lives to prevent this from happening as the surest safeguard against the Shadow ever being resurrected, for they believed that the Shadow would be freed from his eternal imprisonment should the Divine Commandment ever be undone by reversing the meaning of the words written on the Scroll.

Source: the secret Fellowship of the Three One-eared Hares;
origin – discovered in the ruins of the citadel monastery of Labrang,
spiritual centre of the old Western Empire.

CHAPTER 17

THE SINGING SANDS

Many weeks earlier, leaving only hours after An Lushan and Lianxang had set off on their journey, Rokshan too had turned his back on his home and begun his long journey towards the Flame Mountains in the Land of Fire, as Shou Lao had entreated him to.

It was his first journey east and the going was tough. Over the first few days the inside of his thighs were rubbed raw, and the sway and lurch of the camel as they made their way across the sun-scorched steppe made his stomach queasy. Numbed by the plodding monotony, he decided to walk instead, making his feet sore and blistered.

The camels travelled nose to tail in a long line. It was a large caravan, split into groups of five to ten camels tied together by a rope looped through wooden nose pegs. Each animal, whether it was camel, buffalo, horse or mule, wore a small bronze bell around its neck, which made a dull clanging as the caravan made its slow, ponderous progress.

As the days wore on, Rokshan proved his worth in the task of dung-collecting. Also Gupta – the chief cameleer – had taught him a few tricks of the trade: today's lesson was how to tie the camels together and insert their wooden nose pegs.

'You have to make it trust you,' Gupta said. Rokshan had managed to get the camel to sit down, but only after a lot of noisy protesting.

'Now take the peg.'

'Me?' Rokshan said, alarmed. He really didn't want to get any closer to the camel, which was belching and farting ferociously – the fetid smell of its breath was overpowering. In between belches, it drew back its lips and made the strangest gurgling noises, as if it was being strangled.

'That's it – make the clacking noises I showed you, to soothe it. Approach it like you mean business but not like you're threatening it,' Gupta said.

Rokshan did as he was told, but only so he wouldn't lose face with his new friend.

'Hold out the nuts and hay – that way it'll be more interested in the food than in what you're going to do to it,' Gupta advised.

Nervously Rokshan held out his hand with the un-appetizing mixture.

'And don't forget to push the peg through all in one go with your other hand as it takes the treat.'

This was the tricky part, and it could be dangerous if the camel decided to take a bite at the hand offering the food – as they quite commonly did; Rokshan knew that a camel bite could leave you without a finger, or two even.

'Do it all in one go,' Gupta said, quietly enjoying Rokshan's awkwardness but trying to encourage him too. As soon as the camel saw the food, it stopped its protesting and started to nibble appreciatively at the offering.

Before it knew what was happening, Rokshan had produced the peg, slotted it perfectly in one large nostril and pushed it gently but firmly through. The camel gave a sharp snort and a disdainful belch before resuming its contented chewing, eyeing him suspiciously.

'Yes! I did it! I did it!' Rokshan danced a little jig of delight, feeling extremely proud of himself.

'Not bad for a rich merchant's son,' laughed Gupta. 'You'll be snipping their you-know-whats off next,' he joked. 'Now that really is fun. You can make quite a decent living being a camel-pegger, you know.'

'No, thank you,' Rokshan said firmly. 'I think I'll stick to being a special envoy.'

'Maybe in your next life! For now, I'll tell Chen Ming that we have one more expert cameleer in our caravan.'

Rokshan watched him thread his way through the long line of pack animals with their cameleers and drivers patiently walking beside them. He reminded himself to find him again when they made camp that evening, just so he could see the expression on Chen Ming's face when Gupta told him of his camel-tending skills.

The caravan usually stopped before sunset. Sometimes there might be a small hamlet with an inn that only remained open because of the caravan trade. Chen Ming and his cameleers would stay at the inn, while the rest of the caravan made camp and slept in sturdy tents made of animal skins and a coarse felt-like material. When they broke camp in the morning, it was also Rokshan's job to help load up the camels.

At first he had been impatient, piling up whatever came to hand, but the results had been disastrous; he'd spent whole days scrabbling on and off his camel as his bad packing unravelled.

Gupta had come to his rescue. 'You have to have a system,' he'd explained patiently. 'First, take the blankets and a saddle-cloth and put them around the two humps . . . like so . . .' He carefully wound them round. 'Then, when you've taken the tent down, use the frame' – these were slatted, slightly curved panels of wood which fitted on either side of the camel – 'like this,' he added, neatly tying them in place. 'Now take the big round saddlebags . . .' These were nearly as large as a grown man, stuffed full with the finest Sogdian wool, which Gupta showed Rokshan how to drape over the wood panels. Finally he'd gather up the small bags of his belongings and cooking pots and put them on top of one saddlebag. On the other saddlebag he'd sling a hunting knife in a scabbard, a small sword – just in case of bandit attacks – a bow and a quiver of arrows. Water was carried in lightweight, hollowed-out gourds.

Of course there was Abu, the caravan monkey. Every morning he would be at Rokshan's tent, chattering and skittering about. Abu helped as much as he could; this usually involved unloading everything Rokshan had just loaded up, or pulling the wool out of the bags, or running off with the pots and other essential pieces of equipment.

But the relentless routine of desert travel took its toll on everyone's spirits.

'It feels like we've been tramping for ever across these plains,' Rokshan said to Gupta towards the end of the second week. The chief cameleer's hawk-like face betrayed no emotion but his eyes narrowed as he shielded them against the shimmering anvil of the sun.

There was no end to it: the steppe stretched from one end of the horizon to the other, broken only by the odd lonely outpost – a military garrison or trading post perhaps – barely discernible in the hazy distance. Rokshan had noticed the increased level of activity at the garrisons, and they'd come across imperial troops more than once.

'Only a few more days of this,' Gupta told him, 'then we'll get to the Red Sandy Wastes; after that it'll get a little cooler as we approach the foothills of the Mountains of Hami – and then on to the Terek Dhavan Pass – another cycle of the moon and then half again . . . maybe a little more.' He grinned through cracked lips, trying to cheer Rokshan up.

But one weary day blurred into another as they left the steppe behind and reached the Red Sandy Wastes, just as Gupta had said. It was a different landscape at last, but they soon longed for the grassy steppe again. Even this late in the season, it was like a furnace during the day; the wind blew dusty clouds into the air, kicking up a reddy-grey haze that got in everybody's clothes and hair and made their eyes itch – once they started scratching, they couldn't stop. And Rokshan couldn't help shuddering as he recalled Kan's ghostly stories about the Singing Sands, which lay nearby.

He longed for the mournful note of the caravan master's horn at dusk, signalling the day's march was at an end; but how he dreaded the cheery tinkle of the bell at dawn as the priest went up and down the caravan blessing all the travellers, calling them to make their prayers to the dragon spirits of earth, wind, fire and air. His plaintive, sing-song chant would echo through the camp as he prayed to the dragon spirits not to curse them with earthquakes, desert storms or extreme weather of any kind.

For days they trekked across li after li of sand and gravel, broken only by razor-edged clumps of wiry grass, camel sage and small thorny bushes. It was drawing towards the end of the short summer season, and the leaves of the poplar trees in the oases were just starting to turn from green to golden yellow, heralding the severe winter weather to come. Already the temperature at night was starting to drop uncomfortably.

Nearly a cycle and a half of the moon into the journey, the caravan had halted for the night at a well in a deserted hamlet on the edge of the wastes. The distant peaks of the Mountains of Hami glowed a dusty reddy-pink in the setting sun.

Rokshan was making his way through the caravan as everyone prepared to bed down for the night. The smell of campfires and cooking hung over the camp as the evening meal was prepared. In the gathering dusk the cameleers were checking their cargo and settling the camels and other pack animals. The more devout among them had lit small shrines and were murmuring incantations as they burned incense in small bronze models of whatever animal sign they had been born under. Rokshan noticed that the dragon, the snake and the horse seemed the most common, and wondered if the more superstitious of the travellers were anxious to appease the potent spirits of the fabled valleys of the Kingdom of the Wild Horsemen as they drew near their lands.

He hadn't seen Chen Ming for a day or two and decided to seek out their old family friend. When Rokshan was small, they had spent many happy hours together while the caravan master tried to teach him everything he knew about buying and selling on the trade routes. Everything they didn't teach the pupils at the school about trading in the cut-throat business world of the Empire, Rokshan had learned from Chen Ming – exactly what quantities of wool, carpets, glass and gems were required to trade through each oasis town; the quantities and different types of currency needed; which customs posts to bribe by what amount; and how to open gaps in the large bales of wool to allow the desert sand to seep in, increasing their weight and so increasing profits too. Now he was learning at first hand how tough the life of a caravan traveller really was.

As he approached the caravan master's encampment, Rokshan felt an odd feeling come over him. He looked up at the mist-shrouded Mountains of Hami and, beside them, the mighty Pamir range, home to the sacred breeding grounds of the Wild Horsemen. Suddenly he felt drawn towards them, wherever they were. The feeling was so strong that he stopped dead in his tracks, only carrying on when some small children, giggling loudly, prodded him with a stick just to make sure he wasn't playing a game they could join in.

Chen Ming was sitting by his campfire, sipping a glass of tea. He told Rokshan to make himself comfortable on the cushions that were spread around next to low tables laden with bowls of fruit and dates and ornate silver ewers of wine.

'Pour yourself some tea. It will refresh you after the day's journey,' Chen Ming said gruffly, but looking kindly at him.

Rokshan did as he was told and sat down. They sipped the bitter-sweet drink in companionable silence before discussing the journey; the caravan was one of the bigger ones travelling along the trade routes, and the practical organizational details of making a success of such a large enterprise fascinated Rokshan.

As they chatted, dusk turned to velvety night and the stars began to glitter. Rokshan tossed the occasional sprig of camel sage onto the campfire, enjoying watching the flames crackle and flare into the darkness. After a while they both fell silent and Rokshan's thoughts turned to home, as they always did, and to the old storyteller's message.

'How long have you known Shou Lao?' he asked the caravan master.

'Why do you ask?' Chen Ming stood up to refill their tea glasses, shadows dancing across his fierce-looking face in the flickering light of the campfire.

'Nobody knows how old he really is, or where he actually comes from, do they?' Rokshan meant it as more of a statement than a question. 'My father says he remembers his grandparents telling him stories that they said their parents had heard from Shou Lao.'

'Perhaps it's true then what people say about him: that he must be as old as the world itself and must know all its secrets,' Chen Ming said with a rumbling laugh as he sat down again. 'I don't know, my young friend.' He shrugged. 'But soon you'll be able to ask someone far wiser than me about these things.'

'Who?' Rokshan asked, sitting up excitedly.

'The abbot of Labrang is a wise man, one whose frugal hospitality I have enjoyed for many years in my travels on the trade routes. In a few days' time we will eat our evening meal together – assuming we get there,' Chen Ming added sombrely.

'The abbot of Labrang!' Rokshan whistled softly in surprise. Labrang was the largest Buddhist monastery in the

Kingdom of Sogdiana – well known for its massive statue of a leaping dragon, reputed to be made of solid gold, which amazed pilgrims from all over the kingdom.

'What do you mean, *assuming we get there?* Is there any reason why we shouldn't?' he asked, suddenly alert to Chen Ming's veiled note of warning.

'You must have noticed the level of military activity at the forts and garrisons we've passed – more soldiers on the road than I've ever seen at this time of year: the emperor must be getting impatient with the Horsemen.'

Rokshan recalled the military supply wagons they had passed, fully laden with piles of wood, foodstuffs and animal fodder, sure signs of an army preparing to dig in for a long winter.

Just as he was thinking that if they were going to be stopped, it would've happened already, he heard a distant rumbling noise, as if a giant bass drum was being struck rapidly and repeatedly. Chen Ming glanced up; he had heard it too, and now, on top of the distant booming, floated out the sweetest voice of a woman singing.

Chen Ming rapidly made the sign of the dragon on his forehead, lips and breast before leaping up. Already there was a commotion as Gupta and his most trusted cameleers hurried through the camp, ordering everyone into their tents, having first checked that their pack animals and livestock were securely tethered.

'Is it the Singing Sands, Chen Ming?' Rokshan asked in awe.

The caravan master nodded fiercely. 'Quickly! Back to your tent, and stop your ears with whatever you can find. Do not follow the siren song, Rokshan, for you will never find your way back. Go!' Chen Ming strode off to join his cameleers.

As he stumbled back to his tent, Rokshan noticed that an eerie silence had descended on the camp. Crying children were being gathered up and hurried into shelter by their worried-looking parents, and the animals were restless. The drivers moved quickly among the packhorses, making sure they were securely tied, offering soothing words to calm them. The larger animals were hobbled – the camels were given special attention with a chorus of clacking and clicking from the cameleers as they moved them closer to their night shelters and bound them securely. The rumbling sounded further away now, but sweet snatches of song carried on the still night air and seemed to dance around him.

Chen Ming's warning, and also what both Kan and Gupta had told Rokshan, clamoured in his head – those who follow the song of the Singing Sands leave the well-trodden path and stray onto what seems like another well-used track, which then just fades into the sands. Hopelessly lost, the victims would wander for days, getting weaker and weaker, before lying down to die. Only their bones would remain, bleached sparkling white by the sun and scoured clean by the wind and sand.

Rokshan crawled into his tent and put a hand to his ear, huddling in the blankets for warmth against the bitter chill of the desert night, but also for protection against the siren call of the Singing Sands.

He didn't know whether it was the cold that woke him later that night, or the single note, throbbing and low-pitched, that made his body shiver. The note was held for a long time, dipping sharply at the end. He scrambled up from under the blankets and poked his head out of the tent.

Only the screech of an owl pierced the inky quiet that lay over the camp. He gazed up at the brilliant, star-drenched sky of the desert night, relieved that the danger of the Singing Sands seemed to have passed and convinced he must have imagined the strange noise.

He'd just settled himself down and was drifting off to sleep again when a faint eerie wail drifted across the desert . . .

It came and went, now almost too far away to hear, now clamouring loudly again, calling his name. As if in a dream, he felt himself slowly getting up and going outside.

He looked around but couldn't see anyone. The voice was coming from the giant sand dunes they had passed earlier that day. They were some way off, but he could just make out their dark mass rearing into the night sky. Rokshan thought he glimpsed a hooded, cloaked figure beckoning to him as he stumbled towards them.

As he got closer, Rokshan heard the voice calling him more clearly; it was a strong male voice that he recognized from his childhood. He stumbled and fell on the uneven rough sand, cursing as he cut his hand on a sharp stone. There it was again – he knew that voice but just couldn't put a face to it. Half running, half stumbling, he staggered on.

Now the voice seemed to be a woman's, a chant with snatches of a familiar melody.

'Where are you?' he shouted, scrambling up the mountainous dune. 'I'm coming . . .' But he felt weak and could barely continue. The sand gave way beneath his feet, and the harder he tried to claw his way up, the further he seemed to slip down. He would never get to the top; he felt himself falling faster now and the melody abruptly turned into a triumphant scream as he tumbled over and over into the yawning blackness of a bottomless chasm.

'Rokshan . . . Wake up, wake up. It's Gupta. Wake up!' Somebody was shaking him. He opened his eyes and Gupta's worried face swam into view.

'Bad dream.' The cameleer grinned as Rokshan sat up groggily. 'Lucky you didn't wander too far from the tent. You must have been sleepwalking. I was woken up by what I thought was one of the camp dogs, but then it didn't sound quite like a dog, so I went to investigate, and found you rolling around here.' Gupta looked at him curiously.

'Thank you,' Rokshan muttered, embarrassed at his strange behaviour. 'I thought . . . I dreamed I was climbing those huge sand dunes we passed earlier. I could hear voices, and then the most beautiful singing.'

'You would've had to walk many li to reach those sand dunes; that's why what we heard earlier sounded so faint,' Gupta said matter-of-factly as he walked Rokshan back to his tent. 'Get some sleep now; it's another three candle-rings or so before we set off. And put a bandage round that cut to your hand – it looks nasty.'

Rokshan looked at his hand in surprise; so it couldn't have been a dream then, he thought.

Neither he nor anyone else heard a crow give a raucous cry as it wheeled round the dunes and flew west, back towards Maracanda.

CHAPTER 18

THE MONASTERY OF LABRANG

Rokshan stared at the grisly road marking with foreboding: the grinning skull of a camel, bleached white by the relentless desert sun and placed on top of its upended ribcage. The sun had passed directly overhead at least four hours ago, leaving only another one, perhaps two candle-rings' travel before they reached the monastery, he calculated.

'Bandits,' Gupta said impassively as Rokshan gaped at the pile of bones. The cameleer put his arm reassuringly around him. 'It's their calling card. There was a massacre here – twenty, twenty-five years ago. A group of Buddhist monks and nuns on their way to the monastery for the Feast of the Dead. The bandits must have known about their cargo – rolls of gold leaf for gilding the statue of the Golden Buddha of Labrang. They crucified all thirty of them, and then set them alight for good measure. Some of the older monks at the monastery swear they heard their screams carrying on the wind. And smelled their burning flesh.' Gupta clapped Rokshan on the back. 'That's what happens in these parts, my friend. But don't worry; the bandits wouldn't dare ambush a caravan of the legendary Chen Ming.'

'Why not?' Rokshan asked, ashen-faced.

'Because they'd be too frightened of what he'd do to them,' Gupta replied, deadly serious.

Rokshan felt sick, and wished for what must have been the hundredth time since setting out from Maracanda – one and a half cycles of the moon ago – that he was back in the library at school, with just his books for company. He still couldn't quite believe that he'd been right to do what Shou Lao had said he must; and he was always thinking of his poor father – how he longed to hear his voice!

The foothills of the Mountains of Hami gradually inched closer on the horizon as, towards early evening, they at last approached the citadel monastery of Labrang. The citadel had five sets of ramparts and was tucked into the foothills of the mountains. The high sandstone walls reflected the crimson-golden glow of the evening sun, and carved into the rock above, an enormous compassionate Buddha – more than five times the height of the tallest towers of the monastery – smiled benignly down on the building, filling all those who passed beneath his serene gaze with feelings of reverence and peaceful tranquillity after their long, gruelling journey. Rokshan gazed at it in awe; he had never seen such a magnificent carving, and he marvelled that there might be yet more wonders ahead for him to see.

The ramparts had been built as protection against bandit attacks after the massacre of the thirty nuns and monks. Behind its protective walls, the largest monastery in the Kingdom of Sogdiana lay serenely, its massive golden statue of a leaping dragon secure. The elders of Maracanda had ensured that the second batch of gold leaf got through, a year or so after the massacre, by providing a crack troop of the Imperial Light Cavalry – by order of the emperor – to accompany it.

Before approaching the first rampart they passed a shrine which was built of clay in the traditional design, hexagonally shaped with a low rounded tower. A small bronze bell mounted at the top of the tower tolled mournfully with an irregular two or three peals whenever the wind gusted strongly enough. Around the base of the tower, Rokshan counted thirty skulls on top of a pile of bones.

'Victims of the massacre,' Gupta said as they dismounted

and bowed respectfully to their memory. Rokshan was about to reply when, with a jolt, he noticed a small inscription at the base of the tower. He recognized it instantly – it was the same archaic writing he'd seen on the scrolls in the school library, just after Shou Lao's storytelling. At the foot of the inscription was a colourful ceramic tile with the familiar depiction of three one-eared hares, chasing each other in a circle. Gupta noticed the look of surprise on his face.

'What is it? You look as if you've seen an evil spirit of the road.'

'Don't you see?' Rokshan said, pointing to the picture on the tile.

'Oh, the three one-eared hares. That's been here as long as I can remember.' Gupta jumped lightly back onto his camel. 'No one really knows what it means. I've asked the older monks in the monastery – they just say it's sacred to the memory of the victims of the massacre. Come on, we'll be last through the gates,' he shouted as he clicked and clacked his camel into a loping, swaying trot towards the citadel.

Wearily Rokshan mounted up and passed through the gates, troubled by a niggling, nervous feeling he couldn't shake off.

After they had unloaded the animals and settled them down for the night, an enthusiastic boy monk, delighted to welcome strangers his own age, gave Rokshan a tour of the monastery. Being the largest in the kingdom, it was a village in itself, with outlying buildings, all neatly symmetrical and pagoda-shaped, surrounding the large inner courtyard.

Rokshan gasped as he saw for the first time the statue of the leaping dragon in the middle of the courtyard. It was twice as high as a grown man and was so expertly crafted that it seemed almost alive, sinuously rearing, with flattened wings and head twisting round, as if daring any onlooker to follow it in its flight skywards. In the dying light it looked frighteningly lifelike: its thin reptilian head snarled down at them and Rokshan swore he saw the trailing whiskers on either side of its open mouth twitch slightly in the light wind. It had two huge emeralds for eyes which seemed to flash a green fire as he walked around it.

The courtyard was an open-ended square, with the monks' individual cells forming three sides. Behind the golden dragon at the open end of the square there were steps leading up to a temple. A huge bronze bell hung above the entrance; a heavy wooden pole for striking it was suspended horizontally by a rope. Rokshan asked to look at the shrine, which housed a sacred relic of Han Garid, the lord of the thunder dragons himself – so the monk had told him in hushed tones – but only the monks or very special visitors were allowed to enter the place. As if to emphasize this his guide had nodded towards the warrior monks who guarded the entrance, staring implacably ahead and standing as still as statues.

That evening the abbot entertained Chen Ming, his chief cameleers and, to his surprise, Rokshan, to a simple but satisfying evening meal. This was held in the cavernous main hall, whose brick walls were brightly decorated with frescoes showing Chinese and foreign monks, as well as singers and dancers.

The meal was eaten in silence, in accordance with monastic tradition. As the simple wooden bowls and spoons were being cleared away, the abbot beckoned Chen Ming over to his side. A whispered conversation followed, with the abbot and a startled-looking Chen Ming glancing towards Rokshan. Eventually the caravan master got up and approached him, his face serious.

'The abbot would like to speak to you. You must kneel when he addresses you. He is inviting you to their evening worship. This is a great honour. Be sure to bow low. Go!' he said, patting Rokshan's shoulder.

Rokshan approached the abbot, bowing low, as instructed, before kneeling. The abbot was dressed in the traditional saffron robes but was distinguished from the other monks by his headdress, a large red crescent shape with gold patterning.

'Peace, Rokshan. Do not be afraid.'

The abbot spoke quietly and with a strong accent which Rokshan strained to understand.

'Is it a slave or a master that you seek, Rokshan? If it is a slave, he will always despise you. If it is a master, you have one; therefore you are already a slave and you do not need to seek either.'

'Venerable Father?' Rokshan asked, puzzled.

'Your will, Rokshan, is your master. Therefore you are your own slave. You try to shape the world, to make it bend to your will. And then you are unhappy when the world pays no heed. Your will urges you not to believe what you have been told, and to be disdainful of the signs you have been shown. But your heart knows them to be true. I speak as I have seen, because I have read your heart. You must join us, Rokshan, and you must continue on your journey. We, the followers of Ahura Mazda, can help you.'

'Most Venerable Abbot, my heart may know that what I have been told is true, and also the signs that I have been shown. But my will is strong when it tells me not to believe, and I do not have the knowledge or courage, on my own, to do what I have been asked.'

'Join us, and you will find the courage that was always within you, only much deeper and stronger than you thought possible. As for knowledge, remember, truth bears not one name only. The sage is not one person only.'

Rokshan bowed his head.

The deep, reverberating note of the temple bell broke the heavy silence that filled the hall. Still Rokshan knelt, head bowed.

'Rokshan, will you join us in prayer?'

'Yes, Venerable Father.'

'For you have made your choice.' It was a statement rather than a question.

'Yes, Venerable Father.'

'It is bravely and wisely done, Rokshan.'

'Thank you,' he said respectfully, but not fully understanding quite what he had agreed to. He glanced up at the abbot, who smiled serenely ahead, his gaze fixed on some far point.

At last he rose. The monks all stood and bowed before filing silently out. Chen Ming came over to join Rokshan and, bowing to the abbot, echoed his words.

'Indeed, it is bravely and wisely done, my young friend.'

'Chen Ming, will you come with me?' It suddenly occurred to Rokshan that there was still much about his old friend that he did not know.

'As an honoured guest accompanying you, I am invited to join the community in prayer too, if that's what you mean. As for accompanying you on your journey, that is not for me to decide,' Chen Ming replied.

The last of the monks left the hall, followed by the abbot and his two guests. As the temple bell continued to toll, they walked along the covered walkway which linked the main hall to the inner courtyard of the monastery. As they passed the leaping dragon and approached the steps to the temple, the monks formed a line for them to walk through, pressing their hands together in front of their faces and bowing in the traditional gesture of welcome.

The abbot led the way into the temple, followed by Rokshan and Chen Ming. The rest of the monks quietly sat down cross-legged on the floor, forming a semicircle around the shrine.

This was a large, coffin-shaped reliquary of solid silver, sitting on a tiered golden platform. The lid was shaped like a curved roof tile decorated with gilded lotus flowers, the edges encrusted with pearls in the shape of plum flowers. The two doors were surmounted by a demon's head with a bronze ring suspended from its mouth. Looking around the temple, Rokshan noticed that two of the walls were decorated with colourful frescoes of the Buddha's path towards enlightenment and scenes from paradise; a third – and the ceiling – was bare. With a start he realized that a familiar pattern bordered the paintings – the three one-eared hares, broken up by the more common motif of coiling dragons chasing the Flaming Pearl, which represented the sun. On the far wall, about thirty paces away, the same motif filled the whole area.

As a group of four monks with wind or stringed instruments stepped up to the shrine, the abbot knelt down beside a giant conch and, putting the thinner end of the spiral-shaped shell to his mouth, blew a single deep bass note. This signalled the beginning of the worship, and the monks started to chant. The abbot uttered a dirge-like prayer above the chant, accompanied by the droning of the wind instruments and the plucking of the two-stringed pipas.

Rokshan was familiar with this form of worship, and waited patiently for the chant to reach its climax, usually signalled by another blast from the giant conch shell. The intention was to put the worshipper into a meditative trance. Sure enough, he felt his eyelids grow heavy as the rich, spicy fumes from the incense burner and the hemp oil from the flickering lamps started to fill the temple with thick layers of perfumed smoke.

As the chanting of the monks grew louder, Rokshan felt himself being pulled towards the far wall. He looked around to check if he was actually moving, and was surprised to see his body sitting in exactly the same place. Growing more alarmed now, he tried to resist, but he was experiencing the strangest feeling of being taken out of his body; being pulled towards the three one-eared hares. With rising panic, he saw that the hares too were now moving, chasing each other round and round in their perpetual dance.

'Chen Ming!' he screamed, but the caravan master sat impassively next to his physical body, as if there was nothing wrong.

Gradually he felt himself rising up into a crouching position, as if preparing to run. He looked at the hares and realized that they were running round a dragon's skull, with two plumes of smoke coming out of its mouth. Now he became one with the hares and was running, slowly at first, then faster and faster, until he thought his lungs would burst.

Just when he thought he could run no further and the pounding in his head started to become unbearable, he felt himself being lifted up, lighter than air. A feeling of intense joy and peace came over him, as if he was being carried downstream by a calmly flowing river. The words of Shou Lao about the three hares representing the harmony of Light, Life and Truth rang in his head: *Each is inseparable, one from the other, in the dance of life . . . And to understand our own dance, we have to listen to our hearts as if they were one, shared by all men.*

He seemed to hear the hearts of all men beating as one with all their yearnings and passions, their joys and grief; it built up like an enormous dam inside him and his power expanded to contain it all; and then, with a deafening blast, he was thrown back down and he was running again – running with the energy of the life-force he had just felt so deeply.

Now he felt he could run for ever, so fast he couldn't stop, but the single bass note of the conch blasted and echoed across the temple. The chanting stopped abruptly. He looked around and was surprised to find himself in a hunched, foetal position. Chen Ming helped him up with a look of concern on his face.

A hushed silence filled the temple, broken only by Rokshan's gasps for breath. The abbot spoke.

'Rokshan, very few are chosen to run with the three hares. Those who are have been chosen by Ahura Mazda himself, the Wise Lord. You are welcome as one of the Fellowship of the Three One-eared Hares. Will you join us in the fellowship and make the journey that Shou Lao spoke to you about in Maracanda?'

'I will, Venerable Father,' Rokshan replied, feeling light-headed but more clearly fixed on his purpose; though he wondered if the abbot had known that this would happen, and if it had been witnessed by the community of monks.

'Even though death and pain may be your constant companion – and I speak not only of physical pain, but the pain that lances human hearts?' the abbot pressed him.

'Yes, Venerable Father.'

'Then know this,' the abbot proclaimed, 'before Zerafshan, whom you know as your uncle, proved himself unworthy at the last to become one of our Elect – the highest ranking in the Ahura Mazda priesthood – he had been deputed since your birth, as close blood-kin, to be your guardian in the priesthood until you came of age. He was to have been your guide and mentor as you came to take your place as one of the Elect; for this is your clear destiny, known since your birth. Now, in his deluded lust for power, he wants you for a different purpose that we can only guess at. He holds us in contempt for not allowing him to become one of us, but he underestimates our combined strength.'

Rokshan glanced anxiously at Chen Ming before voicing his fears to the abbot.

'But Venerable Abbot, Zerafshan is said to be intent on leading the Horsemen in open rebellion against the emperor. Any association with him is punishable by death.'

'And we have heard tell that he will call off the rebellion

if you are delivered to him. You must find out what his true intention is, Rokshan. He says he serves only the Wild Horsemen, and through them their charges, the sacred dragon horses. Why? We may only guess at his purpose. It may be that he will need to be stopped from following the path he has chosen.'

'This is a heavy burden, Venerable Father,' Rokshan whispered, bowing his head and feeling his resolve of just a few minutes before starting to drain away.

Was this part of his initiation into the Elect? That he should agree, unquestioningly, to do something that he didn't fully understand? Why had he been chosen for this? The realization that perhaps, after all, he did not have the courage to accept what was being asked of him filled him with a deep shame. Rokshan wrestled with his truth: he knew that this was the turning point; that, after all, he did have a choice.

'Why was I destined from birth, Venerable Father? How could this be?' He had to have the answers; he had to know the whole truth before he could accept what the Elect asked of him.

'Do not doubt, Rokshan, that the Lord of Evil, the Shadow-without-a-name, stirs. You will know his story – how the Wise Lord made his Divine Commandment to seal him in eternal imprisonment. We know that his messenger, Corhanuk, recorded the Divine Commandment on the Sacred Scroll; should it ever be found, we are sworn to guard against its falling into the wrong hands. Now we fear that the Evil One's servants are abroad in the world, seeking to satisfy his desires – desires we recognize through our guardianship of the holy scriptures of the Wise Lord. The Shadow's age-old envy and resentment will at last find expression, so he believes, in a terrible revenge against the world of men and, through them, the Wise Lord. He will stop at nothing to ensure that whoever he snares in his web of deceit does his bidding.' The abbot gazed into that far place only he could see.

'And you are certain that this . . . *revenge* will come about unless we do what Shou Lao asked?' Rokshan said quietly.

'It is ordained in the stars and in the holy texts,' the abbot replied with quiet certainty. 'The holy books of Ahura Mazda, the Wise Lord, and *The Book of Angra Mainyu*, or *The Book of the Dead*, as it is commonly known, contain many prophecies and predictions charted in the stars. Shou Lao's riddle comes from *The Book of Angra Mainyu*, and *The Book of Ahura Mazda* predicted the emperor's obsession with the dragon horses of the Wild Horsemen, which will surely lead, ultimately, to his downfall.

'There will be a sign in the Heavens – an alignment of the stars – that signals to the people their right to overthrow the emperor,' the abbot continued, 'but we are not so sure now that it is the emperor who needs to be halted in his purpose—' The abbot suddenly stopped and looked intently at Rokshan. 'This is how the Elect knows these things, Rokshan. We must know what Zerafshan intends.'

He signalled to Chen Ming, who got up and came across to where they sat. Taking hold of Rokshan's hair the abbot drew it aside, exposing his deformed ear.

'No one can deny that you have been marked with the sign of the ancient priesthood. Those who do not believe – and there are many – may laugh and say it is just a coincidence,' he said, 'but you have asked, and it is only right to tell you. The date and hour of your birth in the Year of the Dragon aligns exactly with the astrological predictions that give the people their mandate for the rightful rebellion I just spoke of. This is why you have been sworn to the ancient priesthood since the day of your birth. Your deformed ear, which has always singled you out, was – to us – merely proof of the correctness of the prediction.'

Here the abbot paused and looked up. 'The configuration of the stars that was foretold has already started to come about,' he added. 'If you need further proof that you are chosen, there is one final prophecy contained in our scriptures, one that the Elect has kept secret these past hundreds of years, the subject of great debate amongst us and little understood – until now.'

The abbot signalled to a monk standing nearby, who carefully handed him an ancient-looking scroll. 'Hear the Prophecy of the Prince,' he intoned reverently, 'for it is in our days that his time has come:

> *A prince from the day of your birth on the holy mountains;*
> *From the womb before the dawn I begot and marked you.*
> *The Shadow has sworn an oath he will not change;*
> *You are his chosen servant for ever.*

'The prophecy also says:

> *Sit at my right hand, for I will make your enemies my footstool.*
> *You will wield from Thai Shan, the Mountain of the East, your Staff*
>   *of Power;*
> *Staff-wielder! Rule in the midst of all your foes;*
> *As the Shadow rules all the souls who return to Thai Shan, the*
>   *Mountain of the Dead.'*

The abbot rolled the scroll up carefully and seemed lost in contemplation before he spoke again.

'Zerafshan would be this prince, my young friend – a prince of darkness – and he intends to use you, in a way we have not been able to fathom, to achieve his ends. This is why you are to take his place as the Twelfth of the Elect: to find out his precise purpose. Whatever that is, you must stop him, even if your journey leads to the ends of the Earth. For Shou Lao has told me your journey will take you to the east, across the Flame

Mountains in the Land of Fire, where you must help the Guardian Monk in his eternal vigil in the court of the Crimson King.'

Rokshan became aware of the intense silence in the temple; the monks had their eyes closed and were deep in meditation. The abbot was telling him what Shou Lao had told him – and more – but he still had no idea exactly what this meant, and wondered desperately how he was meant to find out.

'You will not be on your own, Rokshan.' The abbot looked at Rokshan benevolently. 'Chen Ming's caravan will get as close as it can to the pass of Terek Dhavan, but you must go up the pass as inconspicuously as possible, travelling as a nomad of those parts. One of my warrior monks will be your guide, to alert you of danger. You have been given the gifts of the animal spirit of the Elect, the hare – his speed, agility and cunning; use them. I too have a gift for you . . .'

The abbot once again signalled to the monk, who knelt before the silver reliquary in the centre of the temple and opened its double doors. He took out a small object wrapped in a silk cloth and brought it to the abbot.

'Receive this gift. It will help you on your journey,' the abbot said solemnly as he unwrapped it and handed it to Rokshan.

The bronze amulet was of an unusual design, and had been polished so much that he could only just make out the engraving etched into its border. He twisted it around.

'The Three One-eared Hares of the Fellowship,' Rokshan said, intrigued as he realized what it was.

'Use it only when your life is in mortal danger,' the abbot warned.

'Thank you,' Rokshan said, bowing deeply. 'One final question, Venerable Father . . .' He couldn't leave without asking it of the abbot. 'Where shall we find the court of the

Crimson King? Is he really the gatekeeper of Hell that the stories tell of? And the Guardian Monk – who is he, and what is his eternal vigil?'

'The Crimson King is the servant of the Shadow and keeper of the Four Riders of Hell, whose mounts are Fear, Pain, Loneliness and Despair. The Riders' only purpose, if they are ever released, is to unleash evil such that the balance of harmony in the world is disjointed, and men will come to serve him who has summoned and commands the Riders. But as long as the Guardian Monk remains in the court of the Crimson King, keeping watch over him and assigning the punishments of the souls of the damned, this shall never come to pass . . .

'The Crimson King is kept chained with his charges, deep in the bowels of the Flame Mountains, in eternal punishment for being the henchman of the Shadow in his rebellion against the Wise Lord. He receives the souls of the damned after they have been assigned their punishments – all those who, through their wickedness, have lost their place in the perpetual Wheel of Rebirth.'

'So I must go to the Crimson King, in . . . Hell?' Rokshan was afraid almost to ask it. 'Damning my own soul too?'

'Not if the Guardian Monk is there. This is the only certainty I can give you,' was the abbot's sombre response.

Rokshan nodded, feeling dazed and exhausted by everything that had happened. Just then the temple gong sounded.

'Our worship is over. The monks will return to their cells for the night, and you have an early start. You must make haste on the road eastwards, to the Summit of the Goddess that travellers call the Terek Dhavan Pass. May Kuan Yin watch over you,' the abbot said, making the sign of the dragon and then pressing his hands together in the traditional sign of farewell.

Rokshan returned the gesture, noticing with surprise and wonder that the deep cut on his hand had quite healed. The abbot, closing his eyes, started to murmur an invocation. Chen Ming nodded towards the temple steps, indicating that they should leave.

As they walked out of the temple together, the tall caravan master looked at Rokshan with a mixture of pride and affection and respect.

'What shall I call you now?' he asked, only half joking.

'What you've always called me,' Rokshan shot back, trying to laugh, but only managing a rueful smile. He knew his life had changed for ever; that he could never go back to what he had been. His dreams of following in his father's footsteps after a short but successful career as a special envoy seemed distant and somehow unimportant now.

As he and Chen Ming crossed the square, a monk – already dressed for travelling – came to meet them. He had long tangled hair and wore rough, loose-fitting brown robes that came to just below his knees. A grey cloak was slung around his hip on a shoulder-sash, and a short rope weighted at each end with polished ivory balls was tucked in with his cloak. In one hand he held a short staff of gnarled wood with a bulbous, knotted end.

'Greetings, Rokshan, Caravan Master,' he said, bowing to both in turn. 'Warrior Sung Yuan, here to serve you on the abbot's command. You will not see me on the trail – I will not travel with the caravan, for not all need to know of your mission. But I will be close at hand if you require my help.'

Rokshan returned the bow, but before he could say anything, the warrior monk turned silently and loped away.

The amulet clinked in his pocket against the coin of the three hares that Shou Lao had given him, and he wondered again how different his life was going to be now as the Twelfth Elect of the Fellowship of the Hares. The abbot had given him a mission that he had accepted and could not go back on – he must confront Zerafshan, using the stealth and cunning of the hare to find out if his uncle really was intent on becoming the Prince of Darkness of the prophecy.

How was he to prevent this, if it was his uncle's true intention? And how were the Wild Horsemen involved? The abbot had said it was of the utmost importance that he find out, and he intended to do everything in his power to uncover the answers to all these questions.

CHAPTER 19

GENERAL ARKAN SHAKAR

It was past the third watch of the night when a distant rumble began to send slight tremors through the camp.

Half a cycle of the moon after leaving the citadel monastery, they had at last reached the lowlands of the Pamir Mountains on the borders of the Kingdom of the Wild Horsemen. Here they would meet the Jaxartes River and follow it upstream; at the valley's head they would cross the Terek Dhavan Pass – which the abbot and Shou Lao called the Summit of the Goddess – leading directly into the land of the Horsemen.

The caravan's goats and sheep bleated anxiously as the distant rumble intensified. Shouts of alarm echoed across the camp. Camels and buffaloes pulled at their tethering ropes and pawed the now shaking ground, their grunts growing more urgent as the rumble grew into the rhythmic pounding of what sounded like a thousand galloping horses surging across the desert.

'Stampede! Stampede! Stoke your fires! Pass it on!'

At once the caravan was a tumult of orderly panic as everyone scrambled to get ready to meet what was assumed to be a stampede of wild horses. But above the thunderous pounding Rokshan thought he caught the rattle and clink of armour and weaponry.

Gupta had heard it too. '*Ambush!*' he shouted above the rising crescendo. 'Look to your cargo and animals . . . Arm yourselves and draw swords . . . Stand firm in position.'

The caravan had formed into an arrowhead shape to face

the stampede. This was not a common occurrence on the trading routes, but when it did happen, every caravan knew that the most effective way to head it off was to split the herd head on. It took great courage to stand steady at the tip of the arrow formation in the face of such a thundering mass, but it had not been known to fail.

However, this formation was not ideal for withstanding a bandit attack, but it was too late to change it. A hundred pairs of fearful eyes strained into the blackness, but a thick cloud of dust obscured the raging storm of noise that was heading straight for them.

'It sounds like there are hundreds of them – and there are only fifty of us. We haven't got a chance!' Rokshan shouted.

They were positioned at the rear of the formation. Gupta looked grim and determined, as if ready to defend the caravan to the last man – even if that was him. All Rokshan could think was that he wasn't meant to die here without even getting to the Kingdom of the Wild Horsemen and finding out what his uncle had become.

Chen Ming galloped up and down each side of the arrow formation, yelling encouragement to his camel drivers and guards before reining in his horse at the front of the arrow to face the attack.

The distant rumble became a thundering roar of pounding hooves as the dust cloud parted. Five war chariots burst through it and hurtled towards them. Fanning out behind them was a troop of cavalry at full gallop, at least one hundred strong, Rokshan guessed.

'Four horses to each chariot and each carrying a swordsman and archer plus the charioteer – they're not bandits! Only imperial war chariots are big enough for that,' the caravan guard next to him shouted excitedly.

'What're they doing so far west?' Rokshan yelled back. 'Why are they attacking with no warning?'

The chariots were now only a stone's throw from the caravan. Chen Ming yelled the order to raise their spears and at once, up and down the v-formation, the guards and armed camel-drivers stepped forward with their spears held in the throwing position, ready to hurl at the charioteers.

Suddenly one of the chariots surged forward ahead of the others and made straight for Chen Ming. In the moonlight they could now see that the lead chariot had a canopy and was richly decorated with colourful dragon-and-phoenix patterns. All four horses had their manes cut and their tails tied, and wore silver head-nets with gold plaques on their foreheads.

'Look at the horses pulling the lead chariot and the way it's decorated!' Gupta pointed out to Rokshan. 'No doubt about it; that's a general of the imperial army.'

The chariot came to a sudden halt in a swirl of dust not far from where Chen Ming stood. The tall figure standing behind the charioteer spread out his arms and the cavalry behind him swirled round to left and right, surrounded the caravan and then skilfully reined in their mounts. There was an eerie silence as everyone in the caravan waited for the inevitable charge. A wildcat howled in the stillness of the night. The only other sound was the occasional whinny and snort of a restless horse as it champed at its bit, steadying itself after the headlong gallop across the desert.

'Caravan Master, state your name and destination,' the tall figure in the lead chariot called out, his voice carrying clearly in the thin desert air.

'Chen Ming of Maracanda, Caravan Master, bound for Chang'an,' came the reply. 'And you, sir – what is your business, accosting a peaceable, law-abiding caravan in the night? We have paid all duties due at the imperial customs posts. Is there something irregular I am unaware of? A new regulation of some sort that has not yet reached this far-flung outpost of his celestial highness's mighty Empire?'

'No, Caravan Master, you have not breached any regulations,' the tall figure replied. 'I am General Arkan Shakar and this' – he gestured to his men – 'is the Thirteenth Troop, Special Reconnaissance, of his imperial highness's Light Cavalry. I am commanded by his celestial highness to track down the rebel known as Zerafshan, formerly commander of the Imperial Cavalry Corps, last known whereabouts Kara Shahr – or Black Town, as it is known locally – one hundred li east of Kashgar along the northern road of the imperial trading routes. Caravan Master, think carefully before you reply: Kara Shahr harboured the rebel and now no longer exists. Imperial troops have razed it to the ground, beheaded five thousand of its inhabitants and taken fifteen thousand prisoners. Have you seen or heard of the rebel known as Zerafshan in these parts?'

Chen Ming betrayed no trace of emotion as he listened to what the general said.

Rokshan couldn't believe what he'd just heard. 'Black Town – that's at least one week's travelling from the Kingdom of the Horsemen once you're over the pass, isn't it?' he whispered to Gupta.

'Roughly, with a fair wind. More important, Black Town's where the caravan master's people are from originally. He's not going to be happy about that,' the cameleer replied.

'My lord' – Chen Ming's baritone voice rang out in formal, measured tones – 'what heinous crime has this rebel, Zerafshan, committed to merit such terrible reprisal against the peaceable people of the Kingdom of Agni and its capital, Kara Shahr?'

'Sedition and incitement to revolt against his celestial highness, Caravan Master,' came the general's curt reply.

'Sedition and incitement to revolt? Who is stirring up rebellion – the Horsemen?' Chen Ming asked.

'Led by the former Commander Zerafshan . . . yes. He has failed in his covert mission to subjugate the Wild Horsemen and so guarantee unlimited access to their dragon horses for the expansion and future glory of his celestial highness's imperial army. He has turned traitor instead, becoming the acknowledged leader of the Wild Horsemen. Within the last six months he has come out of hiding, leading a crack troop of Horsemen who have conducted a series of raids on imperial customs posts in the Kingdom of Agni, and most recently along this section of the imperial trading route. Up until one month ago he was using Kara Shahr as his base, entering into an alliance with the Kingdom of Agni, whose people are also expert horsemen – a fact you are no doubt aware of, Caravan Master,' the general said.

'Sounds like the general knows all about Chen Ming. And Chen Ming knows Zerafshan from the old days,' Gupta hissed out of the side of his mouth.

'My lord,' Chen Ming said, having pretended to consider General Arkan Shaker's summary of the rebel Zerafshan's anti-imperial activities, 'I cannot report a sighting of the rebel you speak of. I lead a peaceable trading caravan. We travel by the northern trade route, and will be going over the Terek Dhavan Pass.'

'That will not be possible, Caravan Master,' the general barked. 'Imperial forces have now closed the pass to all traffic apart from the military. You must take your caravan via the southern trading route. Turn back, now . . . that is an order.'

'But that will mean an additional half a year's travel, through warring states . . . It is impossible . . . I protest in the strongest terms . . .'

'Protest all you like,' the general responded grimly, 'but if you disobey my order, I shall commandeer your entire caravan, to be disposed of at his imperial highness's pleasure – do I make myself clear? I shall send a detachment of my troop to ensure my order is obeyed. That is all.'

Chen Ming nodded curtly in acknowledgement. The

general gave the signal to advance, and the Thirteenth Troop, Special Reconnaissance, of his imperial highness's Light Cavalry wheeled round and, at a brisk trot, made off in the direction they'd come from.

While the caravan prepared for a much earlier than expected departure, Chen Ming summoned Gupta; the two of them were deep in discussion in the caravan master's tent, debating what was the best course of action to comply with the general's order. Rokshan stamped his feet and blew on his hands to keep warm in the bitter chill of the desert night, waiting to be called. He gazed up at the glittering panorama of the night sky, ablaze as if a million diamonds had been tossed across a velvet blanket of midnight blue.

As he paced up and down, the abbot's words floated back to him: *He says he serves only the Wild Horsemen, and through them their charges, the sacred dragon horses. Why? We may only guess at his purpose.* Was the abbot right? he wondered. Did the answers to these questions really lie at the heart of the storyteller's riddle?

It all churned around in his head until it hurt; maybe only Zerafshan knew the answers, he thought. Then he would have to find out from him somehow. With this worrying thought gnawing away at him, he was relieved when Gupta stuck his head out of the tent and told him to come in.

He was grateful for the brazier that burned cheerfully in the middle of the tent and warmed himself up while he listened to what Chen Ming had to say.

'It is an opportune moment, Rokshan, for you to split off from the caravan. Just be careful to avoid the detachment of cavalry the general said he'd send to keep an eye on us – they may ask some awkward questions, even of a wandering nomad.'

'It sounds like you knew this was going to happen,' Rokshan said.

'Something like it.' Chen Ming shrugged. 'In fact, I'm

surprised we got as far as we did . . . But that has been to our advantage, getting us as close as we have to the pass. Now, my young friend,' he said, beaming and clapping him round the shoulder, 'you have no time to lose: the abbot's "scout" has already set off ahead of you; you must not be too far behind him.'

'He has set off already?' Rokshan asked in surprise.

'Of course,' Chen Ming laughed. 'He is a warrior monk – be sure to take heed of whatever he tells you. The warrior monks are expert trackers, masters of the martial arts, silent assassins: you will need all the help he can give. Now go and gather your things – you must leave before first light.'

Trudging back through the camp, Rokshan heard the shrill screech of an owl, hunting in the dark watches of the night. He imagined it plummeting silently down on its prey and felt a pang of pity for its victim. Just for a moment he suddenly knew what it must feel like to be hunted. He quickened his pace, trusting that the warrior monk was as silent and deadly as Chen Ming claimed.

Chapter 20

The Snow Devils of Terek Dhavan

He made his departure before the caravan began to stir in the first light of dawn. Mounted on a sturdy Tarpan steppe pony, he'd checked and re-checked his supplies – additional warm clothing, bedding, dried food and concealed weapons.

Rokshan was glad to be on horseback again and had prayed to Kuan Yin to watch over him as he began his ascent up the valleys to the Terek Dhavan Pass and the Summit of the Goddess. Chen Ming had told him to start by following the normal route that the big caravans took when the pass was open. But after the first two passes on the way up to the highest of them – the Terek Dhavan, which took travellers over the mountains – he was to branch off in search of Zerafshan and the rebels' encampment at the summit.

Rokshan could barely contain his excitement at venturing into a part of the Kingdom of the Wild Horsemen that very few travellers had seen. But his stomach churned as he recalled the ancient law of the Horsemen, and he prayed fervently that it really was a thing of the past.

Looking around as he made his way up, he felt dwarfed by the glacial twin peaks of Khan Tengri, the Summit of the Goddess, towering straight ahead. Behind him, the grey-yellow vastness of the Taklamakan Desert stretched forbiddingly to the horizon.

He knew there were permanent settlements of herders and farmers in the valleys extending almost halfway up, and in the warm months nomads lived even higher, although they might have been ordered to leave now. Zerafshan and his followers would be living off the land as high as they could go, and beyond, in the valleys of the Horsemen.

Rokshan saw no sign of the warrior monk, and a creeping fear spread through him that perhaps he was on his own, after all. He tried to convince himself that it was all clear ahead, and nothing was lurking behind either.

The route he was following up the river valley began to change. He passed a cold, lonely night, grateful for the company of his pony which, to keep his spirits up, he decided to name Lucky. On the second day the going was slow and difficult: he struggled across marshy ground, which eventually gave way to shingle and gravel and sometimes bare rock.

As he climbed higher, the encroaching valley walls closed in. With increasing foreboding, Rokshan hoped he might come across some other nomads, but he saw no one; the warrior monk remained invisible. He wasn't used to the altitude, and after only three days began to experience shortness of breath and headaches. He grew lightheaded, and began to imagine that *kuei* – evil spirits of the road – were everywhere.

At this height the temperature started to drop rapidly before dusk. He knew enough from what Chen Ming had told him that snowstorms were not uncommon, even at this time of year. That evening, as he traversed a gently sloping plateau on his way up to the second of the four passes, dusk seemed to fall more quickly.

A bitterly cold wind sprang up and he anxiously looked for a sheltered place to make camp for the night. He had just stopped and was unloading what he needed when he spotted the monk in the fading light. He was halfway up the valley – a lone figure bounding down the rocky escarpment at incredible speed.

'Sung Yuan . . . Better pack everything up, just in case,' Rokshan muttered to himself, gathering his stuff together and securing it all tightly on Lucky as the monk approached at a loping run.

'Greetings, Rokshan.' He bowed. 'Warrior Sung Yuan is here to serve you. We have little time – a storm approaches, and I fear what it may bring with it. We must seek shelter. Please stay close to me at all times.'

Rokshan set off up in the direction Sung Yuan had come from, pulling the reluctant Lucky after him. The sky had been a dirty leaden grey all day and now it started to snow; a thick blanket of snowflakes whirled about them as dusk turned to dark unnaturally quickly. Within seconds they could hardly see three paces in front of them.

Rokshan shouted to Sung Yuan, who he thought was just ahead of him, but his words were whipped away by the gusting wind tearing at him with icy, grasping fingers.

'We must take shelter now, it's getting worse. Where are you?' he yelled into the storm. Had he lost Sung Yuan? he thought in a growing panic. He gasped as something rammed into his stomach.

'Take the end of my staff,' the monk shouted, his face looming out at him through the whirling snow, 'and don't let go!'

They struggled on for a few minutes before Sung Yuan stopped. Lucky stood forlornly in front of them, his mane thick with snow and his reins hanging loose.

'Where are we heading?' Rokshan shouted at the monk, who didn't reply but jabbed his arm in front of him, indicating that they should push on through the blinding snow.

'We should stop here,' Rokshan continued. 'We can't see where we're going . . .'

He tried to make the pony lie down to shelter beside him, but Lucky was whinnying with fear. Sung Yuan stood with his head slightly to one side, as if listening to something. Rokshan, too, thought he could hear something, floating in and out of the gusting wind. There it was again – a single deep bass note, just like the conch shell in the temple at Labrang.

Sung Yuan tugged at Rokshan and his lips moved, but the wind was blowing so hard it was impossible to make out what he said. Suddenly a ferocious blast lifted them off their feet and flung them to the ground. Sung Yuan picked himself up and hung onto Lucky's neck to keep him from bolting. The deep bass note sounded again, and over the raging blizzard they caught snatches of an eerie chant.

His eyes smarting against the driving snow, Rokshan squinted into the boiling, white maelstrom. It was much clearer now: a steady, rhythmic 'Omm . . . ommm . . .' like monks chanting, punctuated by a single drumbeat. It made the hairs on the back of his neck stand on end. Lucky was now mad with fear and reared up, flinging Sung Yuan clear before he bolted away. Rokshan scrambled up, clawing the snow out of his eyes and mouth.

'Omm . . . omm . . .' The chanting grew louder and seemed to be all around them now.

'What are they?' he yelled at Sung Yuan.

'Kuei . . . troubled spirits, sometimes very bad. Something evil has happened in the mountains and they want our life spirits.'

Sung Yuan had managed to grab the bag of weapons off the pony before he bolted, and tossed Rokshan a short sword. He crouched there, looking around, ready to attack whatever it was that was coming. The chanting was deafening now, but still they couldn't see who or what it was. Then they saw them: kuei – snow devils.

Through the blur of driving snow, massed ranks of sinuous, writhing creatures made of ice and snow – as tall as a man but with four tentacles each for arms – slowly advanced. Their faces had mouths but no eyes, noses or ears. They did not need to see or smell; they could sense where their victim was from the waves of fear their prey gave off. They rolled and writhed towards them. Sung Yuan was still crouching, his rope of ivory balls in one hand, his twirling staff in the other. Rokshan stood beside him, transfixed with terror.

The chanting of the snow devils was now a pulsating roar in his head and his body was being pulled this way and that; he began to twist and turn as if he was himself a snow devil. They were close enough now to lash out with their long, tentacle-like arms.

Then, with a blood-curdling cry, Sung Yuan sprang into the front line of the creatures, his rope of deadly ivory balls whirling as he brought it smashing down onto the heads of the snow devils. He was so close to them that their long wriggling tentacles were useless. He scythed through them, and soon a whole row lay with pulped heads and a mass of twitching tentacles strewn all around. Relentlessly another line replaced those Sung Yuan had killed, and when he had dispatched those too, another wave appeared.

Dredging up courage he didn't know he had, Rokshan ran in behind him, finishing off with his short sword those Sung Yuan hadn't killed outright, which were rearing up to fight again. Wave after wave of the creatures came on at them, and the monk began to falter, overcome with exhaustion. He cried out as his arm was caught a slashing blow. His staff fell to the ground and his arm hung uselessly, frozen solid by the touch of the snow devil's tentacle.

'Run! You can outrun them, Rokshan — run! Use the speed of the hare you have been gifted with,' Sung Yuan yelled. There was a muffled scream as he went down under a heaving, writhing mass of the creatures, fighting valiantly to the end.

But it was too late. The snow devils' chanting stopped abruptly: Rokshan was surrounded by them, and the speed and agility of the hare could not help him now. The snow had eased and he could see them, rank upon rank, stretching far back into the gloom. Now they started to sway, gently, hypnotically, from side to side, their tentacles hanging loosely by their sides. Still the wind howled and gusted around them, and Rokshan's head throbbed with the rhythmic chanting of a few moments before. He was shivering with fear and cold, but was determined to be as brave as Sung Yuan. He wasn't giving up without a fight.

He hardly saw it when one of the snow devils suddenly shot out a tentacle and caught him a stinging blow on his upper arm. He gasped in pain at the force of it and felt his arm turning numb; instinctively he rubbed it to get some sort of feeling back – but he could feel his whole body beginning to freeze, as if encased in a huge block of ice. Everything started to turn black and he veered in and out of consciousness.

Feeling as if his whole body was about to be shattered into a million shards of ice, he dropped to his knees, still feebly rubbing his arm. The snow devils continued their swaying dance of death, sensing their victim's helplessness. Another tentacle lashed out, this time catching him on the side of his head. He fell back into the snow, clutching his head in agony. *If only I could get some feeling back in this arm*, he thought drowsily as the blackness began to engulf him. He gripped it and suddenly felt the amulet that he had worn since the abbot had given it to him in the temple.

He feebly rubbed the amulet and, as he drifted into the darkness, he became aware of a distant voice calling his name.

'*Rokshan, it is not your time . . . Rokshan . . . it is not your time.*' Again it called: '*Rokshan . . . it is not your time.*'

While the voice was still calling him, there was a deafening thunderclap, and a jet of intense silvery-white fire, like a meteorite, sizzled into the mass of snow devils. Steam erupted in a mushroom cloud as those at the centre evaporated. Rokshan himself was thrown clear by the blast.

Barely conscious, he watched as the surviving snow devils

writhed in their death throes; the unearthly wails of those
trying to escape the furnace-like heat were terrible to hear.
Suddenly he was astonished to see a giant warrior step out of
the tower of fire, wielding a huge double-handed sword that
glowed white-hot.

'Who summons Guan Di, god of warriors and protector
against evil?' he shouted in a thunderous voice that rolled in
echoing shock waves around the valley. 'Begone, snow sprites,
back to your dungeon of ice in the bowels of the Earth.' The
giant laid about him with his glowing sword, slicing swathes
of snow devils to his left and right. Soon his deadly work was
done, and only little hummocks in the snow showed where the
creatures had been.

Guan Di looked about him. The tower of fire cast an eerie
orange-yellow light. The blizzard had passed, and the stars
clustered brightly in the clear night sky. Rokshan watched
through a daze of semi-consciousness, thinking he must be
dreaming. There was no sign of Sung Yuan.

'Where is my summoner?' the giant thundered. 'Snow
sprites cannot summon – only mortals who are about to die
unjustly.'

Rokshan moaned and feebly raised his arm, waves of
nausea overcoming him. It was sufficient to attract the giant's
attention. In three huge strides he was beside him. Kneeling
down, he gently lifted him up, holding him like a baby in the
crook of his arm.

'Ice-cold from the cruel bite of the snow sprites,' Rokshan
heard him murmur, 'the boy mortal will die without the elixir
from the Summit of the Goddess to heal him. I shall deliver
him there without delay – we have little time.'

As Guan Di wrapped him in his thick red cloak and set out
northwards towards the mountain of Khan Tengri and the
Summit of the Goddess, Rokshan finally lapsed into total
unconsciousness.

CHAPTER 21

GUAN DI

Rokshan felt as warm as a baby but could not place the smell – a mixture of leather, wool, sweat and incense. The light too was strange, a sort of red glow, and the regular, rhythmic pounding seemed to come from far below him. He tried to twist round but found it difficult to move.

Guan Di stopped in mid-stride as he felt him stirring. The red glow disappeared abruptly as the cloak around him was peeled aside and an enormous face peered down at him, blotting out everything else.

'By the gods, *what*, or should I say *who*, are *you*?' Rokshan shouted, squirming in the giant's firm but gentle hold. 'Put me down, now. Please.' He was set down with a steadying hand and tottered back in disbelief. He had assumed the giant had been a delirious hallucination.

'God, yes,' his rescuer responded. 'A minor one, if truth be told, but if you're going to swear by us you should know who I am. Guan Di, god of warriors, merchants and scholars, at your service.' The giant bowed low, with an exaggerated flourish. 'I believe you could qualify as a merchant and scholar, possibly not as a warrior, however, judging by what happened with those snow sprites.' The giant's chuckle was like far-off, rumbling thunder.

'We were completely outnumbered, and anyway, I was practically stung to death,' Rokshan said angrily, trying too late to check himself.

Guan Di folded his enormous muscled arms and

looked down sternly at him, waiting expectantly.

Rokshan looked sheepish. 'I owe my life to you . . . thank you.' He gazed up in awe at Guan Di. 'But how did you get here, wherever here is? Where are we? How long have I been unconscious? Is Sung Yuan all right? And my pony?'

'Questions, questions, young mortal,' Guan Di chuckled. 'It is early in the morning following your attack. I am here because you summoned me, I cannot tell you more. And where is it we go? To the Pool of the Two Peaks on the Summit of the Goddess, for the goddess's elixir to heal the bite of the snow sprites.'

'But I feel well enough,' Rokshan protested.

'You will feel well now, but the ice fever of the snow sprites always returns, stronger each time, until eventually you will die of it,' Guan Di said matter-of-factly. 'For that reason we must hurry. The second fever will come quickly.'

Rokshan tried to take this in. Gingerly he felt his arm and rubbed the side of his head. He wondered if the snow devils had been sent deliberately to warn him off – but who would've sent them? His uncle? The Horsemen? He felt the numb despair of defeat steal over him – the Twelfth of the Elect had failed before he'd even started.

'But where is Sung Yuan . . . and my pony?' he asked again. 'What have you done with them?'

'The pony survives – and will join us when he will. As for the monk – killed either by the blizzard or the snow sprites.' Guan Di shrugged. 'He is not my concern. I owe allegiance only to my summoner . . . and now we must go.' He stooped to pick Rokshan up and swept him onto his back.

The giant maintained a steady pace for the rest of that day. Rokshan had some meagre supplies to keep him going – a piece of stale bread, dried meat and fruit – in a bag that he'd taken off Lucky before the attack, and he filled up his water pouch before the river ran dry further up the mountain valleys. Guan Di didn't seem to need any nourishment.

Now, in the far distance, they could see for the first time the two peaks of the Summit of the Goddess, majestically dominating the skyline. Thin wisps of cloud clung to the summits. A smaller peak nestled to the side of them, and there, right on the edge and only just visible, perched a small hut. Rokshan could just make out a pennant fluttering above a clump of tall bamboo nearby.

Its design was clearly visible to Guan Di with his long sight, however, and he recognized what was depicted on the black background straight away: a golden dragon horse, more dragon than horse, but its head was a grinning skull.

'Does someone live there?' Rokshan asked curiously.

'This is the first time I have seen signs of human life on the summit,' Guan Di replied cautiously. 'The nomads of these parts have never settled so high. We shall ask them if they know who it may be – their summer settlement is not far, if my memory serves me, and we will be with them very soon.'

Rokshan shaded his eyes and peered ahead again. Could the hut perhaps be some dwelling for the Horsemen? Had his uncle Zerafshan been there too? Was he getting nearer to his goal now?

As they carried on at Guan Di's relentless pace, the un-mistakable smell of decay carried on the light breeze. The green pasture turned to patchy scrub, and the river became silted up and then dried to a parched trickle. It started to become abnormally warm for the altitude and time of year, the air becoming thick with a heavy tropical hum as thunderclouds built up and the sky darkened.

Jagged lightning flashes on the summit lit up the hut, and as they approached the nomads' settlement, Rokshan could now clearly see the sinister death's-head pennant, flying proud in the strengthening wind and lashing rain.

'This is what happened before the snow devils attacked –

a sudden storm . . .' he shouted into Guan Di's ear as thunder rumbled across the valley.

'There will not be snow sprites here – fire devils perhaps, but I cannot explain this warmth,' Guan Di replied, puzzled.

For a moment Rokshan started to relive the terror of the snow devils' attack, still so fresh in his mind. The smell of rotting meat wafting on the wind jolted him back to the present.

Guan Di tapped him lightly on the leg. 'See, the nomad village is ahead.'

'Yes, but what's that smell?'

Guan Di did not reply but quickened his pace. There were no signs of life in or around the village – the everyday sounds that you would usually expect to see and hear, even from a distance.

'Why are there no children playing; no villagers; no goats or horses?' Rokshan wondered aloud.

'Something is amiss,' the giant agreed, suddenly stopping in mid-stride.

'What is it, Guan Di? Why have you stopped?'

Rokshan shielded his eyes against the rain. There was a low wooden pallisade encircling the settlement. He could see two entrance gates built into it, with taller posts on either side. The posts seemed to be topped with round objects, but he couldn't make out what they were. He looked harder, and noticed they were dotted all around the pallisade, not just on the entrance posts.

'What are they, Guan Di – you can see from here – those round things?'

'I can see, but it is not something I would ever want to see. A terrible evil has taken place here . . .'

As they approached, Guan Di cut his usual loping stride down to a wary walk and constantly looked about him, as if anticipating an ambush. After a few moments he stopped again.

Now it was quite clear what the round objects were: heads, human heads. Maybe two dozen or more – men, women and children. And these were just the ones on their side of the settlement.

The skulls must have been there for some time. Most had gaping sockets where carrion birds had pecked out the eyes. Grimacing death grins mouthed silently at them where their lips had once been. Rokshan noticed an infant's tiny skull drilled with holes, and felt a wave of nausea.

'Why? Who has done this, Guan Di? What crime had these people committed? And the women and children too?' Questions screamed through Rokshan's head. 'Put me down, quickly, I feel sick!' He retched violently, his stomach heaving, his head reeling. 'We should try . . . we must check the village to see if there are any survivors,' he heard himself say in a horrified daze. 'Maybe they'll be able to tell us what happened here. Guan Di – go round the other side and we'll meet in the middle. It's a small place; we won't be out of sight of each other.'

Guan Di nodded in agreement, his huge, craggy face a contorted mask of pain and anger.

The rotting, sickly-sweet smell of death was over-powering when Rokshan entered the pallisade. Glancing around, he saw that its entire length was skewered with heads. The settlement was small but spread out. It had a main thoroughfare crossed by some unpaved streets. It was difficult to tell if it had once been crowded with shops and stores; with customs houses, inns, blacksmiths and shepherds' huts – because everything within the palisade had been destroyed by fire. Only a few smoking embers remained.

Rokshan's mind reeled . . . All burned. Not content with massacring all the inhabitants, whoever had done this had razed everything to the ground . . . Why such vengeance? What had these people done? Was this anything to do with the

Horsemen? He had heard of their cruelty – but this . . . Was this what he should expect of the people his uncle had befriended?

He noticed that Guan Di had knelt down and was examining something towards the centre of the settlement. He signalled to Rokshan to come over. Those villagers who had not been decapitated had been rounded up and set ablaze in a vast funeral pyre. Scores of charred bodies lay heaped on top of each other. Scattered around the edge of the mound were more mangled remains, which looked as if they had been gnawed at by wild animals.

The yellow imperial pennant that fluttered from a lance at the top of the pyre told Rokshan all he needed to know. Revulsion and anger filled him as he staggered against Guan Di, hardly able to speak.

'Guan Di, this is the emperor's doing, a warning for the Horsemen of what he means to do to them – and anyone else thinking of rebelling against him.'

'And punishment for them too.' Guan Di nodded sombrely, gazing at the carnage. 'Everyone knows the Horsemen are roaming far from their valleys, attacking the emperor's outposts. For centuries they have shared their fertile land with the nomadic people of your kingdom and neighbouring Agni. But now' – Guan Di shook his head sadly, looking around at the carnage – 'now it seems the emperor wants the Horsemen's valleys just for himself.'

He lapsed into a brooding silence. Rokshan pointed at the imperial pennant and began to say something, but as he did so, a sharp, shooting pain stabbed up the arm which had been stung by the snow devils. He cried out in pain and slumped to the ground.

'Come. We have spent too much time amongst this horror. The ice fever must be driven out,' Guan Di said as he carefully lifted him up, turned his back on the funeral pyre and set off towards the Summit of the Goddess.

CHAPTER 22

THE POOL OF THE TWO PEAKS

Guan Di travelled at a loping run, making a steady ascent up the mountain of Khan Tegri to the Pool of the Two Peaks. The light had already begun to fade when they left the village, so they soon stopped to spend an uncomfortable, anxious night beside a deserted shepherd's hut.

Rokshan was sinking fast, only semi-conscious, his body shaking with cold, in the grip of the ice fever. Guan Di wrapped his enormous cloak around him and hugged him close to his chest in an effort to keep him warm. But gradually even the shivering stopped, and a deathly blue tinge spread over Rokshan's face.

'I'm dying, aren't I, Guan Di?' he whispered, his voice cracking.

The giant hugged him closer. 'The spirits of the pool will restore you,' he reassured him.

They set out again in the pale, washed light of dawn. Time was running out for Rokshan, and Guan Di set a fast pace. It was early afternoon when they at last approached the pool. By then Rokshan was slipping in and out of consciousness. The giant feared it might already be too late as he said a prayer over him.

'Awake, little one; soon you will be washed and whole again, cleansed in the healing pool. The dragon spirits of water will bathe you and drive out for ever the poison of the snow sprites from your soul. My task will then be accomplished, until you have need of me once more.'

Rowan trees surrounded the pool, which was the size of a small lake. The water was a clear blue-green. In the middle lay a small island where a mighty willow dipped its drooping branches into the water. To the east, the smaller of the peaks reared up. The wooden hut with its death's-head pennant was now clearly visible, but Guan Di paid it no attention as he knelt by the side of the pool and gently laid Rokshan down.

He undressed him and wrapped him in his red cloak, then waded halfway out to the island. He laid him in the water, unfurling him from his cloak and murmuring healing invocations all the while; he held him for a while little longer before, with a final chant of supplication, letting him go.

Rokshan's limp body slipped beneath the surface as Guan Di bowed; then the giant seemed to slowly melt into the pool, leaving just a ripple behind him.

An hour or so later, dusk began to shroud the mountaintops. A freezing mist rose from the pool, billowing across its surface. Rokshan felt cool water lapping at his feet; it was peaceful here, he thought, but he was cold and hungry. Suddenly he sat up and looked around: where was he? He saw his clothes in a neat pile just a little way along the shore and quickly clambered into them.

Gradually he recalled what had happened: this must be the Pool of the Two Peaks, but where was Guan Di? And how had he reached the shore? His last recollection was of the giant's enormous red cloak wrapped around him; he'd been floating and had never felt so peaceful. Then he had been sinking and . . . he groped in his memory . . . what had happened then? Try as he might, he could not recall; *something* had happened – he was sure of it. Whatever it was, he had shaken off the death fever of the snow devils, and he knew for certain that he owed his life to Guan Di.

He looked out over the lake. A cold breeze whispered through the willow, and a heron stood one-legged on the shore of the small island. It cocked its head, looking for fish, and then, with a slow and deliberate gait, moved further into the water to try its luck.

Rokshan shivered, and drawing his thick quilted jacket around him looked up to the two peaks, which swirled in and out of thick cloud. Pinnacles of granite emerged when the clouds parted, while huge rocky outcrops, dotted with conifers and mountain ash, were gradually veiled and then vanished from sight.

As the chilly mist swirled about him, Rokshan felt the clammy vapour of loneliness settle on his soul, thicken, and become black as the night which had suddenly fallen, enveloping him. Waves of self-pity washed over him: he wished all this had never happened and he rubbed vigorously at the amulet to try and bring Guan Di back, but he knew it was hopeless.

He looked up to the summit's two peaks, towards the wooden hut with its fluttering pennant, and prayed for the strength to do what he knew he must. At last hunger drove him on. It had been over five years since he'd seen his uncle, he mused; would he recognize him? But at least if he did indeed live in the hut, he would surely have something to eat.

Rokshan was filling his water pouch when a nervous but familiar-sounding whinny from the sparse woods surrounding the pool made him jump.

'Lucky?' he called quietly. 'Is that you? Come here, boy, come on . . .'

As he approached the trees, Lucky emerged, looking bedraggled and exhausted but very pleased to see Rokshan. He nuzzled up to him, whickering with pleasure.

'It is you! Lucky by name, lucky by nature! Where have you been?' Rokshan cried, throwing himself on Lucky's neck. 'You followed us all the way up here, you brave little pony! You don't know how pleased I am to see you.'

As if in response, Lucky nuzzled him again, pushing

against him so that they were facing in the direction of the hut.

'Are you as hungry as I am?' Rokshan laughed. 'Then we'll go together.'

He took up the reins, climbed into the saddle and, suddenly feeling much braver and stronger, set out on the last part of his journey to find the uncle who, he was now quite certain, was the rebel leader of the Wild Horsemen.

PART FOUR

ROKSHAN AND THE HORSEMEN

The Legend of the Dragon Horse

The following is recorded in The Book of Ahura Mazda, the Wise Lord

When the defeated dragons were reborn in the Pool of Life, some were reborn as half horse and half dragon, the legend tells.

The emperors of old believed that a certain magnificent species of horse, found in the central west of the Empire, were descendants of these mythical creatures which one day would carry them to immortality in Heaven. Thus they became known as the 'heavenly horses', and the emperors gathered to themselves as many of these horses as they could.

In spite of this, the true guardians of the descendants of the heavenly horses were known as the Wild Horsemen. Over the generations they had formed a bond of understanding with the magnificent breed, which throughout the Empire were popularly called 'dragon horses', after the legend. It became a bond that was universally known, respected and even feared throughout the Empire because, it was whispered, there was a dark secret at the heart of the Horsemen's special understanding of what they called their 'sacred mounts', a secret which only the legendary horse-singers of the plains, known as the Serenadhi, could unlock.

One horse above all others of its kind was considered by the Horsemen to be a direct descendant of the most fearsome of the rebellious dragon spirits - Han Garid, lord of the thunder dragons. The Wild Horsemen call Han Garid's descendant the 'lord of the horses'.

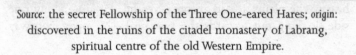

Source: the secret Fellowship of the Three One-eared Hares; *origin:* discovered in the ruins of the citadel monastery of Labrang, spiritual centre of the old Western Empire.

CHAPTER 23

ZERAFSHAN

Night enveloped Rokshan as he wound his way up through the straggling copses of conifers and mountain ash, towards the smaller peak. The mist had thinned as they climbed and the moon, which was almost full, shone through the scudding clouds. Suddenly Rokshan's pony came to a halt.

'Come on, Lucky, what's the matter?' Rokshan urged him on, but he stubbornly refused to budge. 'Something's bothering you, I know.' He tried to sound reassuring but found himself suppressing a shudder as he looked ahead.

His heart was hammering: close to, the bamboo thicket seemed much denser and taller, but there was now no mistaking the design on the pennant streaming above it in the gusting wind, the skull grinning over a sinuous, writhing body.

'Nearly there now,' Rokshan said, feeling he had to keep his voice down as they drew near. He dismounted and rummaged in the saddlebags for something to take Lucky's mind off whatever it was that was bothering him. 'Here we are – this'll cheer you up. Come on, boy,' he said enticingly, feeding him some dried fruit.

Just then a crow flew up and cawed noisily at them from the top of the bamboo thicket, in a sinister call of welcome. Warily, Rokshan led his pony into the clearing. The hut was much larger than he had expected – perhaps it had once been the summer retreat of a rich nobleman seeking to escape the heat of the plains. It had an open veranda running along one side, looking out towards the two peaks. An open doorway yawned blackly, the door occasionally banging in the wind as if warning strangers away.

Rokshan stopped, his heart pounding, tied Lucky to a post, and then, giving him an anxious pat, headed for the doorway. Suddenly the crow swooped down and flew straight across his path, brushing his face with its beating wings before making off. He raised his arms in surprise and, stumbling through the doorway, tripped and fell. Before he could scramble up, the door had slammed shut on him; he peered into the hut nervously but all he could hear was a low muted chuckle.

'Come, Rokshan – or are you going to lie there all night?' a rich, melodic voice said out of the darkness.

'H-hello, Uncle,' Rokshan said sheepishly, hurriedly getting to his feet; he looked around for some sign of his uncle but couldn't see him anywhere.

Silence. Moments like centuries passed: the only sound that could be heard was the wind gusting through the bamboos and, further off, a distant moan as it blustered around the pinnacles of the two peaks.

As his eyes grew accustomed to the gloom, Rokshan could see a small red light flickering dimly at the other end of the hut, ten or twelve paces away; behind it was a raised platform. At first he thought this was an altar, but gradually he could make out the contours of someone lying on it, facing him.

At last Zerafshan got up from the couch. He was dressed in a long robe of black silk adorned with the same grinning dragon skull and body as the pennant which fluttered outside, and his right hand gripped a staff of the blackest ebony, richly carved with entwined serpents.

His head was shaved halfway back across his skull, and long, luxuriant black hair streaked with white fell to his shoulders. His eyes were deep-set and burned with the single-minded zeal of one who is fixed on his purpose, and the expression on his long, rather melancholy-looking face reflected this. The robe he wore was open at the chest and Rokshan noticed that the same dragon was tattood on his hair-less chest. Hanging from a simple leather thong around his neck was a silver torc, fashioned to look like a coil of rope; its clasp resembled a cicada with outstretched wings and two claw-like feet. Rokshan recognized the cicada as a symbol of immortality, and wondered why his uncle didn't wear the torc fixed around his neck.

'Greetings, Uncle.' He could not help his voice catching in surprise at his uncle's appearance. 'It has been many years since I saw you last, at our home in Maracanda.'

'Rokshan! Is it really you? I barely recognize you! Let me look at you – you have grown so and . . . well, in another year or two will be as tall as me! Now, let me see, how many years has it been? Can it really have been five years? However long it's been, it doesn't matter – welcome to you,' Zerafshan said warmly, spreading his arms and looking at him intently. 'You must be weary after your travels. I'm afraid my humble hut does not offer much of a welcome for you' – he moved around the room, lighting some lamps with a long taper – 'but I have some meat we can cook, if we were to build a fire – you are hungry?' His uncle looked at him with sharp, enquiring eyes.

Rokshan noticed his thin smile, and wondered what had happened to the old infectious grin he remembered.

'Is . . . is this where you live, Uncle?' he asked, looking around at the simple furnishings. A long table ran the length of one side of the room and was covered in a messy jumble of scrolls. Glancing at them, Rokshan realized that they were com-plicated diagrams of astral constellations and plotted horoscopes; many were covered with notes written in a very neat but cramped hand.

Zerafshan followed his glance. 'Still interested in astrology,

Rokshan? It has become something of a preoccupation of mine too. When you are recovered from your travels, I have some fascinating star charts to show you. But in answer to your question – no, this is not where I live, not for any significant periods of time, anyway. When I am not walking the valleys amongst the people I have adopted as my own, I come here to be alone, to study my charts, to ponder the future and my place in it – to think of my old life, and what I do now . . .' He looked pensively at his nephew. 'Tell me, how is the family – how is my brother, your father? And how is your brother, An Lushan? He is already building quite a reputation as a merchant, I hear.'

'My brother is well, but my father . . .' Rokshan paused before telling him about his father's imprisonment, even though something told him his uncle must know already.

'My brother imprisoned on the whim of the emperor? This is intolerable,' Zerafshan snapped when he'd heard Rokshan out, tidying up all his scrolls and astrological charts in a burst of activity, as if trying to calm himself down.

'I almost died on the way up here, Uncle; we were attacked by—'

'We?' Zerafshan interrupted, suddenly stopping what he was doing.

Rokshan was careful to omit any mention of Guan Di, explaining that he had set off with a wandering monk as a guide, having travelled with one of the scores of caravans that travelled the trade routes.

'Who attacked you?' his uncle asked.

'*What*, Uncle, would be a more accurate description,' Rokshan said, and he told him about the snow devils – and the death of his companion.

'The spirits of the mountain roads are said to be restless,' Zerafshan said matter-of-factly, 'and so it has proved. You were lucky to escape with your life.'

Rokshan nodded, but he was thinking more of the horror

of what they had come across at the nomad settlement. Before he could tell Zerafshan about this, however, his uncle continued speaking.

'The Horsemen have a healthy respect for the kuei of these parts,' he said, looking towards the open veranda. 'But come – you are safe now, and with all this talk you must grow faint with hunger. I shall light the fire outside and then let's eat while the night is still fine, and you can ask me all the questions you want about what I've been doing here with the Horsemen these past few years – that's what you'd like to know more about, isn't it?'

A little later they settled back around the fire. Zerafshan had cooked them an excellent supper and Rokshan was finding it difficult to keep his eyes open.

'Look at the stars, Rokshan,' his uncle said, gazing upwards. 'I learned during my time at court that the emperor sets his life's compass by them, and those of his people. It will surprise him one day when what is written in the stars comes about.'

'What do you mean, Uncle? Do you set so much store by what the stars can tell us?' Rokshan looked up at the diamond-studded night sky, ablaze with sparkling brilliance.

'Rokshan, you surprise me! You were always interested in the study of astrology when you were a small boy. Surely you've kept this interest up?'

'As much as I need to for my studies. I may know a little more than the average student—'

'Average student? You were always more than that. But I too have been a student – of the Horsemen. I have learned much about these people over the years since I came among them to do the emperor's bidding – things they'll never teach you at the school. The Horsemen are my family now, Rokshan, as I hope they will become yours.'

'I must know why you wanted me here,' Rokshan said, wondering uncomfortably what his uncle meant.

Zerafshan nodded. 'Well, let's start with the rumours. There are those who say I have become many things,' he began. 'They say I am a prophet, or a soothsayer – a spellbinder and master of dreams; others say I am a necromancer of some ancient, outlawed sect. But they are all fools, because no one can know what I've kept locked up inside me for so many years . . .'

For a second Rokshan thought he saw tears misting over his uncle's eyes but it was difficult to tell in the flickering firelight.

'I was appointed special envoy of the emperor to the Kingdom of the Wild Horsemen – this much you know. But it was all a front – the emperor's desire to possess all the sacred charges of the Horsemen became a consuming obsession, and he would not listen to reason. The Horsemen even agreed to increase by five-fold their yearly tribute of two horses, but even that wasn't enough. Eventually—'

'Eventually you became one of them – you must have heard, Uncle,' Rokshan said, 'that you are accused of inciting the Horsemen to open rebellion; anyone associated with you is liable to arrest and—'

'Imprisonment, like your father. I know, which only goes to prove that the emperor will do anything to force me to deliver what is undeliverable. He has betrayed me – and when I am the Horsemen's acknowledged leader, I will make him pay for that.' The venom in Zerafshan's voice made Rokshan flinch.

'But if you're not their acknowledged leader, leave them! Let the Horsemen get on with their rebellion themselves,' he said eagerly. 'Come back with me to Maracanda and tell the Council everything; then they will free my father.'

He looked earnestly at Zerafshan, hoping against hope that he would just say yes; then everything the abbot had said about his uncle wouldn't matter, and his father would be freed.

'Would that it were as simple as that,' Zerafshan said

brusquely, dashing Rokshan's hopes in an instant and making him feel ashamed he'd even thought it.

'Are you saying the Horsemen won't let you go?' Rokshan asked.

A blustery wind had sprung up and blew sparks from the fire into a whirling dance, scattering them into the night sky, where they faded and disappeared. The larger of the two peaks swirled in and out of the gathering stormclouds.

'They wouldn't go as far as that . . . but . . . I have come too far,' Zerafshan said, giving Rokshan an appraising look. All this time he had been fingering the silver torc that hung against his chest.

'Too far? What do you mean?' Rokshan asked.

'The Horsemen have come to believe that it is fate that has delivered me to them. Never before has anyone who is not their khagan – their leader – had such clear visons from the wearing of their Collar, such as I have . . .' He lifted the torc in his hand and slowly turned it round, watching as Rokshan looked at it in fascination. 'This Collar is what I speak of, Rokshan; it is sacred to the Horsemen, normally worn only by their khagan.' There was a tremor in his voice as he put his hand on Rokshan's shoulder. 'To some who wear it, it gives visions,' he continued in a quiet murmur, 'and the visions it has granted me confirm that I am to be the Horsemen's leader in their fight for freedom from the tyranny of the emperor.'

Rokshan looked in alarm at Zerafshan's staring eyes. 'This is treasonable talk, Uncle – enough to get our whole family executed. Visions? From their leader's Collar? How can that be? And why do you not wear it around your neck? How does it give you these visions? And why have you, who are not a Horseman, been allowed to wear it? You talk of the emperor and his tyranny – I must tell you of what I saw on my way up here. A nomad settlement—'

Just then a thunderclap detonated directly overhead. They

gatherered up the bowls and cooking implements and dashed towards the veranda to take shelter. Another deafening crash shook the wooden hut to its foundations. Large drops of rain spattered on the veranda steps, polka-dotting the plain wooden boards. Soon the taller of the two peaks was obscured by a steaming curtain of water.

Zerafshan hurried Rokshan inside. The storm seemed to unsettle him and he began to pace around the room with a worried frown. His hazel eyes sparked a fiery reddish brown as lightning crackled, freezing them in a split-second flash of brilliant silver-white light. He picked up one scroll, and then another, as if uncertain what to do.

'Uncle? The star charts – why don't you show them to me now?' Rokshan said, a little nervously.

'Yes, yes, the star charts ... help me unroll them,' Zerafshan said enthusiastically, handing him a scroll.

As they laid out four or five of the largest charts on the long table, Zerafshan darted from one to the next, tapping his finger on one, rolling it up and then spreading out another, all the while muttering and whispering to himself.

At last he jabbed a finger at a complicated-looking star chart. 'Look! What does this constellation tell you?'

Rokshan glanced at it and smiled in recognition. 'This depicts the Pole Star in the constellation of the White Tiger when it is in conjunction with Jupiter and Mercury, more commonly known as the Dragon of the Eclipse. It is supposed to bring whoever's born under it good luck all their lives. Really, Uncle, this is one of the commonest patterns of the stars – I bought an almanac of the coming Year of the Dragon based on this very star pattern in the market at Maracanda not long before we set out!'

'Very well, very well. And this one?' Zerafshan pointed at another chart that was even more cluttered with his neat, spidery handwriting.

Rokshan looked hard at it, frowning in concentration. 'I . . . I don't recognize it,' he said.

'It is an imperial star chart – the emperor's astrologers chart one every year to mark another glorious period of the emperor's divine rule – so he would have us believe.' Zerafshan almost spat it out. 'Take away all the fanciful interpretations and doodlings, as I have done here, and we have the chart for the year eight hundred and four – the year of your birth; a year when for a brief period of time there was a strange configuration of the stars and planets visible in the heavens. I know for sure that it was marked by the imperial astrologers.'

'But . . . why is it so significant, Uncle?'

'Significant? It is more than just significant . . .' Zerafshan seemed to stare through him, his eyes lit with the zeal of the fanatic. 'It is no coincidence that the year of your birth marked the renewal of the imperial interest in the dragon horses of the Wild Horsemen which, as the world knows, has grown into an all-consuming obsession. And that same strange configuration of the stars and planets is now once again becoming visible in the Heavens – reflecting the earthly disharmony caused by the emperor's obsession.' Zerafshan's voice dropped to a whisper as he suddenly seized Rokshan by the shoulders. 'It is the sign that the imperial astrologers feared to predict: it is the heavenly affirmation that will make our cause just – the stars themselves have pronounced their own verdict on this abomination of a ruler, revoking Heaven's mandate for the emperor to rule, giving the people the right to overthrow him!'

Rokshan was stunned. His uncle's words confirmed everything the abbot had said. Zerafshan *was* planning a rebellion: this was treason; suicidal folly. It suddenly struck him that this must have been a lonely place for his uncle, among a people not his own: all these years with the Horsemen must have bent his mind to this madness.

But what of the deeper purpose the abbot had mentioned?

His mind raced . . . Clearly Zerafshan had no intention of calling off the rebellion just because he, Rokshan, had been delivered to him. What else was he plotting? To find out, he was going to have to go along with whatever his uncle planned for him, wherever it might lead . . . The realization hit him like a punch in the stomach.

In an effort to control his growing sense of panic, he recalled the abbot's words: *You have been given the gifts of the animal spirit of the Elect, the hare – his speed, agility and cunning; use them.* Now he understood what the abbot had intended with these gifts: he was going to have to think on his feet and make quick decisions if he was to succeed in his task as one of the Elect.

Zerafshan, wrapped up in his astrological predictions and plans for rebellion and revolution throughout the Empire, barely noticed Rokshan's shocked reaction and strode over to the veranda as the thunder grumbled over the mountains, the storm now passing over. He looked out intently. 'Can you hear it? Listen . . . No, you wouldn't be able to,' he muttered, giving him a quick glance. 'They are still too far away – my Collar can sometimes heighten my senses when I am seeking something.'

To his astonishment – which he was very careful to conceal – Rokshan *could* hear it; or at least feel it as the slightest of tremors – far off but unmistakable: the light, rhythmic pounding of galloping hooves. But he wasn't going to tell his uncle about the special powers he had been gifted with.

'The Horsemen – the Horsemen are coming, Rokshan!' Zerafshan gripped him in a fever of suppressed excitement. 'They're coming up the pass from the north-east – from the Plain of the Dead, where they have laid to rest their last khagan. Over the next cycle of the moon they will all gather – all the different clans – to choose and acknowledge their new leader!'

CHAPTER 24

ON THE WAY TO THE VALLEYS OF THE HORSEMEN

The next day dawned bright and clear, and Rokshan braced himself against the cold as he went outside. The snow-capped mountains reflected the rising sun in a dazzling golden glow and wispy clouds scudded over the peaks. He looked around, whistling for Lucky, and thought how different a place could look in the light of day; last night when he had crept up, he'd been fearful of what he might find.

'Lucky, you look like you could do with a good brush down. I really haven't been looking after you properly, have I?' He patted the pony's neck affectionately and, rooting around in his saddlebag, found an old brush.

Grooming Lucky helped him to order his thoughts. Questions raced through his mind: what was his uncle's true intention? Did he have enough power over the Horsemen to lead them in rebellion against the emperor? Or were the Horsemen leading him?

He wasn't their acknowledged leader – the Horsemen were gathering to make their choice . . . He must be intending to put himself forward! But how did his uncle expect him to help in that? Did Zerafshan – by virtue of his 'visions' – really have enough influence to win their backing? It didn't seem possible, although he had once been a commander in the imperial army, a respected military figure with plenty of successful campaigns against marauding barbarians to his credit – that was how he had come to the attention of the emperor in the first place; perhaps the Horsemen considered him a safe bet for leading their rebellion.

Rokshan knew he wasn't going to find out the answers to any of these questions until he'd seen his uncle with the Horsemen and was able to judge how much influence he had over them – or whether it was the other way round. The Wild Horsemen! His heart jumped: after the Darhad, these were the most reclusive people in the Empire; before now they'd never ventured into the towns or big cities – why should they? The mountain valleys and Plains of Jalhal'a, where their dragon horses galloped free, provided them with all they needed.

Rokshan remembered the arrival of the imperial messengers in Maracanda, when he'd seen his first dragon horses – and how one in particular had had such an effect on him. He smiled to himself; he couldn't wait to be amongst the Horsemen and their mounts.

'We should be so lucky, Lucky!' he joked, leaning his head against the pony's neck. He laughed as Lucky tried to nuzzle him, twisting his head round.

Just then he suddenly felt that he was being watched, and glancing towards the hut, he saw his uncle on the veranda, observing him.

'Good morning, Uncle.'

Zerafshan nodded in acknowledgement, staff in hand and a bag slung over his shoulder. 'Gather your bags,' he said after a moment. 'We're going to meet the Horsemen. It will be midday or so before we reach the first of their valleys.'

'What about my pony, Uncle – will we ride?'

'No – untether him so he can wander where he will. He'll come to no harm here,' he said, stepping back inside. 'Let us leave at once.'

Zerafshan had a long stride and set a fast pace. It was still and clear in the bright sunshine, as if everything had been washed clean by the storm. They were following a steep path that led down from the smaller peak, where Zerafshan's hut was, before winding its way across and up again towards the higher peak.

'Uncle, is it true what they say about the Horsemen's punishment, when they find strangers in their valleys?' This had been nagging Rokshan since he'd first set out up the pass.

'Cutting out their tongues and blinding them? I have not seen or heard of the punishment being inflicted since I have been among the Horsemen. Do not be fearful, Rokshan. I have enough influence among them to guarantee your safety. The khagan who has just died was from the topmost of their valleys, nearest to my hut. He was the first clan leader I befriended when I came amongst them for the first time. Only later did he become the khagan of all the Horsemen. He was much loved and respected – it was he who allowed me to wear the Collar.'

Rokshan wanted to know more about this Collar but they had come to a large clearing about three-quarters of the way up the peak. In the middle stood a large hexagon-shaped temple, with supporting pillars at each corner and a domed roof. A wide sweep of steps led up to an entrance arch flanked by two large braziers. Behind the temple the taller peak reared up, a sheer slab of granite dotted with conifers. Horses' hooves had clearly trampled the ground around the building.

'What is this place, Uncle?' Rokshan asked, staring at the horse's skull above the entrance arch; each gaping eye-socket housed a candle.

'This is the temple of the Horsemen, where they'll acknowledge their new khagan once he has been chosen,' Zerafshan said, striding up the steps. 'I must leave something here . . . Wait for me,' he added before disappearing through the entrance.

Rokshan decided to risk sneaking a quick look inside from the top of the steps. He bounded up and looked round, making sure that he couldn't be seen. Peering through the entrance, he caught a glimpse of more horses' skulls hanging all the way round. He also noticed the front of the large altar stone, which was decorated with the shadowy outline of a black bird.

Zerafshan was busy unlocking something behind the altar; then he slipped the thong and Collar from around his neck and, stooping, put them in what Rokshan thought must be some sort of shrine. As his uncle locked up the shrine, Rokshan quickly leaped back down the steps, glad to be out of a place that had a strange, unsettling atmosphere.

'Come' – Zerafshan beckoned as he reappeared at the top of the steps – 'we still have a way to go.'

The path now led down from the heights of the two peaks. At times it became narrow and treacherous, and Rokshan understood why they had left his pony behind. After two or three hours, the ground began to level out and the wooded slopes on either side became denser. Even though they had descended to the level of the tree line, they were still very high when Zerafshan stopped to gaze out over an outcrop of rock.

'Look: the Fifth Valley of the Horsemen – the highest of the five,' he said simply, sweeping his arm out in front of him.

It was a beautiful, tranquil sight. Far below them a river snaked lazily through the valley. The afternoon sun reflected off the sheer, golden sandstone cliffs, and the rumpled foothills stretched as far as the eye could see. Huge boulders dotted the ground, as if they had been dropped haphazardly by giant hands.

In amongst the tall grasses and plentiful shrubs and bushes that grew on either side of the river, horses grazed contentedly, undisturbed, it seemed, by the presence of humans: right at the end of the valley they could just make out orderly groupings of wooden huts with ant-like figures moving around. They could also see a steady stream of riders entering the valley.

'As the river makes its way down, there are four more

settlements like the one you see here – the Fourth, Third, Second and First Valleys, in descending order; eventually all the chosen of the Horsemen clans will gather at the highest of these – this one – which is closest to their temple,' Zerafshan explained.

Rokshan nodded; he sensed that the deep tranquillity in this place had been nurtured over the centuries, undisturbed by man-made conflict and fiercely guarded by the Horsemen. He noticed the intent expression on his uncle's face, and began to understand what it was that had drawn him to these people.

'If I told you that the emperor had ordered me to crush the Wild Horsemen and break their spirit for ever – such was his greed for their dragon horses – you would find it difficult to believe, would you not?' Zerafshan suddenly asked, turning from the idyllic scene.

'I . . . y-yes, Uncle,' Rokshan stammered, the question taking him completely by surprise. 'But you had no choice: anyone refusing a command of the emperor is executed for treason . . .'

'Perhaps I did have a choice, Rokshan, but in the end it was denied me. What does that make it? An opportunity missed, perhaps.'

Rokshan could only murmur in agreement.

'Many years ago,' Zerafshan continued, 'I was sent on a mission by the Elect of the Fellowship of the Hares to become their eyes and ears in the imperial court – you have heard of this secret society, I imagine?'

His uncle gave him a searching look. The thought suddenly flashed through Rokshan's mind: did Zerafshan somehow know that he was now the Twelfth Elect? He couldn't tell – all he could do was mumble that he'd only heard of it through the briefest of mentions in history lessons at the school – and listen. Their feet scrunched heavily on the path as they made their way down.

'The success I had should have reaped its own reward, but the Elect were jealous, and deemed that I had become a slave to worldly power and ambition, so they forbade me entry into their ranks – fools! Even though they knew I was the emperor's favourite, so that he trusted me above all others to plan the killing of a people. The emperor hates the Horsemen and their way of life; their independence of spirit that in ages past took them far and wide, roaming free – what if all the people of the Empire were to demand their freedom? Can you understand, Rokshan? I was sent to destroy the Horsemen and all they stand for – what they have always stood for.'

'He has already started his campaign of bloody murder, Uncle.' Rokshan described in detail the terrible scene of carnage and bloodshed they'd come across. 'Couldn't the Horsemen have protected the nomads?' He was determined to get some sort of explanation from his uncle.

'The Horsemen guard their borders jealously. Why would they be persuaded by me to risk their own lives defending the nomads? Besides, the nomads had strayed too far into their winter pastures,' Zerafshan said brusquely, as if that explained everything.

'They aren't just any nomads – they are highlanders, Sogdian highlanders, Uncle . . . Our people, who have always shared the mountains with the Horsemen. You don't mean the Horsemen would've condoned what the emperor did?' Rokshan looked at the tall figure of his uncle in disbelief, shocked at what appeared to be his casual disregard.

'Very few can follow the path the Horsemen tread, to be sure,' Zerafshan replied evenly, 'especially those who are not of them. Certainly, at first, it was not a path of my choosing – but how else was I to do the emperor's bidding, unless I became accepted as one of their own?'

Zerafshan glanced at him, a thin smile on his face. 'But you will understand more once you have met them –

perhaps they will make you one of their own too, if you wish it.'

They walked on, Zerafshan's words hanging heavily between them.

'The Horsemen you heard last night . . .' Rokshan asked to fill the awkward silence. 'Would they have come the same way as we have just come?'

'Well observed – you're wondering, if they came this way, how is it possible they rode down such a steep and sometimes treacherous track, especially as the Horsemen's mounts are larger than ordinary horses? The riding skills of the Horsemen are legendary, are they not?'

Rokshan nodded enthusiastically.

'As children, we hear tales about them at our mothers' knees, but everything you've heard is as nothing compared to the sight of a child of the Horsemen dancing on the back of his mount at full gallop. It is as if they become one with their horse; so negotiating a track like this is as easy as breathing to them.'

'Now, that I *have* to see,' Rokshan scoffed. 'I know it took my friend Kanandak, the acrobat, years of practice just to stand on a trotting circus horse and do tricks – the number of times I saw him fall off!' At the thought of his friend, he suddenly realized how much he missed him.

Zerafshan smiled. 'I am taking you to meet Cetu, a Waymaster of the Horse. He was among the first of the Horsemen I got to know when I first came among them. He knows more about dragon horses than anyone else in the world. He has taught me much, and will be able to answer all your questions.'

Chapter 25

The Waymaster

The valley was much wider than it had looked from afar, and as they tracked round a bend of the river, they heard shouts and the unmistakable pounding of horses' hooves. Zerafshan waved Rokshan over and, pushing past the tall grasses that edged the riverbank, they cautiously peered through.

A group of a dozen or more young children on horseback – boys and girls who couldn't have been more than nine or ten years old, Rokshan thought – were galloping down a rough track, two abreast.

Suddenly one of the leading pair of boys jumped up into a crouching position – still at full gallop – and leaped onto his companion's mount, landing neatly astride behind the rider, who then promptly repeated the manoeuvre, taking command of the riderless horse in one flowing movement. Down the line, one after the other, all the pairs performed the same feat, so quickly that Rokshan gasped in admiration. An older Horseman who galloped alongside them cracked his whip and, wheeling round, they thundered back up the track.

The whoops and shouts of the young riders rang in their ears as they gazed after them. The horses were just as Rokshan remembered them – all sinuous grace and muscular, noble bearing. They galloped effortlessly, carrying their heads proudly. Suddenly he experienced a familiar feeling – he searched around in his mind and there it was: this sense of oneness with the horses that he'd felt when the imperial messengers came to Maracanda. As they disappeared up the track, he thought he discerned wispy colours trailing behind them. As he rubbed his eyes, he realized that the colours, faint as they were, were in his mind.

Zerafshan gave him a curious look before explaining about the young riders. 'They train for half a day every day, as soon as they are big enough to ride a full-grown mount. Before that they ride the younger dragon horses as soon as their backs are strong enough to take the weight of a six- or seven-year-old boy – or girl. Boys and girls of the Horsemen are treated equally when it comes to riding skills.'

'And the girls are trained in the use of arms too?' Rokshan asked, staring after the riders with a look of wonder and disbelief on his face. The Horsemen were renowned for their archery skills in the saddle.

'A few, if they display particular prowess – you will have time enough to find all this out for yourself,' Zerafshan said over his shoulder as he made his way back to the track that led along the river.

Up ahead, a group of mounted Horsemen were approaching, splashing their way upriver. Zerafshan stopped and hailed them.

'Greetings, Horsemen. You are following the progress of your young warriors? We have already admired their practice.'

'Hail, Zerafshan!' they chorused, each thumping a fist to their chests and dipping their heads in salute.

'We are early arrivals from the First Valley clan, led by Gandhara,' one of them continued, referring to the lowest of the mountain settlements. 'We are enjoying our cousins' hospitality here.'

'How many more of you will be coming?' Zerafshan asked.

'There should be many more of us as the conclave approaches. Gandhara is already being spoken of as the khagan-elect: he has the backing of the Horsemen from the Plains of Jalhal'a.'

'Your closest neighbours? That is not surprising. Other clanspeople are gathering already?'

'Deputations from the other valleys are on their way, but we have no word from the plains yet of when, or whether, people from their clan will attend.'

'There will be no conclave without them,' Zerafshan said tersely.

The lead Horseman nodded in agreement, looking a little suspiciously at Rokshan as he joined Zerafshan. 'And who is this young stranger who accompanies you?'

Rokshan couldn't take his eyes off the Horsemen and -women. Their faces were deeply lined and leathery, as if they were always outdoors in the sun and wind, never long out of the saddle. Each wore a long sleeveless coat of animal skin lined with thick fur; on their back they carried a bow and a quiver of arrows; a larger quiver was attached to the saddle, which rested on a brightly coloured woollen rug. A long sheath housed a short throwing javelin. Their hair was cropped short and the men wore beards of varying length. But it was the horses themselves that drew Rokshan's attention. He shook his head as, for just an instant, a kaleidoscope of colours seemed to hum and sing in his mind. He thought he heard a horse whicker softly in his ear, but he was snapped back to reality when Zerafshan put his hand on his shoulder and answered the question.

'He is a kinsman,' Zerafshan replied shortly, 'who has brought me news from Maracanda.'

The Horsemen gave them both a long searching look before saluting Zerafshan again and moving off. Rokshan let out a sigh of relief . . . it didn't bear thinking about, but for a moment grisly images of the Horsemen's traditional punishment for strangers caught wandering in their valleys had flashed through his head. Soon, despite the grim expression on his uncle's face, Rokshan's burning curiosity got the better of him.

'Uncle, who is this Gandhara? Is he a good choice to be the new khagan of the Horsemen?'

'He is an ambitious young leader of the lowest valley clan who has made no secret of his desire to be khagan. He thinks he can lead his people in open rebellion against the emperor, but has no idea of the might of the imperial army. Their lines of communication would be dangerously stretched if they venture out of their valleys – a classic error of strategy in any military campaign – and they would be annihilated. He is a hot-headed fool! I have told them countless times – they will never defeat the imperial army outside their valleys: best to stay on their own ground and wait for the enemy to come to them – which they will when the emperor finally loses patience. It'll be a long, hard campaign – but a worthwhile one if it means the destruction of the imperial army and the deposing of the emperor.'

As they talked, they had veered away from the riverbank and, judging from the rising hubbub, were now making their way into what Rokshan assumed was the central meeting place of the highest valley clan.

The square was unpaved and lined on three sides by covered market stalls selling everything from vegetables and dried meat, to tack, weaponry, intricately carved statuettes of rearing horses and fearsome-looking warriors, patterned woven rugs and blankets and much more.

Goats and small pot-bellied pigs rooted around the food stalls, bleating and grunting in an excited chorus. It struck Rokshan straight away that the market didn't smell the same as the ones back in Maracanda: there were very few spices for sale – a faint smell of sweat mixed with the sharp tang of leather and earthy smell of vegetables hung in the air.

He started to head for a stall selling wooden balls and skittles and curious-looking sticks with streamers of brightly coloured twine, but Zerafshan grabbed his arm and, shouting to be heard above the calls of the stallholders, told him to stay close. A gang of noisy children swooped down on them, instantly recognizing that Rokshan was not from those parts, and started dancing around, poking and pulling at him.

'Enough, children — begone or I'll set the imperial army on you!' Zerafshan warned good-humouredly, flapping his arms and forging a path through. Rokshan followed in his wake, still surrounded by laughing, shouting children. A lot of people seemed to recognize his uncle, some giving little bows as they swept across the square.

'This is where your friend Cetu lives, Uncle?' Rokshan asked, glancing behind him as they headed off down a track that led to the settlement they had seen from the hills above. Zerafshan gave a little nod.

The home of the Horseman they sought was set apart, a simply constructed wooden building, larger than the other huts; the big barn door had a smaller opening that stood slightly ajar. Attached to this building was a smaller hut much like the others; a thin wisp of smoke rose from a covered opening in the roof.

'Cetu, old friend, are you there?' Zerafshan banged on the smaller door. He didn't wait for a reply and went in, motioning for Rokshan to follow. Thick, roughly hewn wooden uprights supported the front of the barn; Rokshan peered through the cross-beams into the gloomy interior. The smell of stables and horses was unmistakable, but he was disappointed to see that it was empty apart from some scrawny-looking chickens scratching about in the hay.

He followed Zerafshan down a dark, narrow passageway leading off from the barn and joined him in a smaller chamber which obviously served as bedroom, living area and kitchen all in one: a plain cot stood in one corner and a simple table with chairs occupied the centre of the room. Crouched by the fire, tending a bubbling pot suspended over a stone hearth that stretched almost the whole length of the room, was a small, wiry old man.

'Zerafshan! An unexpected guest – and you're not alone!' he said, springing up to greet them. His movements were surprisingly light and supple for a man of his years.

He had thick, white, shoulder-length hair. Perched on his head was a battered crownless hat of blue felt. His face was deeply lined and his curious, almond-shaped eyes reminded Rokshan of a cat. It was a watchful, wise face.

'My . . . nephew, Rokshan, whom I have spoken to you about,' Zerafshan murmured. They both bowed respectfully.

'Sit, boy – you are hungry? Please accept some plain cooking from an old Horseman,' Cetu said with a twinkle in his eye. Rokshan made appreciative noises – whatever it was that Cetu was cooking, it certainly didn't smell plain. The old man quickly produced some bowls, knives and bread, and without further ado they fell on what was offered them.

'Gandhara has moved very quickly – to win the support of the Plains of Jalhal'a clan is a masterstroke,' Cetu said thoughtfully, after Zerafshan had recounted what the Horsemen travelling upriver had told them. 'Have you considered you might have underestimated him, Zerafshan? There are mutterings about you, perched like a brooding eagle atop the summit—'

'*Who* are these people you speak to, Cetu? I would have you tell me,' Zerafshan railed good-humouredly. 'The people see me often as I make my way up and down the valleys.'

'Not often enough for their liking, it would seem,' the old Horseman replied benignly. 'A prophet is always forsaken in his own land, Zerafshan, even if that land is adopted – you know this is as true in the Kingdom of the Horsemen as it would be in Sogdiana,' he added shrewdly.

'Now that Rokshan is with us, we can take steps to overcome that,' Zerafshan said matter-of-factly, 'as we have discussed.'

'Indeed, we can take steps . . .' Cetu said, rubbing his chin, giving Rokshan an appraising look. 'It may take longer than we would wish – but I have warned you of this,' he added.

Rokshan returned the old Horseman's look; he didn't like the sound of this. 'What *steps* are you talking about, Uncle?' he asked, trying not to sound too concerned.

'Cetu, you are the Waymaster – tell Rokshan about the Way of the Horse.' Zerafshan got up and went over to the opening that served as a window, where he stood gazing out, leaning on his staff.

'Very well, as you wish,' Cetu murmured, clearing the bowls away. Sitting down again, he gathered himself momentarily before he spoke. 'I am a master – a guide, if you like – of the Way of the Horse. Zerafshan tells me this is barely known about in the Empire . . .' He shook his head, looking at Rokshan as if he couldn't believe this was the case.

'Very little is known about it,' Rokshan replied truthfully, 'and what little we do know consists of old wives' tales about savage initiation rites that few young Horsemen survive – that sort of thing.'

'The Way of the Horse is testing, but it is not *savage*.' Cetu laughed. 'There are three paths that make up the Way,' he went on. 'The path of horsemanship – in which all the skills of the saddle are taught and, more importantly, the lore of the Horseman in knowing the mind of his mount. The second path is that of marksmanship with the bow and fighting with the short javelin – we are renowned for our prowess with both in battle. But the third path . . .' Cetu paused, searching for the right words. 'The third path can only be shown; it cannot be taught . . . and not all are required to be shown it.'

'Which path is that?' Rokshan asked, intrigued.

'It is what men look for whenever they turn to a leader for guidance and inspiration.' Cetu's eyes narrowed. 'If you do not possess it naturally, then it must be earned – through bravery, or sacrifice. Zerafshan . . . he has the gift of leadership, and he has also earned our respect and, in many cases, our loyalty too—'

'By standing up to the emperor?' Rokshan said, glancing towards his uncle.

'Yes, that – and of course his military campaigns for the emperor, which we heard of in our valleys. He has persuaded us that we can win our freedom by fighting, here in our own territory, and be rid at last of the accursed tribute we have to pay to the emperor: this is the vision your uncle has promised will come about; only he can achieve it for us, not Gandhara. Gandhara does not have the experience, despite what he may tell you.'

'How long does it take to complete the Way of the Horse?' Rokshan asked.

'Some say it is never finished, until the day we die,' Cetu replied, 'but that is philosophers' talk. All the children of our people learn the first two paths, starting as soon as they're old enough to ride a horse. I observe, encourage, offer guidance whenever it is needed – or sought.'

'So it is the third path that mainly concerns you?' Rokshan asked.

Cetu nodded. 'I do not pretend to be able to teach leadership, but for a Horseman to lead his people, he must know more than just the mind of his mount. Any skilled rider will say he understands his horse – you are a Sogdian, skilled already in horsemanship.'

'But your dragon horses are different from ordinary horses, I know that, Waymaster,' Rokshan offered humbly.

'But do you know how different, Rokshan?' Zerafshan asked suddenly, turning and coming to join them.

'Their speed, lightness of foot, and their ancestry – anyone can tell they're different, just by looking at them.' Rokshan looked at his uncle as he sat down.

Zerafshan nodded but said nothing, instead clasping his hands together and tapping them meditatively against his lips. 'Knowing the mind of your mount is one thing; being able to talk to it is quite another,' he said at last.

'Uncle . . . ?' Rokshan asked politely, as if he hadn't quite heard correctly.

'It is not so . . . *unlikely* as it sounds, if you consider their ancestry − their *true* ancestry: descendants of the first-born creatures of creation, adored by the Wise Lord, who made everything in Heaven and Earth,' Zerafshan replied. 'What they were originally − *that* part of the legend sometimes gets forgotten. You see, they have not lost what the Wise Lord granted them, such was his love for them—'

'Do you mean the gift of . . . speech, Uncle? You're saying the dragon horses − here, today − they can *talk*, like we're talking now?' Rokshan said, wide-eyed with disbelief.

'No, they do not speak like you or me, but the Horsemen can discern their feelings and emotions, and some − very few of us − can go beyond this to form a bond so strong and deep that the horse's mind opens to us − and when two minds are connected in this way − when they mindjoin, there is no need for speech. It is the purest form, the very *heart* of the Way of the Horse,' Zerafshan said, his voice tight with excitement as he leaned forward and gripped Rokshan's arm so hard it hurt. 'No other people can do this, Rokshan: it is what Cetu will teach you; it is the innermost secret of the Horsemen, guarded for centuries. It is a secret any Horseman would be prepared to lay down his life for − something you would have to be prepared to die for.'

'*Die* for?' Rokshan was incredulous. 'Why should I die for a secret that until now I've known nothing about? I'm not a Horseman; I haven't learned any parts of this Way of theirs.'

'Zerafshan assures me that your horsemanship is good, for one who isn't of our people.' Cetu gave a little shrug. 'This can be improved. As for skill with the bow and lance, even my old arms can still wield the weapons for which we are famed throughout the Empire well enough to impart my skill.' He chuckled.

'Cetu . . . *Waymaster*, forgive me, but are you mad too?' Rokshan burst out, unable to contain himself. 'What you're talking about must take years to master, especially as I haven't completed the other two paths. I'm *not* a Horseman' – he looked at Zerafshan – 'and never will be.' He paused, then went on more calmly, 'Just as you'll never be one of them, Uncle, however much you may think they accept you. Can you *mind-speak*, or whatever you call it? Even if I wanted to, why do you want me to learn this Way of the Horse in the first place? Surely there are other young Horsemen who are already well practised in it?'

'Three good questions that occurred to you just as soon you'd gained control of yourself – that's good, Rokshan,' Zerafshan replied encouragingly, 'because control over your emotions is vital if you are to succeed in the Way.'

'If I am to succeed? Why do you assume I'm going to even *attempt* it, Uncle?' Rokshan asked.

'Unless you do, the Horsemen will never accept me as their leader. And if I do not lead them, they will be destroyed. Think, Rokshan! The emperor will have succeeded – I cannot allow that. For that reason alone, you must attempt the Way.' Zerafshan's tone was steely.

And as Rokshan began to think a little more clearly, he was surprised to feel a growing sense of excitement. What if he succeeded in this Way of theirs? Imagine what it would be like to join minds with a horse, he told himself – it'd be like *becoming* one of them, a magnificent dragon horse! He recalled the dragon horses in Maracanda and the sense of yearning oneness that had come over him. And just now, when he saw the young children being taught their riding skills . . . His heart started to beat faster at the prospect of what his uncle and Cetu were talking about – but he needed to find out more.

'Why will the Horsemen not accept you as their leader unless I do it?' he asked.

Zerafshan was about to reply but then paused, glancing at Cetu, who shook his head ever so slightly, before he answered.

'The reason is simple. The visions imparted to me by the Collar of the Horseman are clear – that it is I who should lead them in their fight for freedom. But I cannot mindjoin – my visions are so powerful that I would not be able to withstand the rigours of the mindjoin as well. In order to lead the Horsemen, the khagan-to-be must have the absolute confidence of his peers that he is advanced enough in the Way of the Horse to be able to mindjoin with Stargazer, who is their lord of the horses. As I cannot do this without losing my mind, you will do it in my place; in so doing you will become the khagan-elect and finally khagan when you have reached your manhood, at sixteen years. Until that time I will rule in your place, and lead the Horsemen to freedom.'

Rokshan blinked in stunned disbelief.

'It is not a question of choice, Rokshan; this is your path,' Zerafshan continued matter-of-factly. 'Do the stars themselves deceive us? No, they cannot; it is impossible. You and I, our paths are inseparable, our destinies intertwined – the charts that plot the movements of the stars prove this. Just think back, not so long ago, to Maracanda, when you saw the imperial messengers and the dragon horses they rode – they moved you, didn't they? They stirred up feelings so strong you didn't know what had come over you, did you?'

'How do you know this?' Rokshan asked quietly, fear suddenly clutching at his guts. What else might his uncle know?

'Sometimes the Collar gives me visions of the utmost clarity; sometimes it allows me to glimpse the future;

sometimes it enables me to' – Zerafshan cast around for the right words – 'to be with someone in mind and soul, experiencing, if only for a few short seconds, what they are seeing and feeling.'

'You were with me in Maracanda, in my mind?'

'Yes, as sudden as a flash of lightning – but in that brief moment I shared with you what you were feeling. Imagine!'

Zerafshan suddenly got up from the table and stood behind Rokshan, his hands softly kneading his temples as if trying to coax the memory out.

'Imagine yourself back in the intensity of that moment in Maracanda; now multiply it by a hundred times and you will have just an inkling of what it will feel like when you see Stargazer for the first time – you will want only one thing at that moment: to be joined and of one mind with the most noble and beautiful creature that the Wise Lord has ever created. Then, Rokshan, in all truth I say to you – you will know you were born for that moment!'

CHAPTER 26

THE THIRD VALLEY

A stillness descended on the room. Even the noise from the market seemed to have faded, and the fire was reduced to dying embers.

It seemed to Rokshan that he didn't really have any option but to go along, for the moment, with what his uncle proposed – and the more he thought about it, the more exciting it seemed. The Waymaster seemed kindly enough – tough too, but he had a wisdom that Rokshan felt drawn to. His mind was still whirling at the thought of somehow being able to communicate with the dragon horses.

'Choosing our leader has never been done this way before, and it took much persuasion on the part of your uncle before he convinced me, but' – Cetu's eyes narrowed – 'if the alternative is defeat, then tradition has to make way for expediency, and we must move with the times. I am with Zerafshan in this.'

He got up and gave Rokshan a reassuring pat on the shoulder as he went to put some logs on the fire. He took a battered leather flask from a stone ledge above the hearth and poured a tawny-coloured drink into wooden tumblers.

'Drink it,' he said, offering one to Rokshan. 'Fortified wine from the best red grapes of Kocho; it will fire your spirit.'

It smelled strong. Rokshan wrinkled his nose as he raised it to his lips, remembering the delicate, fragrant white wine from the same grape – his father's favourite – that he had drunk at their last family supper in Maracanda; it seemed a lifetime ago. He wasn't sure whether it was the fearsomely strong drink or the memory of that supper that made his eyes water.

He coughed violently and sniffed cautiously at his tumbler, catching Cetu's eye. 'Laced with barleyfire, to give you inner strength.' The old Horseman grinned.

Rokshan grimaced back; barleyfire was a well-known and widely traded spirit, distilled from barley with the robust flavours of juniper and sloe berries to mask its ferocious strength, but he had never come across it mixed with wine before.

Zerafshan took a deep draught and then raised his tumbler to them. 'To the Way of the Horse, the pupil and the master. Come, Cetu! Why don't you start straight away. There is much to do. If Gandhara is already being seen as the khagan-elect, I must speak with the other clan leaders on our way to the plains. We must delay no longer.'

Cetu nodded in agreement. 'We'll show Rokshan something of the different lore of each of the clans as we make our way down,' he said.

Zerafshan smacked his hands together, a satisfied smile on his face. 'It is agreed then! Let's be on our way.'

Cetu gave a nod, and without another word Zerafshan left the room.

'There is just enough daylight left for us to reach the settlement of flax-gatherers, where we can pass the night,' Cetu said, looking Rokshan up and down. 'If you are to learn the life of a Horseman, you must dress like one – an old friend of mine there will have something for you.' He shrugged on his coat and headed down the little passageway after Zerafshan.

Rokshan joined him outside, jumping in surprise as Cetu suddenly gave a piercing whistle. As if from nowhere, a beautiful chestnut mare cantered up to them. He gazed with wonder at the brilliant-white winged serpent emblazoned on her forehead. The three dark stripes on her back rippled with easy supple movement. Her dark-green eyes, flecked with gold, held him deep in her gaze, then, with a toss of her head and a little whinny of approval, she shook her long silken mane and flicked her tail excitedly, as if she recognized him.

'Seems like she knows you already,' Cetu said, holding the reins and murmuring something in her ear in a language Rokshan did not recognize. 'Her name is Breeze Whisperer,' he said encouragingly as Rokshan made friends with her by stroking her neck and muzzle and talking in a quiet friendly voice. She tossed her head and blew appreciatively in response to the attention. Inexplicably, all the tension of the last few days suddenly seemed to melt away, and Rokshan felt a deep joy, as if he had been reunited with someone he loved but hadn't seen for a long time.

'She is ready for you.' Cetu smiled, cupping his hands.

Rokshan nodded eagerly and, putting his foot in the makeshift stirrup, jumped as lightly as he could onto the mare's back. In one swift, easy motion, the old Horseman settled himself in front of him. Zerafshan now reappeared, mounted on a beautiful black stallion; Rokshan noticed the ease with which his uncle handled him. A long sheath, which usually carried the Horsemen's short javelin, housed his staff.

'Breeze Whisperer . . . it's a beautiful name!' Rokshan said as they set off.

'You like it?' Cetu half turned in the saddle. 'She is as light to ride as the soft summer wind in our valleys, and she comes and goes as she pleases.'

As they made their way down, people shouted greetings to them. Some called Cetu by name, while others made hurried bows as they recognized Zerafshan. Rokshan attracted some curious stares but he wasn't bothered by them – his heart was bursting at the thrill of riding a dragon horse.

The rhythm of Breeze Whisperer's effortless canter had a

mesmerizing effect: he could feel a pulsing energy deep within her and longed to be able to unlock and possess it for himself. He was sure he felt a current pass between him and the beautiful mare; stranger still, just occasionally he caught flashes of this current as a rainbow of colours, shimmering through his head like a heat haze – it was so quick and faint he couldn't tell if he was imagining it.

He closed his eyes and, as the colours became stronger, let himself fade into them. He marvelled at the wonder of it and wished it would never end. Cetu had been very quiet throughout the ride. Reluctantly opening his eyes again, Rokshan noticed with a start that the day was drawing to a close: the setting sun painted the sky with smudges of reds and pinks edged with silver. As the colours he'd felt also began to fade, Rokshan wondered what they could mean. As if she'd read his thoughts, Breeze Whisperer tossed her head and whinnied loudly, making both him and Cetu laugh.

They had been following the course of the river as it wound its way down; as they rounded a bend, they saw the village nestling in the fold of the valley. It was bigger than the others they had passed through – Rokshan counted four barn-like buildings, all larger than Cetu's. A patchwork of long narrow fields were dotted with piles of yellowy brown fibrous plants, waiting to be gathered in. In the twilight, women made their way from one pile to the next, cramming as many of the plants as they could into the baskets strapped to their backs.

'What are they harvesting, so late in the season?' Rokshan asked curiously.

'These are the flax-gatherers I spoke of,' Cetu said. 'They are bringing in the last crop. It'll make good twine; the best will be woven into linen.'

A group of young children came rushing out of the village to greet them. Rokshan was amazed to see they were all mounted, bareback, on small ponies. Six or seven of them careered towards them, whooping and shouting as they recognized Cetu. Three even younger children were mounted behind them, trailing long streamers of multicoloured twine attached to sticks, swishing and flicking them and shouting to each other, completely absorbed in the game.

As they approached, Rokshan noticed with a start that what he'd taken to be small ponies were in fact young dragon-horse colts. They seemed to sense straight away that he was a stranger but were unabashed in their curiosity as they blew noisily to each other and tried to nuzzle him. Breeze Whisperer whinnied an admonishment and tossed her head, signalling for the colts to behave as they should to a stranger.

'Cetu, Cetu!' piped one of the younger children. 'Look at my dragon-fire!'

'Look at mine – it's much hotter!' squealed another as they set to, bashing each other with the long sticks.

'Children . . . children!' Cetu laughed. 'Your dragon-fire is like a furnace – you'll burn each other if you're not careful, and your mothers will send you to bed with no supper if they see you fighting. Peace!' He held up his hands in mock alarm and the younger children cantered off, laughing and chattering, leaving the old Waymaster shaking his head in amused exasperation.

'The string-sticks, Uncle . . . I noticed some for sale in the market, just like the ones the children were playing with,' Rokshan said, wanting to understand the game.

'They make them here in the Fourth Valley,' Zerafshan replied, trotting beside him. 'All the children play with them, pretending it is the dragon-fire of their horses' ancestors. Cetu says playing games like that prepares them for reading the minds of their mounts as they grow older, teaching them to think in the colours of their horses' feelings.'

'A sort of alphabet of colours, you mean?'

'You could think of it like that – all Horsemen can do it.

Getting beyond that is a real test – a gift granted to few; a gift I believe you possess, deep within you: only a Waymaster of Cetu's skill and experience can draw it out – and draw it out he will. He – you – must succeed in this.'

Tiny seeds of hope and self-belief had been growing in Rokshan following the strange, wonderful feelings he'd experienced riding Breeze Whisperer. Was that the beginning of the union of minds between human and horse they'd spoken about? he wondered. Maybe he could do this after all.

But as he heard the stern finality in his uncle's voice, Rokshan's optimism evaporated, and he wondered gloomily how he was expected to catch up with children who had been born with this ability.

And then the voice of the abbot and the Prophecy of the Prince came floating back to him – and fear and doubt began to gnaw further at his fragile confidence. Would the Elect want him to follow Zerafshan and do his bidding, as he had agreed to? The abbot had claimed that his uncle had chosen to be a prince of darkness, but how? Zerafshan was determined to lead the Horsemen in their fight for freedom against a despotic emperor: surely this was the path of righteousness, fighting for a just cause?

As his mind grappled with all these concerns, Rokshan determined to put them to one side and concentrate on learning the Way of the Horse – or as much as he could in the time he had; somehow he knew that everything, in the end, might depend on this.

CHAPTER 27

CETU'S SECRET

'Draw the arrow between your forefinger and middle finger!
What's your thumb doing – saying hello? Tuck it into the
palm!' Cetu barked at him.

After only three days, Rokshan's bow fingers were agony;
he grimaced as he doggedly followed Cetu's orders. While
Zerafshan had galloped off to meet with the clan leaders,
Rokshan and Cetu had sought out the Waymaster's friend, who
had given Rokshan a long Horsemen's coat, which he wore
over a thick wool waistcoat and leggings; these, along with the
lightweight but sturdy boots and fur-lined, conical leather hat,
made him feel that at least he *looked* like a Horseman now.

In the Third Valley their day began at dawn each day, alter-
nating between training with javelin and bow. Cetu was
working on Rokshan's riding techniques at the same time, as
the weapons were used on horseback. He'd had to work hard
– the Waymaster wanted the basic levels of the Way mastered
before the Dragon Festival, when those select Horsemen who
had the backing of their clans staked their claim to be the new
khagan.

Cetu seemed satisfied with his pupil's progress, especially
his improved riding skills. 'Not bad, for a Sogdian merchant's
son,' he teased one morning.

Rokshan was feeling particularly pleased with himself;
he'd just completed a successful run of the rings. This involved
hooking his javelin through a succession of wooden rings
which Cetu had set up over a distance of about half a li. It had

to be done at full gallop and, because the javelins were barely longer than a man's arm, involved leaning right out of the saddle in order to reach the rings.

'That was with your good arm; now go the other way, using your left arm,' Cetu instructed him.

Rokshan protested, asking yet again when they were going to start on the mindjoining.

'Has it not occurred to you that all this practice serves another purpose besides that of weapons training?' Cetu was making his way up the course he'd set, patiently replacing the rings on their posts.

'How is that?' Rokshan asked, leaning over on Breeze Whisperer and handing him a ring.

'All the time you have been riding Breeze Whisperer, doing the exercises, she has been forming a bond with you. Your mind has been focused completely on what you have been tasked to do – as it has to be. She understands that singularity of purpose, and uses it to help you perform the exercises better than you normally would by anticipating your every need. Weren't you especially pleased at what you did just now?'

'Yes, of course.'

Cetu shrugged his shoulders as if it was obvious. 'Breeze Whisperer knows this, and will strive to help you perform even better next time.'

'I understand . . . I think,' Rokshan said, a little doubtfully. 'But I thought it was the other way round: she is meant to be opening her mind so that I can discern her emotions.'

'This is what they all think – all the young boys. You are no different. Now, the girls . . . that is a different matter. Somehow – and in all my years as Waymaster, I am still not able to explain it fully – but somehow all the girls under my tutelage seem to have known this intuitively, grasping it straight away.'

'Grasp what?' Rokshan asked, feeling stupid.

'That before dragon horses will lay themselves open to human contact, they will want to know *your* mind before letting you into theirs. Seems exactly the right way round to me.'

'But Cetu, I think Breeze Whisperer has done this already!' Rokshan exclaimed excitedly, telling him about the strong currents that had passed between him and the Waymaster's mount when he'd first ridden her.

Cetu nodded. 'I felt it too, but I didn't want to press you on it. She was attracted to you from the start, my young friend. There are plenty of young Horsemen – and women – who never experience such a feeling, certainly not with the strength or depth you felt it.' The Waymaster gave Rokshan an appraising look, as he had done increasingly these last few days: never had he known such a bond develop so quickly between pupil and horse; he knew he'd have to take extra care in directing and channelling the precious gift his young charge seemed to have.

Rokshan was oblivious to this: it seemed so natural to him, and he was growing increasingly impatient to mindjoin with his mount. Now seemed the right moment to ask the question he was increasingly desperate to know the answer to. 'So, my uncle . . . could he . . . did he know the mind of his mount at any level?'

'He was able to discern certain feelings from the stream of colours you can see like a raging torrent, once your mount permits you to delve into this level of their consciousness . . . but I warned him to go no further.'

'You . . . warned him *not* to? Why?'

They were almost at the start of the course again; Cetu seemed strangely reluctant to answer, but Rokshan felt he had to know and pressed the Waymaster, who sighed and leaned his head against the dragon horse as he stroked her neck.

'When I warned him, it was because I had already seen

how the Collar affected him: he believes – as do I – that it gives him a clear vision of the future.'

'What glimpse of the future did he see, Cetu? Tell me about this Collar.' Rokshan was burning with curiosity now.

'It is something you should hear from his lips, though I know that every time he wore the Collar of the old khaghan it was the same . . .'

'What, Cetu? What did he see?' Rokshan asked, bursting to know the answer.

'A noise like a rushing wind envelops him and bears him away to a dry, dusty plain that stretches away on all sides. The sun blazes mercilessly, beating down on the massed ranks of Horsemen stretching to the shimmering, heat-hazed horizon – there are tens of thousands of us, he says. Your uncle sits astride a magnificent grey that must surely be Stargazer, lord of the horses, even though he has seen him only once, from afar. He thumps his fist on his breast in salute, and a deafening noise like a hundred thunderclaps echoes across the plain as the vast army of Horsemen return his salute, accompanied by a deep-throated roar: "Hail, Zerafshan, khagan of the Horsemen!" '

'And it is always the same, this . . . dream?' Rokshan asked quietly, imagining himself on that dusty plain.

'Always. No other Horseman, khagan or not, has ever had the same vision, repeated over and over . . . Which is why some of us attach such significance to it. By the same token, I did not think that his mind, or the mind of his dragon horse, would be able to withstand the strength of two charges, one from the mindjoining of the deepest part of the Way, and the other from wearing the Collar.'

'I understand. So, this mindjoining . . . it really can be dangerous?' Rokshan asked.

'Sometimes fatal,' Cetu said quietly. 'Mindjoining cannot be measured like water in a jug, or like mixing barleyfire with wine. It can sometimes be . . . misjudged, so that the mind of the person attempting it becomes trapped and intertwined with that of the dragon horse – and remember, these are creatures whose ancestors have been touched by the divine spirit. By all accounts it is a terrible experience: one minute you feel in the depths of your soul that you are trapped in an uncontrollable maelstrom of minds, and then you are suddenly free. Except . . . you are not free . . .'

'What do you mean, *not free?*'

'Because the experience has been so painful at such a deep level of your consciousness, you are left with horribly distorted perceptions: the sound of a pebble being tapped on a rock will assault your ears like a hundred thunderclaps, reverberating up to the sky and then streaming back down to earth like liquid silver. Some imagined they were gods who can capture the wind – I have known men throw themselves off cliff tops in their madness. As for the horses . . .' Cetu shook his head.

'Do the dragon horses suffer when this happens?'

'Perhaps more so . . . They have seen the darkest, innermost secrets of a man's mind, and it drives them mad too. They are shunned by others of their kind, and they slowly starve themselves to death. When we can, we end it quickly for them.'

There was a silence between them. What he'd just heard excited but also appalled Rokshan.

'When I was about your age . . .' Cetu started, but fell silent, a sad, faraway look in his eyes as he gazed past Rokshan.

'Do not speak of it, Cetu, if it pains you.' Rokshan was shocked to see the old Waymaster so affected by this memory; he had obviously kept it locked deep within his heart.

'No, you should know . . . My father was stricken in this way as he probed and delved, seeking the heart of the Way. Such was his love for his mount that he was convinced that their bond would allow him to be one with its mind, and he would know pure communion with a creature that carries within its soul a part of the spirit of the Wise Lord. Perhaps their love for each other was too great – I don't know – but it turned my father into a raving madman. In a brief moment of lucidity, he begged me to put an end to his misery, and his mount too . . .'

'And . . . did you?' Rokshan was almost too horrified to ask.

'Yes. My mother never forgave me, and sometimes I think Breeze Whisperer thinks worse of me for doing what I did.'

'Breeze Whisperer?'

'My father's mount was her grandsire, Storm Gatherer.'

'Storm Gatherer? That is the name of my uncle's dragon horse.'

'Yes; he is named after his grandsire. Storm Gatherer and Breeze Whisperer – they are brother and sister. From that moment I resolved to become a Waymaster so I could stop what befell my father happening to others. I could only do this if I became the very best judge of a horse and its rider. So for many years I trod the path of the Way – many times, with many different masters. Eventually one of them judged that I had attained an understanding such that I could teach it to others.'

Rokshan looked at Cetu with renewed respect and, he suddenly realized, a deep affection. 'This is why you never put yourself forward to be your people's khagan?' It was another question Rokshan had wanted to ask him.

'Me?' Cetu laughed but Rokshan detected a vein of sadness there. 'Perhaps I am too old now, but, yes, I have made it my life's work to teach others, not lead them.'

'I will not let you down, Waymaster,' Rokshan said humbly and with as much determination as he could muster.

'These are brave words, Rokshan.' Cetu gave him a searching look. 'Zerafshan will already be at the Second Valley and we will now join him there. Gandhara's people in the First Valley tame the wild spirit of the dragon horses just enough to prepare them for the first touch of the rider on their backs – this is the lore of the people of the Second Valley, where the young dragon horses arrive, fresh from the First. Breeze Whisperer will be greatly excited to see her young cousins, still with a little wildness left in them: the yin and yang of the spirit of our dragon horses reflects the balance of the universe – wildness opposing control, control opposing wildness; the two opposites make one whole . . .' Cetu mused on this a while as he stroked Breeze Whisperer's muzzle. 'And with her emotions at such a pitch of excitement, we will see if she will let you share her feelings,' he added, almost absently.

'Happiness, you mean?' Rokshan asked hesitantly.

'The distilled essence of happiness. Pure joy, my young friend; pure joy.' Cetu clapped his hands together. 'Enough talk! I want to see you do the javelin rings again – with your left hand this time. Mount up!'

'But I wanted you to tell me about the Collar – where did it come from, and how does it get its power?'

Breeze Whisperer, who had been waiting patiently, whickered excitedly and tossed her head.

'Come, my young friend, even Breeze Whisperer agrees – more practice! She loves to work with young riders. More practice and then I'll tell you.' Cetu slapped Breeze Whisperer's haunches before Rokshan could protest any more.

With one bound, she was away; within just a few moments she had reached a full gallop and the first of the rings was coming up fast.

Left arm, Rokshan thought; I must get in close . . . As if she'd read his mind and before he'd even nudged her flank with his heel, he felt Breeze Whisperer correct her line of approach so they would almost brush the short pole as they galloped by.

Judging it carefully, he leaned out of the saddle and, looking down its length as he'd been taught, lined the javelin up with the exact centre of the ring. He felt Breeze Whisperer slow imperceptibly for the hook and marvelled at the oneness he felt with her when they had to work closely on exercises such as this.

Just as he was about to stab with the javelin, Breeze Whisperer veered to the right. Rokshan lunged wildly but missed the ring by an arm's length and almost fell out of the saddle, struggling to regain his seat.

'What're you doing?' he shouted as Breeze Whisperer trotted about, flicking her tail and shaking her head. 'We're meant to be going down the line!' He dismounted and flung the javelin down in disgust as Cetu came up, chuckling.

'I don't see what's so funny,' Rokshan muttered, glowering at him.

'But you said you'd had enough practice with the javelin; Breeze Whisperer is just agreeing with you, that's all!' Cetu took her bridle and whispered some soft words of command to her. 'Come' – he held out his arm – 'she is impatient to see her cousins in the next valley. I'll tell you why, if you make it up with her. I'll collect the rings.'

Rokshan laughed, finally seeing the funny side of it. He stroked Breeze Whisperer's velvety muzzle and spoke gently to her while Cetu gathered up the rings and packed them safely away in the saddlebag. As Breeze Whisperer tossed her head again, a dazzling flash of colours streamed through his head and he leaped back in shocked surprise. 'You *are* impatient, aren't you?' He laughed, a little nervously at first, but then grinned broadly as he realized that Breeze Whisperer was beginning to share more of her thoughts with him. Suddenly he too was seized by an urgent need to be going and had to stop himself from shouting at Cetu to make haste.

As they cantered off, Cetu said the words his pupil had most wanted to hear:

'Soon you will experience what it is to really know the first levels of the mind of your mount. You are ready.'

CHAPTER 28

THE SECOND VALLEY

After a day and a night they reached the Second Valley. The long narrow corral that penned in the dragon horses stretched almost its entire length; even from where they stood at the head of the valley, the dust thrown up as they galloped from one end to the other got into Rokshan's eyes.

In the corral the Horsemen expertly split the herd into groups of three or four and guided them towards one of three exits leading into smaller pens. Breeze Whisperer whinnied and pranced excitedly, shaking her head this way and that.

'What're they doing?' Rokshan asked, tearing his eyes away from the spectacle and trying unsuccessfully to calm Breeze Whisperer.

'They're selecting the mounts who will be most easily led and preparing them for the first touch of the saddle, and then a rider, on their backs. And they are looking in particular for white mares without any markings on their backs.'

Rokshan nodded, wondering what was special about the white mares. 'But how can they tell one from the other in all that chaos?'

'It is their lore. These Horsemen have developed their senses to a point where they can recognize in every dragon horse the colour notes that signal their temperament and disposition. They can distinguish between those whose nature is headstrong and unruly, or nervous and flighty, and those which are calmer, more placid and biddable.'

'The colours tell them all that?' Rokshan said, amazed.

'What then is the colour of the placid, more biddable ones?'

'A deep, deep bluish maroon, running like the bedrock of a river under the torrent of all their other feelings. They would see it instantly in Breeze Whisperer.'

'Let me try now, Cetu – please! I want to see her happiness, as you described it. How can it harm me?'

'Patience, my young friend, patience. First we must find Zerafshan. He said to meet us here. Come, Breeze Whisperer – she will grow more excited the nearer we get to the corral.'

They headed towards the low-roofed huts at the end of the valley with the corral to their left. As they approached, Rokshan felt the current of anticipation running through Breeze Whisperer. The thunder of hooves and explosive cracks of the Horsemen's whips as they marshalled the dragon horses mixed together in an intoxicating swirl of noise and dust. The Horsemen shouted to each other, pointing out individual mounts and expertly separating them before driving them towards the smaller pens.

Rokshan and Cetu were now riding alongside the herd, separated only by a stout wooden fence, just high enough to stop them jumping over. Breeze Whisperer started her prancing again and Cetu suddenly leaned forward, whispered in her ear and then nimbly dismounted.

Rokshan lunged for the reins in panic. 'What are you doing, Cetu?' he shouted in alarm.

'Give her her head – let her go, Rokshan! Open your mind and swim with the current . . . Do not fight against it!'

Rokshan only just heard the last of the Waymaster's instructions: Breeze Whisperer needed no further encouragement and shot forward. Within a few seconds she was at full gallop, her long mane streaming in the wind and flicking him in the eyes; they were going so fast it felt like her hooves were barely touching the ground. Rokshan gripped with his legs until they ached and prayed he wouldn't fall off. Now Breeze

Whisperer settled into her stride and turned to look at the dragon horses galloping alongside her on the other side of the fence; Rokshan was still concentrating hard on staying on, but he swore he could see the gold flecks in her left eye pulsing with stars as she raced along, whinnying an ecstatic greeting to her cousins from the plains.

He glanced away and realized he was no longer hanging on for dear life: *Open your mind . . . swim with the current* − Cetu's words rang in his head. He didn't know how to open his mind, so he tried shutting his eyes, and again he saw the stars shimmering in Breeze Whisperer's eyes.

Before he realized what was happening, he felt a strong current sweeping him down a long dark tunnel. At the end of it he could hear a roaring and tumbling of water, like a waterfall. Now he was being dragged along as if by a swollen river, except that he was being pummelled not by water but by colours that pulsated in deepest shades of green, blue and yellow, while stars of purple with dazzling haloes of silver exploded all around him.

'Breeze Whisperer!' he yelled with joy. 'I can *see* your happiness . . . I've never been so happy . . .' He rolled over and over in the colours as they embraced him, drenching him so thoroughly that he didn't notice they were pulling him down, deeper and deeper into the current.

Then he felt himself being yanked back, as if by a lasso, and he hit the ground − so hard it jolted him painfully back to reality.

'Awake! Go no further!'

Was that Cetu's voice? he wondered. It didn't sound like Cetu.

'Rokshan!'

He was coughing and spluttering as if he'd nearly drowned. Groggily he tried to focus, and the curious, un-smiling faces of two young Horsemen swam into view.

'Where's Cetu? What happened?' he said, his voice sounding strangely far away.

'About two li further down the valley where you left him. He said your horse had run away with you and asked us to catch up with you.'

'Run away? No . . . I . . .' Rokshan was unsure about telling these two strangers what he'd just experienced. 'Thank you,' he said gratefully as the younger one offered him his water pouch.

'Seeing your first deep mind-colours can be disorientating,' the Horseman observed carefully, taking back the pouch with a nod. 'Cetu told us you were attempting it for the first time. He expected Breeze Whisperer to double back towards him once she'd reached the end of the corral, but she just kept on going.'

'Even a venerable old Waymaster can sometimes get things wrong,' his companion joked.

'But isn't it the most exciting thing in the world!' Rokshan exclaimed.

'You will always remember the first time, until the day you die,' the older Horseman replied matter-of-factly. 'And now we have work to do. We'll lead you back – are you strong enough? Your mount tried to let you down gently but you fell off with a bump.'

Rokshan did indeed feel a little shaky. He got up and limped over to Breeze Whisperer, who was now grazing calmly and contentedly nearby. Almost immediately he detected a change in their relationship: he was no longer the raw novice; it was like a faint aura that surrounded them, and within it he sensed a warmer connection and a mutual respect.

They made their way back to where Cetu was patiently waiting for them, a small speck way across the valley. Rokshan felt an overwhelming sense of contentment steal over him.

'Cetu said you are kinsman to Zerafshan, the soothsayer?'

the younger Horseman asked as they approached the Waymaster. Rokshan nodded.

'He must feel the loss of our dead khagan keenly,' the other said.

'Why?' Rokshan asked, suddenly alert.

'He was of the Fifth Valley clan, and in his old age spent much time secluded with your kinsman in his hut on the summit, and in the temple. He was fascinated by Zerafshan's knowledge of the stars, and what they can tell us; he believed they foretold the coming of your kinsman among us, and he allowed him to wear the sacred Collar. No other khagan would have permitted this.'

The Horsemen held their fists to their hearts as they came alongside Cetu, then peeled away to rejoin their companions in the corral.

'May the dragon spirits be with you, Rokshan. We will see you at the festival,' they called back.

'My thanks – and with you!' he shouted after them.

'Well?' Cetu demanded, hurrying up to him, taking Breeze Whisperer's reins and murmuring quietly to her as Rokshan jumped down.

Rokshan described in detail his sense of being completely enveloped in torrents of colour as he was drawn into the first layers of Breeze Whisperer's mind.

'These were just the topmost levels you encountered, like a river splashing and tumbling in shallow rapids which suddenly deepen and become treacherous, full of swirling eddies and currents. This was the submerging sensation you felt, but it was not deliberate – you just didn't know to look out for it, that's all. Next time you will recognize the feeling straight away.'

'And when I do, what then?'

'Stay alert. Be in control. Allow yourself to be pulled down into the deeper layers but be conscious of what is happening.

You were so ecstatic at what you were experiencing for the first time, you were almost overcome by emotion . . . *Breeze Whisperer's* emotions. I have seen it happen before, many times. This may be a young Horseman's only experience of mind-joining: he may too frightened to try it again – but there is no shame in that.'

Rokshan wondered about this as they left the dust and noise of the corral behind them and made their way towards the village. He felt proud to have started mindjoining and was filled with a steely determination to tread the deeper, inner path to the very heart of the Way. He felt Breeze Whisperer tense momentarily beneath him, as if reflecting his newfound deter-mination – a swirl of maroon tinged with a resolute shade of cobalt grey filled his mind as he tried to offer his thanks for her encouragement and for letting him join with her. In response, Breeze Whisperer whinnied loudly and tossed her head, and his heart filled with love and pride; he knew he had her whole-hearted devotion.

A cold wind was blowing and Rokshan was just thinking how ravenously hungry he was when he saw his uncle cantering out towards them on Storm Gatherer.

Drawing in beside them, he enquired after their progress, nodding as he took in Cetu's detailed description of everything they'd covered over the last few days, including his mind-joining with Breeze Whisperer.

'Excellent, Rokshan! Cetu will make a Horseman of you yet,' Zerafshan joked, patting Breeze Whisperer's neck and smiling at him. 'Now, we must make haste,' he said urgently, spurring Storm Gatherer forward.

A freezing drizzle began to fall as the horses broke effort-lessly into a gallop, hurrying towards the First Valley, and the Festival of the Dragon.

Chapter 29

The Festival of the Dragon

The sleet had turned to driving rain as they made their way down. Now well below the tree line, they had decided to take shelter in the thick woodland that stretched away on both sides of the valley, offering protection from the worst of the deluge.

'So, you are pleased with your progress in the Way?' Zerafshan asked Rokshan, leaning forward to coax a flame from a pile of kindling.

'Yes, I think I've made a good start, but . . .'

'But it'll take far longer than you hoped it would, because you now have an inkling of how difficult it is,' Zerafshan finished. 'It is only natural to think like that when we embark on something that seems so arduous and challenging – it's frightening, and we want to back away from it. Do you remember when I visited the family in Maracanda once and you were terrified of riding my warhorse? With a little coaxing and cajoling from me – and your mother – you screwed up your courage, and there! You did it.'

'Of course I remember – it was one of the proudest moments of my life.'

'You couldn't have been more than seven or eight years old . . .' Zerafshan was silent as they both recalled the memory. 'I had exactly the same feeling as that little seven-year-old boy when the old khagan allowed me to wear the Collar of the Horseman for the first time,' he continued quietly, staring into space, then exclaimed suddenly, 'Fear! How it corrodes the soul.'

'The old khagan must have trusted you greatly to allow you to do that,' Rokshan said, seeing his chance to find out more about the Collar. 'How did the Horsemen come by it, and why is it so sacred?'

'There are in fact two Collars. No one knows their true origins – who made them, and why. But I can tell you what we learn as children, at our mothers' knees,' Cetu said, who had been listening intently while he prepared what little food they had; he positioned a pot on some stones over the fire.

'Long ago, when the Horsemen roamed wild and free across all Known and Unknown Lands, they chanced upon the two Collars; they discovered that one of them worked a magic on the wearer – a magic that can drain weaker men of all reason with visions of such beauty. The magic was so strong, our ancestors called it the divine Collar of the Wise Lord. Only this one is ever worn by the living: the one in the possession of our khagans – and your uncle.' Cetu tasted the food and nodded appreciatively to himself before continuing. 'Guided by the visions, the Horsemen gradually stopped their wanderings, and settled here – the green valleys you passed through on your way up to the summit mark the borders of our kingdom. You can serve it now . . .'

Rokshan looked blankly at him.

'The food – it's ready!' Cetu chuckled.

'What about the other Collar?' Rokshan asked, spooning out the rich dried meat and fruit stew. Cetu had added the traditional curd biscuits to thicken it. To wash it down, he tossed over a leather bottle of water.

'Ah, the second, lesser Collar – we call it the Collar of the Dead.' Cetu slurped hungrily at the surprisingly tasty stew. 'Well, this Collar gave no earthly visions, so the Horsemen of old dedicated it to the dead, to help them on their long journey into night. Our ancestors thought the lesser Collar might be used by the dead in a way that we, the living, could not hope to understand. It is worn by each khagan when he is laid to rest in the Towers of Silence, on the Plain of the Dead, just like his predecessors – thus is the wisdom of generations passed on.'

'But . . . what use is wisdom that is passed on to the dead from the dead?' Rokshan asked, mystified.

'Each khagan-elect goes to pray to the spirits of the ancestors on the Plain of the Dead before he takes on the mantle of leader,' Cetu explained patiently, 'hoping that by wearing the Collar of the Dead for one night, he will receive the accumulated wisdom of centuries. He takes the Collar from the dead khagan's predecessor and puts it on; he remains there for a day and a night, before it is time for him to pass the Collar to the khagan who has just died, and rejoin the living.'

'And how is the new khagan elected?' Rokshan asked.

'Whichever clan leader wins the backing of four of the other five leaders becomes khagan-elect. As there are six clans in all, this allows for only one dissenting voice. Traditionally the successful khagan-elect will have achieved the highest level of the Way and will be expected, if called upon, to mindjoin with the lord of the horses. But many khagans never have to do this. The choice will be made at the Festival of the Dragon – here the khagan-elect will be acknowledged by the people. If nobody wins the backing they need' – Cetu shrugged – 'we wait a while – four, six, maybe even twelve cycles of the moon – until we are ready for another festival.'

He wiped his bowl clean with a piece of bread and looked at Rokshan, who was silent as he took it all in.

Zerafshan broke the silence. 'Well, whatever wisdom may have been passed on from the dead to the living in the distant past,' he said, wiping his mouth and putting his bowl aside, 'I know what the Horsemen's old leader told me had been passed on to him.'

'What was that?' Rokshan asked.

' "Here we try to live as my forebears dreamed of: at one

with the natural order of the universe – man, the Earth and all its creatures, the sky, stars, sun and moon; in a true balance of harmonious living . . ." Those were his exact words, and in time I came to realize that he, of all the Horsemen's khagans, was the visionary and prophet of his people, exhorting them to throw off the yoke of the emperor's rule and allow all people, not just the Horsemen, to live according to the old ways.'

'And the vision that the Collar gave your uncle when he wore it confirms him as the leader who will bring us victory, and our freedom,' Cetu added approvingly.

'Yes,' Zerafshan replied simply, 'and I will bring about what the old khagan foretold, if the Horsemen will allow me.'

Rokshan's mind was churning. The balance and harmony his uncle had spoken of was what the ancient priesthood of the Fellowship of the Three One-eared Hares strove towards – but they had rejected Zerafshan, and according to the abbot, his uncle was following the path of darkness. All his old fears and doubts rose to the surface, but he determined to stick to his course – he had little choice in the matter, he acknowledged grimly.

The following day the slanting dawn rays of a late autumn sun rose on the First Valley, painting it a ghostly burnished gold. Rokshan was struck by the size of the settlement, which was larger than any they'd passed through. The squat, low-roofed huts he was used to stretched all the way down the valley, rather than being clustered at one end. Wisps of smoke curled from the huts and hung in the still air of the early morning.

The large circular enclosure at the far end was surrounded by a high protective fence, and beyond that, extending as far as he could see, were the dry, dusty Plains of Jalhal'a, the fiefdom of the Plains Horsemen, cousins to the Horsemen of the valleys; these people remained aloof, considering their lore to be the most significant of all that was passed down and taught in each of the valleys. After all, they argued, they shared their land with the legendary Serenadhi, horse-singers who, alone of all the Horsemen, sing the song that reaches the souls of the wild dragon horses, turning their spirits towards man.

Rokshan's eyes were drawn towards the centre of the enclosure and an enormous wooden statue of a rearing dragon, its writhing coils so expertly crafted that it seemed eerily life-like. Like the famous golden statue at Labrang, this dragon leaped upwards with flattened wings, its head twisting round as if daring any onlooker to follow it in its flight skywards.

'It is a likeness of Han Garid, lord of the thunder dragons,' Cetu said, following his gaze, 'most powerful of all the dragons which the Wise Lord allowed to be reborn again after they had risen against Him and mankind, as the kindly spirits of nature and fire they had once been. Stargazer is directly descended from Han Garid.' He spurred Breeze Whisperer on and made his way down into the valley. 'Come, let us see what the Festival of the Dragon has to show us. People from across the valleys bring all sorts of stuff to trade and barter here – you can pick up the most excellent barleyfire!'

Already the valley was stirring with signs of life. Richly coloured circular tents had been erected around the enclosure, and people were already setting up their stalls and laying out their goods and produce in anticipation of a busy market day. Rokshan sensed Breeze Whisperer's excitement mirroring his own; he couldn't wait to go exploring.

In the crush of the festival, he soon lost Cetu, but he wasn't too concerned – there was so much to see. As the morning wore on, the enclosure came alive and Rokshan almost felt as if he was back home: it rang with the shouts and cries of the people of the different clans. Cetu was right – Rokshan lost count of the number of stallholders selling barleyfire; but he was more interested in sampling the herbs, smoked cheeses, pickled mushrooms, flavoured dried meat and wind-dried curds – all deliciously tasty compared to some of the more mouldy offerings he'd sampled travelling down the valleys.

He sampled *airag*, the salty, sour-tasting fermented milk that was the staple drink of the First Valley and Plains Horsemen – and vowed never to drink it again, wondering if he'd ever get the disgusting taste out of his mouth. He swooped on the foods he recognized and ate so many roast chestnuts he thought his stomach would burst.

The smell of meat and herbs and an even more powerful, mulled version of barleyfire hung over everything, mingling with the odour of the horse leathers that were for sale everywhere. Even bigger up close, the wooden festival dragon loomed over everything.

The influx of people steadily increased and by midday – Rokshan calculated – the enclosure was already reaching bursting point.

Escaping from the throng, he wandered through the deserted side streets, chancing on Cetu in a small tannery shop just off the main enclosure.

'Come in, boy, come in,' wheezed the shopkeeper – a short man of tremendous girth whose skin looked like he had tanned it along with all the hides that hung on the wall. The smell was sharp and pungent. 'Your Waymaster has been telling me all sorts of stories' – the tanner winked – 'some of them so tall only a Waymaster could get away with it!'

'Tall maybe, but good enough as payment for stabling Breeze Whisperer for however long we're going to be with the good people of the First Valley, Master Tanner!' Cetu laughed, raising his tumbler and toasting his benefactor's health.

'Indeed, indeed . . .' The fat tanner chuckled, settling down with a heartfelt sigh. 'But these are troubled times, Master of the Way,' he said, his jowly face suddenly looking very serious as he blessed himself with the sign of the dragon.

Rokshan nodded politely, murmuring that he had heard some things in the marketplace that puzzled him.

'To be sure, to be sure . . .' Cetu murmured drowsily – Rokshan wondered if he'd had one too many tumblers of barleyfire.

'Such as, my young friend?' the tanner asked sharply.

'Well, one stallholder asked me if I'd heard about the white mares of the plains: they've always been born with coats of the purest snowy white, unblemished for their sacrifice to the Jade Spirit, he said, but none of the brood mares can bring them forth now – all the sacrificial mares are being born with the three stripes common to all other dragon horses. What does it mean, Cetu?'

Both of them looked expectantly at the Waymaster.

'I too have heard this,' he said at last, 'but I do not know what it means – how should we know? It has never happened before. If the Serenadhi come with the Plains Horsemen, we shall have to ask them.'

'The horse-singers?' The tanner blessed himself again. 'They have not attended a festival for . . . for as many years as I can remember.'

Cetu stood up. 'You're right; it was a long time ago. But I do remember: I would've been about the same age as my young charge here. Come, Rokshan, time is passing and we must be there to see what unfolds. Thank you for your hospitality, Master Tanner.' He bowed. 'Our horse needs to rest after our journey – there will be too many people in the square to take her with us. I shall return for her soon. Until then!'

'Wait, Cetu! I just want to see Breeze Whisperer.' Rokshan leaped up; he'd suddenly been overwhelmed by such a strong feeling of sadness. Cetu pointed towards the small yard round the back, telling him to be quick.

Rokshan hurried to where Breeze Whisperer was stabled.

He was relieved to see she was comfortable enough, with plenty of fresh hay and water, but he had to stop and shake his head as wave after wave of the deepest blue filled his mind.

'What's the matter?' he asked gently, stroking her muzzle tenderly. 'You want to come with us, don't you? But it's too much of a throng out there and we won't be gone long – we'll be back soon.'

He tried to reassure her but he sensed that she wasn't simply fed up at being left behind. When Cetu called him, she whickered softly; he turned to go reluctantly.

Rokshan hurriedly thanked the tanner for his hospitality and followed Cetu out; the shopkeeper watched them go, a worried frown puckering his brow.

Later that afternoon they stood by the platform that had been erected in front of the festival dragon. When they'd left the shop, Cetu had been strangely silent, dismissing Rokshan's questions about the sacrificial mares of the Jade Spirit with a wave of his hand and a muttered 'Later . . . later.' However, he had stopped short when Rokshan told him about Breeze Whisperer's deep sadness.

'I too felt it, and was glad you went to offer her comfort,' the Waymaster replied, looking approvingly at Rokshan before his expression turned deadly serious. 'My guess is that she senses something very important is about to happen, and so of course she wants to be with us. Only one thing could be so important to her that she would try to tell us . . .' Cetu glanced up at the enormous coiled dragon.

Rokshan followed his gaze. Now draped in a wonderful woven cloth, the rearing dragon almost seemed to be moving. The material shimmered and glowed in the dying light, its hues of gold and green shading into blood-red, blue and silver against a background of scales. Massive braziers had been placed around it, ready to be lit at dusk.

'What, Cetu? What is it that's so important to her?' Rokshan asked quietly.

'The horse-singers, my young friend: they are coming, I'm sure of it. Breeze Whisperer will sense their presence from many li away – the Serenadhi sang the song of the wind to her when she was barely more than a filly on the Plains of Jalhal'a; they tame the untrammelled spirits of the wild dragon horses through their mind-songs, a part of the Way known only to them. She respects them, but she is fearful too – fearful of what tidings they may bring.'

Rokshan's stomach churned, not just at the prospect of bad tidings; for here was yet another part of the Way that he was expected to learn. All the same, he felt excited at the thought of seeing the legendary horse-singers.

Now the setting sun cast a fiery red pall over the enclosure, making the festival dragon's iridescent colours glow, covering it in a deep vermilion; its golden mask snarled down at the crowd, who were strangely quiet now, an expectant hush hovering over them. Gandhara, clan leader of the First Valley – who believed he was the strongest contender for khagan – paced impatiently outside his tent. The other clan chiefs – Akthal of the Second Valley, Mukhravee of the Third Valley and Sethrim of the Fourth Valley – were already in the camp and they now waited only for the clan leader of the Plains Horsemen.

At a signal from Gandhara, the braziers were lit. Within a few moments the flames were crackling and licking hungrily all round the festival dragon, sending sparks shooting up into the night sky; the dragon's face seemed to move in the flickering firelight.

Suddenly there was a commotion on the watchtower: one of the guards was pointing excitedly as the other put his horn to his lips and blew a series of long, piercing notes that shattered the crisp, dry cold of the evening air. As the last of the guard's warning blasts faded, a hushed silence fell on the crowd. Everyone's ears strained to catch what they were denied sight of, but they felt it first: a light thrumming, almost imperceptible at first, then growing in intensity until it was an insistent drumming of hundreds of hooves, making the ground tremble.

Now there could be no mistake – the Plains Horsemen were coming, and in force.

At first it was impossible to see anything in the gloom but gradually a long line of horsemen appeared, stretching as far as the eye could see to left and right, riding at full gallop.

Cetu let out a long, low whistle. 'Unheard of ... un-believable,' he muttered under his breath.

'What? Are there more than usual?' Rokshan asked, his heart hammering.

'Hundreds more: the plains clan leader's father attended the festival to mark the last khagan's approval by the clans – I was not much older than you at the time – but he came with hardly more than a score of men – and only a few women.'

'Women? You mean warriors?'

'The Serenadhi of the plains – the horse-singers we spoke about – they have come, as Breeze Whisperer knew they would.'

The line of riders came to a halt just outside the gates, the dust they'd raised from their headlong gallop swirling about them. The noisy blowing and whinnying of hundreds of dragon horses up and down the line silenced the crowd and for a moment no one breathed. Rokshan's heart was beating like a hammer at the sight; he could feel the horses' energy so strongly he wanted to reach out for it. One rider stepped forward, followed by three others close behind, and then waited.

Rokshan stole a glance at Cetu, whose cat-like eyes had narrowed in anticipation. Where was Zerafshan? He craned his head over the crowd but there were far too many people for him to identify one individual.

Gandhara moved to greet the new arrivals. 'Hail,

Draxurion of the Plains. I, Gandhara of the First Valley, and my fellow clan leaders, on behalf of all your valley kinsmen – we welcome you, and the Serenadhi.'

Draxurion was a tall man not yet in his middle years, with a long, stern face. His black hair was tied in a bun at the back of his head and he wore the sleeveless coat of the Horsemen cut short over thick woollen leggings. His mount was a magnificent chestnut stallion and was the largest dragon horse Rokshan had seen. Tearing his eyes away, he stared in fascination at the Serenadhi – three women riders who were unlike any others he had seen in the valleys.

The dragon horses they rode were all black mares, and Rokshan immediately sensed there was something different about them as they stepped forward, their heads turning inquisitively, their nostrils flared. They kept up a neighing conversation punctuated by noisy blowing and pawing of their hooves, then stopped just behind the clan leader.

At first Rokshan thought his eyes were deceiving him, but he could see no evidence of reins or saddles apart from two thin knotted cords threaded through their mares' long silky manes. Looking more closely, he saw that the women of the Serenadhi rode with only the lightest of saddles; their leggings were made of the thinnest material and they wore moccasins for nimbleness and speed. Their short, sleeveless coats were the same as Draxurion's. They were small and lithe, with dark, intelligent faces; luxuriant black hair tumbled down their backs. Rokshan sensed an aura about them that was at once magical and mysterious, and with a rush of empathy he recognized the extent of Breeze Whisperer's anguish at not being there with them to share this moment.

Gandhara pointed the way to his tent. Draxurion dismounted and disappeared inside, followed by the other clan leaders. The Serenadhi jumped down nimbly and moved silently behind them.

'Cetu, here comes Zerafshan.' Rokshan pointed across the square.

Cetu nodded. 'He has come at the appointed time.'

Zerafshan strode across the marketplace, weaving his way between the knots of stragglers.

'Zerafshan – at last!' Cetu exclaimed as he approached. 'All the clan leaders are now gathered' – he gestured towards Gandhara's tent – 'and the Serenadhi too. We are honoured indeed. You have a captive audience!'

'What, we're just going to barge in there?' Rokshan asked, alarmed. 'Don't we have to be invited or something?'

Cetu pretended to look offended. 'Invited, Rokshan? Me, a Waymaster of the Horse? I think not,' he huffed indignantly. 'I will be accepted as unofficial representative of the Fifth Valley clan as my people have not had sufficient time to agree on a leader. I most certainly do not require an invitation!'

'Indeed not, Cetu,' Zerafshan said, suppressing a smile. 'The clan leaders are fully expecting me to attend too. Come, my old friend, let's not waste a moment longer.'

'Do not underestimate the significance of the Serenadhi's presence here,' Cetu warned, his hand on Zerafshan's arm. 'They may be here out of respect to mark the election of a new khagan, but they are a strange sisterhood – the plains people treat them with the utmost respect, as should we.'

Rokshan's feelings of apprehension were swept away as they entered the tent – he was astonished by its sumptuousness. Gandhara was obviously intent on impressing the other clan leaders. It was hung with rich silks and brocades; dazzling gold and silver ornaments adorned the walls and roof, and thick furs covered the floor. All the clan leaders reclined on floor cushions around a low table laden with bowls of fruit and sweetmeats, and steaming platters of rice and meat. Rokshan felt his mouth water. The leaders were exchanging greetings, but the murmur of conversation stopped as they caught sight of Rokshan.

'My ... kinsman, Rokshan,' Zerafshan announced. Rokshan bowed a little awkwardly.

Draxurion looked at Zerafshan shrewdly. 'I know of your friendship with our old khagan – may his spirit's journey be swift and sure in the Wheel of Rebirth,' he said, clearly meaning to waste no time on the diplomatic niceties that Rokshan had been taught at the school. 'I have heard too that he allowed you to wear the Collar, and that he was convinced you should lead us to freedom, but you must know that it is Gandhara who has the backing of the other clan leaders, my friend.'

Zerafshan gave the smallest of shrugs, careful to maintain his impartiality. 'The Serenadhi . . . Who is their choice, or do they simply follow your lead?' he asked.

Rokshan glanced at the leader of the Serenadhi, who had remained standing next to Draxurion. She returned his glance with a smouldering intensity that unnerved him, and he quickly looked away again as he felt a current pass between them.

Draxurion seemed troubled by the question. 'The Serenadhi are here neither to endorse nor to acknowledge any would-be leader. They come to warn us,' he said. 'We will hear it from Sumiyaa, leader of the sisterhood. What she has to say is of the utmost importance for all of us.'

Sumiyaa stepped forward. The hiss of whispered asides instantly dried up.

'Hear us, Horsemen of the valleys, Waymaster, Zerafshan the soothsayer and his kinsman, Rokshan. The Serenadhi are of one mind when we sing to the dragon spirits that live within the horses of the plains, and so I speak for all my sisters now.

'For generations we have sung the songs passed down to us from the lips of Chu Jung when he calmed the raging dragons and wrought the spirits of wind and earth, air and water and all the natural elements of the world. But now the dragon spirits of the horses of the plains turn from us, as if they do not want to hear our song. In despair, we summoned a *raga*, a spirit-song so pure and true it can call the very lord of the horses himself, binding itself to his soul so that we can follow him wherever he will lead us to find the source of the pain we are causing him.'

The sing-song lilt of Sumiyaa's voice had a hypnotic effect, and Rokshan felt a strong, magical presence in the tent that filled him with hope and joy and sadness all at the same time.

'At last Stargazer came to us, leading us away from the plains into the very heart of the desert. There we stayed with him, but we could not understand what he tried to tell us. Then we followed him back across the plains, sometimes losing him for days, but always the sweet song of the *raga* led us to him. He waits now on the Plain of the Dead, within the Towers of Silence. We do not know why, and we cannot follow him into that place. Nor can any Horseman who is not either bearing the khagan who has died, or is the khagan-elect. The soothsayer, Zerafshan, cannot know the mind of his mount, but he comes to you with the blessing of the old khagan, and out of all of you, it is Zerafshan – with his military experience and service at the imperial court – who knows the mind of the emperor, he who now moves against us. Zerafshan must lead us, Horsemen, even though it is against the tradition of our people: our ancestors never had to bear the cruel yoke of a tyrant who demands ever more of our precious mounts.'

At this a loud buzz of approval went round the table; Rokshan noticed a barely disguised scowl on Gandhara's face as Sumiyaa held up her hand for silence, once again fixing Rokshan with a look that seemed to penetrate into the core of his being.

'Zerafshan cannot know the mind of his mount, but we discern that his kinsman, Rokshan, can. Therefore *he* must go to that place where the lord of the horses waits. Let Rokshan be the means by which we find out what troubles our sacred mounts, as well as fulfilling the vision of the old khagan in winning the battle for freedom. In this way, our gift may be restored to us: it is a path that must be followed to find the answer. The Serenadhi have spoken: this is our counsel.'

There was silence in the tent. Sumiyaa's lilting voice echoed in Rokshan's head like the chiming of bells and he wondered if the others felt it too. He found it difficult to concentrate; it was almost as if he was dreaming.

'The Serenadhi's warning is clear.' Gandhara spoke up at last. 'We must fight, and fight now, before we are crushed and lose our dragon horses for ever. But with respect, there is no time to waste sending an untried boy to the Plain of the Dead. I will be khagan-elect: back me and I will do as the Serenadhi have counselled. We cannot elect someone as our leader who is not even a Horseman.' He waved his hand dismissively at Zerafshan. 'It would be sacrilegious, and a grave offence against the spirits of our ancestors.'

'There is something I would add, clan leaders,' Cetu said. 'I respect what the Serenadhi have told us, but if Rokshan were to make this attempt, I fear it could kill him. He has only just started out on the Way. To be sure, he has made good progress, but to try to speak with Stargazer before he has properly learned the mind of his mount and explored all the different levels' – Cetu shook his head – 'it is madness. As his Waymaster, I could not condone it. Let Gandhara go, if he is so intent on proving his worthiness to lead us.'

There was startled surprise at Cetu's thinly veiled contempt and Zerafshan seized his chance.

'If what the Serenadhi say is true, if the Horsemen's gift of speaking with the dragon horses is deserting you – and the Serenadhi are always the first to exercise this wonderful gift – you as a people are fated to wither and die. In one stroke the very point of your existence is removed and something irreplaceable is gone for ever. Heed the words of your

Serenadhi, Horsemen, I urge you! I can help you defeat the emperor! Even now I know the plans he will be drawing up, the strategy he will be finalizing with his generals – remember, I was once his most trusted commander.

'With Rokshan at my side and with the blessing of the Serenadhi, nothing can stop us from overthrowing the emperor and turning your old khagan's vision into reality by winning first your freedom, and then the freedom of all the people of the Empire. Let the Horsemen become the champions of the people! I beg you to allow Rokshan to accept the challenge the Serenadhi speak of. He will not fail, I promise you, for he who you see before you is my son, and he has been marked since birth as a sign of this destiny.' Zerafshan's voice rang with a note of triumph round the tent.

Rokshan, stunned and disbelieving, dropped the cup of water he had just poured himself. He felt numb with shock and struggled to collect his thoughts, shaking his head in amazement: what was he talking about? Could Zerafshan truly be his father? His mind whirled and it slowly dawned on him – if he *was* his father, then Jiang Zemin had, after all, spoken the truth that fateful night in Maracanda: his mother had been in love with Zerafshan, the ambitious favourite of the emperor, and she must have married Naha as a way of remaining close to him, even after her marriage.

In a flash of insight that filled him with pain and anger, he realized this was why his mother had always treated him as her favourite, and why An Lushan had never been able to find a place in her affections. He felt the hurt of his brother's rejection as if he was experiencing it himself for the first time. But deep down a sullen, confused rage began to boil: why had the man he'd loved all his life as his father never told him?

'What is this mark that singles him out?' Gandhara asked scornfully, a look of utter disbelief on his face. 'You presume too much, Zerafshan – show us!'

'That is easily done . . . Rokshan, show them.'

Starting at the voice of the man he'd always thought of as his uncle, Rokshan gathered up his long hair and revealed his deformed left ear, at the same time looking around the table proudly, as if daring the clan leaders to comment. His revelation was met by a low murmur of astonished surprise.

'The mark of the secret Fellowship of the Three One-eared Hares,' Zerafshan declared, 'long outlawed by the emperors as a dangerous underground sect because of its belief in freedom for all as the bedrock of a harmonious universe. The fellowship entrusted me with Rokshan's guardianship at birth, and it is because of me that he stands here before you. Like the fellowship, the Serenadhi know he has a gift. They have said as much. They have asked a lot of my son, and it is a dangerous path he embarks on – I hope with your blessing,' he continued. 'But I have no doubt that he will succeed in what the Serenadhi have asked. Let him prove that his gift is true!'

All the clan chiefs apart from Gandhara nodded their approval.

Draxurion, clan leader of the Plains Horsemen, turned his attention to Rokshan. 'Rokshan, you will not go alone. The Serenadhi and I will accompany you and your Waymaster to the Plain of the Dead, about ten days' travel from here. Go now and prepare yourself. We will leave at sunrise tomorrow.'

CHAPTER 30

THE PLAIN OF THE DEAD

Rokshan sliced off some shavings from the block of dried tea and tossed them with a coarse mix of herbal leaves and some roots into the big pot over the fire, grimacing as he added roasted millet to the brew and stirred the thin slush; however many times he made it, he still couldn't bring himself to like the traditional drink of the Plains Horsemen.

'Harmattan!' He gritted the word out through clenched teeth as he stirred, his lips dry and sore with the cold. The Plains Horsemen's word for the icy wind that blew from the Taklamakan Desert was one of the first he had learned: harmattan – 'ice cleaver' – a wind so cold it chilled the soul. He was grateful for the long Horseman's coat and deerskin leggings that protected him from the worst of it.

At dawn on the morning following the Festival of the Dragon, Draxurion and his escort, the three riders of the Serenadhi, Rokshan and Cetu, had set out at a fierce pace across the Plains of Jalhal'a to the Plain of the Dead. They had crossed the salt-caked mudflats of the ancient lake of Lop Nor, where the fierce wind had sculpted the surface into hard, shallow waves. At last, after ten days' hard riding, they had come to the Wastes of Astana.

Cetu rode Storm Gatherer, having left Zerafshan at the First Valley to plan the defence of the Horsemen's kingdom with the other clan leaders, which meant Rokshan had Breeze Whisperer to himself. The further they travelled together, the closer their connection – and Rokshan was both alarmed and excited by her growing anticipation as they approached the Plain of the Dead. Sometimes this was signalled by a cloudburst of colour filling his mind, followed by a current between them so strong that he felt completely at one with her. He had also started to probe beneath the surface, very gingerly at first but growing bolder as he sensed her acceptance of him; she was less playful now, almost as if she understood the importance of his task. As they stopped to make camp for the night, he resolved to ask Cetu about his progress.

He gazed into the bubbling pot and his thoughts turned, as they'd done constantly since the meeting, to the man he'd always known as his father. Before Zerafshan's revelation he had longed to hear the sound of Naha's voice once more, to hear his laugh as he drank a cup of his favourite Kocho wine; but now all he felt was emptiness and sad bewilderment.

Eventually, his mind exhausted and no nearer to making sense of any of it, he closed his heart, shutting it all out; once he'd done this, he felt a steeliness creep into the fibre of his being, hardening his determination to succeed. Cetu, who had been teaching him everything he could about the inner path of the Way, noticed the change in him as his training progressed. Gone was the serious but warm-hearted boy he had known; he sensed a new purpose, tempered with an iron resolve.

Rokshan acknowledged Cetu as he approached, drawn to the smell of supper. The Waymaster squatted down by the fire, blowing into his hands. Rokshan busied himself with the tea broth, silently handing the old Horseman a bowl with some strips of dried meat; the thin gruel disappeared quickly as he noisily slurped the last drops. They had come to the flat Wastes of Astana, which stretched as far as the eye could see. In the brief summer months they would be as hot as a furnace, but in the grey twilight of winter there was an unearthly silence that made them talk in a whisper.

'Just beyond the wastes lies the Plain of the Dead,' Cetu said when he had finished his meal. 'You have mastered completely all the commands and gestures every Horseman uses and you are . . . *comfortable*' – he chose the word carefully – 'when you mindjoin at the first levels. In the two or three days left to us the Serenadhi will lead you to the deeper, inner path of the Way that we have only just touched on. Use your new-found strength, Rokshan: Breeze Whisperer is alert to it – this is why she has opened up to you more these last few days.'

'You have noticed it too, Cetu?' Rokshan asked excitedly. He had hardly dared hope it was true, thinking perhaps it was just the presence of the Serenadhi that had made him so much more attuned to the colours in the first layers of Breeze Whisperer's mind. Since his experience in the Third Valley, he could sense these first layers completely naturally and without fear of the currents beneath them as he started to probe deeper.

'It is almost as if Breeze Whisperer had chosen you as her rider – this is why she has opened up more quickly to you,' Cetu replied, a little sadly, 'but it'll be different with the Serenadhi.'

'How will it be different, Cetu, from what I have experienced already with Breeze Whisperer?' Rokshan asked quietly.

'You expect me to know the mind of the Serenadhi?' Cetu's eyes crinkled and he smiled one of his cat-like smiles. 'Best to expect nothing. When they speak to you, keep your mind empty, yet open at the same time. Then be ready for rapid changes of thought and mood – they can give you the insight you need to take you not just to the heart of the Way – that moment of pure union – but somehow beyond that, to the very source of everything that is, between us and the dragon horses. Then you will be ready for the lord of the horses.'

'I think I understand . . . Because the Serenadhi are the first to use the Horsemen's gifts with the wild dragon horses, to someone unfamiliar with their lore it must seem like going to the beginning of things.'

'Yes, and going to the beginning of things, as you put it, time after time with each wild dragon horse they first make contact with – this has made the Serenadhi what they are. Some say they are prophetesses, and their mind-songs can drive men mad.'

As they spoke, Sumiyaa approached, her movements so lithe and silent she seemed to glide towards them. They both stood up, Rokshan watching her closely with a mixture of respect and fascination as she bowed in greeting. And he sensed an immediate bond between the sisters and Breeze Whisperer; he rejoiced with his horse in her brief moment of reunion with the horse-singers.

'My sisters and I have been conferring amongst ourselves these past few days,' she said in her sing-song voice, as if speaking did not come entirely naturally to her, 'and it is time. We will take you across the wastes, Rokshan, on your own. You must ride with us, on our mounts – leave Breeze Whisperer with Cetu; your Waymaster will rejoin you at the entrance to the Towers of Silence in three days. We will set out straight away.'

'Now, with night approaching?' Rokshan asked. He felt Breeze Whisperer's disappointment that they were to be parted and that the Serenadhi were going – a wave of greens and golds tinged with the violets of her connection with the sisters. He responded automatically with a message of reassurance and love. He *would* be back, he assured her.

'Night, day – it makes no difference to us,' Sumiyaa replied mysteriously.

'I'll just gather a few of my things,' Rokshan said, getting up. Now that it was actually happening, he felt excited but also more than a little nervous.

'You are ready for this, my young friend,' Cetu said. 'Now

you must demonstrate the strength of mind and courage of one whom the stars have singled out. The Serenadhi will guide you; may the dragon spirits of the plains be with you.'

Sumiyaa had come to Rokshan's side and, taking his hand, led him to where her beautiful black mare waited, her ears flicking with impatience. He was relieved to see a lightweight saddle on her and, at Sumiyaa's invitation, mounted up. She jumped up in front of him, and within a few moments they were galloping into the heart of the Wastes of Astana.

CHAPTER 31

STARGAZER AND THE TOWERS OF SILENCE

They had ridden across the wastes for most of the night before stopping to eat, but then, instead of falling into an exhausted sleep, had kept going into the twilit, desolate expanse until Rokshan couldn't tell whether it was night or day and whether they had been riding for hours or weeks.

The effortless gallop of the Serenadhi's black mares began to beat out a melody and he caught snatches of song switching back and forth between the sisters and their mounts. The mares dipped their heads as if they too were singing, galloping faster now until it seemed they were floating over the ground. Sumiyaa's long hair streamed out behind her and Rokshan wasn't sure if she spoke aloud or whether her sing-song voice was echoing in his mind: 'Hear the song of the Serenadhi, Rokshan . . .'

Then he was surrounded by shimmering waves of melody. Amazed, he reached out, trying to grasp the colours, but as he touched them, they dissolved, fading away until, from afar, he heard the strains of a childhood song his mother had sung to him.

Suddenly the blast of a conch shell sounded, jolting him back to his initiation into the Fellowship of the Hares, so that for a moment he was there in the monastery at Labrang. The blast resounded louder and louder until it seemed his body shook with the violence of the noise; he cried out in terror as he felt himself falling, and then lay panting and sweating on the ground just as he had lain on the monastery floor all that time ago.

The frightened whinnies of what sounded like a thousand horses echoed in his head, but he didn't know whether he was dreaming now or whether it was real. The alarm of the horses sounded louder and more urgent now – but he could see no sign of them.

Then suddenly he saw the colours of the Serenadhi's song as clearly as if the sisters were weaving the melody with their fingers as they sang. It was the most beautiful song he'd ever heard, and he wanted it to go on for ever.

Sumiyaa spoke to him once more: 'Rokshan, we have woven this song into your heart and locked it in the deepest, most secret chambers of your mind. It is the song of all the *ragas* the sisters have ever summoned – receive it as our gift to you. When you recall it, the dragon spirits may recognize it as the sum of everything the sisters have sung to them through the ages, but we cannot be sure because our powers have diminished. It will help you to open their minds to you, but beware before you step through this door: you may not be able to find it again until it has closed, and then it will remain shut for ever.'

The Spirit of the Four Winds heard their song and, entranced by the beauty of it, came to them. Together they followed where the *raga* of *ragas* led them, riding the Spirit to the four corners of the Earth. Rokshan didn't know whether they were gone for just one candle-ring or a hundred, but he didn't want it to end . . . and then they left him. Where they went, he didn't know.

The voice sounded very far away and he wished whoever it was would stop poking him in the ribs.

'Wake up! It's me, Cetu. Wake up!'

Blearily Rokshan rubbed his eyes and found himself staring into the cat-like eyes of his Waymaster.

'It is the third day, as the sisters decreed. Look – the Towers of Silence,' Cetu said, pointing to what appeared to be an enormous cloud mushrooming in the sky. 'Clouds of vultures and carrion crows feeding on the flesh – what's left of it – and bones of the old khagan.'

A little shiver of fear went down Rokshan's spine. This was the place where he had to go – alone. Snatches of song echoed through his head, and suddenly he felt his heart bursting with a wonderful sense of fulfilment.

'Cetu . . . I . . . I've been told something so important, but . . . I can't remember what it is. It is there, in my heart and mind, but I can only *feel* it . . . Help me remember, please!'

'This is the way of the Serenadhi,' Cetu said gently, offering him some water. 'Nobody knows how, but you will remember what they have told you when the time comes. They have sung the songs of the wind and touched your soul with mysteries only they know of. Their path is not part of the Way for every Horseman, but be sure of this: what they have given you can only be unlocked through the heart; their gift is not a magician's spell, but something that will remain with you for ever. Now, go! I will wait for you here.'

Rokshan embraced the old Waymaster. 'How will I know if Stargazer is to be found in the Towers of Silence?'

'The pupil will be found by the master when he is ready,' was all Cetu had to say. 'Have faith, Rokshan! You have shown more prowess in the Way than any young Horseman I have taught, and you have ridden with the Serenadhi – an opportunity given to few. If the prophecy is true, the lord of the horses will open his thoughts to you, and it is through you and your father that the vision of the old khagan is to be fulfilled and the Serenadhi's gift restored.' He handed him a saddlebag. 'I will be waiting here for you. It is no more than a few hours' walk to the ridge that separates the towers from the Plain of the Dead. Farewell.'

* * *

Rokshan made his way across on foot; the Waymaster had gradually become a little dot on the horizon. The noise of the carrion birds grew louder; soon it was impossible to think, such was the raucous, greedy cacophony. He walked fast, as if he had been given renewed energy by the Serenadhi. At last he reached the top of the rocky escarpment that formed a natural barrier to the Towers of Silence. There before him, stretching away as far as he could see, was a lonely place of death that he hoped he would never have to look on again.

Everywhere he turned, small towers twice the height of a man dotted the desert like giant pimples. Each was built on a mound and was large enough to support a funeral bier on which the remains of bodies were laid out individually, in accordance with the tradition of the Horsemen – raised above the ground, so that their mortal remains would not defile the earth. Here the bodies would dry out in the sun and be picked clean by the crows and vultures. The sides of the towers were smooth and he wondered how the biers were raised onto them.

Overhead, crows wheeled and cawed, impatiently waiting their turn while the vultures feasted on the bones of the last khagan. The fetid smell carried on the dry desert air made Rokshan feel faint, and bile rose in his throat.

He took a long draught of water and decided to keep going: the more hours of daylight he had the better, he thought as he half slid, half walked down the loose stones and shale.

The birds warned of his approach with raucous cries, reluctantly abandoning their feast. Whitened bones from ancient biers and towers long crumbled into dust gleamed in the dusk as he picked his way fearfully through the maze of the last resting place of the khagans. Rokshan had no intention of stopping. If he had to, he'd walk right across this field of the dead and back again, leaving it exactly where he'd entered it; anything would be better than stopping here.

Gradually he left the noisy cries of the birds behind, and only the gusting of the wind around the towers broke the pall of silence shrouding the Plain of the Dead. Rokshan felt as if he was the last person left on Earth and wished that Cetu was with him.

'I understand why they're called the Towers of Silence,' he muttered to himself to keep his spirits up, hoping that Stargazer was here, despite the dangers of mindjoining with him.

Suddenly, behind him, he heard a little flurry of stones slipping down one of the mounds.

'Who's there?' he cried, whirling round.

The pale towers stood like silent sentinels, stretching away as far as he could see. The sun was now fading in a blaze of smudged reds and purples. Nervously he started to trudge on again when something else caught his attention: in the distance a great yellow-brown cloud spiralled upwards, spreading and obliterating the rapidly darkening sky. Now it was billowing and twisting like an enormous sail; he caught flashes of a rolling wave of red – whatever it was, it was heading straight for the Towers of Silence. The wind gusted and swirled, whipping up a sandstorm that would smother everything in its path.

With the light fading quickly now, Rokshan looked around with growing alarm: he had to find shelter or he'd be suffocated. Frantically he scrabbled inside Cetu's saddlebag for some rope, but the piece he found was much too short to reach the top of the nearby tower.

The swirling sandstorm was approaching fast, battering its way across the plain. In desperation Rokshan clawed at the loose stones of the mound to make a hole big enough to crawl into. Then, suddenly, he stopped: above the howl of the wind he heard a sound that almost made him weep with relief – the urgent whinny of a horse who must have sensed he was in danger.

'Stargazer!' Rokshan shouted with all his might, and again: 'Stargazer!'

Then, through the maelstrom, he could just make out the ghostly shape of a horse straining every sinew to outrun the storm. Then he saw a magnificent grey dragon horse, galloping so fast his hooves were a blur that hardly seemed to touch the ground. He slowed to a canter and came to a halt beside Rokshan, his bearing noble and intelligent, full of quivering, suppressed energy.

Instinctively, Rokshan dropped to his knees. 'Stargazer, lord of the horses,' he acknowledged, overcome with awe at the strength and towering size of the horse. The aura of majesty pulsed around him and Rokshan immediately sensed the pure power glowing at his spirit's core.

Suddenly Stargazer neighed loudly – a burst of silver-blue tinged with red exploded in Rokshan's head, which would have rocked him off his feet if he'd been standing. With the storm almost upon them, he understood straight away what he was being told to do: he leaped up onto Stargazer's broad back.

In a moment they had shot ahead of the storm and were speeding back the way he'd come. The wind whipped against his face, and his hair streamed out behind him as Stargazer picked his way effortlessly through the towers, increasing the distance between them and the sandstorm. They reached the edge of the field of dead and ran parallel with the ridge. Rokshan yelled with joy at the exhilaration of the gallop – the Horsemen called it the dance of the wind. He felt himself connecting so closely with the lord of the horses that it no longer felt as if he was riding a horse. His long hair flew behind him as Stargazer picked up speed and soon the landscape became a blur. Rokshan yelled with exhilaration, urging Stargazer to go faster, but remembering to use the pureness of the moment to empty his mind as Cetu had taught him.

Mentally he braced himself, readying himself for the

sensation of swimming in the currents of Stargazer's first level of emotions. Straightaway he caught the faint, shimmering waves of the melody that the Serenadhi had woven; now it rang in his head, and the ear of his heart heard again its joyful, magical essence. He felt Stargazer's mind gently probing his, and shock waves of colour exploded through his whole body. But now Rokshan's heart froze as he sensed huge breakers crashing towards him; roiling coloured spume danced on the tops of the waves as far as he could see and, too late, he remembered Cetu's warning about controlling the ecstasy of the moment.

Suddenly he felt his mind being drained of the fury of the mindjoining. In its place he felt a gentle, glowing pulse, almost as if Stargazer was reassuring him that all was well. They were well clear of the storm now and the great horse slowed to a canter, and then a walk, coming to a halt by one of the towers at the extreme end of the escarpment.

Trembling with excitement, Rokshan jumped down; gently stroking the velvety muzzle, he looked into Stargazer's fiery, gold-flecked green eyes. He stared deeper and was drenched in a gently undulating blue, which lapped against the edges of his mind like a lake on a summer's day. Abruptly the blue disappeared and he staggered back as his mind was buffeted by waves of raw red against a backdrop of black and purple, like enormous bruises: the lord of the horses was trying to tell him something desperately sad about this place.

Rokshan tried in vain to respond in the same way, arranging his jumbled thoughts into an artist's palette of colours, but in the excitement of the moment he couldn't stop words breaking to the surface. He rubbed his temples in frustration and kicked the wall of the tower. He leaned against it and hung his head, wondering what to do, not noticing that the storm they'd so easily outpaced just minutes before was bearing down on them again.

Stargazer neighed loudly and nuzzled him in the back to attract his attention. Rokshan looked up and saw what he was trying to tell him.

'We're not going to be able to cross the ridge in time,' he yelled in panic.

Climb into the tower. I will wait for you.

Rokshan froze in surprise. The moaning of the wind was growing louder and louder, but he was sure he had heard a voice in his mind – a strong but gentle voice. Stargazer hadn't spoken aloud, but Rokshan knew immediately what he was telling him, as clearly as if he had actually spoken: *Of all the towers, you must shelter in this one.*

He had no time to think about it as the storm was almost upon them. He jumped onto Stargazer's back and reached up to the top of the wall. He hauled himself over, landing heavily on the other side amongst a pile of bones.

Rokshan scrambled as far from the bones as he could, his heart hammering. The funeral bier of whichever khagan it was that the tower had housed originally had collapsed many years before, and the corpse had long since been stripped of its flesh. In the rapidly fading light the bones gleamed dully; they had been picked over and lay in an untidy pile with the ragged remains of a cloak – the skull grinned up at the sky.

He only half took in all this as just one thought filled his head: Stargazer had spoken to him! He had come through the mindjoining, and the lord of the horses had opened his mind to him. He felt dizzy as Stargazer's thoughts tumbled and echoed through his mind – not as actual words but in a way that he could somehow make sense of.

The wind gathered strength and whipped the desert sands into a dancing wall of death. Rokshan huddled into his thick fur-lined coat as the night sky was blotted out completely by the raging maelstrom. The thick, choking sand enveloped the tower, making it difficult to breathe, and he rolled over, yanking

his coat over his head in a desperate effort to escape the suffocating fury of the storm. His breath came in short, rasping
gasps as he struggled to draw air into his lungs. In his panic he
called on Kuan Yin to calm the dragon spirits of the winds.

'Mother of mercy and protector of travellers, hear my
prayer. Protect Stargazer, who lies in the eye of the storm,' he
mouthed to himself, feeling as if his chest was about to
explode. He screamed silently, 'No! I am not fated to die now!
Hear me, spirits of the plain . . . Stargazer, help me . . .'

It was as if the great horse had read his thoughts: Rokshan
heard his loud, whinnying call from the other side of the wall
and knew then that the storm had passed; he could hear it
raging over the ridge. Suddenly he thought of Cetu and prayed
that he had managed to find shelter; if he hadn't, he would
have to be found quickly.

'Stargazer – here!' He hurried over to the pile of bones to
get a good run at the wall. Kicking the ragged cloak out of the
way, he stopped in astonishment as something skidded across
the thick yellow dust that coated the floor. The silver was dirty
and black with age, but there was no mistaking the rope-like
coil of its design and the cicada clasp.

Reverently, his heart hammering, he picked up the other
Collar of the Horsemen. He rubbed the clasp carefully against
his sleeve and the iridescent wings shone through the grime.

'Dragon spirits of storm and rain,' he prayed, 'show
me what Zerafshan intends. What is his real purpose? Let me
know what is in his mind . . .' Before he could have any doubts,
he raised the Collar and fitted it around his neck, hesitating just
a fraction before he pressed the clasp shut.

So intent had he been on the Collar, he had closed his
mind to everything else, and failed to hear Stargazer's warning:
Beware of the Collar, Rokshan. Only the dead wear it . . .

Suddenly there was a noise like the rushing of wind and
he was alone in an enormous cavern, roughly hewn out of

black rock. It had no roof, but the night sky was starless. A pair of massive gates loomed before him, cut into the very rock. From beyond them came a crescendo of shrieks and pitiful wails that froze his soul. It grew louder and louder – a maddening vortex of pain that battered against the impenetrable gates and around the cavern. Now he could see them – shadowy spirits of the damned pressed together in a writhing, seething mass; tears of black, poisoned blood oozed from their eyes and down their faces, dripping to their feet, where it was licked up by blind giant maggots.

The huge gates inched slowly open and the spirits redoubled their wails as they were pulled by an invisible force towards them. Beyond, Rokshan caught a glimpse of a small bowed figure before which the spirits of the damned prostrated themselves, howling for mercy. This must be the Guardian Monk the abbot had told him about, Rokshan thought. Sure enough, the Guardian Monk was reading the records of their lives. Noting the list of evil, dark deeds reflected in the wretched spirits before him, he pronounced their punishments accordingly. Ghoul-like creatures herded the spirits towards the flaming furnace of Hell, where the Crimson King screamed in an ecstasy of anticipation at the prospect of more victims, through all eternity.

With frantic, fumbling fingers Rokshan undid the clasp and wrenched off the Collar. His chest was heaving and his face and hair were drenched with sweat. Huddled on the floor of the tower, he barely heard Stargazer's whinnies of alarm.

'I have witnessed a vision of Hell,' Rokshan gasped to himself, recalling what the abbot had told him and realizing he had just seen the court of the Crimson King, the place where he had been told he must go. 'But *as long as the Guardian Monk remains in the court of the Crimson King, keeping watch over him and assigning the punishments of the souls of the damned, this shall never come to pass . . . and the Four Riders of Hell – Fear, Pain, Loneliness and Despair, will never be released . . .'* he whispered, remembering the words of the abbot.

'It is a path that must be followed to find the answer,' the Serenadhi had said; was this the path they too had meant for him? He stared at the Collar, turning it over and over in his hands . . . Should he take it with him? He acknowledged the enormity of such a theft from the Horsemen.

But simultaneously he felt a growing certainty that swept aside any tiny, lingering doubts. Carefully placing the Collar in the inner pocket of his coat, he murmured a grateful prayer to invoke the abilities of the hare he had been gifted with and ran towards the opposite wall, bounding over to land neatly on Stargazer's back.

He had to find Cetu quickly: the suspicion was growing that what he'd witnessed might in some way he didn't yet understand be central to Zerafshan's plans, and in his heart of hearts he wasn't sure that his uncle's – no, his *father's* – plans had anything at all to do with winning freedom and independence for anyone – not for the Horsemen, nor for any other people of the Empire.

He urged the great horse into a gallop, following the line of the ridge to find the place where he'd first entered the Towers of Silence. Just as he thought that the horror of the vision of Hell was fading as the purity and power of Stargazer flowed through him, he was buffeted again by waves of raw red and great, bruised swathes of black and purple; now the darkening colours turned into a swelling ocean stretching as far as he could see. No horizon contained it, no sky overshadowed it, and there was deep pain and sadness rising from the depths, which he now heard as a lament, like the *ragas* of the Serenadhi. The rhythm of the gallop had a hypnotic, mesmerizing effect, and now Rokshan's mind was so consumed by the pain of Stargazer's vision that he became one with him, hearing a voice through the sadness of the spirit-song:

What you hear is the lament of all ages past which I carry in my heart's core, Rokshan. It is the cry of every man, every woman and every child who suffered the jealous rage and fury of the dragon spirits when they turned against mankind. It is the despair of all my brothers and sisters at the realization of what we became before the Wise Lord in his mercy allowed us to be reborn as the spirits of fire and nature. It is the lament of the fallen guardian spirits who can never serve or be with the Wise Lord again because of their sinful rebellion. It is a raga without end, as long as time itself holds. It goes back to the beginning of time itself, when the Wise Lord's purpose became clear, and Wisdom was born. Having heard just a small part of it will give you courage and strength in the conflict to come, and in what you must do.

Now you have heard the song of all things with the ear of your heart, Rokshan, but you must never look into the inner eye of my soul, for there the spirit of Han Garid, my ancestor from aeons past, lies dormant but simmering, a cauldron ready to ignite into his rage of ages past when he wreaked destruction on your kind and assaulted the Heavens in his rebellion against the Wise Lord. Now I release you – be strong! With my inner eye I have seen all your hopes and fears, everything that has made and shaped you, and what you are to become – do not be afraid.

Rokshan was surprised to find himself still joyously galloping astride Stargazer. But his head felt clear and he was filled with a quiet strength of purpose – and he knew he was no longer alone. The weighty burden of what Shou Lao had asked of him and what the abbot had tasked him with lifted miraculously, and a feeling of great humbleness came over him.

'Thank you, Stargazer, for making me bolder,' he murmured, his heart swelling with pride. He sensed Stargazer's thoughts like gently probing tendrils and laughed aloud.

'We will speak again, Stargazer, of that I am certain! But we must find a friend of mine who will be worried. And I cannot wait to see the expression on his face when he sees us!'

Stargazer tossed his head and whinnied loudly in response as they crossed the ridge, leaving the Towers of Silence behind them.

PART FIVE

PATHS TO THE SUMMIT

The Myth of the Higher Guardian Spirits' Rebellion against the Wise Lord

The following is recorded in The Book of Ahura Mazda, the Wise Lord

It was said that Chu Jung, Spirit of Fire and Heavenly Executioner, wept burning tears as he clawed at the earth deep in the forests that covered the world: he was burying for ever the Talisman of dragon-fire whose power he had been tempted to use against his divine master, the Wise Lord, by the leader of the rebel guardian spirits – known for ever afterwards only as the Shadow-without-a-name.

The Nameless One had been joined in his rebellion by two other higher guardian spirits. They were the Crimson King, whose punishment was to be made the keeper of Hell and its Four Riders of Fear, Pain, Loneliness and Despair. The second was the Jade Spirit, who repented at the last and was made keeper of the Wheel of Rebirth. A third to join them, Beshbaliq, was a lower guardian spirit, and for his punishment he was sent to join the Crimson King in the depths of Hell.

The Wise Lord's creation of the Arch of Darkness bound the Shadow for all eternity outside the universe of all living things, beyond even time itself. Mankind called the darkness night, because before this they had only ever known light, and for ever afterwards men were always afraid of the dark, whispering that it spawned nameless, shadowy creatures.

So it was that the Shadow was able to exert his evil influence over the Wise Lord's weaker creatures, plotting to use them for his own ends to break free from his eternal punishment. His faithful servant, Corhanuk – who had stolen the Staff of Chu Jung – vowed to help him in this quest, ceaselessly plotting and planning for the day when his master would once again be free to stalk the Earth. Always he searched for the Talisman of Chu Jung, to unite it with the Staff he had stolen from the Heavenly Executioner in order to release its divinely granted power.

The lower guardian spirit, Beshbaliq, was allowed to keep his name. In time, he became adept at moving between the lower spirit-world and the middle world of men and women, serving his master well by possessing those who were to be drawn into the Evil One's service.

Source: the secret Fellowship of the Three One-eared Hares;
origin – discovered in the ruins of the citadel monastery of
Labrang, spiritual centre of the old Western Empire.

CHAPTER 32

THE GATHERING STORM

Many, many li to the north of Maracanda, a full cycle and a half of the moon before Rokshan rode out of the Plain of the Dead on Stargazer, his brother – An Lushan – was being drawn into a world which, if he did not know it at the time, was in truth irrevocably intertwined with the prophetic words of Shou Lao, the storyteller.

It was nearly half a cycle of the moon since he had left Lianxang and the settlement of the Darhad to head back towards Maracanda, where his father waited anxiously for news of his sons. But An Lushan's thoughts were no longer with his father – these were bent more and more towards the statuette he had found in the Dark Forests.

Qalim and Bhathra, the two escorts who had accompanied him from Maracanda, were with him now, watching furtively as their master went a few paces away from the campfire and carefully unwrapped the statuette from his bag, as he had done every night since they had set out. They exchanged fearful looks, both hurriedly blessing themselves with the sign of the dragon; one glanced towards their horses, muttering he would have to go and settle them if they became too agitated. How they both longed to be back home with their families again!

An Lushan reverently laid the statuette down, lost in contemplation of it as it gently glowed and pulsed. The exquisitely crafted gold, bronze and silver figure of a leaping dragon, snarling and serpent-like, was studded with precious stones that flashed all the colours of the rainbow as he picked it up again, turning it this way and that.

Tonight, suddenly, it pulsed more strongly, sending beams of coloured light around the encampment, enfolding them in an eerie, multicoloured glow. The colours wheeled across An Lushan's face, his eyes reflecting the changing hues like a kaleidoscope, his expression set in a glaze of anticipation. He thrust his arm upwards, and the statuette shot out a piercing beam of coloured light that streamed up into the night sky as if a giant had hurled a flaming lance at the moon. An Lushan seemed to snap out of his rapture and clasped the statuette tightly between both hands, as if trying to extinguish it. Gradually its pulsing glow dimmed and then went out altogether. Quickly he wrapped it up again, depositing it safely back in his bag.

Not far behind him, Lianxang smiled with relief as she caught the brief flash in the night sky. She had set out in pursuit of An Lushan not long after the Darhad had come across the yawning chasm in the forests. The old spellweaver felt certain that the stranger they'd glimpsed when An Lushan went missing, the inexplicable rent in the earth and his abrupt departure were all somehow linked.

Sarangerel had sent her spirit-bird speeding on her way to ask the advice of those *wiser than her*, she'd said; however, not knowing how long it would take to return with an answer, the Darhad were responsible for tracking the stranger they had invited into their midst to confirm what had taken place in the forests. And who better than Lianxang to coax the truth out of him?

Lianxang also had her own reasons for wanting to catch up with him. It seemed miraculous, but the blight that had attacked the trees had started to recede – so they might be able to go ahead with their plans after all! She couldn't wait to tell An Lushan the good news: if the blight did not recur, they could both return and finalize the trading agreement, just as they'd always planned.

But An Lushan was no longer thinking about the timber, and even if he'd known, he would not have cared that their trading rival, Boghos, had abandoned his expedition into the Dark Forests as his men fell sick and died from a mysterious fever; for his mind was focused to the exclusion of all else on the statuette. Lianxang was also far from his thoughts as, overnight, a wind straight from the north began to blow. By dawn snow was falling heavily. The gusting wind whipped up swirling flurries so that it was impossible to see more than a few paces in front of them.

Quickly they broke camp to search for shelter, heading for the crest of the ridge at the end of a small valley. Struggling up and crossing over to the other side, they stumbled across an opening in the rock face which widened into a cave; it was just big enough for them to lead their horses through. They soon made themselves comfortable: Qalim managed to coax a small fire from the scraps of kindling they always carried for emergencies.

An Lushan huddled into his furs and gazed at the flames flickering in the gusty draughts from the snowstorm. His straggly beard was longer now and his thick black hair fell around his shoulders. His thoughts turned again to the words of the stranger he'd encountered in the Dark Forests: *Whatever you want shall be yours for the asking . . . You will be a hero for solving the riddle . . . If my master favours you, he may decide what I speak of is yours to keep . . . Such power in the hands of one man . . .*

What if the ancient legends and myths were true? This was the question he kept asking himself. It had become so much a part of his inner thoughts that he barely noticed he was shrugging his shoulders in response to the question that looped round and round his mind . . . *Such power* . . . But how was he to use this power? And how could it secure the release of his father like the wood-gatherer had promised?

He had never been interested in the legends of the past like Rokshan – how An'an wished his brother was here now! But the mysterious revelation in the Dark Forests was surely proof of the legend of Chu Jung. Had the mythical tree that had sprung up at the bidding of one of the most powerful of the Wise Lord's guardian spirits been a tree just like any other, an effective hiding place for something the guardian spirit had wanted to hide from men for ever . . . *something he now possessed?* And was it, of all the woods in the world, the Dark Forests that Chu Jung had chosen as a hiding place, just as the Darhad had always believed?

Just then a particularly strong gust of wind blasted a flurry of snow into the cave. The horses suddenly seemed restless, stamping their hooves and whickering nervously. The fire guttered and died.

Muttering, Qalim hauled himself up to tend it. An Lushan thought he heard him whispering encouragement as he blew gently on the embers and the flames flickered back into life.

'If the flames had tongues, I wonder what they'd tell us?' he joked, to pass the time.

'Master?' Qalim replied, looking at him with a puzzled expression.

'You were talking to the fire . . . Were you expecting a reply?' An Lushan grinned.

'I . . . I don't know what you mean, master,' Qalim said, settling himself back down near the horses and nudging Bhathra, who was dozing with his head lolling on his chest. Whatever was the matter with his master, he needed Bhathra awake and alert in case he did anything they weren't expecting – which seemed increasingly likely.

'It doesn't matter,' An Lushan replied irritably. But there it was again! He could definitely hear a faint whispering, which now seemed to be coming from many different directions.

He stared at Qalim, who quickly looked away.

Now An Lushan could hear snatches of a voice calling him from the inky darkness at the back of the cave. And then suddenly it changed again to a whisper, which came in waves, washing over him.

Then, unmistakably, he heard a hypnotic, silken voice, rich and resonant; when it stopped he longed to hear it again, but now it was so close he shrank in terror from its touch.

In time you shall know what I would have you do, and you will have all the answers you need. You will remember these words, for it is the Shadow that speaks, An Lushan . . .

'What . . . what would you have me do?' He could hardly speak the words as the cold clammy grip of fear seized him; he didn't know whether he spoke aloud or had sunk into a terrible nightmare: the voice of the Shadow burrowed like writhing tentacles into his mind.

You helped me, An Lushan, and in return I must help you. I feel your concern for your father: you wonder about the power the wood-gatherer spoke of, and how it will secure his release. The power of what you have in your possession is such that it can do this, and much, much more — if you wish.

An Lushan shook his head violently from side to side as he felt himself being pulled down; now he was falling, slowly tumbling . . . down and down, until he felt he had been falling all his life. At last he was lying beside a lake; the water was black as night and he could feel its chill. And it had suddenly become dark . . . so dark.

He began to shake with fear. In the gloom he could only just see that the crow had appeared, hopping about by the water's edge; it cocked its head and fixed him with a baleful stare. He heard its familiar jerky voice in his head, for the same creature had spoken to him once before, on their journey to the people of the Darhad.

My master and I have long waited for you, An Lushan. I am Corhanuk, messenger to the Shadow and the darkest regions of the Lower World. I will show you your deepest desires and wishes. In time, when these are realized, men will tremble merely at the mention of your name.

He struggled as he felt himself being pulled down again . . . Then he screamed as he was hit in the face—

'Master! Wake up! It is a bad dream . . .' Qalim stooped over him, gently slapping his cheeks to wake him, an anxious look on his face; Bhathra hovered at his side.

An Lushan jerked upright. Despite the cold, he was covered in sweat.

'You were staring at the fire, and then you must have dropped off to sleep,' Qalim said, offering him a cloth.

'Thank you,' he muttered, dabbing at his face. 'Yes, a bad dream . . .' He glanced nervously towards the back of the cave as snatches of it came back to him; the desire to get out of there was overwhelming. 'Has the snow let up? We should be on our way. Let's go now,' he said, gathering up his cloak.

One of the horses whinnied a warning as a shadow fell across the narrow opening in the rock face, blocking out the dull winter daylight that filtered into the cave. The shadow materialized into the unmistakable shape of a Darhad tribeswoman wielding a spear; she hesitated warily at the mouth of the cave.

'Lianxang! What are you doing here?' An Lushan asked in surprise. Bhathra and Qalim flanked him, eyes alert with suspicion, their hands resting lightly on the hilts of their scimitars.

'No word of welcome, An'an?' she said, hiding her surprise at his dishevelled appearance. There was a hunted, haunted look in his eyes she'd never seen before. 'Zayach and two others stand watch outside,' she added. 'There is room enough for them?'

'Of course . . . tell them to join us,' An Lushan replied, signalling to Qalim to revive the fire.

Moments later, the tribesmen filed in and sat cross-legged

by the fire that Qalim had coaxed back into life, while Bhathra filled an earthenware pot with snow to make a warming drink.

'It is good to see you, Lianxang . . . really it is,' An Lushan said softly. 'But quite a shock too – I thought your grandmother was reluctant to let you go . . .' He settled himself by the fire, motioning for her to sit beside him. He noticed everyone staring at him.

'An'an, this is important to our people,' Lianxang said slowly. 'We want you to try and remember what happened in the forest. The two scouts who had been sent out to look for you – they penetrated deeper into the woods before we could get word to them that you were safe. Not only did we see a stranger, but they also came across something that has troubled us deeply . . . Sarangerel especially . . .'

'What? What was it they discovered?' An Lushan asked innocently.

'A great rent in the Earth – more than a pit, a sort of . . . underground cavern, so deep it was almost impossible to see the bottom of it.'

'If you're asking me if I saw this great hole in the Earth – no, I didn't.' An Lushan surprised himself: the lie rolled off his tongue so smoothly. 'Do you think I wouldn't have told you if I had?' he asked indignantly.

'No, of course not,' Lianxang assured him, 'but we – Sarangerel – just wanted to be doubly sure. She's worried that the stranger we saw and the pit are somehow connected; after all, he was in the same part of the forest as the pit. Are you absolutely certain you never saw anyone when you were lost?'

'No one,' An Lushan said emphatically, 'as I told you at the time. You have come all this way to ask me that? How long have you been following us?'

'We set out a few days after you left us. It was not difficult to track you – there are other routes you could have taken, but they wouldn't have been known to you,' Lianxang said, 'and we wanted to be sure you were returning to Maracanda.'

'But . . . where else would I be going?' An Lushan spread his arms in a show of incomprehension.

'What about the lights – bright flashes, explosions of colour – that have accompanied you: only a blind man would have missed them,' Lianxang added. 'What were these? What caused them?'

'You're asking me?' An Lushan's tone was incredulous. 'We have wondered the same. Aren't they something that occurs in these parts, when the stars are configured in a certain way in the winter months?' He shrugged.

Qalim and Bhathra stared fixedly at the fire, avoiding any looks that might have been cast their way.

'The dancing lights of the Land of Ice are many days' travel from the northernmost reaches of our forests, which themselves are at least one cycle of the moon from our southernmost winter settlement,' Zayach observed quietly, joining the conversation for the first time.

'Well, perhaps they have travelled south – it can only be a good omen!' An Lushan exclaimed.

Qalim jumped up and hurriedly set about offering round some freshly brewed tea to fill the awkward silence.

'Perhaps you are right, Zayach,' Lianxang said brightly after they had all taken some appreciative sips. 'After all, the forests have started to recover . . .' She watched An Lushan closely, observing his reaction.

'The blight? The trees are recovering? This is wonderful news, Lianxang,' An Lushan said excitedly, the memory of his plans flooding back into his mind. 'Now nothing will get in my way . . .' He trailed off, catching her startled glance.

'We will accompany you, be sure of that,' Zayach said, his voice steely.

'What, all the way to Maracanda? And then turn round and go all the way back again? That makes no sense.' An Lushan's tone stopped just short of contempt, but it was not lost on them – Lianxang's look of dismay was plain to see.

'Nevertheless, this is the spellweaver's direct command: her granddaughter will not deny it – or us,' Zayach replied with calm indifference to An Lushan's rudeness.

'If the old wom—' An Lushan stopped himself just in time. 'If *Sarangerel* wishes it, who am I to deny her?' He laughed humourlessly, getting up and kicking over the fire before stalking over to the cave mouth to peer out. 'The snow has cleared; we should continue on our way,' he said brusquely. 'It will take us at least half a cycle of the moon to reach Maracanda, and I have unfinished business there. Travel with us if you will, Zayach, or save yourself the trouble and return to the settlement – it makes no difference to me.'

An Lushan wrapped his cloak around him and, with a dismissive glance at the trackers of the Darhad, strode out of the cave.

CHAPTER 33

BESHBALIQ AND THE DEMON WRAITHS

Lianxang looked up at the crow cawing loudly as it wheeled high above them. It was strange, she thought, but the nearer they'd got to Maracanda, the more often it had appeared, and always at dusk. Up ahead, An Lushan couldn't seem to take his eyes off it.

Now at last, far off on the horizon, she could just glimpse the massive walls of the Western Empire's capital city, the red clay of the huge fortification reflecting a ruddy glow in the late afternoon sun. She allowed herself a smile – she was returning much sooner than she'd expected, and she couldn't wait to see her second family again; even Merchant Naha's imprisonment couldn't dampen her enthusiasm. Her smile vanished at the insistent cawing of the ugly bird . . . If only she knew what was troubling her friend.

'Not long, An'an,' she said as she trotted up beside him. Late afternoon dipped into the gloom of encircling twilight and she knew they wouldn't make it through the city gates that night. It would probably be early evening the following day before they reached the city.

At first An Lushan didn't respond, his attention wholly focused on the crow wheeling overhead.

'An'an . . . I'm talking to you.'

'I know. We should make camp soon. I'm tired,' he said at last, tearing his gaze away.

'We should carry on a little longer – less far to travel tomorrow then.'

'You go on. I'll stop soon – I need to rest.'

'And leave you on your own? We wouldn't do that!' It was said lightly, but over the last few days she'd noticed with increasing concern the dark rings under his eyes and his shrunken, haggard appearance – what was happening to him? 'An'an, when we get to the city, I'm going to take you to the best healer Maracanda can offer. You're' – she hesitated, not wanting to draw his anger – 'you're not yourself, and haven't been ever since we joined you, half a cycle of the moon ago now. Will you let me do that?' she asked gently.

'Yes, if you wish,' he murmured, so quietly she could barely hear him.

The truth was that he yearned to be on his own: the statuette seemed to exert a stronger and stronger pull over him the nearer they got to Maracanda, and the longing to hold it and bathe in its glowing colours was becoming overwhelming. If only he could do that, then perhaps the dreams and nightmares he'd been having lately would go away – though they seemed so real to him now that sometimes he couldn't be sure if he was dreaming at all.

The silken, caressing voice that came to him night after night had grown more insistent: it didn't matter whether he was awake or dreaming, he could ignore it no longer – he must do as he was bidden, or he would go mad.

The raucous caw turned to a sudden shriek of alarm before the crow suddenly banked and flew off to the north. A faint, shrill cry caught Lianxang's attention.

'Could it really be . . . ?' she muttered to herself, looking up and scanning the rapidly darkening sky with a thrill of hope. The cry had attracted the attention of the escorts and the Darhad too. A great bird was circling lazily, effortlessly riding the air currents, gradually wheeling closer until there could be no mistaking it.

'A royal eagle!' Qalim said excitedly as he rode up. 'What

can it be doing here?' He looked curiously at Lianxang, who was staring up at it, a rapt expression on her face as she listened intently to the volley of shrill cries.

As it continued to wheel directly above them, she suddenly raised her arm as if in salute, and the great bird gave a final screech and then soared away. She watched it until it was just the tiniest speck in the sky, grateful for the renewed hope it had given her but wondering at its message: whatever came to pass, she must stay with An'an and never leave his side.

The Maracandian escorts noticed the Darhad's gestures, touching their foreheads as the eagle soared away, and made their own sign of the dragon for good measure, trying to convince themselves that it was a favourable omen. An Lushan barely noticed it, murmuring listlessly at Lianxang's excited chatter.

When they had made camp, he was so exhausted that he had hardly eaten anything before excusing himself, saying he needed to sleep. He dreamed terrible dreams that night, groaning and muttering. It was a cold night, but he was sweating so much that the clothes he slept in were sodden.

Suddenly he reared up, clutching his head at the voice which reverberated within it and then seemed to him to swirl around the encampment:

It is the Shadow who speaks, An Lushan. Now your time has come, if you have the courage and will to seize it. Your mortal plans have come to nought: your earthly father has abandoned you and no longer waits for you in your City of Dreams. But I will give you vengeance when you do my bidding.

The Talisman of Chu Jung is yours, An Lushan! All the special powers that the Wise Lord gave his highest guardian spirit are concentrated in it. For now, we have only one purpose: to unite it with the Staff that my faithful messenger, Corhanuk, has kept safe through the ages. The Staff is in the safekeeping of another of my servants, and he awaits you at the Summit of the Goddess. Go now — Corhanuk will guide you. And you will not be without forces of your own to command: just as my lieutenant of old, Beshbaliq, commanded legions of demons, so too will you have recourse to the forces of evil. The girl of the Darhad has some herbs and potions of the spellweaver: tell her to throw them on the fire, and Beshbaliq will come, reborn at last in you . . .

Lianxang woke to find An Lushan looming over her. 'An'an! You startled me,' she said, yawning and rubbing her eyes. 'Another one of your dreams?'

'Yes. I can't get back to sleep . . . Where are they – the herbs and potions you told me Sarangerel uses to unweave bad dreams? I know you have them – go and bring them over here,' he said, looking at her strangely.

Alarmed, Lianxang went to fetch her bags while An Lushan heaped wood on the glowing embers of the fire, making it crackle into life. Muttering to himself, he rummaged through the cotton bags and pillboxes she brought over to him that contained the spellweaver's assorted herbs and potions. He sniffed at a root. 'Aconite – a pretty flower when it blooms, but looks can be deceptive: its roots are deadly . . . but you know that,' he said to Lianxang in a chilling, deadpan voice.

He rubbed his fingers in some bright red powder and sniffed at it cautiously. 'Cinnebar – or mercury sulphide, as your alchemists will tell you: also poisonous, if I'm not mistaken – these are powerful ingredients, even for a spellweaver's granddaughter,' he observed, his eyes narrowing to black pinhead points that she could feel boring into her. 'Gather them up,' he ordered with abrupt ferocity, 'and throw them all on the fire.'

Something in his voice made her obey his instructions instantly, her hands trembling as she did so: how had he known to select the strongest ingredients, known only to a spellweaver and used for exorcism in cases of the most extreme possession by demons? Had her spirit-bird tried to warn her? She had thought it only wanted her to stay with An Lushan, but perhaps there had been a deeper warning in the message it had brought. And now, somehow, she found herself moving as if in a dream, unable to resist An Lushan's command.

He himself was oblivious to everything now: he raised his arms, chanting an invocation. The flames died momentarily, then shot up in a towering blaze of red and purple. Thick black smoke licked around the base of the fire and then swirled upwards, dancing in and out of the flames. An Lushan's chanting intensified and he beckoned to the smoking inferno, as if trying to draw the smoke and flames to him.

Zayach and the other Darhad tribesmen watched, frozen in horror, as the smoke enveloped them. Bhathra and Qalim cowered by the packhorses, trying in vain to calm them as they whinnied in growing alarm, tugging at their halters in their efforts to break free.

'Come, demon wraiths of Beshbaliq,' An Lushan screamed as his arms flailed. 'Come, my spirits from Hell!'

The flames subsided like a fountain, and the smoke around the base of the fire swirled in a twisting, billowing flurry, forming a wraith-like figure dressed in black from top to toe; a turban covered his head and face – apart from a narrow slit for the eyes, which glinted, red and unblinking. An Lushan turned round, and Lianxang gave a cry of dismay at the unmistakable change in his appearance. He grew taller and a shadow rippled over his face, subtly distorting his features and twisting his face into a cruel mask.

At his command, the demon wraith stepped away from the fire, its movements fluid. Its hands were almost transparent but it had no difficulty in drawing the light scimitar belted around its middle, fastened by a silver buckle in the shape of a dragon's skull. The creature touched the scimitar, flat-bladed, to its forehead in a gesture of allegiance to An Lushan, and then stood to one side.

The flames shot up again, the black smoke swirled, and another creature, identical to the first, emerged from the billowing smoke. This happened many times over, but still An

Lushan continued his invocation, his face contorted in triumph as he assembled his horde of hell-creatures.

Frozen in horror, Lianxang mechanically counted forty of them. All identical, they stood in an orderly line, two-deep, perfectly still except for an occasional undulating ripple, like corn swaying in the wind. Each one held its scimitar to its forehead, as if awaiting orders.

Now An Lushan seemed to grow taller still and his voice was like thunder as he called forth mounts for his demon wraiths. Again the flames shot up and black smoke swirled about them, so thickly it was impossible to see anything, but what they heard struck terror into their hearts: at first one, then another and then yet another, building into a crescendo of demonic whinnies of what sounded like horses – though Lianxang shuddered at what they really were. As the smoke cleared at last, they could see the full horror of what had been summoned from the gates of Hell.

The demon wraiths were mounted on their hell-horses, and An Lushan looked with exhausted satisfaction at his assembled riders. The semi-transparent, rippling effect of the demon wraiths did not extend to their mounts – they were a full hand higher than the sturdy steppe ponies of the caravans, and their red eyes shone like hot coals, their sleek coats glinting like polished jet. Slavering and pawing the ground, they called to each other in a deep snarl, baring their teeth, which were long and sharp, like a tiger's. Their hooves were three-toed and ended in viciously sharp points. Without saddle or reins, the wraiths were as one with their mounts, scimitars set in salute, awaiting their master's command. Some of them had lances decorated with fluttering pennants bearing the grinning gold dragon's skulls.

A cold, gusting wind had sprung up, bringing storm-clouds rolling in across the pearl-dawn sky. An Lushan mounted one of his hell-horses and rode up and down the line of patiently waiting demon wraiths, like a general inspecting his troops. Stopping at the head of them, he drew his scimitar and, holding it aloft, acknowledged his creatures' gesture of allegiance.

'Behold your leader, hell-wraiths!' he cried. 'Do you swear to serve me? I, who am Beshbaliq, reborn lieutenant of your Shadow lord.'

As one, the demon wraiths swept their scimitars down and then held them aloft, mimicking their acknowledged leader but uttering not a sound. Lianxang watched in guilty horror at what she had helped summon from the depths of Hell. An Lushan had used her herbs to call forth these monsters! She was a spellweaver-to-be. What had she *done*? Why hadn't she found the courage to resist him? *Lieutenant of your Shadow lord* – what had he become, acknowledging as his master the incarnation of darkness, death and evil? She had not guessed at the true extent of his possession.

She recoiled as An Lushan shouted at her to join him at the head of the column. His eyes blazed and, still powerless to resist, she did as he commanded.

'Demon wraiths!' he shouted triumphantly, his face twisting into a malicious grinning mask as the dark shadow rippled across it. Deliberately he pointed his scimitar at his two escorts and the Darhad tribesmen. 'Kill them!'

Lianxang shouted something in her own tongue. Her words had an instant effect: Zayach and the tribesmen leaped onto their ponies, struggling to control the terrified animals. Qalim and Bhathra were the better horsemen and were already astride their mounts and galloping away, riding for their lives.

'After them – kill them all!' An Lushan barked. Instantly and as one, the demon wraiths thundered after them, the snarls of the hell-horses making a terrifying accompaniment to the blood-curdling howls of their riders.

'Ride – ride for your lives!' Lianxang screamed after

them, backing away from An Lushan as he advanced on her, a look of such fury on his face she hardly recognized him. 'No . . . An'an . . . you are not yourself . . .' she whimpered, her face grimacing in pain and fear as he backed her closer and closer to the still blazing fire. He unsheathed his scimitar and tossed it from hand to hand as his eyes transfixed her.

Suddenly his blade whirled at lightning speed. She heard it whistle past her cheek, felt the moment of contact as it slashed the right side of her face; curiously it felt like only the lightest of scratches, but the razor-sharp blade left a deep, crescent-shaped gash from the side of her forehead to the underside of her chin. She gasped in shock as blood poured from the wound.

'Do not defy me again . . . *ever*,' An Lushan said, wiping the side of her face. Her blood was warm and sticky between his fingers; he smeared it on his face.

High-pitched screams drifted faintly across the plain, but the Darhad tribesmen were too far away in the grey half-light for Lianxang to see what was happening to them.

Moments later the unearthly whinnies of the hell-horses and the shouts of their riders could be heard as they thundered back to the encampment; Lianxang saw with a cry of horror that the riders bore aloft the severed heads of her tribespeople and An Lushan's two loyal escorts, skewered on top of their lances.

They dismounted with their gruesome trophies and bowed deeply in front of their leader. Lianxang felt a wave of nausea and retched violently.

'What will you do now? Will you kill me too?' she asked, her voice shaking. 'Maracanda is only half a day away, An'an,' she reasoned with him, in the forlorn hope that he wasn't already beyond reason. 'Your father . . . We must negotiate with Jiang Zemin to win his free—'

'It is too late. He has abandoned me. I have no father.'

An Lushan turned on his heel. 'Now I have to do the work my Shadow lord has entrusted me with. He has given me a gift beyond measure, but it is incomplete still.'

'What gift?' Lianxang had no idea what he was talking about. 'Show me . . . please.'

He hesitated, then strode over to his bag. With fumbling, trembling hands he unwound the blanket in which he kept the Talisman and reverently lifted it up as if making an offering. As soon as it was in his hands the statuette glowed, its beams undimmed by the early morning light.

'This is the Talisman of Chu Jung, Spirit of Fire and Heavenly Executioner, soon to be joined as one with his Staff,' An Lushan proclaimed softly, giving her just a glimpse of the exquisitively crafted figure before clasping it to his chest.

The Talisman of Chu Jung! Lianxang hadn't understood the other parts of the message but now that she saw what was in An'an's possession, it all fitted together. She forced herself to focus through her pain and fear. This is what he had come across in the cavernous rent in the Earth! With a jolt, she realized that the long-cherished legend of her people was true – it was their beloved forests after all that had been the secret hiding place of Chu Jung's powerful Talisman: theirs had truly been a sacred guardianship. She knew that, on its own, the Talisman's magic was unusable – it had to be united with the Staff of Chu Jung for its potency to be released. But An'an seemed to know where this was to be found. Now she undestood what she had to do – this part of the message from Sarangerel's spirit-bird had been absolutely clear: whatever happened, she must stay with him. Her guts churned at the prospect: how was she going to make him understand the enormous evil of what he might do – and prevent him doing it?

'An'an,' she pleaded, 'you must understand – it is too powerful for any man to control, and will destroy you—'

'But I am no longer a man!' An Lushan laughed a strange barking laugh. 'Together, my Shadow lord and I will command the magic of Chu Jung to do our bidding—'

'Your master's bidding, you mean,' she said despairingly, knowing that he was being taken to a place beyond her reach. 'Why would your Shadow lord share anything with you once you have given him what he wants? His word is false – do not listen to him, An'an!'

The strange, shadow-like effect rippled across his face again as the spirit of Beshbaliq began to possess him, creeping like a malignant growth into the darkest corners of his soul.

'Enough – unless you want this side of your face matching the other!' He brushed the flat blade of his scimitar across her unmarked cheek before sweeping her up onto his hell-horse.

He looked at his motionless ranks of demon wraiths and, with a shouted command answered by a crescendo of snarls and howls, An Lushan and his horde galloped off towards the east, to the Summit of the Goddess.

CHAPTER 34

MURDER ON THE TRADE ROADS

The mounts of the demon wraiths were indefatigable. They galloped by day, avoiding the established trade routes, and also by night. The large crow accompanied them; Lianxang had noticed An Lushan deep in conversation, it seemed, with the ugly bird.

The demon wraiths and their hell-horses needed no sleep, and when they ate, it was more for the pleasure of killing than the need to assuage their hunger – they lived off human flesh, and rumours of a marauding horde of bandits that were said to be evil spirits escaped from Hell began sweeping along the trade routes.

Travelling twice as fast as ordinary horses and far out-stripping the plodding pace of the caravans, they swept down from the direction of the land of the Darhad, veering eastwards past Maracanda and passing the citadel monastery of Labrang in a fraction of the time – just half a cycle of the moon – the lumbering caravan of Chen Ming had taken to cover the distance. As Rokshan left Chen Ming's caravan to make his way up to the pass, An Lushan and his demon horde were already heading eastwards, also in the direction of the pass, only three quarters of a moon or so behind him.

The killing and violence had become their trademark, fill-ing Lianxang with disgust and horror. She prayed that whatever had possessed An Lushan would depart for ever and that he would be returned to his senses. But she knew it was a forlorn hope and hardened her heart to what must be done – to what

Sarangerel and her people would expect of her, even if it meant sacrificing her life: the spirit-bird's message had been absolutely clear on this. She steeled herself to be strong, to empty herself of any feelings she might once have had for An Lushan, seeing only the monster he had become . . . and waited patiently.

A loud, raucous cawing heralded the crow's return from a reconnaissance of a recently spotted caravan. The ungainly bird – which An Lushan had revealed to Lianxang was no less than Corhanuk himself, servant of the Shadow – had trailed them all the way from Maracanda when they had first set out. It seemed a lifetime ago now, Lianxang reflected miserably as the crow hopped excitedly around An Lushan.

A great prize awaits you, Beshbaliq. It is a caravan of Vartkhis Boghos, the richest merchant in all Known Lands.

An Lushan wheeled his horse round in surprise. The name jogged memories which struggled to surface through the raging sea of demonic possession that had become his mind . . . Dim, flickering images of another life swirled in and out, but then faded and were lost to him.

Only merchants as rich as Vartkhis Boghos could afford such caravans: it was the size of a small army. There must have been at least five hundred camels, buffaloes and other pack animals, with camel-drivers, guards and camp followers numbering about two hundred. The smoke from their cooking fires drifted lazily up and hung in a huge hazy pall over the camp.

An Lushan could not have known it, but amongst the dozens of lowly camel-drivers was his own father, Naha. Through a combination of hard negotiation and judiciously placed bribes, he had managed to gain his freedom from the grim citadel of Maracanda – but only at great personal price. The condition had been the forfeiture of his fortune and family home, and permanent exile from his beloved Maracanda. Not only this: he had to suffer the humiliation of working for his lifelong bitter rival as the lowest of the low – a dung collector, picking up the waste of the bad-tempered animals as they trudged across the deserts and steppes. It was a bitter pill to swallow, but he had accepted it nonetheless. If it gave him his life and the freedom to restore his fortune, he reasoned, it was a chance worth taking. Far more important to him, now at last he could find out what had happened to his two sons.

Unaware of his father's presence, An Lushan looked down from a rocky escarpment. Barely a full cycle of the moon out from Maracanda and making its way across the still frozen steppe, the caravan of Vartkhis Boghos was camped in a lee of some gently undulating hills – perfect to give them cover until they attacked.

An Lushan drew his scimitar as he felt the heat from the Talisman against his chest. His eyes narrowed as the now familiar lust for killing settled like a blood-soaked shroud about him, blinding him to all else. Lianxang felt his body tense and shuddered at his mount's demonic whinny.

'No more killing, An'an,' she pleaded. 'You are An Lushan, of Maracanda, skilful trader, elder brother of Rokshan. Your father is Naha Vaish—' Her words had become a mantra which she repeated before every such attack, hoping that they would trigger some sort of response from him, but they fell on deaf ears.

The crow flew up at her as she spoke, beating its wings around her and pecking at her face before An Lushan waved it away and shoved her off the hell-horse.

Winding his black turban around so that it covered his face apart from a narrow slit for his eyes, An Lushan drew his scimitar and brought it chopping down – the signal to charge. Spurring their snarling mounts into a gallop, the demon wraiths streamed down the escarpment and charged across the stony scrub that lay between them and the caravan.

Young children playing on the edge of the camp stared for a moment before running for their lives, yelling and waving their arms to attract the attention of those in the main camp.

In the gathering dusk the camel-drivers were checking their cargo and bedding the pack animals down for the night. The smell of campfires and cooking hung over the caravan as the evening meal was prepared. Suddenly the alarm was sounded: three urgent blasts blasted from the first cameleer's long curving yak-horn.

Vartkhis Boghos glanced up from his accounts and, cursing, strode quickly out of his tent. What was amiss now? Had the gods not cursed him enough, with the utter failure of his timber venture in the Dark Forests – the loss of thousands of *taals*, never mind the men? His eyes narrowed as he saw the charging bandit horde.

'By the gods, what sort of horses are those?' he muttered under his breath.

The bandits had regrouped into a column, two abreast, and were heading straight for his tent, which was set apart from the rest of the camp, distinguished by its fluttering yellow and green pennant. As they streamed through the camp, their scimitars scythed and whirled, hacking and slicing as people scrambled for cover.

Boghos noticed with horror an infant crawling right into the path of the lead horseman, who turned his mount aside at the last minute, just as the mother dashed out to scoop the screaming infant into her arms. The rider broke away to pursue her as she twisted in a desperate attempt to escape. But he was too expert a horsemen. Casually, he swung his scimitar at the back of the fleeing woman's neck, half severing her head in one stroke.

The demon wraiths were unstoppable in their blood-lust. Encircling the encampment, they advanced methodically, torching the tents and slaughtering the cowering women and children. The men fought bravely but were no match for the slashing scimitars and thrusting lances of the bandits.

Two or three other wraiths bore down on Boghos, who drew his razor-sharp dagger and, with a despairing cry, flung it at them with all his strength. It hit one of the hell-horses in the chest, but immediately disappeared bloodlessly into its flesh, failing to halt its frenzied charge. Now they were almost upon him as one of the riders dismounted in one flowing movement and advanced towards him.

'Behold, Merchant Boghos: the hell-bandits of Beshbaliq salute you!' The demon wraith's voice sounded hoarse and ragged. But before he could do anything, the lead horseman galloped up, reining in his mount violently.

'Be gone about your work,' An Lushan shouted at the demon wraiths. 'This man is my concern.'

'Are you the leader of this rabble? Call your men off and you can have your pick of the cargo. Or all of it – I don't care, just stop this senseless slaughter,' Boghos cried.

'I am not interested in your paltry cargo, Merchant Boghos,' An Lushan said, unwinding his black turban. 'You knew me once as An Lushan, of the trading house of Vaishravana.'

Boghos gasped in astonishment. This was the young man who he had heard so much about, the son and heir of his life-long trading rival – the man now employed as a miserable dung collector; the same man who now came running up, sword in hand. Despite his lowly station, Naha had armed himself with whatever discarded weapon he could find and joined in the defence of the caravan. His face was bloodied and there was a flesh wound to his right arm.

'Boghos! These creatures . . .' he gasped. 'They are not human and fight like demons – they will kill us all!'

'Then tell your son, who commands them,' Boghos shouted, pointing at An Lushan, 'to call his men off.'

Naha's heart leaped – he had not seen his elder son in many months. But he stared in dismay and disbelief at the change that had come over him. He seemed taller now, his eyes glinted with menace and there was a sense of power emanating from him that Naha felt he could almost touch. There was a strange glow coming from his chest – and what was that aura about him, something that came and went, like the smell of carrion on the wind?

Smoke and flames shot up in the air as the camp was set ablaze. Screams mixed with the clash of sword against scimitar as Boghos's men continued to offer resistance. Naha stepped towards An Lushan, holding out his arms imploringly.

'My son, call your men off, if that is what they are. This cannot be your doing. You . . . you are sick . . . I beseech you, please. Call your men off, and we can talk in Boghos's tent here.'

'I have no earthly father now,' An Lushan replied, his voice flat and emotionless.

'An Lushan, let me explain,' Vartkhis Boghos said smoothly. 'Naha and I have come to an arrangement: your father sold his business to me in exchange for—'

An Lushan cut him short as he casually thrust his lance at him, impaling him in the chest. Boghos's look of astonishment was short-lived as An Lushan's scimitar finished him off with a slash across the throat that almost severed the merchant's head. He crumpled in a bloody heap.

Horrified, Naha started to back away as his son stared at him intently.

At that moment one of the bandits galloped up, reining in his horse between the two men.

'What is it?' An Lushan barked.

'My lord, the caravan is ours for the taking. We have killed most of the guards and camel-drivers and fired the tents. Only a few women and children still live. What would you have us do with them?'

'Kill them,' An Lushan replied without hesitation.

'No! You cannot!' Naha cried.

An Lushan had dismounted and now stood only a few paces away from his father, who was almost overwhelmed by the waves of power laced with something rank and corrupt that rippled around his son.

'What has happened to you, that you would kill defenceless women and children?' Naha said, looking un-comprehendingly at him. 'No son of mine will murder innocents while I am alive!' he suddenly bellowed. 'Let's see if you can fight! Man to man, single combat – come on! Or are you scared?'

An Lushan's eyes narrowed at the taunt and he spun his scimitar expertly, demonstrating his skill with the weapon. The clang of sword against scimitar rang across the burning, devastated camp.

Lianxang, bruised and winded after being thrown off An Lushan's mount, had been watching from the foot of the escarpment and saw the few remaining women and children being herded together – she had to do something before they were massacred, as she knew they would be. It was an idea born of desperation but she quickly pulled out the the last precious remnants of her herbs, powders and medicines that she'd kept carefully hidden by stitching them into a secret pocket in her waistcoat.

She ran down towards the caravan and came upon a loose pony which, terrified by the slaughter and the flames, had tried to gallop away but had become entangled in its loose reins. Lianxang calmed the animal, freeing its hoof, and swung herself up onto its back. With an impassioned cry to the dragon spirits of fire, she spurred the pony back down the escarpment, riding like the wind across the barren ground. She galloped past the huddled group of terrified prisoners, flinging her herbs and powders onto the flames of the burning tents nearby.

The effect was instantaneous. The women and children wailed in terror as flames shot up, twisting and writhing into a fiery serpent, rising higher and higher. Just when it seemed it would touch the sky, it reared back on itself and the enormous serpent's head came plunging back to Earth, hissing like an eruption of steam, its forked black tongue flicking from side to side.

Green smoke streamed from the serpent's mouth as it swept across the camp, turning the air into a damp, thick fog which settled like a shroud, paralysing all that it enveloped – they could breathe and see and hear, but were unable to move. Even the demon wraiths were frozen in mid-gallop.

Lianxang doused a cotton scarf with water from her pouch, wrapping it tightly round her face. Now she would deal with the possessed, evil creature that An Lushan had become – he would be too distracted in his fight with the brave cameleer to notice the approaching green fog. When he was overcome by the fumes, it'd be easier to do what she had to . . .

She shuddered at the thought but, murmuring an invocation to protect her pony against the fog for a few seconds, urged it straight into the billowing cloud as it rolled towards where the two men were fighting to the death.

At first An Lushan's light skirmishing scimitar had proved no match for Naha's heavy sword and he'd been driven back, well away from the fringes of the camp and the fog of the fiery serpent. But he was possessed by an unnatural strength and agility, dodging and parrying Naha's strokes as his father tired. Summoning all his strength, Naha attempted a sweeping stroke to the side of An Lushan in an effort to expose his son's front when he parried, but he jumped over the swinging blade and sliced his scimitar down on his father's sword-hand, hacking into the flesh and bone. The merchant dropped his sword, grunting in agony and clutching his half-severed hand. He fell to his knees and waited for his son to deliver the death-blow.

'Do it quickly, if you are going to do it,' he panted, looking up at his son, 'and may the gods forgive you.'

Lianxang willed the creeping fog on faster – soon it would be too late. She squinted through the green haze as she neared the men, suppressing a scream of shock when she at last recognized the burly figure kneeling in defeat.

An Lushan flung his scimitar aside and stooped to pick up his father's sword. As he did so, he noticed for the first time the unnatural quiet that had fallen over the camp, and the thick fog rolling towards him. He started back in surprise as a rider burst through the haze, grunting in pain as Lianxang's expertly thrown dagger found its mark, embedding itself in his right shoulder.

Filled with demonic strength, An Lushan gripped the heavy sword with his left hand, swinging it back for the executioner's stroke.

But the fog was already clutching at his throat, suffocating and choking. As it curled around him and his kneeling father, he froze. Lianxang sprang forward, knocking the sword out of his hand as he crumpled to the ground. Moving quickly, she hooked her arms under Naha's shoulders and dragged him out of the way of the advancing fog.

Lianxang sank down beside him, overcome by the effects of the fog, racked with violent coughs, her chest heaving as she fought for breath.

'Lianxang, by the sacred teeth of the dragon,' Naha groaned, clutching his wrist. 'I never in my wildest dreams thought I'd see you here. What has happened to my son? What has he become, and what are those . . . those creatures under his command?'

'Merchant Naha, I cannot explain now.' She waved away the last lingering remnants of the green cloud. 'There is no time – I don't know how long the paralysis will last. You must

. . . finish what was started here . . .' She looked towards the still unconscious form of An Lushan.

'Finish?' Naha looked uncomprehendingly at her.

'He is not your son any more – don't you understand?' she cried desperately, all the pain and horror of the ride with the demon wraiths welling up in her. 'It must be done, now!'

Naha shook his head, still trying to understand what had happened. Suddenly Lianxang noticed An Lushan's eyes flicker open and then close again and her heart missed a beat. Realizing there was little time left before he regained consciousness, she didn't hesitate in going over to him and reaching inside his shirt for the Talisman that hung from his neck. She cut the leather cord that secured it and quickly wrapped it in the scarf she had worn round her face before tucking it in the bag slung over her shoulder.

'This is the sacred Talisman of Chu Jung, guarded these past aeons by my people. In the hands of the forces of evil, its power will be unleashed against the world; your son has become part of that evil – he is *possessed*, Merchant Naha: you *must* do it. What further proof do you need?' she implored him despairingly.

He looked at her, his face racked with anguish. 'I cannot . . .' he whispered. 'Possessed or not, he is still my son.'

'Then go! I will do it for my people. He took something that was not his to take, something that was meant to remain hidden in our forests for ever. He has unleashed powers we can only begin to understand. Go! Take the pony.'

She thrust the reins into his hands then, sobbing, put her dagger to An Lushan's neck, gripping the hilt with both hands to plunge the blade deep into his throat. His eyes remained closed and his face looked strangely peaceful, as if he knew that deliverance was finally at hand. 'This is not the friend I loved,' she cried softly to herself, 'but a creature possessed . . . An'an – forgive me,' she whispered, stroking his face, her arms shaking as she tensed to thrust the dagger down—

'Wait, Lianxang, please.' Naha's knuckles were white as he gripped the pony's reins. 'Now you have what you want, let me take him with me. I will keep him safe – he will not harm anyone; perhaps your people will have a cure for him?'

'There is no cure strong enough for what possesses him, Merchant Naha – the most skilled physician in the Empire will tell you that—' She started as An Lushan stirred, groaning softly.

'Then do it now!' Naha's voice was thick with emotion. 'And may your people be damned for ever with the curse of the dragon's breath!'

Just then the crow that had accompanied them all the way from Maracanda came into view, cawing and making a lunging dive straight at Lianxang.

'This bird – it has never left An'an's side; it is the accomplice of your son and guides him in everything he does. Please, Merchant Naha, go! Ride for your life if you ever want to see your other son!' Lianxang cried, waving her arms to scare off the crow. But it spread its wings and its body began to stretch and expand until it stood before them, taller than a man, monstrously transformed into a giant bird.

It ignored An Lushan's father as he heaved himself painfully into the saddle. 'Lianxang, if you see Rokshan, tell him I always loved him as my own son . . . promise me . . .' Naha shouted, looking with horror at the enormous crow before spurring the pony into a gallop, riding as hard as he could away from the camp.

Now the crow craned its head down to within inches of Lianxang's face and opened its huge beak, screeching its familiar call. The thunderous blast threw her off An Lushan and she cowered on the ground with her ears ringing. Looking up seconds later, she saw a tall, hooded figure dressed in black looming over her.

'Spellweaver's heir and high priestess-in-waiting of the Elect: I am Corhanuk, messenger to the Shadow and guide to Beshbaliq. This much you know, if I am not mistaken.'

He spoke softly, his voice melodic, almost hypnotic. From what she could see of his face, it must once have been beautiful: golden hair tumbled to his shoulders and his eyes were of the deepest blue, glittering with an intensity that for a moment drew Lianxang into their depths. Then the veil parted and she saw a hateful creature beneath, twisted and full of self-loathing, its head little more than a skull covered with a layer of black, diseased growths.

'You do not deceive me, Corhanuk .. I can see what you are.' Her voice trembled but somehow she drew strength from her anger. 'You have made a monster of him! I swear by my people that the Staff you stole will not be made one with the Talisman . . .' She shrank back as Corhanuk advanced on her.

'Silence!' he hissed – gone were the musical tones of a moment before. 'You understand little of these affairs. The Staff of Chu Jung is just a beginning. It will be united with the Talisman, and then we will summon the ancient dragons! Terror will be unleashed on the world and my master will undo the Divine Commandment which keeps him sealed in the Arch of Darkness.'

Summon the dragons? What could he mean? Nothing in the spirit-bird's message had warned her about this . . . Lianxang's blood froze as Corhanuk's spectral laughter rang out at her confusion, and she cringed when his hand brushed her shoulder, then seized her bag and shook it. Lianxang watched in despair as the Talisman fell to the ground.

At his behest the demon wraiths quickly bound her hand and foot, sliding two poles through the ropes and slinging her like so much cargo between two of their hell-horses.

Corhanuk strode over to where An Lushan lay and, stretching out his arm, raised him up. The wound to his shoulder seemed to cause him no discomfort as he sprang across to where the Talisman lay and eagerly thrust it into a pocket.

'Ride like the wind, hell-riders!' he thundered, sounding completely renewed. 'To the summit, where our master's loyal servant, the Staff-wielder, awaits!'

PART SIX

WAR AND SACRIFICE

The Legend of the Divine Collars of the Wise Lord

The following is recorded in The Book of Ahura Mazda, the Wise Lord

In ancient days, when the Earth was young and man knew nothing of shame and evil, the Wise Lord wanted to reward the faithful servants who attended him night and day, from the highest to the lowest guardian spirit. So He forged silver Collars, exquisitely crafted as finely coiled rope. He breathed into each one a smallest particle of his divine essence.

During the time when the dragon spirits that ruled the waters and the winds and all the elements manifested themselves in evil and terrorized man, the three rebel guardian spirits who had plotted against the Wise Lord were cast down, and their Collars were cut off by Chu Jung, Spirit of Fire and Heavenly Executioner. To bind up for ever the spirit of the divine that each Collar had been gifted with, the Wise Lord sealed the ends of the severed Collars with a clasp in the shape of a cicada, symbol of immortality, intending it as a sign of the divine essence of the Collars. Then He scattered the three Collars about the world, meaning to hide them for ever from men - but trusting that if they were ever found, the particle of the divine essence they contained and the heightened senses they could impart would bring whosoever wore them closer to Him

It was the tribe known as the Wild Horsemen who, in ages long past when they roamed far and wide across the Earth, came into possession of two of the Collars. The third, the Collar of the Shadow himself, has never been found.

Source: the secret Fellowship of the Three One-eared Hares;
origin – discovered in the ruins of the citadel monastery of Labrang,
spiritual centre of the old Western Empire.

CHAPTER 35

THE SECRET OF THE HORSEMEN'S COLLARS

They slowed to a trot as they approached the ridge again, emerging at the spot where Rokshan had first entered the Towers of Silence.

'Thank the stars . . .' he muttered. 'I'd never have found it again on my own.' He saw with relief that the sandstorm had already blasted its way over the rest of the Plain of the Dead and prayed once more that Cetu had managed to avoid the worst of it.

Stargazer stopped as he sensed Rokshan's uncertainty. The pale gravel shale of the Plain, eerily reflecting the silvery grey moonlight, stretched ahead of them, silent and forbidding. Rokshan looked down at the lord of the horses in humble amazement, knowing that Stargazer had delved into his heart and searched his soul, giving him an inner strength he'd never known before. He knew that Stargazer was infinitely wise, strong and true; he trusted him completely now.

His eyes scanned the horizon, searching for some sign of where Cetu might be . . . There! The tiny, flickering light of a campfire. Stargazer blew noisily and tossed his head, and instinctively Rokshan knew it was his Waymaster waiting there for him.

Stargazer needed no guidance and Rokshan clung onto his streaming mane as they galloped across the plain; it seemed only moments before they came to the encampment where Cetu had kept his lonely vigil. He started towards them as they approached, his eyes widening as he recognized the powerful beauty and unmistakable aura of Stargazer.

As he dropped to one knee in homage, he was almost knocked over by Breeze Whisperer. She skittered shyly up to her lord, blowing gently and returning Stargazer's nickers of greeting. Rokshan jumped down but for a moment couldn't speak as he witnessed the love and devotion between the two horses. Closing his eyes, he felt he could almost touch the current between them; delving deeper, he saw their emotions flowing like a river of colours – perhaps he could share in their delight, he thought, smiling.

'Rokshan! Do not intrude where most would fear to go.' Cetu's note of warning brought him back from the brink, but the pride in his voice was unmistakable: 'So confident already – to even contemplate such a thing! They will be back before dawn,' he added as the two horses whirled joyously together and galloped off across the plain. Rokshan shrugged his shoulders, but he already felt Stargazer's absence, and was a little puzzled by what he saw as his desertion.

They made themselves comfortable by the fire, each with a steaming bowl of broth that Cetu had prepared.

The old Waymaster looked at Rokshan over the rim of his bowl. 'I never doubted you would return, and to have returned with Stargazer is a cause for even greater joy,' he said carefully. 'What has the lord of the horses told you? I could see that the bond between you is already strong. This is wondrous indeed, my young friend . . . What happened amongst our dead?' he asked quietly, setting down his bowl.

Rokshan recounted faithfully what had befallen him while Cetu listened intently, nodding and occasionally asking a question so that he was clear about every detail. Soon Rokshan had to admit that he'd worn the Collar, and described the vision he'd experienced.

'You *wore* the Collar? And this vision it gave you . . . you think it was a vision of Hell – where the old storyteller said you must go? You must tell me all about that. But first . . . I wonder . . . perhaps it was the wearing of the Collar of the Dead that made your joining with Stargazer so rapid? It is, after all, said to impart the wisdom of generations.'

'Perhaps – and was it just coincidence that I sought shelter in the tower of the dead khagan's predecessor? No! Stargazer led me there deliberately,' Rokshan exclaimed excitedly.

Cetu refilled his bowl and said nothing as he took a long sip.

Rokshan thought this might be a good moment to tell him that he'd taken the Collar. 'I brought it with me,' he said softly, reaching into his pocket and holding it up. 'It will help us in knowing what we must—'

At the sight of it Cetu choked on his drink and, coughing violently, spilled his broth. Rokshan leaped up to help him but the Waymaster angrily waved him away.

'You . . . you stole the Collar of the Dead? The dead will reclaim it!' Cetu gasped in between spasms of coughing. 'What possessed you? It is . . . is—' He couldn't finish his sentence and grudgingly accepted the water pouch Rokshan offered him. Gradually his coughing subsided and he stared at the fire, shaking his head and wiping his streaming eyes. 'You will have to return it. At first light, so no one will know of your . . . your madness,' he said severely, not even looking at him.

'Why? It'll just lie there, doing no one any good when it could be helping us.'

'Helping us?'

'Yes, helping us! Now everything points to what the old storyteller told me I must do. First, Stargazer staying with me – there is no faster creature alive to take us to the Flame Mountains! How far away are they – eight hundred li or more? Then the vision I've just had wearing the Collar – surely a place of such nightmares could only be Hell itself? And once we have reached the Flame Mountains, the Collar may lead us to the court of the Crimson King, at the portals of Hell.' Rokshan noticed a flicker of surprise cross Cetu's face.

'Your storyteller may have been wiser than you know, Rokshan. There is an old Horseman's story of one of our earliest khagans and the Collars – it is a tale you would do well to listen to, so you know what we're dealing with,' Cetu sighed.

Rokshan nodded attentively.

'Long ago,' the Waymaster began, 'one of our khagans was driven mad because he wore the greater Collar too often, and for too long. That is why every khagan since has worn the Collar only very sparingly – for this khagan recorded what he saw in his visions. The Crimson King himself appeared to him, demanding the return of both his Collar, and that of Beshbaliq, a lesser guardian spirit: this is why they became known to us as the greater Collar, and the lesser Collar of the Dead – the one you have stolen.' Cetu glared disapprovingly at his wayward pupil. 'More than this, he warned us of a third Collar, which has never been found, and I pray never will be—'

'A third Collar? Who does it belong to – did the vision reveal this?'

'The most powerful Collar of the three' – Cetu paused, searching for the right words – 'is the most potent of divine gifts that could be used against the Wise Lord, for it is the Collar of his most favoured guardian spirit . . . the one who became the Shadow, the Lord of Evil himself.'

Cetu fell silent, his story done. A tale, Rokshan thought, which only a Horseman would have known – and it dawned on him that, like their mindjoining with the dragon horses, this was another secret the Horsemen had kept so closely guarded not even the Elect knew of it. But what was it meant to tell him? And did they have other secrets he didn't know about? He clung to the only certainty he could think of, which was what Shou Lao had told him he must do.

'We must make our way to the Flame Mountains, Cetu, without delay.'

'If I go with you, it will be with the clan chiefs' blessing or not at all,' Cetu said firmly. 'They must know what has happened here . . . I will not hear otherwise. The Serenadhi will surely wish to speak with you too, but they will find us when they wish. As for the Collar you have taken, you must keep it hidden, and tell no one. I wish you had not told me. At first light we must return to the First Valley with all haste.'

Cetu settled himself down, grunting a gruff goodnight before starting to snore softly. Rokshan's mind was too busy for sleep; he gazed up at the stars, wondering if the answers to everything were really written there, as Zerafshan believed – and perhaps, he admitted to himself, he did too: how else would things have come about as they had, if it had not been his destiny? In the far distance he thought he caught the faintest echo of a horse's whinnying cry; after a while his eyes became heavy, and he eventually drifted off.

He dreamed strange dreams that night. He was riding Stargazer across the plains when they were approached by the black dragon horses of the Serenadhi: it was Sumiyaa and two of her sisters. Sumiyaa was giving him a warning.

'The lord of the horses allows you to ride him. It is enough. The dragon spirits of the horses will work their own way, in a fashion we cannot yet grasp. You are part of this – that is all we know. Beware, however, the power of the visions the Collar may show you . . .'

And then, strangest of all:

'Rokshan . . . we will wait for you,' Sumiyaa called in her sing-song voice as the dream faded.

He was woken by a loud whinny – it was dawn and Stargazer and Breeze Whisperer had returned. Rokshan sensed an urgency in Stargazer, as if he was willing them to be on their way as quickly as they could, and there was a new tension to

Breeze Whisperer's aura, he noticed. This concerned him, and as they broke camp, he recounted his dream to Cetu.

'It is as I said – the ways of the Serenadhi are not our ways; they will speak with you when they wish, and have chosen to do so in a dream.' Cetu shrugged. 'But are you *sure* it was a dream, my young friend?' He grinned, picking up his saddle and swinging it onto Breeze Whisperer's back.

Rokshan gasped in amazement: neatly stored under Cetu's saddle was one of the unmistakable lightweight riding seats – it could hardly be called a saddle – that had seemed so curious to him when he had first seen the Serenadhi at the Festival of the Dragon. Coiled on top of it was a length of the fine rope that they entwined through the long manes of their mounts in place of reins.

'Saddle him up – if he'll take it; you'll find riding him much easier, even without the stirrups.' Cetu laughed.

Rokshan laughed too – he would have to make do without them, as he already had. Stargazer's gold-green eyes flashed, his long tail flicking back and forth, and he blew noisily down his nose as if to warn Rokshan off as he approached him.

He threaded the cord through first; murmuring words of encouragement, he felt gentle currents passing between the two horses which he tried to flow into with his thoughts. Just as he stooped to pick up the riding seat, an image of the Serenadhi snapped into his mind with such clarity that he froze.

'What? What is it?' Cetu asked anxiously.

Rokshan gestured for him to be quiet as he saw the three sisters surrounded by ribbons of blue and yellow that twisted this way and that, coiling around them as if to tie them up. In an instant the image was gone. Stargazer whickered softly as Rokshan carefully positioned the seat on his back.

'What was it you showed me?' Rokshan asked gently. 'Are

the sisters in danger? Must we go to them? How shall we find them?'

But nothing else flashed through his head. It was only later that it struck Rokshan: blue and yellow were the imperial colours of the emperor . . .

CHAPTER 36

WAR CLOUDS

They rode hard across the Wastes of Astana and the Plains of Jalhal'a. One morning, with more than a day's ride still ahead of them before they arrived back at the First Valley, they were preparing to set off in the grey light of dawn when they saw two riders approaching at a gallop from the north-east.

As they came nearer, Rokshan felt a shiver course through Stargazer and sensed a low warning note beneath a current of red; Breeze Whisperer too seemed nervous, tossing her head and skittering back and forth. Cetu had dismounted and had his bow ready, arrow nocked.

'Who are you? Stop and speak your names,' he called out.

The riders' horses were flecked with sweat and their heads hung with exhaustion, their chests heaving. Rokshan noticed the riders rode without stirrups, as did many of the Plains Horsemen.

'Are you Horsemen, who would drive your mounts to the brink of death?' the Waymaster observed angrily. 'Speak!

'Peace, Cetu, Waymaster of the Horse,' one of the riders answered, throwing back his hooded fur cloak to reveal his face. 'It is I, Lerikos, brother to the dead Gandhara, formerly clan leader of the First Valley.' He slid off his mount, half dead with fatigue, crumpling on his knees in front of Stargazer. 'May the dragon spirits of the plains be praised . . . Stargazer . . .' he murmured, bowing his head.

'Gandhara – dead?' Cetu queried, numb with shock. 'How? On your feet . . . What is happening in the valleys? Can your companion speak?' he demanded, recovering himself.

'I am Kezenway, son of Lerikos,' the other rider called out with a tremor in his voice, revealing himself to be hardly older than Rokshan. 'Gandhara was killed in a skirmish with the imperial forces, scouts from a mighty host marching from the east across our plains—'

'Imperial forces?' Cetu asked, surprise and alarm in his voice.

'They carried the blue and yellow markings of the emperor's colours, yes,' said Lerikos, 'and have violated the treaty in which they agreed never to enter our plains or valleys. His intention is clear, Cetu: he will destroy our people and capture as many of our dragon horses as he can at the same time.'

Cetu was too stunned to speak.

'What were you doing on the plains? Were you following us?' Rokshan spoke for the first time.

Lerikos got to his feet and bowed. 'Before he was killed, Gandhara sent us to find out if you had succeeded in what the Serenadhi sent you to do and what you had learned from our dead . . .' The grizzled Horseman looked at him appraisingly, noting his saddle and the cord entwined through Stargazer's mane. 'We have the answer to that, if my eyes do not deceive me.'

'They do not, Lerikos,' Cetu snapped, finding his voice again, 'but there is no time for that now. We shall tell the other clan leaders all they need to know when we see them. We must get back to the First Valley with all speed.'

'That will be difficult, Waymaster,' Lerikos replied flatly.

'What do you mean?'

'Zerafshan has taken command of our forces. All the remaining clan leaders report to him, and are digging in: their orders are that each clan must defend its own valley, to the last man. All our dragon horses have been driven up the valleys, along with the old and infirm, and the women and children, and are penned at the highest point in your Fifth Valley. The First Valley will defend itself as best it can, and must hold off the imperial army as long as possible. Similar orders are in place for each clan. By the time the army reaches the Fifth Valley, it will be fatally weakened and we will be able to finish off what remains of it. This is Zerafshan's strategy. A force of the Plains Horsemen under Draxurion has assembled in the First Valley to help their defence. The rest of us are doing all in our power to protect the wild dragon horses of the plains but . . .' Lerikos fell into an exhausted silence.

'But, Lerikos . . . ?' Rokshan prompted gently.

'They are unbiddable without the song of the Serenadhi to speak to their innermost spirits and tell them we mean them no harm. We shall lose them all to the emperor, who will simply round them up by force,' he replied despairingly.

Rokshan struggled to recall something he knew he had learned from the Serenadhi, but he could only glimpse it like a tiny spark of light winking fitfully on the horizon. What was it Cetu had said? *This is the way of the Serenadhi . . . Nobody knows how, but you will remember what they have told you when the time comes.*

Surely the time was now? he raged. Closing his eyes, he willed Stargazer to speak to him, but stepped back in shock and dismay when he saw that the horse's mind was a seething mass of anger and frustration: anger at what was happening to his brothers and sisters, and frustration that he could not go to them because he owed allegiance to his rider.

'Where are the Serenadhi, do you know?' Rokshan asked, wondering if there was any way he could let Stargazer go but knowing in his heart of hearts that it was impossible – nor would Stargazer countenance it, he realized.

'There are rumours that they have been captured by the imperial forces and are being forced to help them round up the wild dragon horses,' Kezenway replied, glancing at his father.

'No! This cannot be!' Cetu cried, hurling his bow to the ground. 'They would have done *anything* to avoid capture . . . They – they would've escaped into the desert. They would not permit their powers to be abused—'

'Nonetheless, there has been no sighting of them since the Festival of the Dragon,' Lerikos replied, 'and the imperial army is now two days' march – three days at most – from the First Valley. We rode hard to increase our lead on them.'

'I have seen them . . . the Serenadhi,' Rokshan said softly into the silence. The two Horsemen looked at him expectantly, making him feel sick at heart: the sisters had given him a gift, but he didn't know what it was, or how to use it. Surely, though, he could inspire them instead? It was he, after all, who rode the lord of the horses!

Stargazer tossed his head and echoed his thoughts as a softly shimmering, warm note of green ran through his mind.

'Come, Cetu,' Rokshan said in a stronger voice. 'Our place is with the men of the First Valley and their Plains cousins. It will give them great joy to see Stargazer, and Stargazer wishes to be there for them – there could be no omen more powerful for them. We must ride like the wind!'

Lerikos nodded approvingly.

'We will get there ahead of you,' Rokshan said to the two Plains Horsemen. 'Rest your mounts a while – we will get word to your kin that you are safe.'

The following day, weary and dusty from their headlong gallop – they had ridden through the night – they approached the tall gates of the First Valley settlement, which were closed and heavily guarded.

'Who approaches the First Valley of the Horsemen?' one of the guards shouted.

'Open the gates – it is Cetu, Waymaster of the Fifth Valley, and Rokshan, mounted on Stargazer, lord of the horses. Open the gates!'

As they rode in, a young Horseman hurried up to them. He gave the Horsemen's salute as he dropped to one knee in acknowledgement of Stargazer, looking with intense curiosity at Rokshan as he sat holding the cord woven into his horse's mane.

'I must ask you respectfully to tell me what your business is here, Waymaster,' he requested.

'Come, Salamundi, since when has a Waymaster accompanied by the lord of the horses and his rider been accountable for his movements through any of the valleys?' Cetu bristled, not in the mood for interrogation.

'Since the clan chiefs all acknowledged Zerafshan as military commander of the Horsemen. All travellers from the plains are to be questioned as to their business,' Salamundi replied coolly.

'Our business?' Cetu muttered under his breath before gathering himself. 'Imperial forces are already on the plains, one . . . two days' march away at most. Defences must be readied and fully manned! Where is Draxurion? Take us to him!'

Salamundi blanched. 'Follow me,' he said quietly, turning smartly on his heel and issuing orders as he led them to Draxurion's tent.

CHAPTER 37

THE BATTLE OF THE FIRST VALLEY

'The hour has come,' Draxurion observed, having listened quietly to everything Cetu and Rokshan had told him. 'More quickly and over the plains in violation of the treaty, from the direction we least expected – but we are ready for them.'

He looked respectfully at Rokshan before walking quickly down the line of men who had gathered in his tent, saluting each one.

'To your posts, Horsemen! The lord of the horses has come among us – ridden by our future khagan, if Zerafshan should lead us to victory. Stargazer will lend us strength and renewed hope. Now go! Check and double-check your preparations while there is still time. Remember, we defend our valleys to the death. No surrender! The emperor will have to pick his way through a mountain of our dead before the gates of the First Valley open to him!' He gave a final salute and strode out of the tent without another word.

'Rokshan, Salamundi – come with me,' Cetu said as he followed the others out. Salamundi hurried after him.

'Rokshan, you must know that your destiny and that of the lord of the horses lie beyond this valley,' said the Waymaster. 'Stargazer cannot fight in this battle; I will ask him and Breeze Whisperer to come with me to a place of safety while you take your place with the archers. I will rejoin you presently. Salamundi, if anything should happen to me, I want you to stay with Rokshan. If all seems lost, there is no dishonour in retreat – the people of the other valleys will need to see Stargazer; it will give them hope. That is, if he does not go to help his brothers and sisters on the plains.'

Salamundi nodded his understanding, grim-faced. Breeze Whisperer whickered softly to her lord, and Stargazer paused; it seemed he was reluctant to go with her. Rokshan stroked his neck, sensing he was torn between loyalty to his rider on one hand and his brothers and sisters on the other. Finally he made his decision, moving away with Breeze Whisperer and Cetu.

Rokshan's heart was thumping as he mounted the steps to the section of the perimeter that he had been assigned to. Only fifteen or sixteen candle-rings had passed since they had gathered in Draxurion's tent, but the tramp of the massed forces of the imperial army as it swept across the Plains of Jalhal'a to the droning beat of a thousand gourd-shaped drums and the shrill wail of bamboo pan-pipes was growing ever louder: it rolled across the plains, along with the clink and rattle of heavily armed chariots and the pounding of thousands of hooves that made the ground shake.

The defenders prayed to the Wise Lord and all the beneficent dragon spirits of the earth, air, fire and water, blessing themselves with the sign of the dragon. Some had lucky charms and tokens which they kissed before stowing them away safely.

Hundreds of Plains Horsemen streamed out of the gates and wheeled to the right, galloping about one li away before lying in wait to attack the left flank of the anticipated chariot charge. More followed them out, wheeling to the left to attack the right flank of the enemy. The remaining Plains Horsemen, led by Draxurion and joined now by Lerikos and Kezenway, fanned out directly in front of the tall gates to defend the entrance. About five hundred men of the First Valley lined the perimeter walls.

Cetu walked among them, offering words of encouragement

and advice, joking with the younger warriors, who looked to him for support, trying not to appear as frightened as they felt.

'Remember to make each arrow count. Aim for the throat – imperial troops are well protected by their armour but this is their weak spot. When it comes to it, use your short lances and aim for the same spot but keep your front covered. Remember what you have been taught and have practised a thousand times. Steady now . . .'

Up and down the line he went, only joining Rokshan and Salamundi's group by the tall gates when they saw the distant cloud of dust rolling towards them.

'Here comes the first wave,' Cetu said grimly. 'Chariots – hundreds of them, judging by that dust cloud, and there'll be cavalry behind them.'

He had to raise his voice above the increasing cacophony. The air shook with the beating of the Horsemen's leather drums, which were strung with bells. Standard-bearers unfurled banners of rearing dragons in dazzling gold, which seemed to leap and snarl as they streamed in the wind. Leading from the front, Draxurion raised his hand and signalled to his hornsman to sound the advance. All along the lines, two deep and about one thousand strong, the Plains Horsemen defending the gates urged their mounts forward at a trot, then a canter, only breaking into a gallop at Draxurion's signal.

Rokshan watched the brave charge against the assembled might of the emperor's elite chariot corps, his heart thumping. Hopelessly outnumbered, the Horsemen were taking the fight directly to the enemy rather than waiting to be overwhelmed by the sheer weight of numbers ranged against them.

There was a thundering roar now as the Horsemen galloped towards the approaching imperial chariots. The dust cloud parted as the chariots burst through, hurtling at break-neck speed towards them. They came in clusters of two, three and five, in a huge diamond formation. But Rokshan's heart sank when he saw what was lumbering along behind them: captured deep in the jungles of the Southern Empire and then trained in the emperor's largest military garrison which defended the imperial capital, a fifty-strong formation of fully armoured war-elephants, their banners of imperial yellow bordered with blue streaming from the howdahs on the elephants' backs, each occupied by two archers.

The elephants' fierce trumpeting sounded above the din as the Horsemen let loose their first volley of arrows at full gallop, veering aside at the last minute to stream round the chariots, then reining in their mounts sharply to penetrate the formation.

The skill and accuracy of the Horsemen in mounted warfare was legendary throughout the Empire, and for good reason: Rokshan watched their first volley cut a deadly swathe among the most important target – the charioteers. The swordsmen or archers were capable of taking the reins from their dead comrades, but the tight diamond formation soon broke up as the Horsemen darted and weaved around the cumbersome four-horse vehicles, picking off the swordsmen and archers with lance and arrow.

Close behind, the archers on the imperial war-elephants saw what was happening and used their height to loose a deadly rain of arrows on the Horsemen. The elephants closed in, seriously hampering the Horsemen's movement: some of their mounts were terrified by the enormous strange creatures. Rokshan sensed their fear in rolling waves of colour, but then was astonished to feel a sudden calm, which he knew must be Stargazer trying to allay the fears of his brothers and sisters; he also sensed Stargazer's frustration at not being with them.

With all their efforts concentrated on calming their snorting, rearing mounts, the Horsemen made much easier targets for the chariot swordsmen, and one by one they fell. Those who escaped the sword were trampled underfoot by the elephants.

'Where are our flanking forces?' Rokshan cried despairingly as he watched the Plains Horsemen being slaughtered.

'They must've caught sight of the elephants as they
advanced and decided to hold back,' Cetu shouted.

Some of the Horsemen's riderless mounts had broken
away from the scene of carnage and were heading for the safety
of the gates when a troop of imperial cavalry – at least two
hundred strong, Rokshan guessed – came into view. Behind
them tramped rank upon rank of imperial foot soldiers, a vast
field of yellow and blue, marching to the shrilling pipes and
the beating of the gourd drums.

The cavalry tore into the re-formed phalanx of chariots,
riding skilfully among them to finish off the survivors of
Draxurion's brave full-frontal attack. Their scimitars flashed in
the wintry afternoon sun as they thrust and lunged at the
dwindling band of Horsemen in the centre. The warriors
formed a circle around their clan leader, who bravely tried to
rally them. Their arrows all spent, they hacked defensively with
their short swords and wielded their lances, but it was a hopeless struggle.

Finally Draxurion and Lerikos stood alone among the
heaped bodies of their dead and dying comrades. The cavalrymen suddenly pulled back from the fray as the archers on the
war-elephants prepared for one last devastating volley. The hail
of arrows cut down the Horsemen instantly: Draxurion fell
without a sound, pierced by a dozen arrows, his lifeless body
crumpling beside that of Lerikos.

Less than half a li from the gates, the imperial troops swept
along, the war-elephants leading the charge with the cavalry
protecting the infantry's flanks.

'Prepare arrows but do not release until the order,' the
command went up and down the perimeter walls.

Rokshan's hands were slippery with sweat but his face was

set as he rehearsed the procedure he had practised with Cetu a hundred times.

'*Aim* – target the drivers perched on the elephants and on the first line of infantry.'

Five hundred bowstrings were pulled taut, some with a tremor, and held there. Less than quarter of a li now, Rokshan calculated . . . Where were their flanking forces? Couldn't they see that now was the perfect time to launch their attack?

Then his mind focused on what he was doing, shutting everything else out: the trumpeting of the war-elephants; the clink and rattle of the chariots; the pounding of the hooves of the cavalry; the tramp of the foot soldiers; the wail of the pipes and rhythmic, mesmerizing beat of the drums; the reek of battle – blood, sweat and fear – over everything. His mind floated above it all, his left eye squinting in line with his bow hand as he lined up his target – an elephant-driver perched on the massive neck of one of the beasts . . . two hundred paces now . . . one hundred . . .

'*Hold* . . . Hold it steady now . . . Steady . . . *Release!*'

Five hundred arrows loosed simultaneously hissed through the air to their targets. Rokshan's elephant-driver toppled soundlessly from his perch, an arrow in his eye, but Rokshan concentrated only on releasing one arrow after another as quickly as he could. The discipline and accuracy of the defenders' fire checked the enemy's advance as half a dozen or more elephants, suddenly freed from the guiding heels and taps of their drivers, charged in all directions. Gaps appeared in the front line of infantry as volley after volley of arrows found their marks. A ragged cheer went up from the defenders as three of the driverless elephants turned tail and charged back among their own ranks, trampling a great swathe through the massed infantry, who were too tightly packed to avoid the beasts' rampage.

Horns sounded to the left and right as the flanking forces

of the remaining Plains Horsemen at last charged to the attack and clashed with the cavalry on both sides of the relentlessly advancing infantry.

'There are too many of them! However fast we kill them, there are always more coming up behind,' Rokshan cried. 'Arrows! I need arrows!'

The youngest warriors, who had been assigned the task of running up and down the line replenishing stocks of arrows, had been working as fast as they could but now stood behind the defenders, their job done.

'None left? All your stocks gone?' Cetu shouted. 'Check the dead – there may be some left unused.'

The advancing foot soldiers halted just out of range of the Horsemen's arrows. Protected by the cavalry on their flanks, who had beaten off the attack from the Horsemen, they now regrouped and prepared to charge the gates and walls.

The war-elephants trumpeted, and the earth shook as the imperial troops roared their response, stamping their feet in time to the beat of the drums. Mounted officers trotted up and down, whipping their men into a frenzy for the final attack. At last the command to advance went up and the troops surged forward. They were met by a hail of arrows and lances. It was the defenders' last volley.

'Save your lances!' Cetu yelled, running up and down the line. 'Defend the walls . . . beat them off any way you can . . . short swords and lances – bare hands if you have nothing else!' he shouted defiantly.

The imperial forces were swarming up makeshift ladders now; as soon as one was hurled down, another took its place. Cetu looked at the gates as a group of elephants charged towards them.

'By the teeth of the dragon,' he swore under his breath, 'we are done for now . . .' There was a splintering crash as the elephants thundered into the heavily barred gates. They held, but Cetu realized it was only a matter of time before they gave way. Imperial troops were on the ramparts now, and more were pouring up the ladders, lashed on by their officers.

Salamundi darted around the thick of the fighting, steering Rokshan by the arm towards where Cetu stood. 'Waymaster!' he roared to make himself heard above the din of battle. 'You must go – now, Waymaster, before it's too late! And take your charge with you.' Salamundi bowed hastily to Rokshan. 'The rider of the lord of the horses has acquitted himself well today, like a true Horseman!' He thumped his chest in the customary salute. 'We will meet again, with the white mares on the plains of the world where the spirits of our ancestors roam free. Farewell!' He turned and rushed back to the fray.

'He's right: the gates will give way soon and we'll all be slaughtered – follow me,' Cetu barked.

Rushing down from the perimeter walls, they ran across the enclosure where the festival dragon still stood, snarling defiantly.

'Where are Stargazer and Breeze Whisperer?' Rokshan shouted.

'Safe, away from this carnage, along with our bags and a few provisions.' Cetu weaved in and out of a maze of narrow streets. Rokshan began to feel dizzy with exhaustion and the release of tension after the battle. Just as he was wondering if Cetu knew where they were going, he stopped, diving into the tannery.

As they led the horses out of the tanner's yard, they heard a rending and splintering followed by a booming thud as the gates finally crashed to the ground. A huge roar went up from the imperial forces. Suddenly Stargazer reared and whinnied as if trying to rally the Horsemen. Rokshan slipped the cord from his hand and stumbled to the ground as, through the fog and clamour of the battle, he saw through Stargazer's inner eye what was happening on the plains: heart-rending neighs from the wild dragon horses rose above the shouts of soldiers and cracks of whips and lasso as they were rounded up by skilled imperial cavalrymen; in the dust and confusion he could make out the black mounts of the Serenadhi, which wheeled and galloped, desperately trying to calm their charges and make their inevitable capture as painless as possible. Rokshan sensed Stargazer's anger and pain as black, towering thunderclouds in his mind.

'Go to them, Stargazer – they need you,' he urged him. 'Our paths will cross again when they will; we must trust to fate for that.'

He felt a flood of warm reassurance in response, and it was all Cetu could do to calm Breeze Whisperer and stop her galloping after Stargazer, who headed like a thunderbolt for the broken, splintered gates of the First Valley.

'Stargazer!' Rokshan suddenly shouted after him, but he knew that the lord of the horses had to be with his own kind, to somehow rescue them from their fate.

Cetu grasped straight away what had happened. 'He is servant to none,' he told Rokshan, 'and will surely join us when he has done all he can for his kind. For now we must ride, Rokshan, like we've never ridden before! The valley clans must have hope, and that is our message to give them.' He leaped astride Breeze Whisperer and offered his hand as Rokshan jumped up behind him. 'Just like when we started out, my young friend!' he laughed, urging Breeze Whisperer on.

She needed no second bidding and galloped like the wind as they made their escape from the slaughter in the First Valley.

CHAPTER 38

STARGAZER AND THE RIDDLE

Dusk was falling and the valleys seemed eerily quiet after the smoke and din of the battle. Breeze Whisperer set a fierce pace. At this speed it would take no more than two candle-rings to reach the Second Valley, Rokshan thought as he listened to the light, rhythmic pounding of her hooves.

An emptiness gnawed away at him as terrible bloody images from the battle flickered through his mind. Salamundi had said he'd acquitted himself well, but all he felt was a sense of guilt and shame at leaving the Horsemen to their fate. Draxurion had said, 'No surrender,' and they would've fought to the last man. Rokshan thought of Kezenway, barely older than him, and wondered how he had felt at the end. And what had become of Stargazer? What if he too was captured? He felt sick at the thought and quickly tried to put it out of his mind.

Breeze Whisperer seemed ill at ease too, tossing her head and whickering when at last they stopped to rest a while, having put a good distance behind them. Rokshan felt her sadness at being separated from Stargazer and tried to reassure her that her lord would do all in his power to help her wild kin of the plains. Cetu was anxious and didn't want to stop for too long, fearing that scouts from the victorious imperial forces might be sent on ahead and catch them unawares.

Scudding clouds couldn't obscure the brilliance of the almost full moon as they approached the empty corral – before, it had been full of dragon horses fresh from the First Valley. Rokshan felt the desolation within Breeze Whisperer and patted her neck fondly. He was also trying to reassure himself as he pondered on what Lerikos had told them: how many hundreds of dragon horses had been herded together and penned at the topmost point of the valleys?

His thoughts turned to the man who had declared himself to be his father. He had barely had time to think about it at all since Zerafshan had made his stunning revelation; he still found it very difficult to think of him as his father.

Then his mind turned to the storyteller. He wondered how Shou Lao had come by the ancient scroll from the Kingdom of the Horsemen – the same scroll that recounted the riddle of the Staff. *The servant of the Nameless One is the one I speak of*, Shou Lao had said. *He serves the Shadow-without-a-name, the Lord of Evil. He pores over the ancient lore and is plotting to use the power of the dragons of old for his own ends. But there is one hope, and one hope only – an ancient scroll unearthed in the Kingdom of the Wild Horsemen, which foretold this very moment . . .*

Was Zerafshan at the bottom of it? His father! Could all this be his doing? Had he come by the scroll just by accident, or had he stolen it from the Elect when he was an initiate, carrying it off to the Kingdom of the Horsemen to brood and plot, eventually coming up with his own mad interpretation of the riddle?

He is plotting to use the power of the dragons of old for his own ends. What did this mean? Rokshan didn't know the answer to any of these questions: he needed to find out. A trickling sense that time was running out grew into a bloody torrent as he imagined the imperial forces scything their way up the valleys as Zerafshan's strategy failed, with every last Horseman being killed to satisfy the emperor.

The Horsemen had put their trust in his father, but Rokshan wasn't so sure: something deep down bothered him. Nervously he fingered the Collar which he kept close to him at all times now, hanging against his chest from a leather cord around his neck.

Lost in these thoughts, he, along with Cetu, was nearly thrown when Breeze Whisperer suddenly slowed and, veering around, cantered alongside the corral, tossing up her head and whinnying loudly. Cetu jumped down when she slowed for a moment, but something made Rokshan stay with her. 'It's all right, Cetu – she's trying to tell me something!' he shouted as the Waymaster grabbed the reins and tried to calm her.

'What is it, Breeze Whisperer? Tell me!'

All at once he felt a current pass between him and the horse, like a gentle breeze wafting through his mind; far off he thought he heard a voice calling him . . . it dawned on him that the lord of the horses was now using Breeze Whisperer as a conduit through which to mindjoin with him. Breeze Whisperer was still now, and he felt calm, gripped by the absolute conviction that nothing in his whole life had been more important than this moment. He knew that there was no need to dismount, that Stargazer wanted him to be one with him through Breeze Whisperer.

Out of the corner of his eye he noticed Cetu approaching and waved him aside urgently. A moment later he plunged into the depths of the first levels of Breeze Whisperer and Stargazer's combined emotions. These were massively strong currents! He fought against a growing sense of panic as he felt their swirling ebb and pull, closing his mind's eye to an exploding kaleido-scope of colour that threatened to disorientate him. Suddenly he was being swirled towards two waterfalls: one raged over a drop which he could hear thundering far below; the other gurgled gently, the water slipping smoothly over the edge. He knew which one he was being drawn towards as he tumbled over the lip and felt himself being deluged by streaming torrents of colour.

He let himself fall. When he thought he couldn't possibly fall any further, he saw he had emerged into a tranquil lagoon, where he was surrounded by Stargazer's thoughts. They were the deepest blue – he imagined himself drowning in their depths . . . It was such a peaceful death, he thought to himself . . . so quiet and warm – all he had to do was let himself drift and float on for ever . . . He thought he would touch the Collar one more time before he slipped away—

As he did so, a fearsome whinny shattered the intense silence and the waters started to boil, becoming full of shadowy shapes plunging far down from the surface of the pool. Looking up, he saw a small circle of sky with clouds scudding across . . . then the sky was covered with thick black stormclouds; jagged lightning flashed and sizzled into the water, spearing down through the depths. And he was naked . . . His body was being slashed and cut. Writhing and twisting, he screamed silently and swam on and on, but now he was in the vastness of the ocean and he would have to swim for ever. The water turned a thickening red, filled with his blood – so much blood he was drowning in it; he couldn't stop himself gulping it down and choking . . . Slowly he sank beneath the waves of blood and started to fall into a black vortex that slowly closed over him.

The stars, shining so brightly in the blackness, were snuffed out like so many candles, and far-off he thought he heard a voice intoning, over and over, 'Remember, you are the Nameless One . . . Remember you are the Nameless One . . .' Then there was a soul-piercing scream, a noise like the rushing of wind, and finally a silence so profound it felt as if he had always been there, in the centre of it; but he was disappearing now, like a wraith. Too late – as he started to gasp for breath – he understood.

Stargazer . . . I . . . I cannot control the conjoining . . . I have gone too far into your spirit soul, and it is killing me.

No, Rokshan, take heart . . . Stargazer's voice was distant, warm but commanding. *I have allowed you to look into the inner eye of my soul, and there you have glimpsed the memory of something so terrible that the Wise*

Lord buried it deep in the spirit soul of my ancestor, Han Garid, when he witnessed the imprisoning of the Shadow; something that has been passed down through the ages to every lord of the horse that has ever been. But now I only have the barest inkling of what it can be; I only know that it is there, and that we were created the most beautiful and swift of all creatures so that we would never come under the sway of man, who must never know this secret. This is the memory that the forces of evil seek to unlock: you will be tested in the ordeal to come, because the Shadow knows of this memory and bends every fibre of his being to retrieve it. Heed my warning, Rokshan! He will beguile you with a choice — you must resist him and those who serve him, as I must, but the ancient magic may be too powerful for all of us. Resist, if you want to save your kind and the dragon horses!

You must remember the Divine Commandment which created what men call night, imprisoning the Shadow for ever — until now. Know too that when I left the Plains of Jalhal'a and was not seen by the Horsemen for many cycles of the moon, I rode with Shou Lao, taking him to warn the people of the lands by the Great Ocean, just as he has warned your people, and those of the desert Kingdom of Kroraynia. We rode to the Land of Temples, and from there to the people of the Thousand Islands; even the far-off northern shores of the Lands of Ice have received him. The Dark Forests, too, have given their own warning to the people of the Darhad . . .

Strike up to the surface now and breathe the air, before you drown in the oneness of the Great Ocean, which fills with the blood of countless souls in the struggle to come. Remember our joining, and what it has revealed to you . . .

Rokshan so badly wanted to talk to Stargazer and understand more as he swam upwards, his lungs bursting. But the mind-link joining him through Breeze Whisperer dimmed and faded away as he surfaced, gasping and heaving for breath — and found himself with his back to Cetu, pinned against his chest, his arms clamped tight by his side.

He struggled to free himself, staggering to the ground as he was suddenly released. Just as quickly Cetu hauled him up again, striking him hard on the face.

'Let go!' he shouted. 'Sever the link completely!'

'How long have I been joined?' Rokshan gasped, seizing hold of him.

'Nearly half the night. I have been in a battle with a madman, possessed by a thousand demons – that's how hard you struggled after you had slid off Breeze Whisperer. It was lucky I was there to catch you. What has she shown you? I have never witnessed such a mindjoining . . .'

Rokshan sat down, his head spinning from what he'd just experienced. He fumbled for the Collar of the Dead. 'Where is it?' he asked sharply.

'You tore it off and threw it away,' Cetu said mildly. 'I gathered it up and wrapped it securely – it is in your coat.'

'I don't think I need it any more . . . Stargazer has told me so much, Cetu! But much of it I cannot understand either. How I wish we could've spoken longer.' Rokshan wiped his face, which was covered in sweat.

'Stargazer?' Cetu asked, looking with concern at Rokshan – had his mind been damaged?

'Yes, he spoke to me through Breeze Whisperer.'

'It is impossible, never have I—'

'It is possible, Cetu, you must not doubt me. She has not been affected?'

'No, as you can see,' Cetu replied, looking round and nodding towards Breeze Whisperer, who grazed contentedly a short distance away.

'Do you know what has happened to the dragon horses of the plains? Has Stargazer succeeded?' Cetu asked quietly.

'I . . . I don't know . . . He had to go – his own kind need him now. But there was much else he told me besides . . . much else.' Rokshan held his head in his hands, staring hard at the ground, trying to fathom it all out.

'Drink, my friend,' Cetu said gently, sitting beside him and passing him a water pouch, 'and tell me what passed between you and Stargazer.'

Rokshan drank deep before he began to speak.

'Tell us more of this Divine Commandment,' Cetu said when Rokshan had told him as much as he could of what he had experienced. 'Many of the old myths are lost to the Horsemen.'

'I only know about it through the Fellowship of the Hares,' Rokshan said. 'The Wise Lord did not intend it to be written down, but when he made his Divine Commandment, he was accompanied by his faithful messenger, Corhanuk – a higher guardian spirit – who was to act as witness to the terrible punishment of the Shadow. Unbeknown to the Wise Lord, Corhanuk was already falling under the Shadow's power – and in future ages was to serve his new master. So when his master was sealed behind the Arch of Darkness, Corhanuk made mischief by recording the words of the Divine Commandment on a scroll, which he loosed in the world of men – the words that could be used, the Fellowship of the Hares believe, to give the Shadow his freedom: this is why the fellowship is dedicated to the Scroll's safekeeping, should it ever be found, so the words of the Divine Commandment will always remain with them, and be kept secret.

'Then, when Chu Jung had done the Wise Lord's bidding and the monstrous dragons were no more, and he had hidden the Talisman, he gave his Staff to Corhanuk to take to the Wise Lord as a gift, but Corhanuk stole it and hid himself and the Staff away from men and all living things. Through the ages he, the Staff and Talisman and the Sacred Scroll were all lost and forgotten about, passing into the mists of myth and legend. And through all those aeons, Corhanuk has served his new master – the Shadow.'

'But . . . can this Divine Commandment ever be undone, if it has been put in place by the Wise Lord himself?' Cetu asked.

'This we do not know, but the abbot told me: "It is enough

that the Sacred Scroll exists: for if it exists, it can be found, and when it is found, the servant of the Shadow will find out, sure enough, how it can be undone." Those were his exact words. Perhaps, now, Corhanuk is working his evil mischief once more and has found this scroll again?'

'Well, we waste time here, my friend,' Cetu said. 'We should heed what Stargazer has told you, and trust that, with his help, we will discover the answers to all these questions and be guided in what to do. He will join us again when he is ready . . . Rokshan? What's the matter?'

'The Staff and Talisman of Chu Jung!' Rokshan murmured, looking as if he'd been hit by a thunderbolt. 'Chu Jung *buried his Talisman somewhere in the forests of the world*, the legend says, and Corhanuk stole the Staff that Chu Jung fashioned from the tree that sprang up where the Talisman had been buried . . . Cetu! Perhaps Stargazer was trying to tell me what forests those were! *The Dark Forests have given their own warning to the people of the Darhad*, he said. And if he was trying to tell me that, it must've been for a reason. The Dark Forests were where my brother was headed, not so long ago. What was Stargazer trying to tell me? Zerafshan lies at the heart of this, I'm sure of that now: we must question him. We must get up to the Fifth Valley, where he prepares the final defences against the imperial forces.'

Cetu nodded his understanding. 'Be assured, I shall go with you – to the ends of the Earth, if that is where you should lead us.' His wise old face crinkled into a broad grin. 'Your Waymaster is not done with you yet, my young friend, even if the lord of the horses has allowed you to mindjoin with him in a fashion I have never known before!'

'And I would have it no other way, Waymaster!' Rokshan laughed before bowing respectfully and leaping up onto Breeze Whisperer's broad back, holding out his arm for Cetu, who did not demur at riding behind him.

Rokshan leaned down and whispered in Breeze Whisperer's ear. With a flick of her mane she broke into a gallop, bearing them both up towards the Fifth Valley and the summit.

CHAPTER 39

SACRIFICE AND VENGEANCE

The eerie emptiness began to unnerve them as they steadily made their way up the valleys. Rokshan had to constantly reassure Breeze Whisperer, who became more distressed and agitated. Along with each valley's entire stock of dragon horses, those who could not fight had been ordered up to the Fifth Valley in accordance with Zerafshan's plan. Only a defensive core of two to three hundred warriors were left in each valley as they had to yield one quarter of their men to bolster the defences of the Fifth Valley, where the deciding battle would be fought.

As they passed through each settlement, they told of the night Rokshan had passed on the Plain of the Dead with Stargazer. The clan leaders were respectful enough, taking this as a sure sign that their decision to back Zerafshan had been proved right, but they were more concerned about the fall of the First Valley's defences.

Towards the end of the third day, they at last approached Cetu's home valley and the old Waymaster's spirits lifted.

The low hum of thousands of people gathered together in one place gradually turned into a tumult as they became aware of the full scale of the exodus.

As far as the eye could see, the Fifth Valley was covered with tents of all sizes. They were sturdy shelters, made from the tough flax the Horsemen produced themselves, overlaid with rough wool and felt. Families had congregated around the settlement; further up the valley, smaller one-, two- and three-man tents were arranged in clusters, according to which valley the warriors came from. Pennants showing the colours and symbols of the different clans fluttered from hastily erected flagpoles around which dormitory-like tents had been put up for the younger boys and girls. The squeals and bleats of pigs and goats added to the ordered chaos of the camp. Appetizing aromas of the evening meals mingled with the woodsmoke of the campfires. Rokshan sniffed appreciatively.

Right at the top of the valley, where he'd first witnessed the skill of the young Horsemen in training, an enormous temporary corral had been built. Rokshan had never seen so many dragon horses in one place before.

'There must be four or five hundred or more,' he said, in awe at the sight.

Cetu nodded. 'About one hundred from each of the valleys.'

Rokshan shook his head sadly. They could sense that the dragon horses were quiet and subdued, as if they accepted but did not understand why the Horsemen wanted them to stay penned in, when normally they would have been roaming free in the valleys.

Cetu agreed with Rokshan that they should head for the temple of the Horsemen, where they were told Zerafshan planned his last stand if the imperial forces were not stopped at the last valley. They could see the summit clearly now, soaring above the temple which nestled high on its slopes. Rokshan gazed at the sheer granite, wondering why he felt so drawn to it; he needed to be with Stargazer, but why did the feeling grow stronger and stronger as they approached the summit? And how could he be with him, if the lord of the horses had chosen to be with his own kind on the Plains of Jalhal'a?

Dusk had fallen and he was glad they'd kept going at a good pace, for the chill wind bit even harder as the temperature fell. Wispy clouds scudded across the sky and the stars glittered brilliantly; a pale moon, almost full, hung low in the sky, glowing luminously.

As the track grew narrower and steeper, they dismounted and continued on foot. They had almost completed the ascent when they heard the single, drawn-out note of a Horseman's horn sounding from the temple.

Cetu glanced up the track. 'The watchman warns of our coming. Come, Breeze Whisperer.'

It was not long before they at last neared the temple. Rokshan had already seen the horse's skull above the entrance arch, but only in daylight; now its gaping eye-sockets flickered eerily, illuminated by an incense candle. Inside, the horses' skulls were lit in the same way, hanging side by side with flaming torches that cast a yellow, flickering light. The two large braziers at either side of the temple steps blazed brightly. In front of them, Zerafshan paced back and forth.

They left Breeze Whisperer with the guards patrolling the outer boundaries of the temple, and together went forward into the enclosure. Zerafshan, staff in hand, stopped when he saw who it was.

'Cetu, Rokshan! At last! You are a welcome sight. Come – come and rest on the steps here and warm yourselves by the fire. You look weary and in need of food and drink.' He clapped his hands, signalling for refreshment to be brought.

'You were expecting us . . . Father?' Rokshan asked, a little suspiciously.

'Why yes, my son . . . But you disappoint me.' There was a slight edge to Zerafshan's voice.

'Oh – how is that?' Rokshan replied, gratefully accepting the broth and barleyfire from one of the guards.

'Do not play with me, boy.' Zerafshan stepped towards Rokshan, looming menacingly over him. 'Where is Stargazer?'

'We don't know.' Cetu's voice was matter-of-fact. 'When we left the First Valley after the battle there, Stargazer went to join his brothers and sisters – to help the wild horses escape, we believe. It was not in our power to stop him and we do not know where he is now.'

'Battle? Has it begun? And from the direction the Horsemen least expected it?' Zerafshan asked eagerly.

Cetu nodded, and told him everything he needed to know, carefully omitting any mention of Rokshan's most recent mindjoining.

'Excellent, excellent.' Zerafshan clapped his hands together. 'Stargazer will join us, of that I have no doubt,' he murmured.

Just then the watchman's horn sounded its mournful note.

'A group of thirty or forty riders making their way up from the lower peak,' he reported. 'And a lone horse half a li ahead of them, galloping faster than the wind,' he added, pointing in wonder.

Stargazer . . . could it really be? But how could he have travelled that distance in so short a time? Rokshan's heart leaped as Cetu squeezed his arm.

'Stargazer must have ridden on the wind – take heart, my young friend,' he whispered, hurrying to where the watchman stood at the top of the steep, narrow path that led up to the temple from a westerly direction. From there the broader paths led down the pass, past the Pool of the Two Peaks.

They watched the group of riders and the horse ahead of them, who slowed only slightly as he reached the steep path.

'It is Stargazer,' Rokshan said, his heart thudding with relief as the lord of the horses cantered into the enclosure.

His sides and face were flecked with foam, his eyes wild and bloodshot. The watchman and guards fell to their knees but Rokshan recognized the urgency of Stargazer's whinny and ran over to him, Cetu hurrying behind. Rokshan sensed a deep exhaustion but his heart leaped as a colour note of subdued elation coursed through his mind. What had happened on the plains? Were the wild dragon horses going to be safe after all?

But Stargazer reared as if in warning at his approach, before kneeling before him.

Zerafshan had been watching approvingly; now he pulled Rokshan away, seizing him by the arm and making for the temple. He bounded up the steps before turning, his arm tightly around Rokshan's shoulder.

'It is as I predicted, Horsemen!' Zerafshan shouted triumphantly to the handful of guards, who looked at him in astonishment. 'My son has succeeded in the task set him by the Serenadhi and has been acknowledged by Stargazer. I will rule as khagan in his place until he comes of age. Now, at last, we shall welcome the black riders!'

'You know who these riders are?' Cetu asked, looking worried as he made his way up the steps, leaving Stargazer restlessly waiting in the temple enclosure.

'Oh yes, Cetu, I know who they are,' Zerafshan replied slowly. 'I have waited a long time for this moment. Now the great plans I have will be revealed to you . . .'

As the watchman's horn sounded again, Zerafshan raised his staff, a wolfish look on his face.

'Do not move, if you value your life,' he warned, still gripping Rokshan tightly by the shoulder as he watched the riders approaching. They were all clothed in black and rode mounts larger even than those of the Horsemen.

In the flickering light of the torches, the sharp-eyed watchman couldn't help but notice the odd-shaped hooves of the strangers' mounts as he challenged them.

'Stay, riders! Who are you and what brings you to the temple of the Horsemen?'

'Stand aside, Horseman. We are known to your leader – that is all you need to know.'

Rokshan's heart froze at the sinister voice that came from the heavily hooded figure; a hoarse, rasping whisper edged with menace that made his blood run cold.

Since leaving the remains of Vartkhis Boghos's caravan, Corhanuk had driven An Lushan and the demon wraiths on relentlessly, covering in just two short weeks what would have taken unusually fast riders more than twice as long. They had left behind them a trail of terror and destruction. Corhanuk had returned to his guise of a crow for much of the journey, taking the form of a rider only as they had neared the summit. An Lushan was at his side, also heavily hooded.

'Let them through,' Zerafshan commanded, raising his staff.

Who were these black riders? Rokshan tried to recall anything from his mindjoining that might give him a clue. Suddenly he remembered what Stargazer had said to him: he, the lord of the horses, had to obey the servants of the Shadow, and it suddenly hit him – the lord of the horses had knelt in front of both him and Zerafshan . . .

His father pointed with his staff and some of the black riders peeled off, spreading round the perimeter. In the darkness, Rokshan couldn't see their faces, which were all uniformly hooded. Two of the riders had a roped bundle between them which he was astonished to see was a body.

The rider who had spoken came forward with his companion. 'I greet you, Zerafshan – Staff-wielder. I, Corhanuk, am accompanied by Beshbaliq, as my master always promised.'

The rasping whisper grated into the still night air . . . Rokshan swayed in shock – Corhanuk, the messenger to the Shadow himself, stood here in front of them in human guise . . . and these black riders – they must be demon wraiths summoned from the depths of Hell, along with their hell-horses. Fear clawed at his guts as he felt Corhanuk's gaze light momentarily on him before turning back to Zerafshan.

'Lord, your servant welcomes you,' Zerafshan said, dropping to one knee. 'Where is the bearer of the Talisman?'

'It is as I promised,' Corhanuk replied, indicating the rider next to him.

'I, Beshbaliq, bear the Talisman.' The other hooded rider beside Corhanuk spoke for the first time.

Rokshan's stomach lurched: there was a terrible familiarity about his voice. The figure threw back his hood and held out before him a carved statuette. Rokshan wondered at the exquisitely crafted Talisman, which glowed and pulsed in his hand, sending out beams of blue, green, white and red light. But he couldn't take his eyes off the rider.

'An'an? Is that really you? Is it possible?' he whispered despairingly. 'But . . . what's happened to you?'

An Lushan made no acknowledgement as Rokshan turned towards Zerafshan, his face wild with anger and confusion.

'What's happened to him?' Zerafshan echoed with his thin smile. 'Only someone with a deep, burning ambition and lust for power could have chosen the path your half-brother has – he has completely justified my choice.'

'Your choice?' A memory came flooding back to Rokshan: the moment at their home in Maracanda when an ugly crow had swooped down to their balcony and cawed noisily for a few moments before they'd shooed it off.

'An Lushan, spirit of Beshbaliq and blood kinsman . . . welcome,' Zerafshan proclaimed, standing with his staff – with a sickening jolt Rokshan realized that this was indeed the Staff of Chu Jung – planted firmly in front of him.

'I bring the lost Talisman, Staff-wielder, to be joined at last with the Staff,' came the reply as a powerful charge pulsed back and forth between them, the Talisman glowing even more strongly in An Lushan's hand. The demon wraiths and their mounts were absolutely still and an expectant hush fell over the clearing.

The Talisman? His brother? Rokshan realized at last what Stargazer had been trying to tell him. He looked out at the handful of Horsemen who, like him, seemed frozen in the moment. His mind reeled: the Talisman had been lost, as he knew from the old legends and from Shou Lao's colourful stories, buried somewhere in the forests of the world, no one knew where . . . until now.

The Darhad's Dark Forests had finally revealed the secret of where Chu Jung had buried his Talisman.

Why did it have to be you who found it, An'an? What happened with the Darhad? Where is Lianxang? Rokshan's head clamoured with a hundred unanswered questions.

An Lushan started to mount the steps to where Rokshan stood with Zerafshan, who was trembling, his hands outstretched.

'Wait!' The hoarse, sepulchral voice of Corhanuk rang out. 'Return what is not yours, mortal, before you take the Talisman. What you call the greater Collar – bring it to me.'

Zerafshan turned and hurried into the temple to retrieve the Collar from the shrine Rokshan had seen when they'd first arrived in the Kingdom of the Horsemen; he handed it reverently to An Lushan and, in return, received the Talisman into his shaking hands. An Lushan passed the Collar to Corhanuk, whose eyes gleamed with a terrible delight. 'Now shall my brother guardian spirirt, the Crimson King, be empowered to break free from his shackles at the gates of Hell,' he proclaimed.

'At last . . . at last,' Zerafshan muttered as he turned the Talisman this way and that; then he lifted the Staff and slammed it down, the Talisman held aloft in his other hand. A peal of thunder rumbled directly overhead as the Talisman's steadily pulsing glow changed to a blinding iridescence, bathing everything in a light as bright as the desert sun. As they all threw up their arms to cover their eyes, the ground shook with a series of tremors. The silence that followed was broken by whinnies of alarm from the guards' dragon horses. Stargazer responded with a series of whickers that seemed to calm them.

Zerafshan held the Talisman high above his head now as the intense light coalesced into a single beam of pulsing power directed at the two peaks. Suddenly there was a deafening crack as the piercing light from the Talisman split the lower of the peaks, shivering it into two like a piece of flint; rocks rained down into the pool it had previously overlooked, making the water churn and boil.

The hell-horses reared in alarm, their snarls echoing around the clearing. Now a low hum started to come from the Talisman. There was another thunderclap and, as if in response, a surge of crackling orange-yellow fire shot out in a blinding flash of concentrated power. The hum grew louder as the Talisman spat out another orange-yellow flame, which sizzled up into the sky in a hurtling, crackling roar. Clouds, whipped along by a bitingly cold wind that had suddenly sprung up, began to take on the shape of writhing, leaping dragons.

'See the fiery breath of the ancient dragons! They will live again!' Zerafshan screamed in exultation. 'Witness the power of the Staff and Talisman! Now shall the Wise Lord tremble!'

With outstretched arms he brought the end of the Staff towards the Talisman and, as they touched, a surge of power fused the two together in an explosion of colour that lit up the temple and then faded into the wood and stone of the structure itself, leaving it glowing and pulsing. Zerafshan held the Staff aloft, with the Talisman now fixed to its end.

'Behold the Staff and Talisman of Chu Jung, slayer of the ancient dragons, united after a thousand millennia!' Zerafshan howled in triumph. 'Now the dragon horses shall live again, reborn in the Pool of the Two Peaks, the fiery breath of their ancestors rekindled, fiercer and stronger after a long sleep of ages, sealed in the Talisman!'

The storyteller's voice echoed in Rokshan's head: *The ancient power is stirring . . . the sleeping dragon awakes . . .*

Shou Lao's voice became mixed up with his mother's and Ah Lin's as the familiar words of the story told to him countless times clanged like alarm bells in his head: 'The evil of the ancient dragons was crushed for ever and then, being reborn in water, they became spirits of nature . . . *some were reborn as horses . . .*'

Images of his mindjoining came rushing back to him: shadowy shapes plunging down from the surface of the pool he had swum in . . . whinnying screams of fear and the waters boiling, matching his own thoughts now as they churned inside him: *The ancient power is stirring . . . the sleeping dragon awakes . . .*

He realized that Stargazer had shown him this, and the truth of what Zerafshan intended dawned on him. The Staff and Talisman had been united, restoring their power – something Chu Jung, their creator, had never intended. Consumed by their jealousy of mankind and tempted by the rebel guardian spirits to rise up with them against the Wise Lord, the once-beautiful first-born creatures of creation had turned into ravening monsters. Now, Zerafshan was going to use the powerful magic of the Staff and the Talisman to transform the dragon horses back into those monsters! But how?

Stargazer neighed urgently as if in response; Rokshan started forward but his father's grip tightened. Stargazer restlessly paced around the Horsemen, who had gathered together in a tight group.

'Seize the dragon horses – take care with Stargazer!' Zerafshan shouted. 'Han Garid, lord of the thunder dragons, will come amongst us again!' He spun Rokshan round to face him, his face twisted by a mad desire for power. 'Now do you understand, my *son*?' he hissed. 'The riddle was a message for me from the Shadow lord himself; all I had to do was unlock its meaning, for only he understood what has never been dreamed of. *Open the far gates* Free me from my bondage, smash the Arch of Darkness! But how, Rokshan – how? *Raise up my body . . . The horse of Heaven has come, mediator for the dragon.* Don't you see? What was transformed once can be transformed back again: the ancestors of the heavenly horses live here, among us! They are all the *mediator for the dragon.* All we lacked were the tools to make it possible . . . *He travels to the Gate of Heaven* – the gates of Heaven and Hell are opposites of the same in the great yin and yang of the universe. The Shadow's Hell shall become his Heaven when he *looks on the Terrace of Jade* once more: the Terrace of Jade is the Earth, my son. If the Shadow looks on it, then he must be in the world once more – as he will be when our work is done!'

Rokshan stared at Zerafshan in despair as he finally understood what his father's plan was, Shou Lao's words echoing in his head: *The sleeping dragon awakes . . . Reborn in the Pool of the Two Peaks.* Is that what he intended – to lead the dragon horses to the pool, to be reborn again? It seemed insane, but if it was so, then he had to stop him at all costs. Zerafshan's plan couldn't work without the dragon horses – he had to go back down to the Fifth Valley and release them, sending them off as far away from Zerafshan and the pool as possible. His father had them all penned there not for their safekeeping but, he suddenly realized, so they'd be close to the pool.

Corhanuk now stepped forward, and Zerafshan sank to his knees in front of the Shadow's chief servant.

'Master,' he acknowledged, holding out the Staff and the Talisman.

'Come, Beshbaliq, take Chu Jung's Talisman and Staff as reward for your loyalty through the ages,' Corhanuk commanded, before turning to the demon wraiths. 'Free the prisoner and bring her into the temple,' he ordered, snapping Rokshan back to the nightmare of what was unfolding. 'A young spellweaver will make a potent blood sacrifice to Han Garid – he will expect no less.'

Two of the demon wraiths hurriedly unslung the roped bundle and took it to the foot of the steps, slashing at the thick ropes. The huddled figure remained cowering on the ground, but the wraiths' scimitars whirled threateningly about her, forcing her to move.

It took Rokshan only a second to recognize who the prisoner was as he raced down the steps. 'Lianxang! What's happened to you . . . and An'an?' He glanced up to where his brother stood next to Zerafshan. There was no sign of recognition in his eyes.

'Rokshan . . .' She shook her head weakly and sagged against him, barely able to stand. 'You remember I told you about the spirit-birds of the Darhad?' she whispered urgently into his good ear. 'My eagle – she has been following us—'

But she could tell him no more as he was pushed aside by the wraiths, who bundled her unceremoniously up the temple steps.

'You can't do this, Zerafshan!' Rokshan shouted angrily as he leaped up after them.

'Take the blood sacrifice to the altar,' Corhanuk commanded, 'and prepare her.'

'You must be present, Rokshan,' Zerafshan insisted. 'For a sacrifice in the temple of the Horsemen to impart its true power, it must be witnessed by the khagan himself – and you, as my successor when you come of age. Come!'

Gesturing to one of his demon wraiths, he turned towards the temple. The wraith grabbed Rokshan by the shoulder and bundled him under the horse-skull arch into the temple itself. Two others followed, while the remainder flowed into position around the temple, standing with their scimitars to their foreheads in the customary gesture of allegiance, red eyes gleaming from beneath their hoods as they blocked entry to anyone else.

As he struggled, Rokshan caught the faint shrill cry of a bird of prey. Through the open sides of the temple, he recognized the silhouette of Lianxang's eagle as she glided serenely on the air currents high above them.

'Come, spirit-bird . . .' he whispered.

Zerafshan ordered Lianxang to be laid on the altar, her arms and legs bound securely. The demon wraiths obeyed, treating her reverently, as befitted a sacrificial victim. Lianxang was too exhausted from the ordeal of her journey to put up any sort of fight.

An Lushan and Corhanuk stood on the right-hand side of the altar while the struggling Rokshan was held on the left.

Zerafshan knelt and opened the shrine behind the altar. Reverently he took out a gold chin strap and a bronze dagger, its gold hilt inlaid with turquoise and decorated with an elaborate dragon design. Now he started to chant an invocation before turning back to the altar, a huge skull in his hands: 'Behold the skull of Han Garid, lord of the thunder dragons of ancient times,' he declared, lowering it onto his head and fastening it with the chin strap. Then he took up the dagger.

Arching her back in desperation, Lianxang cried out – a long, agonized scream that pierced Rokshan's heart – as Zerafshan held the dagger just below her ear, ready to slit her throat. 'Rokshan,' she called out, 'if I am to die, I swore to pass a message on to you, from Naha – yes, he lives! He said he always loved you as a father.'

At these words, something snapped in Rokshan: he tore himself from the grip of the demon wraith and leaped forward, kicking the dagger out of Zerafshan's hand and wrenching the huge dragon skull off his head. Filled with an uncontrollable rage, he smashed the skull down on his father's head again and again. Zerafshan sank to the ground with a dull groan, blood oozing from his wounds.

'Here is your blood sacrifice!' Rokshan shouted.

Corhanuk reacted first, whirling round and knocking Rokshan off his feet, then slamming him head first into the side of the altar, where he lay, stunned.

Just then there was a startled shout from outside as an enormous eagle circled low around the clearing. Corhanuk and An Lushan hurried out of the temple; An Lushan used the Staff to loose a lightning bolt in its direction but the giant bird swooped down and went straight for the centre of the enclosure, raking her massive, razor-sharp talons across whatever she came in contact with.

The hell-horses reared, whinnying in confusion as the eagle shot away and disappeared back into the night sky. Seconds later she repeated her attack, diving down, as silent as an arrow. An Lushan and the demon wraiths fought to control their mounts in the constricted space while the handful of Horsemen who had been with Zerafshan – enraged at the sacrilegious use of their temple – now entered the fray. Again and again the eagle dived, distracting An Lushan, who loosed one bolt after another to no effect. Stargazer too fought bravely; almost as big but far nimbler than the hell-horses, he used his hooves to deadly effect when the demon wraiths fell from their mounts.

Corhanuk was nowhere to be seen – but suddenly an enormous crow rose from the fray, its huge wings beating hard as it sped up into the dark sky, its raucous cry all but drowning out the sound of battle.

But the ungainly crow was no match for the mistress of the skies: again the eagle swooped, swerving to avoid it and then, at the last second, shooting into the temple itself and flying towards the altar, where Lianxang was writhing, trying to free herself from the ropes that bound her.

'Rokshan, untie me!' she screamed.

Rokshan's head was throbbing but he heaved himself up,

only dimly aware of Zerafshan, who was now standing, clutching at the altar for support, the sacrificial dagger once more in his hands. The eagle headed straight for him, her talons gouging deep into his scalp and forehead, and he screamed in pain. The bird's enormous wings knocked the dagger out of his hand as he slashed wildly at her, blood pouring down his face. Suddenly she lunged at his face again with her huge hooked beak – and pecked out one of his eyes.

With an agonized cry, Zerafshan fell to his knees, vainly trying to protect his face against the eagle's savage attack. Soon his hands and face hung in bloody strips; finally he was plunged into darkness for ever as the bird pecked out his other eye.

As Rokshan watched in horror, Lianxang shouted something in a language he didn't recognize: at her command the eagle halted her vicious attack, circled around the altar and, with a screech, flew out of the temple and down the pass. With a screaming caw of rage, Corhanuk assumed his bodily form once more, snatching the Staff from An Lushan to loose a thunderous volley of lightning bolts after the eagle – but it was too late.

Zerafshan crawled around on all fours, whimpering in agony. The floor by the shrine was slippery with his blood. The sounds of battle rang in Rokshan's ears, and all at once he sensed that Stargazer was fighting for his life. He closed his eyes to block out the pitiful sight of his father and was almost engulfed by blazing reds and purples exploding in his head: the message that pulsed through the colours made him recoil for an instant but he could not ignore the command Stargazer gave him.

Your father betrayed the Horsemen's trust, and he condemned an innocent girl to death. He planned the death of my kind, through transformation into living monsters, the creatures we once were. Now he is blind and helpless – it is punishment enough. Be merciful and dispatch him quickly before we make our escape . . .

As if in a dream, Rokshan picked up the dagger which Zerafshan had dropped and stood over him, both hands on the bloody handle, the tip of the blade pricking the back of his neck.

'The Horsemen would say you do not deserve a quick death, Father, but the lord of the horses has commanded I grant you merciful release.'

Before Zerafshan even realized what was happening, Rokshan plunged the dagger down. The blade went deep and his father shuddered briefly before slumping dead by the altar. As he pulled the dagger out Rokshan stood over the body, trembling violently, sickened by what he'd done.

In the clearing, the small group of Horsemen wavered as the demon wraiths, no longer distracted by the swooping attacks of the eagle, began to get the upper hand. The Horsemen fought bravely but the silent, untiring savagery of the demon wraiths was too much for them. One by one they fell under the relentless scimitars and thrusting lances.

Rokshan quickly unbound Lianxang, who slid off the altar and slumped behind it, looking in stunned horror at the blood-soaked body of Zerafshan.

'We must get down to the Fifth Valley and release the dragon horses,' Rokshan said urgently. 'Zerafshan had them all penned there so they'd be near the Pool of the Two Peaks. We must free them. Corhanuk and my brother will not stop just because Zerafshan is dead. You must help us, Lianxang!'

He sprinted to the top of the temple steps; Lianxang, exhausted after her recent ordeals, followed him as quickly as she could. The ground was strewn with the bodies of dead or dying Horsemen. Desperately Rokshan cast about for any sign of Cetu . . .

Instead he saw the tall figure of Corhanuk at the head of the demon wraiths, mounted on Stargazer with An Lushan beside him. The cord that Rokshan had woven into his mane was tightly wrapped around Corhanuk's claw-like hand. Rokshan saw Stargazer dipping and shaking his head, as if trying to warn him. A cloudburst of jagged warning notes exploded in his head, just as he saw Corhanuk levelling the Staff straight at them.

'Get down!' Rokshan screamed at Lianxang.

Stargazer reared and bucked ferociously, twisting Corhanuk out of his saddle as he broke away and made for the temple steps. Corhanuk picked himself up and loosed a bolt, but Rokshan and Lianxang were already halfway down the steps and launching themselves onto Stargazer's broad back.

The scorching blast slammed into the temple, shattering the altar and shrine in a thunderous explosion that rocked the building to its foundations. Before Corhanuk could unleash another one, a Horseman appeared from the shadows behind the temple. Rokshan recognized Cetu and Breeze Whisperer as his Waymaster lifted his bow and loosed an arrow, all in one skilled, fluid movement.

The arrow found its target just below the top of the Staff, whipping it out of Corhanuk's grip; it landed with a thud a dozen paces away from him. With a roar of rage he sprang to retrieve it, An Lushan and the demon wraiths immediately forming a protective shield around him.

'Follow me!' Cetu yelled, realizing that this was their only chance of escape. Breeze Whisperer and Stargazer surged through the entrance at a thunderous gallop, heading for the Fifth Valley in a desperate attempt to rescue the penned dragon horses from their fate.

PART SEVEN

SUMMONING AND TRANSFORMATION

The Creation Myth of the Wise Lord

Fragment from a badly damaged scroll.

When the Wise Lord commanded Chu Jung to subdue the ravening monsters his dragon spirits of fire had become, Chu Jung created a huge pit in the Earth, which he filled with water, putting out the flames of the dragons.

'Raise them up,' the Wise Lord then commanded him. 'All my dragon spirits, of earth and water, of air and fire. For these were my first creatures of creation and I cannot destroy them for ever. Raise them up again, but make them invisible so that my lesser creature, man, will not be frightened of them . . . thus shall my dragon spirits always be reminded of their sin against Me. As for the dragon spirits of fire - man will always need fire, and I shall inspire in him reverence and awe for it such that somewhere in the world of men a flame will always flicker, and so the essence of the dragon spirits of fire will never die. Those who worship me shall worship the eternal flame, which they shall always light in my honour.

'Let the outward forms of my beloved dragon spirits of fire live - but transformed beyond measure with only the smallest spark of their original essence, which will be buried, deep in the souls of the gentlest and most beautiful of creatures. These I shall make so fleet of foot, man will never capture them and learn their deepest, innermost secret. Men will come to call this creature dragon horse, for they will know in their hearts it is descended from the first-born, the purest of my creatures, before they strayed from me.'

Chu Jung knew not how to do this, for he could not fathom the Wise Lord's purpose.

'Take your Talisman and cast the beams of life-giving light over the water where the monstrous forms of my dragon spirits lie,' the Wise Lord told him. 'In this way – and with my powers granted to you to do this – the rebirth I have commanded shall come about.'

Aeons later, the pit of water became known as the Pool of the Two Peaks, revered for its healing powers – and a tribe of men learned how to tame, but only in part, the wild spirit of the dragon horses.

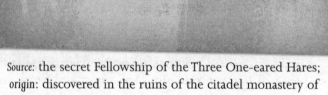

Source: the secret Fellowship of the Three One-eared Hares;
origin: discovered in the ruins of the citadel monastery of
Labrang, spiritual centre of the old Western Empire.

CHAPTER 40

THE SUMMONING

As they streamed back down to the valleys, Rokshan kept looking back, fearful that the demon wraiths would be giving chase. Gold, red, green and blue lightning bolts exploded around the summit.

Lianxang had her arms wrapped tightly round him on Stargazer. 'The Talisman!' she shouted. 'Joined with the Staff, the power it can unleash will be unstoppable. What can we do?'

'We must stop them getting the dragon horses!' Rokshan yelled back. 'Whatever they intend cannot work without them – they want them in the pool!'

'Why?' she asked, but ahead of them Cetu had already dismounted as he reached the narrow part of the path which dropped down into the Fifth Valley.

Stargazer skidded to a halt not far from Cetu, and Rokshan and Lianxang jumped down. Clearly agitated now, he tossed his head again and again, snorting loudly and then twisting round to stare up at the summit, checking for danger. Rokshan's senses were alerted too and he could hardly concentrate on what Lianxang was saying. He could see Stargazer's anxiety in his head like roiling stormclouds, dark and oppressive.

'This is Stargazer, lord of the horses,' Rokshan said, twisting his hands round the cord threaded through Stargazer's mane to stop him shaking his head.

'He is magnificent,' she murmured, stroking his muzzle, 'but how is it that you ride him? Are you truly a Horseman now?' She looked at him appraisingly, taking in the long coat and leggings, and the short lance slung round the saddle, as they hurried towards Cetu, who was gazing across the Fifth Valley.

'This is Cetu, my Waymaster . . .' Rokshan replied distractedly.

The Waymaster bowed to Lianxang as Rokshan hurriedly told him who she was, but there was a flickering knot of concern in his gaze as he turned to look again at what was happening in the Fifth Valley.

'Cetu, we mustn't stop,' Rokshan urged him, following his gaze down the valley. 'I can see what troubles you—'

'What? What is it?' Lianxang asked anxiously.

'The dragon horses – look!' Cetu exclaimed. 'You remember how quiet and dispirited they were on our way up, Rokshan? Now they seem nervous, frightened even . . .'

In the first glimmerings of dawn, they could see that something was very wrong in the enormous corral at the top of the valley. The dragon horses swirled back and forth from one end to the other and they could hear their agitated whinnies. Rokshan felt almost as if he was joining with them through Stargazer as wave after wave of colour rose up from the penned horses – fearful purples and reds boiling together in an intense expression of alarm aimed at their lord and brother. He tried to send messages of reassurance back, but he had no real idea how to stop what he feared was about to befall them. Behind him, the lightning bolts started to come in a continuous volley of ear-splitting explosions.

Suddenly Stargazer reared, yanking the cord out of Rokshan's hand. He staggered back in alarm as bursts of red and purple drenched his consciousness, clouding his vision for a few moments. As clearly as if Stargazer had spoken aloud to him, he knew that the horse must help his brothers and sisters and be their lord in their time of need. While one part of him longed to keep Stargazer at his side, another part acknowledged this need. Understanding, the lord of the horses bowed his head for a moment to Rokshan, then wheeled round and headed for the corral. As the explosions faded, he could hear Stargazer galloping towards the penned horses.

Cetu took Rokshan by the arm as a slight tremor shook the ground. Rokshan shook his head. 'We must get the dragon horses as far away from here as we can – we must help Stargazer herd them away – that is what he is trying to do, I know it!' he shouted.

The tremor became a rumbling roar as what remained of the smaller of the two peaks crumbled and crashed down the mountainside beyond the temple.

As Rokshan turned to go, Cetu shouted out and pointed at what was taking place on the highest point of the other peak.

In the grey morning light An Lushan held the Staff, now united with its Talisman. He stood at the highest point of a massive outcrop of rock as he prepared himself for the summoning of the dragon horses. A short distance from the Horsemen's temple, everything was in place: demon wraiths were standing ready at the western and eastern entrances to the summit. Corhanuk himself stood on the shore of the Pool of the Two Peaks, positioning more demon wraiths around the lake.

Planting his feet firmly against the buffeting wind, An Lushan stood with his black cloak streaming out behind him and his voice ringing out across the valley.

'Hear me, my Shadow lord . . . your Staff-wielder. I invoke the ancient power of the Talisman in your name! Let the dragon horses of the Horsemen be summoned and transformed back into the creatures they once were, to do your bidding – to unleash terror and evil in the world once more!'

He circled the Staff above his head and then pointed it down to the Fifth Valley and the corral where the dragon horses were penned. Streams of iridescent flame erupted from the Talisman, and tremors shook the mountains and valleys. The Horsemen who had been tending the dragon horses fled as balls of fire erupted around them, incinerating the sturdy fencing. The dragon horses whinnied in terror but seemed nervous of their unexpected freedom.

As An Lushan whirled the Staff above his head, a swirling pattern of colours erupted from it, shooting up into the dawn sky and then re-forming into an undulating torrent, like a river in the sky. Suddenly he directed the torrent at the dragon horses far below. Like a river swollen by rains raging down a mountainside, the rush of colours cascaded down towards them, enveloping them in a pulsing skein of blues and greens, purples and gold. The colours settled, mixing into a shimmering haze, all but obscuring the dragon horses from view. A silence settled like a pall around them.

'What is happening?' Lianxang whispered, glancing fearfully at the distant figure on the peak.

Then there was an eruption of noise as the haze suddenly lifted, coalescing back into the torrent of colours that had broken over the herd. Rearing and bucking and whinnying, now more in exultation than in fear, the dragon horses broke into a gallop, moving in one flowing mass up the river of colour that had swept over them and now carried them upwards, towards the summit.

Cetu, Rokshan and Lianxang looked aghast at what was happening, feeling utterly helpless in the face of the power that was being unleashed against the dragon horses. The distant tremor became a pounding roar – the drumming of hundreds of hooves – and the stampeding dragon horses rounded the bend of the river, joining in one swirling mass the winding track that led up to the summit. Rokshan couldn't see Stargazer in amongst them but sensed his acceptance of his fate, along with his brothers and sisters, and his intense feeling of protective loyalty. Despairingly, he felt the bond between them fading as Stargazer concentrated all his energies on his own kind.

The Horsemen who had been guarding the corral were swept up in the stampede and used all their skills to try to swing the herd round. But their mounts could not resist the summons of the Staff and, bucking and rearing, threw their riders off in their mad rush to join the herd.

On they came at a wild gallop, a solid mass of horses. Soon there were too many for the narrowing path and many plunged into the river, surging upstream like salmon driven by relentless instinct to find their spawning grounds. The colours from the Talisman drew them on, snaking around the streaming mass, pulling them on and up . . .

'We will be crushed to death here!' Cetu shouted. 'Climb! Climb!' he yelled again as Lianxang looked around wildly.

The slopes beside the path rose steeply but they grabbed hold of whatever they could, scrabbling frantically to get out of the way of the coming stampede.

The thundering mass numbering many hundreds made the ground tremble and shake as they approached. Now they strung themselves out in ones and twos, slowing to a canter to negotiate the path that snaked up to the summit; for a moment they were lost to sight but soon reappeared, not far off now, a thin cloud of dust rolling before them. Leading them, in a group slightly ahead of the rest, was Stargazer.

'No, Stargazer. Lead them away . . . Turn, turn!' Rokshan screamed both aloud and in his mind, sending waves of colour towards the stallion, but his despairing cry was lost in the surging mass that thundered past them, and then was gone in a cloud of dust mixed with the sharp, pungent smell of horse sweat. He knew from Cetu's anguished look that Breeze Whisperer had also been swept up in the stampede. Silently they ran up the track – if they could do nothing else, they would at least witness the fate of the dragon horses.

The demon wraiths brought the herd down to a trot when they neared the temple clearing, steering the horses skilfully across the enclosure and then down the track to what had been the smaller of the two peaks and on towards the pool. Those horses that could not slow down on the steep track stumbled and fell heavily – their whinnies of pain silenced abruptly as the demon wraiths ended their agony.

As they approached the water, Stargazer shot further ahead of the rest of the herd. Bucking and neighing like a colt, he splashed along the shoreline. The others reached the pool and neighed back, making a tumultuous, quivering wall of noise that echoed around the mountains.

From his vantage point on the taller of the peaks, An Lushan loosed a thunderous bolt of yellow fire, shot through with all the colours of the precious stones of the Talisman – deep ruby-red, sapphire-blue and emerald-green. The lightning bolt exploded into the pool, making it fizz and foam. As the waters settled back, thin gold and green vapours spiralled up and formed into a shape that resembled the writhing dragon of the Talisman.

Cetu, Rokshan and Lianxang stumbled, exhausted, into the temple enclosure and, having first checked that all was clear, scrambled down towards the pool. Finding a concealed spot a safe distance away, they watched in mounting horror as the dragon horses now lined themselves around the pool, whinnying and pawing the ground as if sensing what they were being led to do. The demon wraiths stood a few paces behind them.

Corhanuk gathered some wraiths to him and advanced on Stargazer; they lashed their whips threateningly as they forced him into the water. He reared and bucked defiantly, but they drove him further in until the water covered his haunches; turning, he gave a final despairing whinny before he started swimming away towards the island to escape the sting of the whips.

In answer to his call, as one the herd plunged into the

water and the pool was transformed into a foaming, thrashing mass as the dragon horses followed Stargazer, who was still swimming desperately, his eyes bulging and the veins on his neck clearly visible. His panic and confusion spread to the rest of the herd, but then, as if someone had snapped a command, the horses suddenly stopped struggling and, one by one, slipped soundlessly beneath the surface.

Rokshan gasped; this is what he had been shown in his mindjoin with Stargazer – this was the vision he had seen: the jagged lightning strikes searing into the pool . . . His naked body slashed and cut; he had been writhing and twisting, and now it was happening to his beloved dragon horses. Sobbing with anger and pity, he held his head in his hands, knowing he was powerless to stop it.

Up above, the pool's tranquil surface was restored. An Lushan let loose another lightning bolt, which crackled into the water, sending a jet of steam hissing into the sky; another followed, then another and another so that the pool was now boiling and bubbling, carpeted with fire.

In the depths, brightly coloured lights darted and flashed about, fading as quickly as they'd come. Then, suddenly, all became calm again. Not a ripple broke the surface of the water, no breeze sighed through the branches of the willows. Moments passed. There was a slight tremor on the shoreline, and then the waters of the pool folded back on themselves and were sucked into a whirling vortex.

With a tremendous surge of power, a column of water erupted from the whirlpool, so high it seemed to disappear into the clouds; then it crashed down, causing waves to break on the shore, before shooting up again. The cascading tower of water spun round, faster and faster, in whirling hues of gold, green and blue – and all the time something was stretching, pushing and pulling inside it, as if it was struggling to emerge like a giant moth from its cocoon.

Gradually the heaving, writhing form took on a thin, snake-like body, curved like a bow. It wound its coils up like a spring before catapulting itself up through the column of water, emerging with an ear-piercing screech, its enormous wings beating hard as it sped up towards An Lushan.

The demon wraiths fell to their knees in worship, touching their heads to the ground as the dragon soared directly above its summoner. An Lushan stood with his arms outstretched in triumph and loosed a crackling stream of lightning into the sky, freezing the creature in a flashing sequence of reflected electric-green and gold.

Rokshan gaped at its awesome, terrifying beauty, unconsciously making the sign of the dragon. Even at such a distance he could tell that the creature was huge by the spread of its wings – at least three horses' lengths across – and its body and tail – at least six long. Its long reptilian head bore a single horn that swept back and curved into a sharp point.

'How can this be . . . ?' Cetu kept repeating, his voice shaking. Lianxang looked as awestruck as Rokshan as she made a curious gesture to her forehead. Instinctively they flattened themselves on the ground as the dragon stopped climbing and started to circle around what was left of the two peaks.

'Can he see us from that distance?' Rokshan whispered.

'Dragon-sight is many times sharper than humans',' Cetu replied.

'Is he real, or a sorcerer's conjuring?' Lianxang asked, her voice tinged with disbelief.

'He is real,' Cetu said. 'He is the ancestor of our dragon horse. Hundreds of centuries ago, it was a dragon that could do all the things your legends tell of, which you now witness. See the effortless flight,' he continued in a breathless whisper. 'They can fly without stopping for days and can go without food for a full cycle of the moon – but then, when they eat, they cannot stop until they are sated. They are intelligent, and can mindjoin with any creature that has a language. They are solitary creatures by nature, but they can be fiercely loyal once their trust has been won . . .'

As he spoke, the dragon emitted a deafening shriek, gliding effortlessly around An Lushan, who loosed another bolt of lightning at the pool, summoning a second dragon through the tower of water.

Then he turned his attention to the fearsome beast that swooped and glided around the outcrop of rock where he stood.

The dragon's intelligent, piercing eyes shone a burning red. With another of his unearthly screeches he revealed a mouth full of sharp teeth surrounded by long, whiskery feelers. Two small, stag-like horns grew above his ear-holes, each surmounted by a slight ridge of flesh. Most striking was his brilliant coloration of electric-green and gold, shot through with the palest blue, which made his scaly skin shimmer and glow.

'Hail, Stargazer, born again as Han Garid, lord of the thunder dragons! Receive your dragon-fire!'

An Lushan's triumphant shout echoed around the mountaintops as he pointed the Staff and Talisman directly at Han Garid and fired a lightning bolt of extraordinary power. The lord of the thunder dragons caught the deadly charge directly in his gaping mouth and, with a triumphant roar, spat it out in a hot blast that billowed in a flaming arc before sizzling harmlessly against the unyielding granite.

'Stay, Han Garid – until I have gathered more of your kind to spread terror through the land!' An Lushan gave a mad, barking laugh. 'Human flesh awaits to fill your ravening hunger!'

Rokshan recoiled in horror, tears misting his eyes as he struggled to take it in. How was it possible that Stargazer, the most beautiful, noble lord of the horses who had allowed him into the depths of his innermost soul – how could he have become this fearsome monster? Scrambled thoughts raced in his head: if he was intelligent, would he be able to communicate with him? The thought of a mindjoin with such a beast filled him with terror. Surely it was impossible – he would be driven mad long before he got anywhere near the first level of his mind – and did this creature even *have* levels of feeling?

Now Corhanuk came to join An Lushan in their moment of triumph as he unleashed a lightning bolt at another dragon emerging from the pool. Many came to receive the gift of dragon-fire from their summoner, until the pool yielded no more.

The dragon horde wheeled about the peak like a cloud of giant but slow-moving bats, calling to each other in ear-splitting, savage shrieks. Their distinctive colouring merged into a sea of green and shimmering blue, shot through by orange flames as the dragons spat their fire. Han Garid was the largest of them all, at least half the size again of most of the dragons that emerged from the pool.

Crouching in their hiding place, Lianxang, Cetu and Rokshan put their hands to their ears, hardly able to bear the intensity of the noise. Cetu rocked back and forth on his heels, his eyes shut to block out the sight of what had become of his beloved dragon horses.

'Go, Beshbaliq, master of the dragon hordes!' Corhanuk thundered. 'Destroy the imperial army which even now marches up the pass. Let the dragons feast on flesh and increase their mighty frames! Soon they will be unleashed to follow the Four Riders, to spread fear and terror among mankind and to wreak havoc in the world. Join me after your victory in the court of our brother, the Crimson King, who awaits his freedom from Hell once he has been reunited with his long-lost Collar – he will need no bidding then to release the Four Riders; the demon wraiths will guide you there.'

As Han Garid swooped and dived amongst the dragons,

gathering them for the battle to come, An Lushan pointed the Staff down the pass and commanded the beasts to attack and engulf the unsuspecting forces of the emperor, which would be defenceless against such savage power. The beating of the dragons' wings buffeted the air like a raging storm as they swarmed down the pass, their ravening cries anticipating the slaughter and feasting that was to come . . .

PART EIGHT

DEATH AND REBIRTH

The Legend of the Jade Spirit

The following is recorded in The Book of Ahura Mazda, the Wise Lord

The guardian spirit that became known as the Jade Spirit was the third of the triumvirate of high guardian spirits, he sided with the Shadow and the Crimson King in their rebellion against the Wise Lord.

As the Jade Spirit repented at the last, the Wise Lord rewarded him by making him keeper of the first cycle of the Wheel of Rebirth. All the souls of the dead go before him to be given their final chance to repent, just as the Jade Spirit went before the Wise Lord. They are either taken to be with the Wise Lord to await their reincarnation, or are damned for all eternity, being sent to the court of the Crimson King, where the Guardian Monk keeps his perpetual vigil over the keeper of Hell and assigns the punishments of the souls of the damned.

The Jade Spirit was allowed to retain his Collar and, through it, his divinely given powers – but only on condition that his divine soul was turned into the precious, imperishable element itself: thus he would never be allowed to forget his moment of sinful rebellion and would have an eternity to reflect on the folly of his moment of temptation. So it was that the precious material came to contain the five eternal virtues: compassion, modesty, courage, justice and wisdom.

He was also made the keeper of the world's jade, the most precious of all materials. The most perfect jade of all is found on the bed of the great world river that men called Dolbor, which also flows through the Lower World. The Dolbor trickles like a silver thread from the Five Terraces Mountain in the Land of Perpetual Mist.

Men came to call this the Jade Mountain. Mysterious and inaccessible, eternally shrouded in thick fog, it became known as a land of kuei – full of wandering spirits seeking an audience with the Jade Spirit to repent of their sins.

In time, people became unsure which of all the peaks the Jade Mountain was, or if it even existed. Men feared to go there, for the kuei, it was said, were always restless and would not countenance the tread of living, mortal feet in the Land of Perpetual Mist, always driving those who trespassed there to turn back, never to return.

Source: the secret Fellowship of the Three One-eared Hares; origin: discovered in the ruins of the citadel monastery of Labrang, spiritual centre of the old Western Empire.

CHAPTER 41

A MESSAGE OF HOPE

The sky was a darkening, dirty grey and a cold, squally wind gusted around the temple of the Horsemen. Rokshan, Cetu and Lianxang had spent an uncomfortable hour or two crouched in their hiding place before they were certain it was safe to make their way back up the mountain.

Cetu had insisted on performing the funeral rites for the Horsemen who still lay where they had fallen at the temple. Rokshan and Lianxang helped him build makeshift biers; they burned strongly now, the ashes scattered by the wind. Cetu stood silently by, staring at nothing. The light had gone out of his eyes, which were filled only with despair.

Rokshan stole the occasional concerned glance at his old Waymaster. He too felt despair, but more than this, a terrible sense of loss that Stargazer had gone – and Breeze Whisperer along with him – and all the dragon horses. All the colours in his mind that had connected him with Stargazer and the dragon horses had suddenly left him. It was as if part of his soul had been torn out. Where was Stargazer now? he wondered bitterly. Now and then he felt almost as if the lord of the horses was calling him; odd flashes of familiar colours resonated through his mind, but they were overshadowed by a sudden lancing pain that had him clutching his head in agony. He recalled Stargazer's vision on the Plain of the Dead; here he had seen the lord of the horse's inner eye and the dormant spirit of Han Garid. Was he now somehow connected, through his former bond with Stargazer, to the lord of the thunder dragons? His heart froze at the thought.

An unnatural silence hung over them, but Rokshan knew it was the calm before the storm, and that time was running out. Corhanuk's command to An Lushan had been clear: to meet him in the court of the Crimson King – at the portals of Hell itself – and Rokshan again recalled the words of Shou Lao: *You must cross the Flame Mountains in the Land of Fire, there to seek the Guardian Monk and help him in the eternal vigil he keeps in the court of the Crimson King. All else will fail if you do not succeed in this.*

Rokshan stood by the temple steps, wrestling with the hard, unalterable fact: the Flame Mountains were far to the east, at least three to four full cycles of the moon away, over the most hostile mountains and deserts – how could they possibly hope to get there before Corhanuk, An Lushan (or whatever it was his brother had become) and the demon wraiths?

Smacking his fist into his palm in frustration, he glanced inside the temple. The crumpled body of Zerafshan lay by the altar, and he felt an overwhelming guilt. To have killed his own father – surely he would be damned for all eternity to the twilight life of a *kuei* for it? He wondered if, after all, he had been right to obey Stargazer.

Lost in these melancholy thoughts, he suddenly realized that Lianxang was gesturing to him. She was directing all her conscious energy at something – quite what, Rokshan wasn't sure, but after some moments he caught a familiar shrill cry, faint and far-off . . . there it was again – and getting closer! There was no mistaking the silhouette when it eventually came into view – Lianxang's spirit-bird had returned. As she wheeled closer, Rokshan started to make the sign of the dragon before stopping himself and murmuring a prayer to the goddess of travellers – Lianxang's spirit-bird would have no heartening news for them, of that he was certain.

Lianxang answered the eagle's call and stood in the clearing beside the burning funeral biers, her face raised up and arms outstretched, in communion with the great bird. Cetu and Rokshan stood aside, watching respectfully as the silent dialogue was enacted. At last the eagle gave a final cry of farewell, climbed effortlessly to catch the air currents that would carry her soaring over the mountaintops, and was gone.

Lianxang stood as if in a trance before shaking herself out of her reverie. 'Rokshan, Cetu, listen. My spirit-bird – the great eagle – has been patrolling the borders of your kingdom, and has seen the wild dragon horses that roam beyond your valleys in the rolling Plains of Jalhal'a. She told me that Stargazer called on the Spirit of the Four Winds to blast their pursuers from their path and then they fled – many hundreds of them – towards the great desert, led there by the horse-singers. Stargazer then rode on with the Spirit to rejoin his captive brothers and sisters on the summit – this we know – to share their fate.'

'The Serenadhi! Cetu, they're alive – and Stargazer helped them and his wild horses escape from the imperial forces!' Rokshan cried. 'Don't you see? He wouldn't help the sisters only for them to lead the dragon horses to their deaths in the desert – they must have some plan, I'm sure of it!'

'Maybe so, my young friend.' Cetu nodded slowly. 'Yes . . . maybe so.' He allowed himself the faintest of smiles.

'The Serenadhi told my spirit-bird of no plan,' Lianxang said sharply; 'only to tell you this—'

'What? What did they say?' Rokshan asked quietly.

'They said that even if the Wise Lord has made the sky infinite, nevertheless in His wisdom He has made a doorway to go beyond the Heavens. In the same way, while the Earth must be deep and solid – like the valleys of the Horsemen – there are also many passages that allow us to enter into the Lower World.'

'And for the spirits of the Lower World, Lianxang, to visit ours – yes, this is the belief of the Horsemen,' Cetu replied.

'Then the message of the Serenadhi is clear,' Lianxang said

firmly. 'We must heed what Shou Lao told Rokshan and make haste to find the court of the Crimson King, and *you*, Cetu – so the Serenadhi tell my spirit-bird – can lead us there.'

Rokshan looked at her in bemusement. 'Lianxang, how fast does An Lushan ride with his demon wraiths?' he asked impatiently.

'We rode from within sight of Maracanda to the summit in just over two cycles of the moon. No ordinary rider could do the same journey in less than three.'

'Just over two! Are you sure?'

'I will not forget a day or a night of that journey as long as I live,' Lianxang replied with grim certainty.

'At that pace, they could be at the Flame Mountains before we have even got three-quarters of the way there.' Rokshan turned to his Waymaster. 'Cetu, this is important, do you know of a faster route to the Flame Mountains? We'll have to work out how to find the Guardian Monk once we're there, but can you get us there quickly? What about one of these secret underground ways Lianxang's talking about – there must be a way, otherwise the message of the Serenadhi means nothing!'

'Peace, my young friend . . . there is a way, known only to the Serenadhi, or those whom they have entrusted with its secret.'

'Until now . . .' Rokshan said.

'Yes, until now . . .' Cetu said, sighing deeply. 'These are unprecedented times, and the message from the sisters seems clear: the old ways must speak their secrets. The passageway they point us to is through the Jade Mountain, three quarters of a cycle of the moon away – less if we travel hard; but we will have to journey through the Land of Perpetual Mist to get there. It is a path only a few Horsemen know, north of here. We would have to go directly over the pass, on foot. Through it there is a way to the Lower World; it is known to the Horsemen through our pact with the Jade Spirit. It has long been a tradition of our people – you heard it spoken of in the valleys.'

'The special mares of the plains, those born with coats of the purest snowy white, unblemished for their sacrifice to the Jade Spirit,' Rokshan said, recalling what he'd heard in the marketplace at the Festival of the Dragon. 'But none of the brood mares can bring them forth now – all the sacrificial mares are being born with the three stripes common to all dragon horses.'

'The first time this has ever happened,' Cetu replied sadly. 'Another omen of the evil days that are now upon us.'

'I thought only the Serenadhi enacted the sacrifice – but . . . are you saying that the white mares are actually presented to the Jade Spirit?' Rokshan asked, puzzled.

'Sometimes, once in every two or three generations, the Serenadhi honour a Waymaster by letting him accompany them; this is how I know of what Lianxang has spoken of,' Cetu replied. 'Once I was allowed to travel with them, though not to accompany the mare on her final journey. Each valley clan prays to the dragon spirits that it will be their brood mares that bring the unblemished ones into the world; that time it was the turn of the Fifth Valley clan. There was much joy in our valley then . . .' Cetu gazed into the distance, lost in his memories of happier times.

Lianxang had been listening with increasing anger. 'Why do you allow this sacrifice of your sacred mounts? It is barbaric. My people would not countenance it.'

'The Jade Spirit has nurtured the souls of the dragon horses over all the countless centuries, so that when the time comes he will be able to use their swiftness and strength to leave his eternal prison of jade,' Cetu answered simply. 'It is a great honour for a dragon horse to serve such a high-ranking guardian spirit in this way. The mares go willingly, in joyous anticipation. It is what they are born for: they know they will live again for ever in the Lower World, reborn as spirit-souls amongst their own kind. And when a Horseman dies, the Jade Spirit summons one of the spirit horses to bear their soul heavenwards, to be at one with them. So it is that, even after death, we Horsemen can be together with our dragon horses: the pact with the Jade Spirit ensures that this will always be so.'

'So he will welcome us into his twilight kingdom, but he will surely expect another sacrifice. What will he do when he learns that your . . . *pact* is to be unfulfilled?' Lianxang asked coldly, still unconvinced.

'We will tell him that the forces of evil that have been unleashed are the cause of the brood mares' barrenness – and we will tell him of the transformation of the horses into their dragon ancestors – there are no white mares left to fulfil the pact. This will perhaps assuage his anger, while fuelling his thirst for revenge against the brother guardian spirits who tempted him from the path of the Wise Lord. He will be a powerful ally indeed.' Cetu paused, looking steadily at them both. 'That is, if he decides not to take us as sacrifices instead.' His words of warning hung in the air.

'It is a risk we will have to take,' Rokshan said decisively. 'It's our only chance to get to the court of the Crimson King. We will have to rely on the Jade Spirit to show us the way – and he may also tell us why it is so important for us to get there and help the Guardian Monk – we must make a start now!'

'Corhanuk will also know of a passageway into the spirit world, of that I am certain,' Lianxang said matter-of-factly.

'But we have to try, Lianxang! We have no choice,' Rokshan exhorted her. 'Will your spirit-bird come with us to warn us of danger?'

'She is always with me, in my mind's eye, and deep in my soul. She is as much a part of me as Stargazer was surely part of you. Nothing can ever be the same once you have become one with another creature – but you know this already.'

'One more thing we should be aware of, my young friends,' Cetu said. 'Time is of the essence, but in the Lower World, time can pass strangely. A day in the Kingdom of the Jade Spirit may amount to a full cycle of the moon in our world.'

'And it may work the other way round, as well?'

'I could not say . . .' Cetu shrugged his shoulders, and went to pay his last respects to the dead before they headed north.

CHAPTER 42

THE KINGDOM OF THE JADE SPIRIT

The swirling mists had got thicker until they could barely see an arm's length in front of them. After half a cycle of the moon's hard travelling – at a half-run for as long as Cetu had been able to keep up with them – they had at last come to within a day of the peak they sought.

'Our people know of this land,' Lianxang said. 'It is full of wandering *kuei*.'

'The sisterhood said as much' – Cetu shrugged – 'but it is just legend.'

'They are here,' Lianxang said simply, 'and we are known to them.'

'They know we are here?' Rokshan asked.

'Can't you feel it?' Lianxang asked, amazed.

They were following the course of the River Dolbor. At this point it was only a stream but they could see the precious element it carried, glowing and flickering as it trickled downstream. Rokshan had whistled in delight when he had first seen it, plunging his hands into the icy water and scooping it up by the handful.

'If only Naha could've seen this! He would have had a caravan of mules and packhorses up here in no time!'

He let the nuggets plop back into the stream, making a little waterfall of jade. He would have given anything just then for the man he'd loved all his life as his father to be there with him. With a deep sigh he offered instead a prayer to Kuan Yin that she had seen Naha safely back to Maracanda.

And what of his brother? Could he in truth be blamed if he was possessed? No, Rokshan thought bitterly. One man was to blame, and no one else . . .

'What's the matter?' Lianxang had been watching him.

He started at the sound of her voice. 'Nothing . . .'

'I'm frightened too, you know – of all this,' she said, sitting down beside him, trailing her fingers in the cold water. 'I'm sorry about An'an. I haven't spoken to you properly – I mean, about him . . . I've been praying that there is some way we can get through to him, something that will help him break out of his possession. Yet I fear there is nothing left of the brother and friend we knew; we should not fool ourselves by holding out hope for him,' she said sadly.

'Hope is all we have, isn't it? Isn't that what we're doing here?' Rokshan replied, bitter-sweet memories of his brother flitting like wraiths through his mind.

'I and my people will help you in the task Shou Lao entrusted you with,' Lianxang said, deadly serious. 'That is all we can do. And if it brings An'an back to us . . .'

'Of course, that's what we'd all hope for – but I wish— Oh, it doesn't matter.' Rokshan got up quickly before he could say any more.

'I know you think I should've seen what was happening to An'an and done something about it,' Lianxang said suddenly, catching his arm.

He didn't reply; he had been thinking exactly that.

'Rokshan, listen!' Lianxang's eyes flashed. 'It was too late by the time we were nearing Maracanda! He was a husk – something was sucking all that was good out of him so he could be filled with that . . . *creature* he now is. I tried to stop him! Do you really think he would've done this if I'd been able to reach him? *Do you?*' She pointed at her slashed cheek.

'No, I'm sorry . . . I didn't really—'

'I know, it's all right,' Lianxang said. 'I didn't know how

much I . . . how fond I was of him until it was too late. We'd better get on,' she said, hurrying off so he wouldn't see her tears.

As they walked, Rokshan thought he heard faint, far-off snatches of singing, mixed with the scraping, clinking and tapping of picks and shovels. Then the curtains of mist would part and they'd catch glimpses of the higher levels of the Five Terraces Mountain. Pinpoint shafts of light studded its slopes.

'What is that I can hear, and the lights on the mountain-side?' he called ahead to Cetu.

'It is the mine-sprites, mining and working the jade. The lights are where they open up the shafts to throw out those pieces that are not perfect enough for the Wise Lord. These the river eventually carries down to us. How else do you think the emperors get their jade?' Cetu observed.

As they made camp that night, Lianxang pressed Cetu on the exact means of entry into the Kingdom of the Jade Spirit.

'When the setting sun pierces the gloom of the mist and shines a blood-red shaft of light onto a cleft in the side of the mountain, it is a sign from the Jade Spirit, marking the beginning of a path that will lead us down into the depths of his spirit world . . .' the old Waymaster told them at last, tossing a branch onto the fire.

Rokshan sensed a sadness in him. Perhaps having to reveal centuries-old secrets known only to his own people rankled with him, he thought.

Without another word, the Waymaster settled down under his blanket to sleep. Rokshan's eyes became heavy and he wrapped himself up against the damp chill before he too drifted off.

'Wake up! Rokshan!' It felt like he'd been asleep only minutes, but Lianxang was shaking him by the shoulder. 'Wake up! Look . . .'

The mist had cleared, and the stars shone brilliantly in a cloudless sky. Halfway up the mountain, light blazed from one of the jade mine's opened shafts – a blood-red beam just as Cetu had described.

Quickly they broke camp and set off; within the hour they were approaching the shaft. The red light that poured out was tinged with a jade-green luminescence so brilliant that it was impossible to see what lay beyond the entrance.

'What now?' Rokshan asked, more than a little nervous.

'We go in,' Cetu said. 'I have been no further. On my one visit to this place, this is where I stayed, to await the sisters' return, but as we are on our own, we must take the path they took.'

'But . . . what lies beyond? We cannot see,' Lianxang said anxiously.

'The sisters always returned,' Cetu said hesitatingly.

Rokshan took a deep breath and stepped into the shaft. Instead of being blinded by the light, he immediately had the strangest sensation of floating in an ocean of blackness. It was warm and comfortable, and he felt unafraid. He looked around for Cetu and Lianxang but they were nowhere to be seen. Now he was gently sinking; he wondered where he was being taken to.

With a gentle bump, he landed on a soft surface. He raised his head and saw a distant doorway framed in light, like a beacon in the blackness. Waves lapped gently against it. A woman stood there, long robes of blue and green rippling all about her. She beckoned to Rokshan to come: she looked so serene and beguiling, he couldn't resist. Her slender white arm drew him towards her, but as he approached, she turned away as if to hide her face. He called out to her, his voice sounding strange and far away.

'Welcome, Rokshan. Do not be afraid. Your companions will join you. I am a water spirit of this world's river, the Dolbor. Enter – the Jade Spirit awaits you.'

Her voice was lilting and musical. She gestured towards the doorway, which started to open inwards, revealing a further blaze of blinding light. Rokshan shielded his eyes and stepped through; the door silently swung shut behind him. He turned to see if the water spirit had followed him, but he was alone.

He was in a vast cavern of the palest green jade. Sheer walls, as smooth as glass, soared upwards to a domed roof. His eye was immediately drawn to a magnificently carved throne of solid jade radiating waves of brilliant white light shot through with flashes of pale green which reflected off the walls and roof of the cavern, giving a hypnotic, pulsing effect.

Around the throne stood twelve figures; their bodies were human but each had a different animal head. Rokshan recognized them as the animals of birth and resemblance – the rat was there, along with the ox, tiger, rabbit, dragon, snake, horse, ram, monkey, cockerel, dog and pig. Every soul taken to the Wise Lord to await their reincarnation after they had repented was given the sign of an animal to take with them. These were the semi-divine beings themselves, Rokshan realized, but they were so still he thought they must be statues: they stared at him, unblinking.

Behind the throne flowed the river of the underworld, its fathomless depths silent; at intervals a fountain of water shot up to the vaulted roof of the jade cavern and came crashing noisily down into the river again. All along its banks, stretching away into the distance, hooded figures stood, stooped and penitent.

Rokshan looked at the figure sitting on the throne, who extended his arms in a gesture of welcome.

The calm of the water spirit deserted Rokshan and he approached the throne feeling increasingly afraid. Where were Cetu and Lianxang? As he got nearer, he saw that the occupant of the throne had a human body, but his face was covered by a jade mask studded with opals that shimmered with palest pink and green and deep blue as they caught the light. He was dressed in a white robe which hung in folds across his chest and covered his legs.

Rokshan stopped as he noticed with mounting alarm that a silver torq, exactly the same as those of the Horsemen, hung around the Jade Spirit's neck, but with one difference – it had no cicada-shaped clasp joining its two ends. With a jolt of fear, Rokshan realized that it was all true: the Jade Spirit was a higher guardian spirit who, despite his punishment of eternal imprisonment in this kingdom of jade, must still be favoured by the Wise Lord. Why then did he exude such a restless, questing malevolence? Rokshan looked around in vain for his friends – what had happened to them? he wondered with a growing sense of unease.

As he did so, he felt a gentle probing in his mind, like caressing fingers. As it searched and delved, he heard a voice: *Where are the women of the Serenadhi who accompany the blood sacrifice?*

Rokshan opened his mouth to reply, but found he did not need to. 'Where are my companions? What have you done with them?' he asked, his heart pounding.

At this, the Jade Spirit stirred; from the eye-slits in his mask, green beams of light shone with an intensity that made Rokshan shrink back in fear; the animal spirits moved towards him, encircling him.

Do not dare to question me! You are a mortal and trespass here in the Lower World. They cannot see you, but if I willed it, all those pitiful creatures by the river would fall on you and devour your soul, piece by piece.

Rokshan quaked. 'I did not mean to offend you. The Serenadhi cannot deliver the blood sacrifice – but I have come with my companions, seeking a way to the court of the Crimson King—'

It has come about then, as my animal spirits said it would: evil has again been unleashed in the world. But why do you seek to gain entry where only the souls of the damned go?

'Corhanuk and An— Beshbaliq – they have the Staff of Chu Jung, and have joined it with the Talisman; they have transformed the dragon horses of the Horsemen back into the ancient dragons. Now they go to the court of the Crimson King to do more of their master's bidding. We must stop them before it is too late. Please, can you help us? You once served the Wise Lord—'

The Jade Spirit's eye-slits flashed at the mention of his master's name. *Corhanuk's meddling in the mortal affairs of men and the divine order of the universe are of no concern to me*, he replied contemptuously. *My place is here, for all eternity, to listen to the last pleas of souls seeking forgiveness for their sins against the Wise Lord. If I am seen to be meddling in the affairs of men, I may suffer His renewed wrath and punishment.*

'But they are going to try and loose the Four Riders and free the Shadow from the Arch of Darkness; together they and the dragons will destroy everything that is beautiful in the world! If they succeed, all humankind will become enslaved to the Shadow's will and the Wise Lord will no longer have dominion over the Heavens. What then will become of you?'

How do you know this?

The fountain of water behind the Jade Spirit's throne shot up to the vaulted roof of the cavern and came crashing down again.

'The abbot at the citadel monastery of Labrang told me, and Stargazer, the lord of the horses, has also warned of this . . .'

The Jade Spirit nodded and inclined his head towards the animal spirits. The horse figure stepped forward and knelt before him. Moments passed. Rokshan felt the sweat trickling down his back and willed himself to remain still, hardly daring to breathe as the Jade Spirit continued a silent dialogue with the horse divinity. At last he looked up, his green eye-slits pulsing.

You speak truly, mortal. But my animal spirits urge me to tell you more. The rebirth of the dragons is just the first of the conditions that must be met before the Shadow can be freed. They are to spread fear and terror in preparation for the return of their master. Corhanuk now seeks to fulfil the next condition: he goes to free the Crimson King, who in turn will loose the Four Riders of Hell.

The Four Riders are the most monstrous of the first-born creatures of creation, transformed by their consuming jealousy of mankind, fanned by the Shadow's own greed and lust for power. They are Despair, Pain, Loneliness and Fear made manifest. Once they are in the world, the dragons will flock to follow them and the balance, the very yin and yang of the universe itself, will be lost for ever: chaos will prevail; fear and loneliness will rule in the hearts of men and, in their despair and pain, they will be capable only of evil. In this way evil will prevail in the world and thus will the second condition for the release of the Shadow be met.

'But they must also have the words of the Divine Commandment that put the Arch of Darkness in place – and these have been lost for ever,' Rokshan said, despairing at this terrible vision of the future, 'so they cannot succeed—'

You speak of the Sacred Scroll? Rokshan jumped in fright at the Jade Spirit's derisive laughter, which echoed off the cavernous walls. *You are wrong, mortal. The words of the Divine Comandment were indeed written down by Corhanuk, against the wishes of the Wise Lord, and then loosed in the world. But Corhanuk was with the Wise Lord when he issued the Commandment: each word is seared into his memory, repeated over and over through the countless aeons. Only mortal creatures would need them written down to remember them; this Corhanuk did to beguile and mislead men.*

The Divine Commandment must be read again, with its original meaning reversed, and this Corhanuk can do from memory. Thus will the final condition be met – but it will fail unless the final condition's own requirement is met, and if the final condition fails, all fails – and everything that the Shadow has planned comes to nought.

'What is this requirement?' Rokshan asked, his mind reeling.

The Elect had sought to prevent the Shadow from freeing himself by making sure that the Sacred Scroll was safe in their hands – should it ever be found – but now it seemed the forces of evil had no need of it anyway.

The requirement of the final condition is one that Corhanuk has worked for ceaselessly at the behest of his master, planting the seeds for its fruition by treacherously turning the gifts of the Wise Lord against Him—

'I . . . I don't understand,' Rokshan said.

Consider the divine Collars, mortal! Why do you think they did not turn men back to Him, once they were found, as the Wise Lord intended? Because they had been corrupted by their wearers – those guardian spirits who sought to overthrow the Wise Lord and rule the Heavens and Earth in His place . . .

'So the Horsemen were right about their Collars . . .' Rokshan whispered.

They were right about where they came from – but were ignorant of the Collars' power to corrupt and lead men to evil.

'Why . . . how did they do this?'

The Wise Lord breathed the smallest particle of His essence into each Collar; they were gifts for His faithful servants, from the highest to the lowest guardian spirit.

The two Collars found by the Horsemen were those of the Crimson King and Beshbaliq – this you already know. But neither you nor any mortal could ever know that the taint of their original wearers' evil had already seeped into the Collars, corrupting them. Each time a broken Collar is worn by a mortal, the seed of evil is awakened, and grows . . .

'But what the Horsemen call the lesser Collar, which all the dead khagans have worn – it was supposed to pass on the wisdom of centuries to each new khagan when he passed one night in the Towers of Silence: why was this knowledge of the Collars never revealed to any of them?'

Corhanuk made sure this knowledge was always hidden from the living, and now the passage of time has done its work: through the Collars, stealthily and with patient, malicious cunning, he and his master exerted a mysterious hold over the Horsemen. Thus was the way prepared for their acceptance of Zerafshan, and the fulfilment of the third condition—

'They have fulfilled the third condition already?' Rokshan prayed it wasn't so. 'How?'

He could feel the Jade Spirit's piercing stare as it probed the depths of his soul, making his mind go blank . . .

Have you not understood, mortal? You are the fulfilment!

Rokshan felt only a dumb despair as he tried to make sense of what he'd just been told. 'I . . . but you must be mistaken . . . how could . . . ?'

Do not doubt the word of a higher guardian spirit! The words of the Divine Comandment must be read again in the opposite of their meaning. But even this will fail if they are not read by a warrior who is pure in heart and spirit. You have done the Horsemen's Way, and spoken with the lord of the horses, even obeying his command to end your father's life mercifully; only a warrior pure in heart and spirit could have done this: you are he.

'But I am not a Horseman!' Rokshan cried.

And therefore you are not tainted by the corruption of the Collars as the Horsemen have been, through the generations. Truly you are 'a warrior pure in heart and spirit'. And now you are here, in my power. To deliver you to the portals of Hell would be playing into the hands of Corhanuk and his master . . . Is this your wish?

'Please help us.' Rokshan dropped to his knees in supplication. 'In the name of the Wise Lord, I beg you . . . Do not let the world suffer the Shadow's revenge on all that is good and pure in the hearts of men and women, on all those who are yet to be born, and all those who have lived blameless lives.'

The Jade Spirit sat unmoving and, it seemed, unmoved by Rokshan's plea. But his head was bowed and the beams of light through the eye-slits of his mask shone dimly onto the ground around him. As he looked up, Rokshan thought he caught a glimpse of the ice-green eyes behind the mask, and he wondered if the Jade Spirit's cold, frozen heart – fixed by the

Wise Lord in an eternity of contemplation of his own folly –
had at last been moved to pity.

*I would not have told you what you know now if it was not in my mind
to help you. There is perhaps just a small chance, but first you must give me what
is not yours . . .* The Jade Spirit stroked his Collar, making it quite
clear what he intended.

Carefully Rokshan took the Collar he had taken from the
Plain of the Dead out of his coat pocket and unwrapped it. The
Jade Spirit beckoned to him to come closer, stretching out his
hand. Rokshan mounted the steps, fearful of getting any closer.
He fell to his knees two steps from the top.

Close up, he saw that the Jade Spirit's skin glowed the
faintest pale green just below the surface. The fingers of his
outstretched hand were covered in heavily jewelled rings, the
nails long and sharp.

The Collar of Beshbaliq, he said, his fingers closing around it.
*Never again will the Collar be able to corrupt those who wear it. It would have
been better for you, though, if this had been the Collar of the Crimson King, the
higher guardian spirit. Once his Collar is returned to him, his free will is restored
and he will rise up against the eternal vigil of the Guardian Monk in
order to release the Four Riders of Hell. This is why the Guardian Monk needs
your help, even now as we speak. Go now! And I will send my army to help you.
Let me summon Abarga, who carries the souls of the damned to Hell.
Abarga!*

As the Jade Spirit called out the name, the fountain of
water erupted again from behind his throne and fell back into
the river. The animal spirits resumed their positions beside
their lord, staring straight ahead. Rokshan noticed the river had
not settled back into its glass-like stillness: its surface began to
ripple with waves, which lapped against the banks, gently at
first and then with increasing force. At the same time, from
deep below he could hear a faint rhythmic tramp, as if
hundreds of heavy boots were crunching across ground strewn
with glass.

The hooded, huddled figures along the riverbank began to chant, at first softly, then more loudly as the water was gradually whipped into a boiling fury. The fountain erupted, throwing up a mountainous jet of water that seemed to stop in mid-flow before cascading down again. Then, suddenly, Rokshan saw a shape that lay just below the surface, its vast yellow form filling the whole river.

'Behold!' The Jade Spirit spoke aloud for the first time. 'Abarga Shara Mogoi! Spirit of the Waters, carrier of souls to Hell!' His voice echoed off the soaring walls of jade but was drowned out by the wails of the damned, who must have known their moment of judgement was not far off.

As the Jade Spirit's greeting to Abarga faded away, the faint tramp became a crashing crescendo, and a legion of jade warriors, hundreds strong, marched into view. Rokshan gaped in awe at them, but then gave a shout of joy when he spotted Cetu and Lianxang in the midst of the stone army. Rokshan whispered his thanks to the Jade Spirit and bowed low before bounding down the steps to join them.

The water spirit who had welcomed Rokshan into the palace of jade seemed to float beside them, her long robes of blue and green rippling all about her.

The hooded souls parted to make way for the jade warriors. As they approached the banks, the river was whipped into an even greater fury.

'Cetu!' Lianxang screamed as Abarga's great yellow head and coiled body surfaced, erupting in a cascade of water and malevolent hissing. It swayed as if to a snake charmer's pipes, its head swinging from side to side.

'Mortals are forbidden in the Lower World. Who are you and what is your purpose here?' Abarga's sibilant voice was low and menacing.

'I am Rokshan. I and my friends seek passage to the court of the Crimson King.'

The Jade Spirit raised a hand. 'Take them to the place of torment, Abarga!' he commanded.

Abarga's gleaming eyes of palest green transfixed them before, with a swaying bow, it lowered its scaly body for them to mount. The souls of the damned – pushed forward by the ranks of jade warriors – also began to climb onto the giant snake, where they lay, still and silent.

The warriors then lined the banks, providing a silent escort but waiting on the command from their lord as Abarga slowly swam away from the banks of the Kingdom of the Jade Spirit and then dived down, speeding them all to the fiery portals of Hell.

CHAPTER 43

IN THE COURT OF THE CRIMSON KING

They awoke as if from a deep sleep to see a pair of massive gates cut into the rock ahead of them. They clambered off Abarga, watching the inky black waters of the river meander sluggishly towards the gates.

From beyond the gates came a terrible howling and wailing. The souls of the damned, silently lining the banks, shrank into themselves and sighed a quiet moan of terror.

'This is the entrance to Hell . . .' Rokshan said in a quavering whisper.

The noise grew louder and louder – Rokshan recognized it from his vision on the Plain of the Dead. Now they could see the shadowy spirits, all pressed together in a writhing, seething mass; tears of black, poisoned blood dripped from their eyes, spattering on the ground.

They edged back, shrinking against the wall of the cavern as the huge gates inched slowly open, allowing the waters of the Lower World to flow silently through. Beyond them was a scene of barren desolation: massive pillars of black, craggy granite soared to a roof so high it was lost to view. Sulphurous pools bubbled and boiled, giving off foul-smelling fumes. Along the far walls, as far as the eye could see, streamed rivulets of fire, licking greedily at the noisome air and staining the walls a ghostly greenish-black.

Far off, almost on the horizon of this nightmare world, they could just make out an enormous conflagration and hear its flames roaring and crackling up from the abyss.

The shadowy spirits now gathered up those who had just arrived on the back of Abarga, driving them into the river that wound its brackish way through the featureless terrain. Their wails were redoubled as they were pulled towards the inferno which blazed on the horizon.

'Come, we must hurry,' Cetu said, gesturing towards the gates. 'Before they close and we're locked out here for ever.'

They hurried through the forbidding portals and set off, cautiously following the course of the river towards the raging fires of Hell and the court of the Crimson King. The heat and noise were overwhelming.

'We need to find the Guardian Monk – and avoid being seen by the Crimson King himself,' Rokshan shouted above the din of the crackling inferno. 'We must try and remain hidden.'

'We are in the Lower World now,' Lianxang said. 'Just as spirits are invisible to us in the Upper World – unless, like Corhanuk, they are powerful enough to be able to take on a physical aspect – here we cannot be seen by the souls of the damned. This is as my spirit-bird tells me.'

'So other mortals like An'an could see us?' Rokshan asked, his eyes darting around the terrifying place.

'Yes,' Lianxang replied. 'And the Crimson King and the Guardian Monk – they are higher spirits; they too will be able to see us.'

Roaring flames shot up from the edge of the abyss as they got closer. The river curled around some sulphurous pools and then disappeared between two towering crags of black rock, beyond which the cries and laments of the spirits of the damned could be heard even above the roaring of Hell itself.

'We must climb up there,' Rokshan shouted to Cetu. 'Those crags must be the outposts of where the spirits have been taken.'

Cetu nodded grimly, gazing up at the rocky peaks. Suddenly he shot out his arm and pulled Rokshan to the ground. Lianxang flung herself down between them.

'What is it?' she asked breathlessly.

'I saw something move,' Cetu whispered hoarsely. 'There! They're all over the base of the rocks . . . Look!'

Rokshan squinted again at the crags, and then spotted them too. Their black robes blended perfectly with the rock, but their glinting red eye-slits gave them away.

'The demon wraiths!' he exclaimed. 'Corhanuk must have shown them the way through the Flame Mountains.'

'Then we must have been gone much longer than it seems – as you warned us, Cetu,' Lianxang said. 'But where is Corhanuk . . . and An'an?'

Cetu nodded towards the base of the rocky outcrops. There, his eyes glinting feverishly, An Lushan was signalling to the demon wraiths. Their elastic, viscous bodies flowed easily across the rock like molten lava as they silently streamed along behind him.

'Come on!' Rokshan urged. 'We've got to see what they're doing.'

They sprinted the short distance to the crags and clambered up. Cautiously, Rokshan peered over the edge and gasped at the sight that confronted him.

The roaring inferno licked up over the edge of an abyss beyond two enormous iron gates that glowed red-hot and soared upwards as far as the eye could see. Chained to the gates was a giant figure that seemed human but was impervious to the flames dancing around him. His bulging eyes flashed fire and his mouth was open in a soundless scream, displaying needle-sharp teeth. His legs and feet were bare and he wore only a crimson tunic open to the waist, tied with a trailing white sash. Gold and jewellery adorned his muscular body. In his right hand he held a huge iron club, which he beat against his chains and then slammed into the gates, causing a thunderous clanking that made the ground shake.

'The Crimson King himself,' Lianxang breathed, shrinking back in horror.

Some of the spirits were being dragged down to the right of the gates, where a wide path led through a massive archway and extended down into an inky blackness lit intermittently by feebly sputtering torches. From these further depths of Hell they could hear distant snarls even more ferocious than those of the hell-horses.

In front of the gated abyss sat a hooded figure in a shape-less robe – the Guardian Monk. Head down, he pored over hundreds of scrolls laid out on a large flat piece of rock as each spirit of the damned prostrated itself before him. He seemed to study the scrolls carefully and then, lifting his head, pro-nounced his verdict, pointing either towards the Crimson King and the abyss or to the blackness beyond the archway.

As he lifted his head, they caught a glimpse of a radiant face. Small, goblin-like creatures pranced around him, gleefully escorting each spirit as it received its judgement. Many were pulled and pushed, kicking and wailing, to the gated abyss, where a huge mass of cowering spirits awaited their fate. Others – whose crimes merited further tortures first – were being herded through the archway, where savage punishments awaited them in the depths of Hell. The Crimson King gathered all those who had been condemned to burn alive for all eternity in the unquenchable flames and, straining his bulk against the enormous gates, heaved them open, tumbling his victims down into the roaring inferno.

Rokshan could see the demon wraiths, with An Lushan in the middle of them, amongst the mass of clamouring spirits. Stealthily they made their way closer to where the Guardian Monk sat, poring over his scrolls which contained everything he needed to know about the life of each of the tormented souls that came before him.

An Lushan was standing in front of the Guardian Monk

when one of the hell-goblins pointed an accusatory, long-nailed finger at him and screamed at his master. The demon wraiths immediately formed a protective wall around An Lushan.

'Where is Corhanuk?' Lianxang said, not taking her eyes off what was unfolding before them. 'He must be here too. This is surely a trap, to distract the Guardian Monk . . . We must stop An'an – look what he has in his hands!'

'The Crimson King's Collar,' Rokshan replied. 'Once he gets it back, he'll have the power to release the Four Riders.'

The demon wraiths now surrounded the Guardian Monk. Some of his goblins clamoured at his side, brandishing their clubs; some had slunk away, but the rest now sidled alongside the demon wraiths, needing little persuasion, it seemed, to join forces with their own kind.

An Lushan's black robes streamed out amidst the hot ash as he swept towards the Guardian Monk. 'Your eternal vigil is over!' he screamed over the roaring fires of the abyss. 'I come with the Collar of the Crimson King. I am returning it to him to wear again, so that he can be free of you!'

Accompanied by a handful of his hell-goblins, the Guardian Monk planted himself firmly in front of the Crimson King. Throwing aside the monk's habit, he drew a gleaming sword. As he touched the tip to the claspless Collar that was now revealed around his neck, it ignited in a blinding flash, its blade glowing with a clean white fire. The Guardian Monk himself was transformed, clothed in a white robe that shone so brightly he was surrounded by a shimmering, transcendent glow. His face shone, his eyes aflame as he stood, serene and implacable, his sword held upright with both hands in front of him.

'The Crimson King is mine to guard,' he stated, his voice echoing like a peal of bells around the court of the Crimson King. 'Mine is an eternal vigil that the Wise Lord has appointed.

None can break it, without first destroying me. The Crimson King pays the price for his pride and ambition – as you will.'

At this the Crimson King roared with rage and ran as far as his chains would allow, to within a few paces of the Guardian Monk, before they jerked him back with a crash against the massive gates.

An Lushan's mad, barking laugh rang around the cavernous wastes of Hell as he held the Collar high in the air. 'No!' he shouted. 'You will be the one to pay the price!'

From his position at the top of the rock, Rokshan shuddered. He knew what he had to do . . .

Cetu must have read his thoughts; he gave him a searching look. 'Trap or no trap, he is your brother. Can you kill him?'

'You and Lianxang must draw the demon wraiths and those other creatures away from him so I can get close.' Rokshan looked steadily at the old Waymaster as he fingered the long ceremonial dagger that he had used to kill Zerafshan. 'He is no longer my brother, Cetu, just as Zerafshan was not my father, except by blood. Lianxang – you know this . . .'

Lianxang nodded, brushing aside a tear.

Nothing more needed to be said and they scrambled down as quickly as they could, sprinting across the hot, ashy ground towards An Lushan and the Guardian Monk.

Lianxang darted silently among the hell-goblins, using all the deadly skills of her people with the dagger. Cetu slashed at any who got near him, one hand using his sword, the other thrusting and stabbing with his short lance.

An Lushan swivelled round in anger, directing the demon wraiths against their attackers while the Crimson King wrestled in fury against the chains that bound him as the Guardian Monk remained in front of him, resolute and strong.

Rokshan held the Horsemen's dagger high as he raced – summoning all the agility and speed of the hare – to where An Lushan was urging on his demon horde.

'On, wraiths!' he was shouting. 'Show them no mercy!'

Cetu fought like a man half his years but cried out as his leg caught a deep, raking slash from a wraith's scimitar. Lianxang was being overwhelmed by the hell-goblins, and Rokshan saw her go down with a despairing cry. He slashed at them with his dagger as he came to within striking distance of An Lushan, but within seconds the demon wraiths had blocked his way.

'Seize him! Take him alive!' An Lushan commanded. 'My master has need of him. Bring him to witness what has only ever been dreamed of . . . and the other two – bring them *all* to witness my triumph.'

Rokshan struggled uselessly as the demon wraiths prodded him with the butts of their lances, herding him forward to join Lianxang and Cetu, who was limping badly from his bleeding wound.

Unseen by any of them, a hooded figure was making his way along the path that led down into the depths of Hell. All that could be seen of him were the slivers of his eye-slits, glinting a faint red in the darkness. As he reached the great archway, he lifted his short lance.

An Lushan signalled for the demon wraiths to unleash a volley of lances at the Guardian Monk, but he batted them away as if they were children's playthings.

'None but a higher guardian spirit or the Wise Lord Himself can kill me,' the Guardian Monk's voice rang out. 'You were too easily led, Beshbaliq, by false promises of power and glory, many aeons ago. Why have you let yourself be tempted again?'

As the last faint echoes of his reply reverberated around the cavernous walls, Corhanuk threw off his hood, drew his arm back and hurled the lance at the Guardian Monk with all the strength his malevolent spirit could muster. Thrown faster and more powerfully than by any human arm, it struck the monk in the side with such brutal force it crumpled him to his knees, his sword clattering to the ground.

In silent agony, the Guardian Monk clutched at the lance, its length almost entirely impaled in his side, which gushed blood and water. He looked in bewildered surprise to where Corhanuk emerged from the shadows, laughing triumphantly. The monk had fallen just within reach of the Crimson King, who in one bound fell on top of him with a roar of revenge, his huge hands seizing the unbroken Collar that the Guardian Monk wore around his neck.

With maniacal strength, he twisted it into a garrotte and, slowly and deliberately, started to strangle his former captor to death. Rokshan watched in horror as the Guardian Monk struggled, his once radiant face dimming—

Then a voice sounded in his head, soft, soothing: *Rokshan, I go to be with the Wise Lord at last. He will not be angry with me. Do not lose heart: all is not lost as long as the Evil One remains ignorant of—* Rokshan heard an agonized cry as the Crimson King throttled the last breath out of him.

'No!' Rokshan cried as the body of the Guardian Monk shuddered and went limp, his torment over.

The Crimson King swung his club and heaved at his chains, fixing his fiery gaze on Corhanuk, who tore the Collar from An Lushan's grasp and triumphantly passed it to him.

The guardian spirit clasped it around his neck and flexed his muscles, twisting this way and that as his chains fell away. Immediately he grew in stature, now almost as tall as the gates he had once guarded. Flames leaped around his body, crackling around him as he moved. Opening his mouth and spreading his arms wide as if to embrace his newfound freedom, he unleashed a roar so loud it seemed that the very rocks of Hell would split asunder.

'None shall defy me, ever again! I am free! Let the Wise

Lord tremble in fear, for he shall bow before me and my master when he comes among us!'

The demon wraiths parted, bowing low as the Crimson King stepped away from the gates he had guarded for so many aeons.

Disdainfully he picked up the body of the Guardian Monk and tossed it like a discarded rag into the abyss. He gazed into the flames and, spreading his arms, calmed the raging conflagration into a muted roar. Through the archway the ferocious snarls could now be clearly heard, and the Crimson King gave another triumphant cry which froze their hearts. An Lushan bowed in homage.

Rokshan felt Lianxang's hand grasp his as they backed away in terror. Cetu's head hung down as he leaned against them, his breath coming in short, painful rasps, his leg still bleeding freely. Rokshan tried to think. What could they do? Was all lost, here in the depths of Hell? As he moved to support Cetu, his arm brushed against the amulet the abbot had given him . . . Of course! His amulet – and Guan Di . . .

Could it work here, in the Lower World? His life had to be in mortal danger before Guan Di would come to his aid. There was nothing for it – he had to make one last, desperate effort. Screwing up his courage, he tried to block out the terrifying sight of the Crimson King, now with all his evil potency restored to him. Springing forward with a yell, he charged straight for the demon wraiths.

CHAPTER 44

THE FOUR RIDERS OF HELL

They whirled round as Rokshan rushed towards them, drawing back their lances.

'Guan Di!' Rokshan screamed, rubbing the amulet against his upper arm.

For a few agonizing moments nothing happened, but then he heard an explosion thundering over the flames of the abyss, and saw Guan Di poised in a defensive crouch, wielding his huge double-handed sword, by the craggy wall of rock.

'Where is the boy mortal, my summoner?' the huge warrior god shouted as he ran towards them with his long, loping stride.

The Crimson King turned. 'Who enters my domain un-bidden?' he roared, pointing an accusing finger at Guan Di. 'I know of only one giant who was made a god after his service to Chu Jung – does he now put himself at the service of mere mortals?'

The Crimson King laughed mockingly as he picked up the sword of the fallen Guardian Monk, touching it to his Collar just as the monk had done, making it glow a fiery red as the blade broadened and increased in length, making it a fearsome weapon in his hands.

'Run, mortals!' Guan Di boomed. 'I will hold them off.'

But the demon wraiths were too numerous and quick for them, making escape impossible. An Lushan – now completely possessed by Beshbaliq in all but bodily form – screamed in triumph.

'Imprison them behind the gates,' he ordered. At his command, the demon wraiths dragged Rokshan, Cetu and Lianxang across to the towering gates, shoving them onto the narrow ledge above the yawning abyss of the fires of Hell.

Guan Di passed his sword from one enormous hand to the other as the three allies of evil – Corhanuk, the Crimson King and Beshbaliq – closed in on him. He parried as the Crimson King lunged at him, and sidestepped a double-handed lance thrust from Corhanuk. So quickly it seemed a blur, the Crimson King spun round to one side of the giant, slashing at his legs, while Corhanuk, a lance in each hand, thrust at his heart and stomach. The giant swiped at the lances, slicing them in two, but let out a howl of pain as the Crimson King's sword cut deep into his thigh. He stumbled and went down on one knee. Seizing his chance, the freed guardian of the gates of Hell darted behind him and was about to drive his sword deep into the giant's back.

'Wait!' Rokshan screamed. 'You cannot unsay the Divine Commandment without me! If you kill Guan Di or my friends, I will throw myself over the abyss. Let him go!'

'Stay your hand!' Corhanuk roared to the Crimson King. 'We need the boy – he speaks the truth. And the giant may be useful to us alive . . . for the moment. We will await the command of my master, who comes soon. Seize him!'

Corhanuk gestured to the demon wraiths, who swarmed round the fallen Guan Di, binding him in a tangle of thick ropes and carrying him to the massive gates. Using the chains that had bound the Crimson King, they locked him to the massive iron portals.

'Do the same to them.' Corhanuk gestured to Rokshan, Lianxang and Cetu. 'Take care with the boy mortal – we will have need of him when we are ready. As for the others, we will ask our master what their fate is to be.' Corhanuk's evil laugh was drowned out by the strange, whinnying snarls that once again could be heard from far-off in the depths.

'Your charges await you, brother spirit, and grow impatient,' he said, addressing the Crimson King. 'Go! Release them from their long imprisonment.' He gestured to the archway. 'Send them out to the four corners of the world to spread their evil. Already Han Garid answers their call and gathers his dragon horde here, to serve and follow the Four Riders.'

As the Crimson King turned and raced to free his charges, Rokshan and Lianxang were bound and thrown to the ground beside Guan Di. Cetu, veering in and out of consciousness, was kicked across to lie beside them.

'He is bleeding to death,' Lianxang said, her voice shaking.

'Rokshan . . . and you, girl mortal' – Guan Di's voice was muffled by the ropes and chains around him – 'the Four Riders come: you must not look at them, and stop your ears, otherwise you will be their first victims. Gather up the old one and help him if you can, then settle around me – quickly!'

The urgency in Guan Di's command left no time for explanation and they struggled to do as he had bidden them. The ferocious snarls from beyond the archway grew ever louder, almost drowning out the deranged, yelping laugh of An Lushan, the cackle of the hell-goblins and the wails of the tens of millions of lost souls in the depths of Hell.

Then, far above them, very faint but borne in on the winds of Hell, they heard the beating of hundreds of dragons' wings quivering through the air: Han Garid was assembling his horde in the skies outside, waiting to unleash unimaginable terror upon the world; the dragons' ancient, jealous rage against mankind had been rekindled and could not be contained much longer.

Rokshan cried out in agony as his mind was pummelled by wave after wave of the full fury of the dragons, channelled through their lord, Han Garid; he quailed at the terrifying thought that the lord of the thunder dragons might be calling him, just as he had called on Stargazer on the Plain of the Dead.

And above all this unearthly din, like the scent of carrion on the wind, they smelled wafts of something unspeakably evil.

They screwed their eyes tight shut but it was impossible to block out the stench of fear and raw smell of pain; the bitter taste of loneliness and an empty pit of despair began to fill them as if their minds were being sucked dry. Lianxang moaned and rocked from side to side as she felt the power of the evil that had been summoned. Rokshan's heart pounded and he too began to rock back and forth, shaking his head in a vain attempt to counter the waves of fear, pain, loneliness and despair that assaulted them.

'Look on them here and you will lose your reason, becoming an empty husk and fit only for the fires of Hell,' Guan Di warned. 'I will be your eyes, for I know these creatures of old. The mounts they ride are bigger and more fearsome than those of the demon wraiths. As for the Riders themselves, they are fused with their mounts; their twisted bodies are mis-shapen and their heads are sunk into their chests. They have scaly tails like a lizard's which join with those of their mounts and help to balance them when they fly with their enormous bats' wings, which have talons the size of a mortal's arms. Do not look upon them – I will warn you no more!'

The crescendo of noise reached an unbearable intensity as they sensed the creatures getting nearer. Dimly Rokshan heard the triumphant shout of Corhanuk exhorting the Crimson King and the Four Riders to join with him to help defeat the forces of good gathered at Labrang before speeding to the four corners of the Earth to infect the whole of humankind with their evil.

There was a thunderous clattering of hooves from the direction of the archway and Rokshan heard An Lushan order-ing the demon wraiths to follow the Riders. There was a rush of wind and then, some moments later, a distant, shattering explosion as the Riders burst through the measureless confines of Hell into the Upper World, followed by the unearthly calls of the dragons as they acknowledged their leader.

Feeling sick to the core, Rokshan warily opened one eye, then the other, before looking about. Cool air bathed his face and he gulped in lungfuls of it. He wondered where it came from until he looked up and saw, many, many li away, a gash in what he realized must be the side of the mountain that had sealed the Lower World from the Upper since the beginning of time.

'They have smashed their way through to lead the dragon horde.' Guan Di spat the words out, his face contorted as he struggled against the chains that bound him. 'The newly-winged mounts of the demon wraiths have followed them. Unnatural forces are loosed upon the world again. Many mortals will die now – and evil will reign on Earth . . .'

CHAPTER 45

THE SUMMONING OF THE SHADOW

But Rokshan hardly heard either Guan Di or Corhanuk, even as
Corhanuk triumphantly pronounced the fulfilment of the
second condition for the release of his evil master. A soft
chiming voice filled his head, like a rippling peal of bells, and
his vision became clouded . . .

*And thus will the third — and final — condition soon be fulfilled, even as
my creatures complete the second. But they will need my help to ensure its
complete fulfilment; for chaos to prevail in the world and evil to take root in
men's hearts. Even now the Elect gather their forces of good — puny though they
are — to thwart my plans. But I will smash their power! Never again will
they resist me. Now you shall unsay the words of the Divine Commandment to
summon my shade so I can lead the battle against the Elect and destroy them for
ever — my designs are not be thwarted!*

*Then you will help me unlock the secret that is buried deep within Han
Garid's soul: only he has the memory of the missing word of the Divine
Commandment . . . my name, mortal! You have joined with Stargazer, the
descendant of what Han Garid once was, and you will join with the lord of
the thunder dragons to do my will. Thus will I shed the vestiges of the Shadow
and his shade and, restored to my full power and glory, I shall once again walk
the Earth for all mankind to worship me! I have waited aeons for this moment,
mortal. Do not resist me, and the rewards will be great indeed, beyond your
wildest imaginings. Hear me, Rokshan, it is your Shadow Lord who speaks. Do
not resist me . . .*

The voice faded and his vision cleared. Corhanuk swam
into focus, pacing up and down. Lianxang was looking at him,
her eyes wide with terror. Rokshan's face was ashen and he was

shaking with fear at the realization of what the Shadow wanted of him – his name! This is what he had sought through the ages, and now at last he would have his way – how could he resist the power of the Shadow? And this was just his shade . . . Rokshan tried to sit up but the horror of the Shadow's silken voice that had seemed to stroke his soul made him retch violently and he lay back with a moan.

The gates of Hell were open and the roaring fires in the depths, revived now, licked hungrily over the edge of the abyss. The wails of the spirits of the damned rose up against the soaring black granite walls.

'Silence!' Corhanuk's stern command thundered around the court. 'Beshbaliq, prepare the boy mortal . . .'

He no longer even resembled his brother, Rokshan thought. An Lushan looked on while the demon wraiths unbound Rokshan, shoving him away from the roaring furnace; his face rippled constantly with the presence of the fallen spirit that possessed him, as if his mortal body could no longer contain him.

'Kneel!' An Lushan barked, stepping behind his brother and whipping out a dagger, which he held at his throat. But the dagger was unnecessary; Rokshan dropped to his knees, the whispering evil voice of the Shadow no longer in his head, but its power bending his mind to his will: *Do not resist me . . . Do not resist me . . .*

'Now all is ready!' Corhanuk cried in triumph. 'In time our master shall come among us, free at last to walk the Earth and enslave mankind in preparation for the last battle against our sworn enemy who still rules the Heavens. Hear the words of the Divine Commandment, master, which the warrior pure in heart and spirit who kneels before us will unsay, to summon your shade to us.'

'Say the words exactly as I say them,' An Lushan hissed.

'An'an, please . . . Don't do this . . . Think what you are

about to do! It cannot be undone once I have said the words—'

'Just say *exactly* what I say.' An Lushan yanked Rokshan's hair and pricked the tip of his dagger against his throat.

'I, the Wise Lord, place you . . .' Corhanuk proclaimed.

'I, *the Wise Lord, release you* . . .' An Lushan said, clearly reversing the intended consequences of the words of the Divine Commandment. '*Louder!*' he roared at Rokshan, who repeated his words, his will to resist now almost gone.

'In the perpetual imprisonment of the Arch of Darkness, outside the universe of all things and even time itself,' Corhanuk went on.

'*From the perpetual imprisonment of the Arch of Darkness, outside the universe of all things and even time itself,*' An Lushan said, Rokshan repeating the words after him.

'Here you will forget who and what you were, and you will never again tempt any of my creatures to stray from me . . .' Corhanuk intoned.

'*Here you will remember who and what you were, and you will once again tempt all of my creatures to stray from me,*' An Lushan said, and again Rokshan repeated his words.

'And so, through the aeons of ages to come, your name . . . will be forgotten like the earth from which you were created, and from henceforth you will be known only as the Shadow-without-a-name, even unto the end of time.'

'*And so, through the aeons of ages to come, your name . . . will be remembered, never again to be forgotten, as perpetual as the earth from which you were created. Never again will you be known as the Shadow-without-a-name, even unto the end of time.*'

Rokshan repeated the final words of the Divine Commandment, their meaning reversed by An Lushan. As he finished, there was a tremor in the depths; the flames from the abyss leaped higher and a rushing wave of evil erupted through the archway, beating around the cavernous confines of the portals of Hell.

Amidst the roiling currents of power, twisting, wraith-like shapes began to join into the form of an enormous dragon . . . then a rider . . . then shape-shifting back again into a dragon; now it was growing, becoming enormous and bloated, pushing at the confines of the cavern as if it would burst out, vomiting its evil into the world.

Rokshan clutched his head as he felt probing, coiling tendrils of power wrapping around his mind. 'Merciful goddess,' he whimpered softly, 'what have I done?' Then came a voice, hoarse and rasping as if unused to speech . . . and the words chilled his soul.

'*It is enough . . . The chains that bind me outside the universe have loosened and a crack appears in the Arch . . . My shade is free! On, my faithful servants! The Riders already go about their work and Han Garid goes before us. To Labrang, where we will destroy for ever the force for good that calls itself the Elect; they will then no longer prevent the boy mortal from giving me the name I need.*'

'Yes, my Shadow lord,' Corhanuk replied obediently. 'What would you have us do with the giant and the mortals he protects?'

'*It is a task for Beshbaliq, who has served me well: kill them all but the boy mortal! Remain here with him, Beshbaliq, until I return with Han Garid. I command you to keep him safe! After our victory, the Four Riders and the dragon horde will go into the world. Thus will the second condition be met and then, at last, I shall be ready for the joining. Guard the boy well for me and the kingdom of the Lower World shall be yours to rule over when we return!*'

Beshbaliq bowed low, a sly look of joy on his face that his master had singled him out for such a task.

The wraith-like shapes twisted and darted about them and the sound of the beating of a thousand dragons' wings pounded in their ears as the ghostly, grotesque shape of an enormous rider formed, growing so big even the cavernous reaches of Hell could not contain it.

'Come, Corhanuk, the forces of good await their fate . . .'

The voice of the Shadow swirled and echoed around them as Corhanuk stepped into the swirling mass; the shade of the Shadow beat its enormous wings and, with a triumphant, screeching cry, flew towards the rent in the mountain.

Beshbaliq watched his masters go before stalking towards Lianxang, Cetu and Guan Di, who lay helpless by the huge gates. His fingers twitched impatiently around the lance he carried – the same lance Corhanuk had used to kill the Guardian Monk. A savage grin twisted his face into a demonic mask.

CHAPTER 46

THE PROMISE OF THE JADE SPIRIT

An Lushan strode across the empty vastness of the court of the Crimson King towards where his intended victims lay. The wailing of the damned was muted, with only an occasional roar of flames from the depths and along the banks of the river that wound its way through the barren, sulphurous kingdom of the Lower World.

'Leave them!' Rokshan screamed, but his brother paid him no attention as he stood over Lianxang, his lance poised at her throat. Cetu lay unconscious, his life-blood seeping away.

Guan Di strained and heaved but the chains that had kept the Crimson King bound for aeons were too strong. 'Flee, boy mortal . . . I cannot save you – flee!' he boomed, distracting An Lushan, who looked round as Rokshan shouted at him again, only from twenty or thirty paces away.

Rokshan heard it first: a faint, rhythmic sound, so light it sounded like stiffened brush-strokes against paper . . . it had a sharp, glassy note to it that he thought he recognized.

'The Jade Spirit . . .' he whispered to himself, skidding to a halt. 'He has kept his word; he has sent his warriors . . . Lianxang, Guan Di, they are coming!' he yelled in relief.

An Lushan whipped round with a snarl that turned to astonished surprise as a volley of needle-sharp jade arrows thudded into his chest. He staggered back against the open gates, sinking to his knees.

It took Rokshan only a few moments to reach his side. As he knelt down, An Lushan coughed up a great gout of blood, his eyes closed in a grimace of pain, his hand clutching uselessly at the deadly arrows.

'An'an . . . it's me, Rokshan.'

For a moment An Lushan's eyes flickered and his mouth worked, but no sound came from his lips.

'We must move you . . . away from the abyss.' The heat was becoming unbearable – the flames licked hungrily over the edge only a few paces away. Blood spewed from An Lushan's mouth as he cried out in the agony of his death throes. Rokshan tried to move his brother, but suddenly felt his arm clutching at him, his eyes staring wildly.

'He will not leave me, brother. I – he will always haunt me.' The tortured look in his brother's eyes as his life faded was too much for him to bear. Rokshan bowed his head, his eyes filling with tears as he realized there was little he could do to help his brother in the agony of his last moments.

'I must set my spirit free . . .' An Lushan whispered as he let go of Rokshan's arm and, with an agonized groan, rolled over to the edge of the abyss, twisting away from the outstretched arm that reached out for him in vain.

'No . . . An'an!' Rokshan screamed as the intense heat of the flames forced him back. He stumbled against the gates of Hell in his anguish, his eyes blind with tears. He had loved An Lushan as a brother; now, rage at the injustice of his fate boiled up in him. Shaking the gates of Hell in his grief and fury, he screamed his defiance: 'I will avenge my brother's death, however many lifetimes it takes. Hear me, *my Shadow lord!*' He spat the words out with contempt.

The tramp of the jade warriors became deafening, echoing off the cavernous walls as they approached – rank on rank of them stretching into the distance – far more than they'd first seen in the Kingdom of the Jade Spirit.

Rokshan felt a faint glimmering of hope as he slashed at the ropes binding Lianxang. 'How many are there?' she whispered, her eyes full of horror at An Lushan's end.

'Hundreds! We will soon be free.'

'Quickly, we must see to Cetu,' she said, rubbing her wrists. 'He does not have much time . . .'

'Tell the jade warriors to cut me free,' Guan Di said urgently as Rokshan bent over Cetu. 'I have an elixir for the old one, but we will need the greater healing power of the precious element too.'

Lianxang cradled the old Waymaster's head: his breaths came in short gasps and his face had the grey pallor of approaching death.

The leader of the first cohort marched up to where they lay huddled beside Guan Di. 'I am Jax: the army of jade warriors is yours to command.'

He struck his gauntleted fist a ringing blow against his chest but the voice from behind the mask was surprisingly soft. Thin beams of light from his eye-slits glowed as he spoke. He stood a head taller than a man and wore a mask exactly like that of his master, the Jade Spirit. His suit of armoured jade must have weighed him down but he wore it like the lightest gossamer. Heavy boots of the same material came up to his knees and his sword was sharpened to a needlepoint. On his back he carried a huge bow and a quiver full of jade arrows.

'Tell your men to cut the giant free!' Rokshan cried. 'Quickly!'

Jax signalled for his warriors to help him and swiftly they sliced through the mass of ropes and chains.

Swirling aside his enormous red cloak, Guan Di produced a leather water pouch. Kneeling beside Cetu, he poured a silvery liquid over the deep gash in his thigh. With a hiss, it mixed with the flesh and blood, sealing and closing the wound. Then he passed the pouch to Jax, who added a few drops from the small jade vial that hung from his sword belt, before putting it to Cetu's lips.

The Waymaster coughed and spluttered, then his eyes fluttered open; the colour was restored to his face and he gingerly stretched out his leg, flexing it back and forth with a look of utter disbelief and joy. 'Whoever you are,' he whispered, 'I owe you my life. Mine will be forfeit, if you should ever call upon it.'

'Guan Di and Jax will remember that, Horseman,' the giant chuckled, a deep, cavernous rumbling from his stomach. 'Now . . . we have work to do.' He stood with his hands on his hips, surveying the army of jade warriors. 'So, the Jade Spirit makes good his repentance. The jade warriors are like the precious material they guard, Rokshan – imperishable, impervious to fire. Lances and arrows bounce harmlessly off them, swords shatter against their rock-like bodies: with them at our side, we will be indestructible!'

Jax bowed in acknowledgement. 'My lord knew that it was Corhanuk's intention to release the Four Riders,' he said, 'but the summoning of the shade of the Shadow' – Jax's green eye-slits flashed – 'this he did not anticipate. I do not know how the Nameless One will be stopped now,' he said softly. 'If he were to become flesh and blood again . . .' He left the rest unsaid.

'It will be the end of all things,' Guan Di finished for him. 'No mortal force can halt the Four Riders led by the Nameless One. As for the dragon horde, fire must be met with fire—'

'The dragons may follow the Riders for now' – Jax raised his hand to interrupt Guan Di – 'but my master knows through the Serenadhi that after centuries of mindjoining, the dragon horses have changed. The dragons follow Han Garid and do his bidding, not that of the Four Riders – for Han Garid bears the memory of his life as Stargazer, and all the lords of the horses before him. Our hope rests with Rokshan, the boy mortal, my master said: he must reach into Han Garid's soul and touch that part of him which is still the lord of the horses, and turn the dragons against the Evil One.'

'Then I must speak to Stargazer,' said Rokshan softly; 'or at least to that inner essence of him that still lives within Han Garid. I still have a link with Stargazer – I am sure of it. Through him I have already felt the rage of the dragons.' He paused, shuddering at the thought before steeling himself again. 'If I have felt that, there must be a way back to Stargazer's spirit, however deep it may be buried within Han Garid. But now, speed is of the essence – and I have been gifted with it, but perhaps not in the way we need it now.'

'What do you mean?' Lianxang asked quietly.

'The Shadow must mindjoin with the lord of the thunder dragons to retrieve the name he needs to complete the Divine Commandment,' Rokshan went on, speaking quickly as if the thought would slip away. 'We know he intends this, using me. But he will not make me attempt it before he has removed any threat the forces of good might pose to the success of the joining. The Shadow will choose the time and place – but what if we were to force his hand,' Rokshan said excitedly, 'so that he attempts the joining through me before he is fully ready; before the second condition of evil being spread through the world has been fulfilled. Don't you see? We must ensure there is some good left in the world – I must reach Labrang and challenge the Shadow before it's too late! Without the fulfilment of the second condition, I may be able to resist him – if I can call on that tiny spark of Stargazer to come to me again and help me stand firm against him.'

Though he spoke clearly, in his heart of hearts Rokshan was terrified of the challenge he had thrown down for himself. Surely it was beyond any mortal to do what he was about to attempt? And if he should fail . . .

'Then we have some hope, my young friend.' They all turned at the sound of Cetu's voice as Lianxang helped him up. 'I know of no other who has mindjoined so swiftly and fully with the lord of the horses. My pupil is a worthy champion –

you will not fail us, Rokshan! But how do we get to Han Garid
in time?'

'He will be leading his horde against the Elect and the
forces of good,' Jax said. 'But we are already too late, I fear.
The dragons will be flying behind the Riders. Distance means
nothing to them: Corhanuk, the Four Riders, the demon
wraiths – they will all be there at Labrang, perhaps even now as
we stand here.'

'It is as Jax says,' Guan Di boomed. 'The forces of good
have gathered and stand alone against the massed legions of
darkness: any time that can be gained in halting them there will
help Rokshan do what he must. His plan to offer himself as bait
to trap the Nameless One is worthy of the speed and cunning
of the hare – his presence at Labrang will be what the Nameless
One least expects.'

'But Jax has said we are already too late, master giant,' Cetu
said, a little impatiently.

Guan Di furrowed his massive brow disapprovingly at
him. 'Take heart, mortals! There is a way, if the Spirit of the Four
Winds answers my summons. Come! We must hurry to the rent
in the mountainside.'

Jax gave the signal and they set off with the jade warriors,
following the course of the underworld river to the rhythmic
tramp of the jade army.

Close to, what had looked from afar like a small gash was
an enormous opening through which the wind moaned and
howled. Guan Di told them to wait while he clambered up the
mountainous pile of rocks. Up he climbed, further and further
still, until he was poised on the very lip of the opening. Now
he was just a small figure silhouetted against the blackness of
the night sky, his cloak billowing around him.

'Spirit of the Four Winds – hear me! Guan Di, warrior
god, friend and ally of Chu Jung in the ancient war against the
dragons, calls on your aid! Seek us on the borders of the Lower

World, where once again we need your invisible wings to carry us to battle against the resurrected forces of evil! Answer me, in the name of the Wise Lord who blew life into you at the beginning of time itself. Show yourself, so the mortals whom I protect may see you.'

He stood with his head bowed. The sulphurous pools of fire behind them flickered, hungrily licking up the cavernous walls in explosive jets of flame. They looked around uneasily; the jade warriors were still and silent behind their masks.

The moaning of the wind grew louder until it reached a roaring crescendo. Guan Di spread his arms and started to whirl them round; gradually Rokshan made out the hazy shapes of two towers of gusting wind, which started to rotate, slowly at first but gathering speed until they were spinning like two giant tops.

Guan Di drew the pillars of wind towards him. He rocked on his feet as they battered their way through the enormous gash in the mountainside and down towards the waiting mortals and warriors like two towering tornadoes, shimmering and twisting.

'Step into the tower,' Guan Di shouted, his voice just carrying to them.

The Jade Warriors were already marching two by two into one of the towers. Rokshan grabbed Lianxang's hand and stepped into the milky vortex of the other. Cetu hurriedly followed them.

As soon as they entered the spinning pillar, Rokshan felt himself being hurled through a tunnel towards a tiny pinprick of light. Falling towards it faster and faster, he heard Lianxang shout something, but the wind whipped her words away. He screwed his eyes shut at the battering and roaring in his head, and felt himself slipping away . . .

Moments or hours later – he couldn't tell which – they woke, cold and huddled together. Palest streaks of washed pink heralded the new day. The shrill cry of a hawk pierced the silence of the fading night as it hunted in the first faint light of dawn.

Rokshan almost cried with relief when he recognized the great sandstone ramparts of the citadel monastery of Labrang, tucked into the foothills of the Mountains of Hami. The citadel's five sets of ramparts reflected in a pink glow the dawn rays of the sun.

Lianxang scrambled to her feet, gazing in awe at the mighty edifice. 'Sarangerel has often spoken of this place,' she murmured. 'One day I would come here, she told me, when I was spellweaver . . .'

'And now you are here,' Guan Di rumbled as he came to join them, 'perhaps before your time; yet it is fitting that the people of the Darhad should have you as their witness in the battle to come.'

The enormous bronze gong of the monastery sounded, a deep, mournful tolling.

'It is a call to arms! Come, we must prepare for battle,' Guan Di boomed, setting off at a loping run towards the citadel.

CHAPTER 47

LAST STAND AT LABRANG

A horn sounded, and hundreds of warrior monks, turbaned and clothed in long orange robes came streaming down the ramparts through the gates, cheering wildly at the sight of the jade army and Guan Di.

The abbot himself came to meet them.

'Venerable Abbot' – Rokshan bowed his head in greeting – 'I have brought Guan Di and the jade warriors to help our cause and defend the citadel. Guan Di tells me they are impervious to the fire of the dragons and will be unflinching in their support!'

'You have become a Horseman, Rokshan of Maracanda. This is fitting, for now we must prepare for battle,' the abbot replied, looking at him appraisingly.

'This is Cetu, venerable Abbot,' Rokshan said, 'Waymaster of the Horse, my guide and friend.' Cetu proudly gave the Horsemen's salute.

'We have much to thank you for, Waymaster,' the abbot replied, bowing low, 'and much to talk of. But even as we speak the Four Riders are loosed upon the Earth, turning the people against each other in their madness and terror. Already the imperial capital lies in smoking ruins, destroyed by the fire of the dragons, and now the dragon horde comes this way.' He turned to Guan Di and bowed low. 'We cannot give thanks enough that you are here, mighty one . . .'

Guan Di returned the courtesy, bowing elaborately, 'I am yours to command, if my summoner wills it . . .' He nodded towards Rokshan, who muttered his assent, embarrassed by the giant's deference.

The abbot turned to Jax and again bowed low. 'Your lord, the Jade Spirit, is generous indeed to spare so many of his warriors. We humbly welcome your support, mighty Jax. Never did I expect to see the legendary soldiers of the Kingdom of the Jade Spirit walk amongst us!'

Jax crashed a fist on his chest in salute and marched off, ordering his forces to take up their positions around the ramparts.

The abbot looked at Lianxang, who proudly returned his gaze. 'The spellweaver's granddaughter – I am honoured. Your spirit-bird has been of great service to us. Now, to arms – we have little time. The dragons are coming! Lianxang's spirit-bird tells us they bear down on us ahead of the Four Riders, who await their master's arrival. And each moment the Shadow is outside the confines of the Lower World, his power grows.'

'I must join with Han Garid to forge a link with Stargazer,' Rokshan said to the abbot, 'and through him turn the dragons against the forces of the Shadow. Han Garid remains his own master, just as Stargazer was servant to none – the Nameless One is perhaps not as mindful of this as we are. If I can reach Stargazer, we may be able to control the dragons and use their power to help us defeat the coming evil. And my being here will throw the Shadow off course, especially when I challenge him before the second condition of his release has been fulfilled.'

'You are to mindjoin with the lord of the thunder dragons himself?' The abbot was stunned. 'And this second condition? We know not of this, save that the Nameless One must never know the words of the Divine Commandment.'

'I have learned much, venerable Abbot, of how Corhanuk's meddlesome ways through the ages have been bent always to the same purpose – to fulfilling those conditions the Wise Lord

433

in His wisdom put in place to thwart the Shadow's ambitions. And the way in which these conditions will be met—'

'Which you must tell me about – and your fellow members of the Elect – at a more peaceful time, my son, for it is clear we have much to learn from you,' the abbot said respectfully, bowing humbly before his former novitiate. 'Lianxang,' he continued, turning to the spellweaver-to-be, 'you must help Rokshan; the ways of the Darhad and their spirit-bird are known only to you: use your gifts! Our victory may depend on them.'

'On behalf of the people of the Darhad, I put myself at your service, venerable Abbot,' Lianxang replied.

'May the Wise Lord be with you, and Kuan Yin, goddess of mercy, bless us,' the abbot concluded before hurrying away to attend to the citadel's defences.

Cetu said he needed to rest as his leg still pained him; he left Rokshan and Lianxang to make their way up the ramparts, which were alive with activity and last-minute preparations. Warrior monks thronged the way, rushing to their posts, checking their supplies of arrows and lances or sharpening their swords, looking anxiously out towards the plains and then up to the foothills. Some wore light armour over their faded orange robes; some carried wooden staffs tipped with gold, a traditional weapon – though Rokshan wondered what good these would do against the creatures from Hell. However, he returned their shouts of greeting and encouragement as they hurried on their way. The jade warriors stood at their posts, still and silent, awaiting orders from Jax, who tramped up and down their positions, checking all was in readiness.

As they reached the highest rampart, a group of boy monks carrying spare weapons stopped to look at them. One of them put down his armful of lances with a loud clatter and shyly approached them. Rokshan recognized him as the young novice monk who had shown him around the monastery on his first visit.

He did his best to answer the all his young guide's inquisitive questions as they wound their way up to the topmost point of the highest rampart, which gave them unrestricted views across the plains.

The monk gaped at the jade warriors, who now occupied every available space. 'Do they speak?' he whispered, wide-eyed. 'Does Shou Lao know they are here?'

'Shou Lao? He's here?' Rokshan was amazed and felt a flood of hope at this news. 'The last I'd heard of him he was travelling to the four corners of the world warning everyone to take heed of what he told them.'

'Well, he's here now,' the young monk assured him.

Just then the gong stopped tolling and a succession of horns sounded – urgent warning notes rang from rampart to rampart, and then fell silent. It was a cloudless, bright winter's day and a light wind buffeted the walls.

'There!' Lianxang pointed to the west, where a black smudge appeared on the horizon, moving at speed. Out on the plain, the remaining jade warriors had formed into four wedge shapes, resembling a star. Within this, units of warrior monks were positioned, bows at the ready, forming an inner protective circle. The elaborate red headdress of the abbot himself was easily recognizable. Rokshan looked closer at the tiny figure beside him and, with a start, realized it must indeed be Shou Lao.

To one side, Guan Di was preparing what looked like a huge net, folding it over and over and then tossing it up. He threw it higher and higher until it seemed it would disappear altogether. A massive axe hung from his belt, together with a sling-shot; a pile of huge stones lay next to him.

'Listen . . .' Lianxang whispered.

But Rokshan had already sensed the pent-up fury of the dragons in rolling waves of dark, thunderous power shot through with deep crimson and purple, which beat inside his head like a pounding drumbeat that would never stop; he knew he had to try and block it out or it would drive him mad.

The steady thrumming grew louder, until it sounded like the buffeting of a typhoon; their hands flew up to their ears as they heard the screeching cries of the dragons for the first time. On they came, two hundred or more, in twos and threes, flying at breathtaking speed as they prepared to swoop on the jade warriors on the plain. As they approached, they seemed to fill the sky with a mass of blazing emeralds, blues and brilliant greens shot through with great gouts of orange flame as they blasted bolts of fire that crackled and roared into the sky. Suddenly the leading dragons flattened their wings and dived straight down, their cries now one continuous scream as they speared towards their targets.

As one, the jade warriors drew back their massive bows and nocked their arrows. Inside the formation, the warrior monks did the same.

'Hold your fire!' Guan Di's voice boomed out as he swung his sling above his head, faster and faster, until it was impossible to see, and then with a hiss released a stone twice the size of a man's head. It shot through the air with the speed of a cannonball, striking one of the dragons with a bone-crunching thud.

Momentarily stunned, the creature plummeted, its great wings beating hard at the last to pull it out of its dive. Silently the jade warriors released a hail of arrows. Five hundred of them found their mark. A fearsome screech of pain and rage made the air crackle as the dragons swooped again, spewing bolts of fire at the implacable formation of jade warriors, who kept up their deadly hail of arrows. The immense size and power of the dragons helped them withstand the deadly volleys but they would surely succumb to the arrows in time.

But where was Han Garid? Rokshan could see no sign of him. The huge lord of the thunder dragons would be easily recognizable, and he would surely *feel* his coming long before sighting him. Anxiously he scanned the skies, but he had no sense of him.

Guan Di's arm whirred as he loosed sling-shot after sling-shot, but it was not enough to bring even a single dragon down. Again and again the dragons directed raging bolts of fire against him, but like the jade warriors, he was impervious to their flames.

One or two got through the arrows of the jade warriors and the agonized screams of the brave warrior monks as they were burned up by the dragons' arching gouts of fire were dreadful to hear. Relentlessly the jade warriors increased the speed of their volleys, making the air hum as hundreds of arrows were loosed.

The tactic at last succeeded in driving the dragons back: with a series of screeching calls to each other, they circled overhead out of range for some moments before starting to climb, higher and higher, until they were reduced to black dots in the sky, their cries fading.

But through the chorus of cheers that erupted from the ramparts, Rokshan thought he caught a snatch of another sound he recognized – a fearsome, whinnying snarl; even worse, he sensed terrifying currents of a concentrated evil.

'The Four Riders' – Lianxang clutched at his arm – 'they are coming!'

'What's happening?' the young novice monk asked, wide-eyed with terror as he felt too it.

'Block your ears and keep your eyes shut! Huddle down!'

Rokshan raced up and down the ramparts, telling everyone how to protect themselves. As he rushed down to the fourth rampart, some of the warrior monks were already going mad with fear, hurling themselves against the implacable jade warriors; many threw themselves off the ramparts while others simply stood and wailed inconsolably, their minds emptied of all reason.

The currents of evil were growing stronger; soon they were beating against the stone ramparts. The screams that rose from the battlements became a crescendo of noise like no other Rokshan had heard.

He was on the third rampart now, looking out onto the plain, shouting at Shou Lao, the abbot and Guan Di to help them before they all went mad. He could feel the Four Riders getting closer now but they were still not visible.

Suddenly, above the wails, he thought he heard something else, faint and far away. The soft, chiming voice echoed in his head, freezing his soul.

He cursed himself for not realizing it sooner − the shade of the Shadow was approaching behind the Four Riders, concealing himself behind his creatures so he could direct all his powers against Han Garid and make him his for ever as soon as the power of the Elect lay in the dust.

But, Rokshan grimly assured himself − the Shadow had not reckoned on the spirit of Stargazer, which he knew lay at the heart of the monstrous creature: this was the fatal flaw in the Shadow's carefully laid plans! This and the fact that he, Rokshan, was here to challenge the Nameless One ahead of time. The knot of fear in his stomach disappeared as a sliver of hope entered his soul and the ear of his heart caught snatches of a song he seemed to have known all his life.

His mind grappled with the memory and he recognized the song the Serenadhi had sung. It was the song of generations of horse-singers, one they had locked in his heart . . . and he knew he must return to the fifth rampart, for Stargazer was coming − and was calling him.

CHAPTER 48

DEATH AND REBIRTH

As he rushed back, Rokshan felt another tidal wave of evil rolling towards the citadel. On the horizon four enormous shapes appeared in the vanguard of the renewed assault.

Where was Han Garid? He was so sure he had heard the spirit of Stargazer calling him . . . With growing panic he looked towards the plain, where the abbot and Shou Lao were both kneeling. Then the abbot rose and with his staff described a wide arc. Gradually, to Rokshan's astonishment, a shimmering, rainbow-coloured dome grew out of the ground and covered the inner circle of the star-shaped formation. Shou Lao stepped outside it and was joined by Guan Di. The giant stooped, gathering up some earth; the abbot and Shou Lao did the same, and then all three of them stood with their arms outstretched, letting the earth slip from their fingers.

Rokshan could hear them only faintly – they seemed to be chanting an invocation. Then he recognized Guan Di's booming voice as it called out a summons; it was so clear and strong, it carried across the citadel, across the plains and scrublands to the Red Sandy Wastes and the bleak, barren vastness of the Taklamakan Desert itself:

'Sand demons of the desert! In the name of the Wise Lord, I, Guan Di, summon you to the citadel monastery of Labrang. Come, storm lords, and unleash your fury on the legions from Hell.'

Rokshan looked on in silent amazement. The wind that had been no more than a light breeze all morning sprang up, whipping up eddies of dust across the wide ramparts of the citadel. Now it gusted fiercely, buffeting the walls until it became a howling accompaniment to the noise of the approaching sandstorm.

For, from the west, an enormous tidal wave of sand was travelling as fast as a galloping horse. It was twice as high as the highest of the citadel's ramparts and the same distance across, and it was set on a collision course with the Four Riders. Rokshan could feel the waves of evil that had been crashing against the citadel being beaten back by the towering wall of sand.

'Look!' Rokshan pointed excitedly as Lianxang came to join him. 'On top of the sand wall – little dancing figures . . . it looks as if they've got whips and are lashing the sand.'

At the combined command of Guan Di and Shou Lao, the wall of sand and the howling wind stopped abruptly in front of the formation of jade warriors like a gigantic rippling curtain, cascading but motionless. The giant stooped and took hold of his net, whirling it round and then tossing it skywards so that it bound itself to the sandstorm, becoming one with it and billowing like an enormous sail. Then he was joined by hundreds of the jade warriors as he struggled to control it.

'They're going to use it like a net to bring them down!' Rokshan shouted. Two of the Riders veered away, climbing sharply, but the two that led, one with the Crimson King astride also, flew straight into the whirling, murky mass. Guan Di bellowed in triumph and began to haul the sand-net down, signalling to the jade warriors to do the same.

The Crimson King and his two trapped charges struggled violently but they were completely enmeshed; the sand-demons ensured there was no escape as they rolled the net over and over. With a shuddering crash the Riders thudded to the ground and were immediately surrounded by the jade warriors, their huge bows drawn.

The ragged cheer that came from the ramparts of the citadel was silenced abruptly as, across the distant horizon, the sky began to darken.

'N-night is coming,' stammered the young monk, who refused to leave Rokshan's side. 'But if it is night, where are the stars and moon?'

'It is not night, my friend,' Rokshan breathed quietly. 'Lianxang, are you prepared?'

Lianxang nodded, her gaze fixed on something only she could see. Rokshan peered into the advancing gloom; then, just ahead of the advancing curtain of darkness that seemed to swallow up the sky, he saw a familiar shape, dipping and swooping in front of a much larger, slower creature.

'Use your eagle eye; is it what I think it is?' Rokshan urged her.

Lianxang leaped up onto the parapet and called the shrill cry of her spirit-bird. 'It is my eagle, and Han Garid,' she said grimly. 'Han Garid gathers his dragon horde for a final assault against us with the two remaining Riders. He must already have fallen under the sway of the Nameless One – is there no limit to his power?'

The tide of night was bearing down on them now, and within it the ghostly shape-shifting wraiths of the Shadow's shade writhed and twisted. In their midst Corhanuk was trying to gather in the two remaining Riders and the dragon horde with the Staff and Talisman, but the dragons sensed their lord and waited on his command.

Rokshan had already felt the menace and pent-up fury of the dragons; now, amongst the waves of dark, thunderous power his heart missed a beat as the faintest glimmering spark of silver, fading like the blazing tail of a shooting star, emblazoned itself for a split second in his mind – and then was gone.

Stargazer . . . Now he was certain his spirit was trying to

call him! He sprang up onto the parapet, drawn by the chilling but majestic sight of Han Garid flying just ahead of the rolling blackness that was swallowing up the sky. His huge wings beat effortlessly and his long reptilian head with its single horn moved gracefully from side to side as he surveyed all with his dragon-sight.

Suddenly he let out a deafening screech of anger and alarm, spewing a jet of hot fire and veering to one side as the spirit-bird swooped directly in his path, soared above him and then dived, dropping like a stone in a brave attempt to deflect Han Garid and his dragons away from their attack. Next to the huge dragon the spirit-bird looked like a sparrow . . . it was only a matter of time before she was either consumed by fire or simply outpaced.

'Rokshan, I must be with my spirit-bird,' Lianxang said urgently, 'but not just in mind and spirit: try to understand, and do not think badly of me – it is the only way. She will not succeed otherwise.'

'What? What do you mean?'

'You must join with Han Garid as I join with my spirit-bird. I will keep him from directing the dragon horde against us – it will only be for a few moments but it may give you enough time. You must spring the bait by offering yourself – now!'

With that she spread her arms and closed her eyes, a look of intense concentration spreading over her beautiful scarred face. Then, with her arms still outstretched, she stepped out from the parapet.

'Lianxang!' Rokshan screamed, lunging forward. He leaned over the parapet, watching in frozen horror as she spiralled to her death far below.

Just at that moment, in the skies above, the spirit-bird seemed to grow, a sudden burst of energy flaring around her wingtips as she drew level with the great dragon once more. The lord of the thunder dragons reared around in mid-flight, letting out another piercing screech and blasting a great bolt of fire at the eagle. The great bird tipped her wings to change direction and the flames rushed harmlessly past as she went straight back on the attack, her razor-sharp talons raking ragged strips of flesh from Han Garid's flank.

Rokshan watched, frantic: he could not let Lianxang's sacrifice be wasted, but he could see no mind-colours to step into in the way he'd practised so often with Cetu and Breeze Whisperer. Forcing himself to focus, he concentrated on a single faraway place in his mind's eye.

'Come, Stargazer, for Lianxang's sake, show yourself to me,' he whispered, over and over like a mantra: if he believed it enough, it would surely happen, he told himself.

The eagle still dipped and swooped around the great dragon's head, harrying and clawing as if possessed, at last forcing Han Garid to veer away from the citadel. The dragon horde followed him but dared not blast their hot breaths of fire against the spirit-bird, which stayed close to Han Garid, slashing and pecking and ripping at the great dragon's head and eyes with her hooked, scimitar-like beak.

Suddenly Rokshan was forced to dive below the parapet as the two remaining Riders raced towards the citadel, radiating currents that blasted, one after the other, into the fifth rampart. Not even the jade warriors could withstand such an assault; its ferocity struck at the brittle core of their being, shattering them into a thousand pieces.

'Stargazer!' Rokshan screamed as he witnessed the fate of the jade warriors: surely defeat was upon them – and he had failed. 'Come to me! Come to me!' he shouted again and again.

His heart leaped as he heard a soft chime in his head, but he froze as he recognized the voice of the Shadow.

Why do you resist me, Rokshan? Han Garid is mine. Victory is within our grasp. It does not matter to me how you come to be here – our victory here is assured and in a short time mankind shall bow down and worship me. When you have helped me master Han Garid, join us! The riches of the world will be yours — whatever powers you wish for, I will grant you, to add to those you already have. Join us . . .

With a loud groan, Rokshan stumbled against the parapet. The two Riders soared by, their huge wings brushing the top of the citadel, shattering it like glass.

The Shadow's voice continued to exhort him until it clanged in his head like the huge temple bell. But as the clamour faded, the chimes lapped like fading ripples at the edges of his mind. He was filled with a joyous elation as they began to form the beginnings of a melody — the far-off strains of a song he'd always known came back to him, and with growing clarity he began to understand what it was the Serenadhi had gifted to him.

Rokshan, we have woven this song into your heart and locked it in the deepest, most secret chambers of your mind. It will help you open their minds to you, but beware before you step through this door — you may not be able to find it again until it has closed, and then it will remain shut for ever.

The chiming voice of the Shadow had become the song of generations of horse-singers ringing through his head. The melody was the sweetest song he would ever hear, and now he could see its colours like a shimmering rainbow, and through the colours he could see a door slowly opening. He heard the warning of the Serenadhi again, but now he knew the answer: it didn't matter if he couldn't find the door again, because once he had stepped through, he wouldn't want to go back.

He clambered back up onto the parapet and let the melody grow in his head until he felt it explode in cascading torrents of colour. Spinning it with his fingers, he found he could weave the melody just as he'd seen the Serenadhi do. Concentrating now so intently that he felt himself slipping into a trance, he wove more and more of the colours until they poured down the great sandstone walls of the citadel and cascaded against the shimmering dome to strengthen it against the repeated attacks of the Riders.

Then he directed the swirling torrent in a flaming rainbow of colours across the darkened sky, where Lianxang's spirit-bird still bravely harried and tormented the lord of the thunder dragons. The colours drenched Han Garid, surrounding him in a shimmering skein which pulsed to the gentle rhythm of the desert *raga* of the Serenadhi. The spirit-bird soared upwards, her shrill cry piercing the gloom. Rokshan thanked her and Lianxang in his heart, praying he wasn't too late.

Time itself now stood still, and the cracked but still unbroken Arch of Darkness poured into the yawning, empty vacuum until it filled one end of the horizon to the other. The twisting wraith-like shade of the Shadow coiled its black tendrils around the gently pulsing skein of colours that enveloped Han Garid, squeezing and probing . . .

The warning of the Serenadhi was ringing in his ears but Rokshan didn't hesitate in emptying his mind. Immediately he was engulfed by a swelling wave of purple pain that broke in his head, draining it clear for a moment before swelling and breaking again.

He let his mind free itself of all physical ties as he gathered his life spirit to break as thunderous waves on the shimmering cocoon of colours that enveloped Han Garid. The coiling tendrils of the Shadow lashed around him but he shrugged them aside as he parted the colours as easily as a curtain. The song of the Serenadhi floated through them, giving him strength as the voice of the Shadow echoed around him:

Why do you still resist me, Rokshan? Where you lead I shall follow, as surely as the path we are on will take us to the memory that I seek deep in Han Garid's soul. For I am becoming part of you, driving out all memories of Stargazer in Han Garid's consciousness, and then all memories of yourself and what you are: for I have the power to take your mind from you. Join us, instead! And sit at my right hand . . .

Rokshan felt his mind being slowly squeezed, sucked dry,

and tried to close the inner core of himself, sealing it off from the Shadow's relentless probing. As he was swept along in the treacherous currents of Han Garid's consciousness, he remembered Cetu's words of advice about letting yourself be carried along while retaining a stillness at your centre. But this time it was different: the maelstrom of colours was turning darker; soon he wouldn't be able to see, and if he couldn't see, how would he know where he was going? A growing sense of despair overwhelmed him, and instead of letting himself float along lightly, he began to sink. Desperately he tried to remember how to swim, but he had lost the ability – all memory of it had gone.

Memories of his life began to flash past him, clearly at first, but then faster and faster until they blurred and made no sense. He began to laugh like a madman as he realized that the Shadow was wiping his life away as easily as marks on a wax slate.

Then abruptly it all stopped as he came to the entrance of a long tunnel, and he was falling as the flames of Hell licked around him, faster and faster until he was burning up.

I shall burn to death, and then it will be finished, he screamed silently.

A feeling of relief washed over him as he accepted the end. But as he started to succumb to the blackness closing in around him, he heard a voice, far away but recognizable, and his heart leaped as he recognized Stargazer's warm but commanding tones looping around the tunnel.

Rokshan . . . do not succumb to the Shadow's despair! This is what he intends, and then he will break you just as you lead him to where he thinks his search ends. Remember the vision I showed you when we galloped the dance of the wind on the Plain of the Dead – and the warning I gave of never looking into the inner eye of my soul. Hold out, Rokshan, my spirit-brother! Even as the Nameless One sucks your mind and heart and spirit dry, I am gathering together all memories of the pain and anguish that has ever been in the world to confront and confound the evil one when he breaks beyond my inner eye. Such will be his confusion, it will give us the precious seconds we need before at last the name he seeks is revealed to him through my memory of the punishment meted out to him those countless aeons ago.

For such will be his joy at recovering his name that he will repeat it, over and over. While he does this, recall the original words of the Divine Commandment – this will be the last memory you have before it is taken from you by the Evil One – but this will be his undoing. Because you are joined as one in Han Garid's mind, it will be as if the Shadow is saying the words again: thus shall he condemn himself once again, for all eternity, to be bound outside the universe of all things and even time itself.

The blinding light at the end of the tunnel rushed towards Rokshan and he cried out as the probing tendrils of the Shadow coiled around his mind, crushing all memory and consciousness out of him. He had heard a kindly voice, one he thought he recognized, and it had told him to do something . . . but now he struggled to recall what it had asked him to do, and he cried out in his agony as his mind began to crumble.

Memories of Stargazer, and all the lords of the horses before him – and the bond he'd had with him reeled through his mind – and were gone. Once again he heard the kindly voice.

'Do this one thing for him and his kind, and all humankind, I ask this of you . . . I ask this of you . . .' The voice faded, and Rokshan recoiled as it was replaced by another.

Your feeble, mortal thoughts no longer concern me. The words of the Divine Commandment have already been unsaid. Be gone! You shall wander like a kuei, a cursed spirit, inside your shattered mind for the rest of your pitiful life, knowing no one, recognizing nothing . . .

The Divine Commandment! The mocking laughter of the Shadow rang in his head as he felt his mind being drained of all reason, all memory, everything that made him who he was . . . Yet through all this he silently cried his thanks to the Nameless One, who had named the very thing Stargazer had requested of him.

With the memory rapidly fading, he knelt again in the empty vastness of Hell and recited the words of the Divine Commandment spoken by Corhanuk before An Lushan had forced him to repeat them with the meaning reversed – just as the Shadow triumphantly led him to unlock the long-buried secret he sought from deep in Han Garid's memory, releasing the name that had been forgotten these past aeons.

Now shall the Wise Lord tremble! Never again shall it be taken from me, and all creatures will worship me . . .

'Never . . .' Rokshan whispered. The recollection of what had happened in Hell vanished from his mind as he murmured the last words of the Divine Commandment and said the forgotten name which, just as Stargazer had predicted, the Shadow repeated triumphantly over and over again.

As Rokshan felt his life spirit ebbing away, he caught a glimpse of a monstrous figure coming towards him out of the light of the tunnel.

'I have failed – forgive me, Cetu, and my brave Lianxang,' he murmured, wondering why he could not now remember the name that had flashed into his consciousness just a moment ago; perhaps the Divine Commandment could never be re-enacted by any but the Wise Lord Himself.

What was left of his mind quailed before the advancing figure: the hideous head sunken into the shoulders and the long bony tail seemed familiar but he knew it couldn't be a Fifth Rider of Hell . . . This was the Shadow himself, resurrected to tread the Earth once more.

But as he tried to turn his head, a thin scream drifted across to him, and he was amazed to see the Shadow not almost upon him as he'd imagined, but fading away, disappearing down the tunnel of light that was itself fading . . . And then he heard Stargazer's voice again, but it sounded different.

Be gone, Nameless One, back beyond the arch that was made for you and which you have condemned yourself to for another eternity—

No! The anguished horror of the Shadow as he recognized his own prideful folly was pitiful to hear. *The Commandment is unsaid, my name is remembered, this cannot be . . .*

It can, and is! Rokshan repeated the Commandment as you shouted your name – now forgotten again – but not with its meaning reversed. You have pronounced your own sentence, because the boy mortal is also joined with me in my mind, therefore his thoughts and yours were one and the same. He has taken the name – your name, which you repeated over and over in your pride and arrogance; this he took to make the Divine Commandment the potent word of the Wise Lord again . . . and now the link is broken: be gone!

Condemn me then to a living death, but I shall endure through the ages . . . I shall rise again . . . The fading but defiant tones of the Shadow rose to a final strangulated scream as he disappeared at the end of the tunnel.

'Han Garid?' But Rokshan already knew the answer.

'The Wise Lord in his wisdom made the lords of the horses servants to none, and so it has come about, even in the transformation the Nameless One wrought of us through his servants,' the lord of the thunder dragons replied. 'Now your time has come, Rokshan! Command the dragon horde and show the mortals that we no longer mean them any harm!'

Rokshan felt himself lifted up by the spirit-force of Han Garid and then laughed with joy as he flew with him, perched on his neck, soaring up into the sky that was no longer black, starless night, right to the centre of the great wheeling arc of dragons who had been waiting patiently for their lord. They acknowledged him with a triumphant chorus of screeching calls that carried across the plain. Rokshan cried with exhilaration as the dragons opened their minds and they swooped this way and that, filling the sky with blazing bolts of colour. The song of the Serenadhi carried on the air and Rokshan caught the gouts and blasts of colour, threading them through his fingers and tossing them skywards like gigantic exploding firecrackers. Suddenly he had to hang on as if his life depended on it as Han Garid beat his enormous wings and climbed higher and higher.

Then Han Garid plunged back to earth, heading straight for the mass of dragons which wheeled round in an enormous arc that seemed to fill the sky; the noise of their beating wings rose to a quivering crescendo as they flew faster and faster around a single point. Now they formed a spinning vortex of golds and greens and blues, like a gloriously coloured whirlpool in the sky, and Han Garid had folded his huge wings and was making straight for the epicentre. The air rushed past Rokshan and they were going so fast that he could barely draw breath.

They plunged into the spinning whirlpool of dragons and the feeling of joyous exhilaration turned to one of peace and calm: Rokshan felt himself falling and then being laid down by gentle hands. The dragons wheeled and swooped in a final farewell, and suddenly Rokshan felt an exhaustion that seemed to crush the life out of him; he was too tired even to wonder where Han Garid had gone, but as he felt his life spirit fading, a familiar whinnying call drifted across to him. How he longed to see Stargazer for just one last time! A smile flickered across his face, the thought faded, and he slipped away. The door to Han Garid's soul closed for ever as Rokshan allowed his spirit to become one with Stargazer's so that the lord of the horses could live again, and once more roam the plains and valleys of the Horsemen.

On the ramparts of the citadel and out on the field of battle, they awoke as if from a dream. The shadowy night that had enveloped them rolled away in an instant on their waking, and the creatures intent on destroying them vanished too. A lone crow cawed its raucous cry, circling overhead before flying away to the east. To their astonishment, the jade warriors that had fought so bravely all stood lifeless, as if they'd always been statues, and the giant was nowhere to be seen.

A magnificent grey stallion now pawed the ground and tossed its head next to one of the fallen. And so high they were just tiny specks, the dragons still soared and wheeled, their screeching cries carrying on the wind as they keened for their lord. The people dropped to their knees in respectful wonder – but no shudder of fear went through them at the sight. Instead, they marvelled that creatures of such loathsome appearance, power and ferocity could be commanded by one young boy – for had they not seen him, astride the biggest and most majestic of the thunder dragons? Could it have been Han Garid himself? And together, had they not created the most awesomely beautiful spectacle in the sky? Turning to each other in astonishment, they wondered in their hearts what had become of Han Garid – and where was the boy – and what would become of the dragons if he was gone?

Just then the abbot and Shou Lao emerged from within the circle that the jade warriors had defended so stoutly, and a thin cheer went up. Together they hurried over to where Stargazer waited impatiently by Rokshan. Here, not even a candle-ring past, he had stepped into a storm of flaming rainbow colours which he had summoned with his bare hands – and only a few short moments before, the dragon horde had acknowledged him as the peer and equal of their lord.

The Staff and the Talisman lay abandoned not far from where he lay. The abbot quickly gathered them up and went to join Shou Lao as he bent over Rokshan.

Shou Lao answered the abbot's anxious, questioning look with a nod. 'He lives, but' – the old storyteller looked at Rokshan's face, waving his hand in front of the wildly staring, unblinking eyes – 'but as for his mind – he will need your strongest remedies, and your attention night and day, if he is ever to recover.'

The abbot nodded his understanding, signalling for a bier to be brought to take Rokshan into the citadel. Stargazer nuzzled him aside and, nickering very low, blew gently into Rokshan's face. For a moment his eyes flickered before they slowly closed; then he breathed the smallest of sighs, as if falling asleep. He looked at peace.

Just then a shrill cry made them look up − it was Lianxang's spirit-bird, wheeling towards them. The eagle flew gently down, landing just beside Rokshan. Stretching out a wing, she covered his body as if saying a tender farewell, calling her piercing cries.

'She is telling us something,' the abbot said, turning to Shou Lao.

'She must return to her people, she is saying, but first she will return with the dragons back to the Pool of the Two Peaks. Cetu must lead them and be with them when they are born again. He will go with others of his tribe, who are coming now for him, and will ride Stargazer, who has already been reborn through Rokshan's sacrifice.'

As he spoke, they heard the distinctive thrumming of hooves as two hundred or so Horsemen appeared on the crest of a ridge in the distance, the familiar figures of the Serenadhi on their black mares at their head. The wild dragon horses had survived their desert exile and had come to greet Stargazer, their lord − and to mourn the stricken Rokshan, who had been their lord's spirit-brother. They bore on their backs the remaining Horsemen, who were using all their skills to calm and reassure their inexperienced mounts. The Horsemen remained on the ridge, and only the Serenadhi now rode across to where Rokshan lay, gathering round with heads bowed in thanks. A lone figure emerged from the citadel on one of the monastery's sturdy steppe ponies and rode towards them. As he approached, they saw that it was Cetu.

He dismounted stiffly and bowed first to the sisters, then

to Shou Lao and the abbot, before kneeling down beside Stargazer and lifting Rokshan in his arms. He held him tightly, his eyes filled with tears.

'It was bravely done, my young friend; bravely done and befitting a true khagan of the Horsemen. Our tale shall never be forgotten, as long as there are those of us who live to tell it.'

Gently he laid him down again and, still kneeling, turned towards Stargazer, who tossed his head in acknowledgement. Then he mounted up as best he could, taking a handful of Stargazer's long mane for his reins.

'May the goddess be with you,' Shou Lao called as the abbot invoked the blessing of the Wise Lord.

'You will take care of Rokshan until the day I return?' Cetu said, wheeling Stargazer round. 'And Lianxang, she will be honoured in the custom of her people?'

'It shall be done, and we will build a holy shrine for her and her people, so that her memory and brave deeds will never be forgotten,' the abbot replied.

'She was the bravest of the brave,' Cetu murmured, giving the Horsemen's salute before cantering off to where his people waited for him. Their thunderous acclamation reverberated around the citadel.

The sisters of the Serenadhi lingered a while before turning to go. Only Sumiyaa spoke.

'Rokshan knows that we will wait for him if the door of Stargazer's soul should remain shut for ever, but the lord of the horses would not keep his spirit captive – he knows Rokshan is too much loved among his own kind if his brother spirit would ever wish to return to them. We bless your healers, Father Abbot – may the dragon spirits of the cleansing fire help them mend his mind. We too will return.'

The abbot bowed low towards the sisters as they galloped away, and Shou Lao raised his staff, directing the spirit-bird higher and higher into the sky, her shrill cry leading the dragons back to the pool.

A group of monks approached, carrying two biers, one of them bearing the broken body of Lianxang. Gently they laid Rokshan on the other, and with the abbot at their head, formed a solemn procession across the field of battle back towards the citadel.

The old storyteller gazed to the west, in the direction the Horsemen and dragons had gone, before he too turned towards the citadel, his staff tapping on the hard, frozen ground of the plain.

He had a new tale to tell, one that would be told the world over; one it would wonder at, and take heart from. He tap-tapped his way through the great gates with a weary smile, wondering where in the world he'd go first to tell his story.

One cycle of the moon later . . .

They came at last to the Pool of the Two Peaks, the last two hundred Horsemen led by Cetu, riding Stargazer and acknowledged as their new khagan.

Lianxang's spirit-bird had led the dragons, at such a great height that sometimes they hadn't seen either the bird or the dragons for days as they journeyed as fast as Stargazer could take them to their place of rebirth. Now the eagle swooped down to them for the last time and, beating her great wings, cried her shrill cry to them, her task done.

'Farewell, spirit of Lianxang,' Cetu called as she soared aloft and disappeared, riding the wind currents.

Stargazer reared up in the shallows of the pool and whinnied loud and long, calling the dragons to him. Four hundred or more wheeled like a billowing stormcloud in the sky, silent now but trailing wisps of fire as they gathered expectantly above the pool. The beautiful gold, green and blue hues of their skin merged into a whirling rainbow of colours and there was a noise like a gathering wind as their sinuous bodies straightened and plummeted headlong into the icy depths of the pool.

For a few moments all was silent. The dragon horses waited anxiously on the shoreline, nickering softly and nuzzling one another as if for comfort. Stargazer trotted nervously to and fro. Suddenly, without warning, a wave came rushing towards them, its bow boiling with foaming white spume, followed by another and another, until the shoreline thundered with crashing breakers.

The waves became larger still, forcing the Horsemen to retreat from the shoreline; but their mounts refused to be bidden and plunged into the pool, greeting their brothers and sisters as they were delivered back into the world, tumbling one after the other from the pounding waves.

Spray lashed Cetu's face and mixed with his tears of joy as Breeze Whisperer whinnied with a thrill of recognition at her old rider. Hundreds of dragon horses galloped and pranced along the shore as the Horsemen laughed and cheered.

Then all of them, horse and human alike, paid homage to the lord of the horses and, proudly astride him, Cetu. In the solemn silence of the moment even the mountains seemed to hold their breath, and the new khagan thought he heard the spirit of Rokshan calling him through Stargazer.

Rokshan said that he understood now what the Serenadhi had meant by saying they would wait for him, and that at the end of things, it didn't matter if the door closed and, perhaps, remained shut for ever: he would always be happy – for part of him, the very inner kernel of his spirit, would never be separated from Stargazer.

At last, with an exultant shout, Cetu pointed up to the summit, beyond which lay the Horsemen's beloved valleys.

Stargazer needed no second bidding: he galloped away up the mountain, followed by the thundering mass of reborn dragon horses, wild and free – as they always had been and always would be – until the end of all things.

Open the gates while there is time.
They will draw me up and carry me
To the Holy Mountain of K'unlun.
The Heavenly Horses have come
And the Dragon will follow in their wake.
I shall reach the Gates of Heaven.
I shall see the Palace of God.

Chinese hymn, c. 101 BC

Acknowledgements

I owe a great debt of gratitude to my agent, Broo Doherty, who right from the start encouraged me to keep on writing, having seen the very rough, early drafts, and then through persistent and judicious editing helped me to rewrite them into something presentable. Her calming hand has always been on the tiller in helping to navigate this book through sometimes stormy waters to completion. To Claire Doherty, heartfelt thanks for introducing me to her sister and making it all possible in the first place, and for being such a staunch supporter and loyal friend.

Thanks too to Philippa Dickinson at Random House for taking the initial leap and always keeping faith; to my fantastic editor, Sue Cook, and meticulous copy editor, Sophie Nelson. To Mark and Piers Ward, my brother and nephew respectively, and Katie Day, for reading early drafts and for all their comments and encouragement; Peppe, for always listening and for his infectious optimism, and Peter Johnson at my local Lloyds TSB branch for his flexibility and discretion in the teeth of head office intransigence. Thanks too to my brother-in-law, Peter Fudakowski, and his wife, Minette, for their unstinting support, advice and encouragement.

I am grateful to the London School of Oriental and African Studies and the British Library for their reference works and on-hand help in my initial and later research into the Silk Road, especially to Dr Susan Whitfield, founder and director of the International Dunhuang Project, and all the staff involved in the amazing Silk Road exhibition shown at the British Library in 2004, which provided me with such an invaluable insight into everyday life on the historic trade routes.

Author's Historical Note: The Silk Road

'Great Princes, emperors and Kings, Dukes and Marquises, Counts, Knights and Burgesses! And people of all degrees who desire to get knowledge of the various races of mankind and of the diversities of the sundry regions of the World, take this Book and cause it to be read to you. For ye shall find therein all kinds of wonderful things, and the diverse histories of the great Armenia, and of Persia and of the Land of the Tartars, and of India, and of many another country.'

Marco Polo, *The Book of Ser*, 1298 AD

Thus did the great Venetian trader and explorer, Marco Polo, exhort the world to listen to his tale of the fabulous wonders he had seen on the fabled Silk Road to the east, which is the setting for *Dragon Horse*.

The many different trading routes together made up the greatest road of the ancient world, which linked the Mediterranean to Central Asia, travelled by Alexander the Great, Darius (the 'King of Kings') of Persia, Genghis Khan and Marco Polo. The Silk Road linked the Eastern Roman Empire in the west to China, at the height of its power and cultural glory during the T'ang Dynasty (618–907 AD). Travellers, merchants and adventurers from the west came in search of silk, which was valued as highly as gold.

The different routes stretched for thousands of miles along some of the most inhospitable terrain on the planet, crossing lonely desert tracks and soaring mountain passes, connecting Chang'an, the ancient imperial capital of China, through the oases of central Asia and on to the eastern shores of the Mediterranean Sea.

All kinds of marvels were carried back and forth along the Silk Road. From Persia and the west came dates, peaches, walnuts, fragrant narcissus flowers and the precious perfumes of frankincense and myrrh. From Central Asia came semi-precious jade and lapis lazuli. From India came pepper, sandalwood and cotton, and from China the most secretly guarded treasure and most coveted commodity of all – the luxurious gossamer fabric of silk. The Chinese kept the secrets of sericulture (the production of silk) for at least 2000 years, being the only producer until the sixth century AD.

But the Silk Road was more than just one of the greatest trading routes; it was the ancient world's equivalent of what today we would term the 'information super-highway', providing a two-way avenue for the exchange of some of the most important ideas and technologies that we take for granted in the west: writing, the wheel, weaving, agriculture, riding – to name just a few – all made their way across Asia via the Silk Road. In medieval times, the two most fundamental contributions from the east made their way westward: paper and printing – described as the 'scaffolding of the modern world'. New thinking and practical developments in medicine, astronomy, engineering and weaponry – including the crossbow, siege engines, gunpowder, armour and war-chariots – also made their way to Europe via the Silk Road.

The opulence and grandeur of the emperors of the T'ang Dynasty (during which *Dragon Horse* is set) would have been unimaginable for the average European of that time – in the 'Dark Ages' of European history. By the beginning of the T'ang Dynasty in the seventh century, Chang'an was a bustling and vibrant capital city covering an area of eighty square kilometres, with a population of one million inside the city and another million in surrounding metropolitan areas. It was six times larger than Constantinople, the capital of the Byzantine Empire, comparable to Babylon, Alexandria and Rome at the height of their power.

To give an idea of what, to contemporary European eyes, would have been the unimaginable scale of the place, the great imperial Daming Palace, begun by emperor Taizong in 634, covered about 200 hectares – it was larger than medieval London and roughly twice the size of Louis XIV's palace and grounds at Versailles (built nearly 1000 years later).

In recognition of its political importance in the east, between 652 and 798 AD the eastern Roman emperors sent seven diplomats to Chang'an, the Arabian caliph sent thirty-six, and Persia's 'King of Kings' sent twenty-nine envoys to pay homage at the court of the 'Son of Heaven'. The city itself was thronging with a constantly shifting population (because of the incessant trading back and forth along the ancient trade routes) that would have included Tocharians, Sogdians, Turks, Uighurs, Mongols, Arabs, Persians and Indians.

In this cosmopolitan mix, extraordinary (for the times) religious tolerance meant that Nestorians (an offshoot of Christianity), Manichaeans (a religion founded by the Persian prophet, Mani, in the latter half of the third century) and Zoroastrians (fire-worshippers) from Sogdiana and Persia coexisted with Buddhist students and monks from Kashmir, Japan and Tibet.

In its setting, *Dragon Horse* reflects this religious diversity by bringing together all the various elements of worship depicted in the book: of the spirits of nature – 'dragon spirits'; Buddhism at the citadel monastery of Labrang; Chinese deities like Kuan Yin (goddess of mercy) and Guan Di (god of merchants, soldiers and scholars); the Chinese 'Immortals', including Shou Lao, god of longevity; fire-worship and ancestor-worship

(Lianxang's people of the Darhad). All these are brought together under the auspices of the 'Wise Lord' (Ahura Mazda) of the Zoroastrian tradition, together with an invented 'Creation' myth which reflects the Christian tradition.

Much of *Dragon Horse* is set in the semi-autonomous (during the T'ang Dynasty) Persian, western half of the Silk Road in the Kingdom of Sogdiana, with its regional capital, Maracanda (or Samarkand, as it became known later). The Sogdians were master-traders and it was their language that became the *lingua franca* of the Silk Road during the T'ang era. Towards the eastern end of the Silk Road, the Chinese themselves were so convinced of the Sogdian people's innate talent for trade that they believed their 'mothers fed them sugar in the cradle to honey their voices, and daubed their baby palms with paste to attract profitable things'. (*Shadow of the Silk Road*, Colin Thubron.)

Finally, the Fellowship of the Three One-eared Hares, which is such an integral part of *Dragon Horse*, is based on an actual motif depicted on different artefacts: it occurs with puzzling randomness not only throughout the length of the Silk Road but also in sacred sites across Great Britain, continental Europe and the Middle and Far East. This mysterious, ancient symbol shows three hares chasing each other in a circle. Each of the three ears in the image is shared between the animals so that the illusion is created they each have a pair of ears, whereas in fact they each only have one ear. Nobody has yet worked out what this motif means or what it could have signified.

Striking depictions of three hares joined at the ears have been found in roof bosses of medieval parish churches in Devon and elsewhere in the UK, and in churches, chapels and cathedrals in France and Germany, on thirteenth-century Mongol metalwork from Iran and in cave temples from the Chinese Sui Dynasty of 589–618 AD.

The hare has always had divine and mystical associations both in the east and in the west. Legends often give the animal magical qualities associated with fertility, femininity and the lunar cycle. Dr Tom Greeves, a landscape archaeologist and part of the British research team that has visited sites in China since 2004 to try and find an answer to the mystery, has suggested that the motif was brought to the west along the Silk Road:

'We can deduce from the motif's use in holy places in different religions and cultures, and the prominence it was given, that the symbol had a special significance . . . if we can open a window on something that in the past had relevance and meaning to people separated by thousands of miles and hundreds of years, it could benefit our present-day understanding of the things we share with different cultures and religions.'

The history, different cultures and religions of the Silk Road, the richness and diversity of Chinese mythology and the beneficent dragon of the east – in complete contrast to its ferocious western counterpart – have all inspired me. I hope Dragon Horse will open a window for you into this fascinating world.

Peter Ward

Bibliography and Further Reading

Chinese Mythology, Anthony Christie (Hamlyn, 1968)

Gilded Dragons, Carol Michaelson (British Museum Press, 1999)

The Silk Road: Trade, Travel, War & Faith, Susan Whitfield, (British Library, 2004)

Life along the Silk Road, Susan Whitfield (John Murray, 1999)

The Silk Road: a History, Franck & Brownstone (Facts on File Publications, 1986)

A Chinese Anthology, ed. Raymond Van Over (Picador, 1973)

Sky Burial, Xinran (Chatto & Windus, 2004)

Riding Windhorses – a Journey into the Heart of Mongolian Shamanism, Julie Ann Stewart (Destiny Books, 2004)

The Silk Road Journey with Xuanzang, Sally Hovey Wriggins (Westview Press, 2004)

Tao – the Chinese philosophy of Time and Change, Philip Rawson and Laszlo Legeza (Thames & Hudson, 1973)

The Silk Road – 2,000 years in the Heart of Asia, Frances Wood (British Library, 2004)

China – A Geographical Sketch, Foreign Languages Press (Beijing, 1974)

Animal Wisdom – Guide to the Myth, Folklore and Medicine Power of Animals, Jessica Dawn Palmer (Element/HarperCollins, 2002)

Shadow of the Silk Road, Colin Thubron (Chatto & Windus, 2006)

Monkey: A Journey to the West – a retelling of the Chinese folk novel by Wu Ch'eng-en (1500–1582), translated by David Kherdian (Shambhala Publications Inc., Boston, 1992)

The Essential Chuang Tzu, trans. from the Chinese by Sam Hamill and J. P. Seaton (Shambhala Publications Inc., Boston and London, 1999)

www.threehares.net For latest information on international research into the three hares mystery

ABOUT THE AUTHOR

With his father in military service, Peter Ward grew up in different places all over England including much of his early childhood in Germany and the Far East. He was educated at Ampleforth college before graduating in English & Religious Studies from Leeds University, marking the start of a lifelong interest in Eastern mythology and religions.

He became interested in Chinese ceramics and decorative arts when he worked in the sales rooms of Sotheby's, the antiques auctioneers in London. This fuelled his fascination with the mythology and culture of the East, especially China and tales set around the ancient Silk Road, which inspired him to want to write his own stories.

Dragon Horse is Peter's first novel. It has now been translated into several different languages.

Peter lives with his wife, daughter and two sons in London.